LEGION OF THE DAMNED

WITH ANOTHER ROAR, the Fire Lords Chaplain launched himself from the top of the steps. He hungered for a swift end to the contest and closed with the distracted Excoriator. The gladius cut through the air. Kersh rolled to one side, allowing the blade to fall where he had lain, chipping the stone. Rolling back, the tip of Kersh's boot made contact with the Fire Lord's jaw, sending the Chaplain off balance. By the time Kersh was back on his feet, the Fire Lords Space Marine was coming at him with the envenomed blade, flicking it this way and that, exploring the Excoriator's defences. Kersh danced away on the toes of his boots. He arched and angled his body, retracting his limbs and skipping back out of the blade's path.

A WARHAMMER 40,000 NOVEL

LEGION OF THE DAMNED

ROB SANDERS

BLACK LIBRARY

For TC, Jonah and Elliot – you know why…

A Black Library Publication

First published in Great Britain in 2012 by
The Black Library,
Games Workshop Ltd.,
The Black Library,
Nottingham, NG7 2WS, UK.

10 9 8 7 6 5 4 3 2 1

Cover illustration by Jon Sullivan.
Maps by Rob Sanders and Adrian Wood.
'The Ancient Traveller' illustration by Rhys Pugh.

A CIP record for this book is available from the British Library.

UK ISBN 13: 978 1 84970 142 6
US ISBN 13: 978 1 84970 143 3

See the Black Library on the internet at

www.blacklibrary.com

Find out more about Games Workshop
and the world of Warhammer 40,000 at

www.games-workshop.com

Printed and bound by CPI Group (UK) Ltd, Croydon, CR0 4YY

It is the 41st millennium. For more than a hundred centuries the Emperor has sat immobile on the Golden Throne of Earth. He is the master of mankind by the will of the gods, and master of a million worlds by the might of his inexhaustible armies. He is a rotting carcass writhing invisibly with power from the Dark Age of Technology. He is the Carrion Lord of the Imperium for whom a thousand souls are sacrificed every day, so that he may never truly die.

Yet even in his deathless state, the Emperor continues his eternal vigilance. Mighty battlefleets cross the daemon-infested miasma of the warp, the only route between distant stars, their way lit by the Astronomican, the psychic manifestation of the Emperor's will. Vast armies give battle in His name on uncounted worlds. Greatest amongst his soldiers are the Adeptus Astartes, the Space Marines, bio-engineered super-warriors. Their comrades in arms are legion: the Imperial Guard and countless planetary defence forces, the ever-vigilant Inquisition and the tech-priests of the Adeptus Mechanicus to name only a few. But for all their multitudes, they are barely enough to hold off the ever-present threat from aliens, heretics, mutants - and worse.

To be a man in such times is to be one amongst untold billions. It is to live in the cruellest and most bloody regime imaginable. These are the tales of those times. Forget the power of technology and science, for so much has been forgotten, never to be re-learned. Forget the promise of progress and understanding, for in the grim dark future there is only war. There is no peace amongst the stars, only an eternity of carnage and slaughter, and the laughter of thirsting gods.

ANNO INCOGNITA

PROLOGUE
SIGNS AND WONDERS

THE DEAFENING SILENCE of carnage after the fact.

An ocean of bolt-riddled bodies, as far as the eye could see. Corpse crests and blasted troughs, black with blood and swarming with flesh lice. Plunging breakers of ragged remains and shattered armour, marking the abrupt end of some maniacal charge. The trampled mulch of the fallen: deviants, the daemon-possessed and warriors in desecrated plate. Hideous faces of indescribable rage. A battle-smear of wretched flesh, hammered out of its misery by some merciful trajectory. The Emperor himself, it seemed, guiding the path of each blessed bolt and blast.

Approbator Vaskellen Quast of the Ordo Obsoletus pulled his scented neckerchief down and brought the grille of the meme-vox to his lips. 'Twenty-seven fifty-eight hours, Central Planetary Time. Certus-Minor – Adeptus Ministorum cemetery world.' The stench of gore steaming in the morning heat seared his nostrils, prompting the young acolyte to snort, hock and spit. 'Praga subsector, Segmentum Obscurus.'

Quast clambered carefully across a ridge of corrupt

forms. His advance was frustrated by more than just bodies. Beneath the carpet of bone-jutting butchery lay the cemetery world surface: a crowded expanse of ornate tombstones, mausolea and funerary sculpture. Every square metre of dirt was devoted to the art of burial and the infrastructure that served that hallowed purpose. Space on Certus-Minor existed at a premium, with grave plots and baroque memorial markers almost built one on top of another. This created a landscape of cold, crafted stone. A graveyard on a planetary scale.

The approbator could see little of the surface from where he was standing, covered as it was with the splattered remains of those who had never reached the solace of an Imperial grave, and those who didn't deserve one. Knee-deep in the Chaotics and carnage, Quast felt tense with overwhelming disgust. It was more than just the stench and warming rot. He felt that his very soul was in danger just standing in the presence of the unhallowed dead – that the corrupting influence of the Ruinous Powers was still in evidence in the mutilated remains and that it was aware of his God-Emperor-fearing footsteps.

Behind the acolyte hovered a Valkyrie carrier, as black as a silhouette against the pearly cloud cover of the cemetery world sky and marked only with the sinister insignia of the Ordo Obsoletus. About him stalked Inquisitorial storm troopers from the 52nd Ranger Pelluciad, all field masks, humming weaponry and camo-carapace.

'Ruling pontifex and planetary governor,' Quast continued, 'one Erasmus Oliphant. Tithe grade: Solutio Tertius. Population at last Administratum census estimated at one million Imperial souls. Certus-Minor, revised estimates, post-atrocities: zero.'

The Cholercaust had built its fearful reputation on such barbaric efficiency. The Blood God's servants couldn't help themselves. Survivors weren't a strategic consideration. The Slayer cared little for the tales of victims-in-waiting and what others might do with such information. Its tactics were always the same: uncompromising, overwhelming and savage. Where hearts beat with the defiance of life, the goremongers raged, honouring only the razored edge and baptising worlds in torrents of blood.

'Hadria, Dregeddon IV, L'Orient, Callistus Mundi, Port Koronach, among a hundred other worlds, all similarly butchered. All victims of the Cholercaust Blood Crusade. All planets on the path of the Keeler Comet.'

Quast's vox-bead chirped. 'Proceed.'

'Sir, the *Providence* reports that a large vessel has just translated in-system.'

'Markings and registration?'

'Still collating that information, sir. I can tell you that it has achieved high orbit.'

'Probably a Ministorum heavy transport, bringing in penitents and frater labour from Bona Phidia. Get a visual. Keep me informed. Quast out.'

The approbator let his eyes linger on the charred mountain of rubble that was Obsequa City. The smouldering ruins before Quast had been a beautiful, baroque metrapol. A vision of towers, steeples and spires. Stained-glass and rockrete, dark with age, thrusting for the heavens with reverent majesty. With nearly every square metre of dirt on Certus-Minor devoted to the dead, even the city was considered an extravagance. Like a tiny, ecclesiastical hive, Obsequa City comprised bethels, basilicas and cathedrals that were built tall and tight. The narrow alleys and passages were steep and cobbled, leading up to the crowning monument – the heart of the city in both a physical and spiritual sense – the Umberto II Memorial Mausoleum.

The huge dome of the vault had once dominated the city skyline. Now it was a blasted remnant. A demolished edifice, collapsed in on itself – open and exposed to the elements. It had originally been built to honour and house the bones of Umberto II – Ecclesiarch, High Lord of Terra and prosecuter of innumerable wars of faith. Under Umberto, the Ecclesiarchy's influence across the galaxy grew and the forces of darkness in and around the Eye of Terror made precious little progress. With Umberto's leadership, the common faithful of the Imperium rose up and took the fight back to the Ruinous Powers, standing shoulder to shoulder with their brothers and sisters in the Imperial Guard and the Emperor's Angels of Death. Ancient Terran scholars ascribed the near two thousand years of uneasy peace between the Eleventh Black Crusade and the Gothic War largely to the legacy of Umberto's efforts in the segmentum.

Quast watched the frater burn teams clear bodies about the wrecked city. They were uncovering the arterial routes of the necroplex – the labyrinth of lychways and paths that ran through the crowded memorial burial plots, mausolea and cenoposts. With the main roads leading into Obsequa City clear of death and destruction, the Adeptus Ministorum forces had started to move in heavy equipment and excavators.

Dig-teams swarmed across the city rubble and the ruins of the great Mausoleum. The cemetery world already had a new planetary governor, Pontifex Clemenz-Krycek, newly arrived from St Ethalberg with manpower and instructions to purge the hallowed ground of Certus-Minor of the taint of corruption. The irresistible bureaucracy of the Imperium implemented even in the face of carnage and catastrophe. Quast had felt it prudent to meet Clemenz-Krycek before initiating his investigations. He told the pontifex little of his true purpose there. The driven ecclesiarch seemed not to care, engaged as he was with the small army of frater militia faithful that were piling and incinerating the corrupt forms of the battle-dead and excavating the ruins of the mausoleum. Quast found that the pontifex's vows of devotion to the God-Emperor had done nothing to quell the fire of ambition burning in his veins. Clemenz-Krycek clearly hoped to find Umberto II's bones intact in the spiritual stronghold of the underground vault. Safe from the corruption of Chaos. Even without the ecclesiarch's bones, the pontifex was boldly heralding Umberto II's sacred remains as responsible for the halting of the Cholercaust Blood Crusade.

The investigation of such assertions was well within the

remit of the Ordo Obsoletus, but information already in Quast's possession made him question such a possibility – that and the fire behind the pontifex's eyes. Clemenz-Krycek was already mooting recommendations for Umberto II's veneration to the rank of Imperial Saint – a call that, if approved by the High Ecclesiarch, would undoubtedly improve the pontifex's own prospects in the ranks of the Adeptus Ministorum.

A rusted breastplate creaked underfoot and, with a crack, the approbator's boot slipped down into the stinking chest cavity of a fallen giant. Its armour was a god-pleasing red and one shoulder plate was spiked like an ocean urchin. A studded gauntlet still hate-clenched the shaft of a brute axe, unable – even in death – to surrender the weapon. The monster's helmet was missing and the monstrous head with it. As Quast's boot sank into corruption, liquefied tissue spilled from the neck brace, thick with squirming flesh lice.

'Merda!' Quast spat in gutter Gothic, flicking gobbets of rot from the toe of his boot. The approbator shook his head. He was a savant, a researcher – not a field operative. What he had learned aboard the Ordo Obsoletus Black Ship *Providence*, however, was too important to leave to another. If he had found evidence of an authentic miracle – an event beyond human phenomena, alien curiosity or the pollution of Chaos – then it was his solemn duty to ask challenging questions and hunt for elusive answers. Answers his venerable master, Inquisitor Ehrensperger, had charged him to find.

Quast went to scrape the sole of his boot on the sculpted finish of the Chaos Space Marine's other shoulder plate, only to find himself staring down the brass throat of a fang-filled maw. The symbol of the fell XIIth Legion, wrought in pure hate. The World Eaters.

Quast swiftly retracted his foot, fearful that the effigy itself might assume a bloodthirsty life and snap shut. There had been other Blood Crusades. The Odium Wars. The Coming of the Brazen Host. The Dominion of Fire. The Black

Crusade of the Daemon Prince Doombreed. But not since Armageddon's First War had so many berserker brethren of the World Eaters Traitor Legion gathered under one banner.

'Approbator?'

'Carry on, sergeant.'

The Inquisitorial storm troopers brought forth a prisoner. She was naked but for the scraps of filthy, feral world hide that preserved her modesty. Her matted hair trailed down her back and her flesh was the canvas upon which primitive tattoos were carved and inked. Her emaciated form crawled across the butchery like a hound on a scent, while the two troopers flanked and followed, holding her between them on metal poles and lanyards. The savage began clawing at a mauled body draped across a gravestone that was carved in the fashion of the Imperial aquila.

'Sir, looks like the witch has something.'

Quast wiped his boot on the scalp of a dead cultist and turned back to approach the feverish psyker. She froze with her bare back to them, and then without warning started thrashing this way and that. The lanyards around her neck bit into her thin flesh and the storm troopers on the ends of the poles were yanked back and forth. The Ranger Pelluciad sergeant called to Quast to hold his position.

The witch returned to stillness before turning her head and snarling at the approbator. Her bright eyes rolled over blood-red like a wine glass filling with claret and her entire face suddenly contorted with an agonising rage. She looked along the pole at one of her storm trooper sentinels like a thing possessed. The witch suddenly convulsed and spewed forth a stream of bloody vomit. The blistering gruel splattered the Ranger's helmet and body armour. He tore at his chin strap and started screaming something about burning.

'Hold her down!' the sergeant bawled, and to this end the remaining storm trooper brutally thrust the pole at the witch and the witch to the ground. 'Reinforcements. Now!' the sergeant called into his vox-bead, before drawing his hellpistol and charging across the slaughterscape at the struggling storm trooper and his charge. The trooper had forced the thrashing psyker right down into the stinking carpet of rent armour, jutting bones and festering bodies.

'Sir!'

'Hold her, damn it!'

But the witch was gone. The wasted creature had somehow slipped down into the layers of rotting flesh and ceramite, crawling – swimming almost – through the disintegrating carcasses. The pole suddenly followed, whipped into the cadaver-mound and taking the second storm trooper with it. 'G'Vera!' the sergeant called into his vox-link. 'Corporal, talk to me!'

The mound exploded. A fount of blood blasted up out of the bodies and at the Certusian dawn-sky. How much of it belonged to G'Vera and how much to the surrounding dead was impossible to tell. What was certain was that the corporal was now one of them.

The sergeant began scanning the ground about them with his hellpistol. A limb twitched here. A body moved there. The witch was certainly on the move. 'Sir, arm yourself,' the storm trooper instructed. The approbator had been so sickened at the spectacle that it was the meme-vox that he still clenched in one white-knuckled hand, rather than his laspistol. Fumbling for the weapon, Quast drew his sidearm.

The witch was suddenly before him, slithering out from the slaughter like a serpent. Her body was completely naked now and slick with black blood and spoilage. Her eyes burned hate and her lips had retracted horribly like a predatory cat.

'Approbator!' the sergeant screamed, but Quast found that he couldn't move. Fear clouded his mind and all he could do was gawp as the possessed witch hissed and came in so close as to touch her bloody forehead to his own.

There was a flash. The furious face suddenly disappeared. Snapped out of view. Blasted away. Quast stood, blinking. His face was speckled with the witch's blood and his laspistol still felt a world away. Turning, the approbator saw the reinforcements that the sergeant had called for. Storm trooper sharpshooters, swiftly descended from the Valkyrie transport, with hellguns to chins and scopes to visors. They had executed the psyker from some distance away with a cool nerve, precision marksmanship and supercharged lasfire. As they brought their weapons down, Quast nodded in silent respect.

The sergeant was suddenly beside him, his boot on the witch's ribcage and his hellpistol pointed at what was left of her head. The storm trooper put three more blasts into the creature before he was satisfied.

'Freaks,' the sergeant spat. 'Can't stand them, sir.'

'She was no doubt possessed by some residual evil she found amongst the bodies,' Quast announced, trying to re-establish some kind of authority over the situation, even if it was only intellectual. He found himself looking down on the jumbled cadavers: the hellspawn, Traitor Guardsmen and degenerate World Eaters.

'How are you, sir?'

'Better now, sergeant,' Quast managed.

'Approbator, perhaps we should–'

'Continue,' Quast interjected. 'Perhaps, sergeant, we should continue.' He holstered his laspistol and nodded at the ordo Valkyrie. 'Bring me another.'

The sergeant hesitated, before nodding. 'As you wish, approbator,' he said, before marching off towards the Valkyrie transport. He left Quast alone with the dead and his thoughts.

'The question…' Quast began again, activating the meme-vox and wiping blood from his cheeks with a silk scarf,' … is not what ended this world. The Cholercaust clearly did that. The question is, what ended the Cholercaust?'

Inquisitorial records often identified the Blood God's favoured operating in wretched warbands roaming the galaxy. Greater concentrations were rare, since the XIIth Legion's primordial hate seemed to extend to brother-slayers as well as the innocents of the Imperium. The Cholercaust had been different, however. The planetary populations upon whom it descended were always slaughtered to the last man, woman and child. Failed Adeptus Astartes interventions and Imperial Navy gauntlets had confirmed large numbers of ancient World Eaters vessels in the screaming cultist armada, which seemed to grow with every conquest. Some of those frigates and cruisers identified hadn't been seen since the Horus Heresy, thousands of years before.

Little was known about the champion that led the Blood Crusade, the maniac who had managed the impossible and gathered so many of his murderous brothers to one cause and objective. He was known only as 'the Pilgrim' and led his vast host with religious conviction, following the strange path of a blood-red comet. Celestial cartographers believed it to be the Keeler Comet, a long-period body with a highly eccentric orbit, recorded to have passed through both Segmentum Obscurus and Segmentum Solar nearly ten thousand years before. Euphrati Keeler, the remembrancer of great antiquity, immortalised the comet over El'Phanor in *The Ancient Traveller*, a pict rumoured to hang in the Imperial Palace and reproduced across the Imperium. The comet had found the galaxy much-changed upon its most recent return. The xenos empire of the eldar had fallen, the Imperium had been shattered by civil war and the colossal warp storm known as the Eye of Terror had erupted in its path.

As the Keeler Comet blasted out of the immateriality of the Eye, it became apparent that it too had changed. A blood-red beacon, it appeared to wander with a mind of its own and trailed in its wake the Pilgrim and his Cholercaust Blood Crusade. The daemons, cultists and World Eaters seemed to believe that the cursed comet embodied the will of their Chaos god and would lead them across the stars in a celebration of slaughter, right to the Imperium's finest and Holy Terra itself.

That was until the comet appeared in the skies of a tiny cemetery world in the Praga subsector. Until the Cholercaust came to Certus-Minor and the Blood God's butchers became the butchered.

A shadow screamed above. The thunder of engines

passed straight through Quast and an involuntary instinct shocked the approbator into ducking his head and dropping into a crouch amongst the rot. The wash of the thruster trail bathed the area about Quast in a dry heat. Squinting through the blaze of afterburning engines, the acolyte stood and watched the craft rocket across the corpse-strewn necroplex before banking and taking in the ruins of Obsequa City in a double pass.

Even serving in the ranks of the Holy Emperor's Inquisition, Quast had only seen such a craft once before. It was a Thunderhawk gunship, the Adeptus Astartes' fearsome steed amongst the stars. Spinning around, the approbator saw that another had punched through the sheen of pearly cloud, dropping silently like the first in a controlled freefall, thrusters ready to snatch it from gravity's embrace and slingshot the gunship across the cemetery world surface. A swarm of gunships followed, spearing down through the heavens in formation, before peeling off to take position above the killing fields, around the demolished city.

'Sir, the vessel has made itself known to us,' the vox-bead in Quast's ear announced.

'Proceed.'

'Adeptus Astartes battle-barge *Cerberus*. Golden Throne, she's huge.'

'To which Chapter does this blessed vessel belong?' Quast pushed.

'The Excoriators, approbator.'

Quast nodded. It made sense. Among the warped and wretched servants of Chaos, the acolyte had come across numerous Adeptus Astartes dead, all armoured in the holy plate of the Excoriators Chapter. The defenders of a doomed world.

'Have the captain greet the *Cerberus* and inform the battle-barge commander of our presence in orbit and on the planet surface. Extend my compliments and that of the ordo, then beg an audience for myself with the ranking Adeptus Astartes among their number.'

'What are the Emperor's Angels doing here, sir?'

'I do not know,' the approbator admitted, 'but I intend to find out. Quast out.'

The acolyte left the Valkyrie and its storm trooper contingent and struck out across the slaughter. He walked for the ruined city and the gathering of gunships that hovered with ominous intent above the carnage. Clambering across the twisted dead and the expanse of tombstones beneath, Quast spoke into his meme-vox.

'The Excoriators,' he said, out of breath. 'Battle-brothers of the Great Dorn's seed. Their reputation is for fearsome feats of stamina and attrition. The Codex Astartes records the Excoriators as created from the ranks of the Imperial Fists post-Heresy, during the dark days of the Second Founding. This in recognition of their stalwart defence of the Imperial Palace during the Siege of Terra.'

The approbator's eyes settled upon a particularly horrific visage, daemonflesh that leered murderous lust at Quast, even after its destruction and banishment. For a moment the corpse-thing held his horrid attention before the acolyte forced his eyes closed and stumbled on across the battlefield. 'The Excoriators are listed in the *Mythos Angelica Mortis* as one of the Astartes Praeses,' Quast continued, 'those Space Marine Chapters charged with the solemn duty of guarding the Eye of Terror and the vulnerable regions of Imperial space bordering.'

He slipped a small pair of magnoculars from the folds of his robes and scanned the dun-white lengths of the Excoriators Thunderhawks. 'Markings indicate the presence of the Third, Sixth and Eighth Companies. Three companies and a Chapter battle-barge suggests an undertaking of extreme importance. Cross reference with Telepathica transmittal 44L-21-Digamma/Theta, intercepted from the Stroika-Six Observium Array.'

The approbator attempted to make his presence known to the nearest Thunderhawk. He held up his ordo identification and waved his arm at the craft. The pilot took little notice of the tiny Quast, amongst the bodies and funeral sculpture, and the craft held its station above a corpse-strewn blast crater. The lead Thunderhawk, the scout ship that had preceded the formation of gunships, took another pass, however, once more prompting Quast to crouch down in the blood and the mire.

Grit and grave dust whipped up about the approbator, and turning, Quast came to regard the Thunderhawk that had led the formation down through the thick cloud cover. Its prow section drifted up behind him, hovering like some great predator. Quast stood up in the beast-craft's sights, his robes thrashing about him in the squall of its engines. The tempest invested cadavers with momentary life as bodies trembled and mortis-stiff limbs rocked in the backwash of the Thunderhawk's thrusters.

Once again Quast held out his identification, finding himself turning and stumbling as the Thunderhawk circled, the craft's tail gliding around while the armoured cockpit, heavy bolters and troop section remained fixed on the approbator. The gunship's engines, landing gear and weaponry gleamed with sacred oils and clear maintenance; however, its armour was sallow and abused. The flash-scarring of las-blasts accompanied soot-smeared missile strikes and a nosetip-to-tail mauling of bolt plucks and heavy-gauge auto-fire.

As the bay ramp opened, Excoriators Space Marines filed down the incline and dropped to the ground below in two flanking lines. The Excoriators moved with solemn purpose, the compact brutality of their boltguns breaking up the curvilinear lines of their ceramite. The plate itself was a dirty ivory – shabby in appearance against the polished gleam of the torso cabling – and above the scorn of their half-moon helmet grilles, a pair of dark optics burned with resolution.

The battered cream of their armour became immediately splattered with the ichor of the dead. With the crouch landing of each armoured Angel, Quast fancied he could feel the flesh below him quake. As the gunship circled, the deploying Excoriators began fanning out, boltguns aimed at the carpet of carnage and helmets methodically scanning from left to right. Turning his magnoculars on the other Thunderhawks, Quast found that they too had delivered their Adeptus Astartes payloads to the battlefield about the smoking remains of Obsequa City. And they too seemed to be doing more than a reconnaissance sweep. The Excoriators were looking for something. Or someone.

As the howling wind grew about him, Quast lowered the glasses. The Thunderhawk had completed its deployment and now closed on the approbator. The last thing that the acolyte wanted was confusion, or to cause offence, and so he kept his ordo identification stretched out in front of him, that the living arsenal of the Emperor knew that he was no enemy of the Imperium.

A final figure stepped out of the shadows of the troop bay. His steps were those of a warrior bearing the burden of great age and rank, and as he waited on the edge of the ramp, the Thunderhawk effortlessly drifted forwards. Quast felt like they were both in the eye of a storm. The acolyte staggered back as the gunship rolled right up to him. The Excoriator stepped off the ramp and onto the battlefield. The ramp behind him closed and the craft gently banked and peeled off, leaving the two of them amongst the calm and quiet of the massacre.

Quast was drowned in the shadow of the ceramite hulk. Like the Thunderhawk from which he'd stepped, the Excoriator's armour was blasted and scarred. Unlike his superhuman brethren, however, this figure was decked in battle-plate of deepest black. A blizzard of bolt craters blemished its dark surface, while the criss-cross of blade slashes and claw scratches scored the plate into a mosaic blaze. This once again contrasted with the adamantium gleam of its cables, casings and Imperial aquila, unfolding its glorious wings across the warrior's broad chest. His scuffed gauntlet clenched a great crozius, beneath the mirrored blades of its sculpted eagle head. The shaft of the power weapon extended all the way to the ground and the giant used it like a staff as he took his first steps across the felled bodies towards the approbator.

'Approbator Quast?' the Adeptus Astartes rumbled. When Quast didn't answer, the Excoriator removed his helmet. He peered down at the acolyte over his chestplate, revealing his mangled features, a patchwork of ugly stitching cutting his ancient face into quarters.

Quast couldn't quite find his words in the presence of the Angel. Neither could he hold the intensity of the Excoriator's dark eyes, and found his own drifting down and across the detail of the warrior's scarred battle-plate. Unconsciously leaning in, Quast saw that adorning each nick, each sword slash and bullet hole was an inscription, scratched in High Gothic lettering. The battle-plate was covered in such markings, each gouge and las-burn bearing its own notation, dates and locations: *221751.M41 Gethsemane*; *435405. M41 Delleria Secundus*; *997640.M41 Mallastabergiii* . From the dun sheen of the ivory armour worn by the Excoriators beyond, Quast assumed their plate bore the same mixture of script and scarring.

'Approbator?'

'Yes,' Quast managed, lowering his ordo identification and looking up. 'It was my vessel that hailed your mighty battle-barge.'

'And I thank you for your concision,' the Excoriator said. 'I know you broke with the protocol of your Holy Ordo. In turn forgive me the forthright nature of our approach. For the Adeptus Astartes, like the Emperor's Inquisition, there is often much to accomplish and little time. I am Santiarch Balshazar, Chapter Chaplain of the Excoriators, and I represent the interests of Chapter Master Ichabod, here on this cemetery world.'

'Vaskellen Quast,' the acolyte replied. 'And I represent Lord Ehrensperger and the interests of the Ordo Obsoletus on this planet.' Quast tried to hold the stony gaze of the Excoriators Chaplain but failed a second time.

'The Ordo Obsoletus?'

'We are an ordo minoris, my lord. Santiarch, may I offer my condolences to your Chapter during the test of these times. I understand that the entire Fifth Company was lost in garrisoning this world against the predations of Chaos.'

'Duly noted, approbator. Might you tell me what the Inquisition's interest in our misfortunes might be?'

Quast felt the crushing weight of the Angel's expectation. The authority of seeming immortality in his grave words. The fearful insistence of the Space Marine's physical presence.

'The interest of the Ordo Obsoletus extends to your own interest, Santiarch,' Quast responded with growing confidence.

'Just like the Inquisition,' the Santiarch replied. 'To reply in riddles. Are the Excoriators to suffer the indignity of investigation, approbator?' Balshazar asked. When Quast didn't respond, the Chaplain continued. 'The Emperor's Angels come to Certus-Minor to bury brothers, search for survivors and recover our sacred seed. I suffer your aspersions only to achieve that end all the faster. Now, approbator, tell me, have you encountered any of my battle-brethren?'

'Yes, Santiarch,' Quast confirmed. 'Many of them. All dead, I regret. Some of their bodies are spread out across the battlefield beyond, but the greatest concentration lie about the ruins of Obsequa City. I wish I could assist you further but the Cholercaust is absolute in its insistence to leave us nought but corpse witnesses.'

'Thank you,' the Santiarch replied soberly and strode across the slaughter towards the demolished city.

'Three companies and a Chapter battle-barge,' Quast said as the giant passed, causing the Chaplain to grind to a furious pause. 'Withdrawn from active duty garrisoning the Eye of Terror? That seems a great outlay for such a solemn mission.'

Balshazar turned dangerously, and Quast became very aware of the gleaming blades that adorned the Chaplain's death-dealing staff of office. 'And what would you know of deployments and the Emperor's Angels, mortal, having existed for all but a galactic blink in the greater scheme of the Imperium?'

'Nothing, Santiarch. I beg of you. Explain them to me,

for I fear you are not here on this dead world just for the bodies of your fallen brothers.' Quast gestured about the battlefield at the hovering Thunderhawks and swarms of Excoriators methodically picking through the annihilation. 'What are you looking for, Santiarch? The Adeptus Astartes and the Holy Inquisition have a history of cautious cooperation. Let us build on that heritage. Perhaps I can help you. Perhaps we can help each other. Perhaps together we might truly come to understand what happened here.'

'You are bold for one so young, approbator. I hope your master understands how incorrigible and stupid you really are.'

'He does, Lord Santiarch,' Quast returned. 'It is undoubtedly the reason he sent me.'

Balshazar stared at the acolyte. This time, Quast held his nerve and stared right back. 'Santiarch, please.'

'The Adeptus Astartes do not often share their shame so publically,' the Excoriator said finally. 'The Fifth Company requested reinforcement. The *Cerberus* was en route to Certus-Minor to answer our brothers' call and halt the progress of the Cholercaust. We failed. We failed to reach our battle-brethren in time and they faced an unstoppable enemy alone and in our absence. Our battle-barge was delayed by strange warp currents in the wake of the crimson comet. Our approach vector was direct but flawed, as was my intention in ordering it. If we had not encountered such problems then we might have been here to fight side by side with our brothers and perhaps prevent their destruction.'

Quast nodded. He chose his words carefully.

'Santiarch, I do not doubt the truth of your tribulations and the misfortunes that resulted, but we both know that the *Cerberus* is not here to reinforce the Fifth Company.'

The Excoriators Chaplain began a livid and inevitable advance.

'You would tempt me, mortal, in a place already sodden with bloodshed?'

Quast stumbled back, his heart battering the inside of his ribcage. He tripped back over a severed limb and landed on his backside in the remains of a ruined cadaver. With the Space Marine towering above him, Quast reached inside his robe pockets and produced a vellum scroll which he offered up to the furious Excoriator.

'The Fifth Company did request reinforcement but had little expectation of its arrival,' Quast blurted. The Chaplain snarled and leaning down tore the scroll from the approbator's fingers. As the Excoriator read, Quast climbed awkwardly to his feet and brushed gore from his robes. 'They sent long-range astrotelepathic requests to the Viper Legion at Hellionii Reticuli, Second Company Novamarines stationed at Belis Quora and the Angels Eradicant at Port Kreel. They even sent to the Vanaheim Cordon, in full knowledge of its futility. That the Imperial Fists, the Exorcists and the Grey Knights stationed there would not leave the line of defence for fear that the Keeler Comet and trailing Cholercaust might resume its progress on towards Ancient Terra. The Adeptus Astartes wouldn't leave Terra open to attack to help defend a tiny Ecclesiarchy cemetery world. Their allegiance is to the living, not the dead. The *Cerberus* set out from your home world of Eschara and no astrotelepathic transmission was sent there. You are too distant a prospect, given the time constraints of the Cholercaust's arrival.'

'How did you come by this information?' Balshazar demanded, scanning the vellum transcript in his ceramite fingertips.

Quast hesitated. 'My Lord Ehrensperger maintains a choir of powerful astropaths aboard his personal Black Ship. They have instructions to listen for telepathic messages and to scan those communiqués for motifs relating to the Ordo Obsoletus's work.'

'Your inquisitor lord roams the galaxy, eavesdropping on the communications of others?' Balshazar marvelled. 'Again, how like the Holy Ordos. How pathetic. Then specimens like your good self are dispatched to investigate the promise of information and authenticate its relevance.'

Quast nodded, allowing the slurs to wash over him.

'Our choir intercepted a psychic distress signal in an Adeptus Astartes code, relayed through the Stroika-Six Observium Array but originating from this very world.'

'I should have you flayed for even that,' the Santiarch growled. 'Those were Adeptus Astartes words for Adeptus Astartes ears, information not meant for mere mortals such as yourself.'

'I'm not sure it was meant for the Emperor's Angels, either,' Quast told the Excoriator. 'The message transcript in your hand contains a report of planetary invasion and a request for reinforcement, followed by a direct appeal to the God-Emperor of Mankind for assistance. For intervention. For a miracle.'

Balshazar scanned the words to which the approbator was referring.

'A simple prayer,' the Santiarch said. 'Open reverence to the father of our very own. I hope that such benediction is not absent from the prosecution of your own work, approbator.'

'A prayer,' Quast echoed. 'My master reached the same conclusion. Until I showed him the intended destination of the message.'

Balshazar located the astrotelepathic terminus on the crumpled vellum. 'Ancient Terra…'

Quast nodded. 'The Excoriators did not prevail on Certus-Minor. They are all dead. Yet the Cholercaust was defeated. I do not know what happened here. What I do know is that one of your Librarians made a direct appeal to Holy Terra, to the God-Emperor of Mankind for a miracle, and that appeal seems to have been answered.'

The Space Marine and approbator locked gazes. 'And that is reason enough for the Ordo Obsoletus's involvement, so please, Santiarch, now tell me what you and three companies of your Excoriators are really doing here.'

The Chaplain's mangled face creased with vexation. His anger had dissipated and his brow now furrowed with genuine conflict. As his lips began to form around a response to the approbator's request, the storm trooper sergeant jogged up behind him.

'Approbator!'

'Yes, sergeant,' Quast replied with obvious displeasure. His eyes remained on the hulking Santiarch.

'Report just in. One of the frater burn teams has found a survivor.'

Both Quast and Balshazar turned.

'A cemetery worlder?'

'An Adeptus Astartes.'

Balshazar seemed to sag in his heavy plate.

'We might get answers to our questions, yet,' the Santiarch told Quast.

The approbator gave a brief nod. 'Sergeant, take us to him. Take us to him, right now.'

POST HOC, ERGO PROPTER HOC

PART ONE
TERROR IS THEIR HARBINGER...

CHAPTER ONE
THE DARKNESS

'HOW GOES THE Feast, brother?' called Apothecary Ezrachi, across the frigate *Scarifica*'s tactical-oratorium. Corpus-Captain Shiloh Gideon stood at a rostrum decorated with runeslates and scrolls of vellum. As Ezrachi approached, the small gathering of bondservants about the rostrum peeled away. The Apothecary's right leg was a full bionic replacement and almost as old as Ezrachi himself. While robust and powerful, it sighed with hydraulic insistence and lagged a millisecond behind its flesh-and-bone equivalent, giving the impression of a slight limp.

'The Feast of Blades goes badly,' the corpus-captain lamented. 'For the Excoriators, at least.'

'How many?' inquired the Apothecary as he approached.

'Too many,' Gideon snapped, running a palm across the top of his tonsure-shaven scalp. He grasped hair that grew like a silver crown around his skull in obvious frustration. 'We lost three more to our Successor Chapter kin this morning in honorific contestations. Occam, Basrael and Jabez. Occam fought well, but not well enough. I thought Jabez was dead. I don't think anything is going to stop that

33

Crimson Fist. The Feast may already be theirs.'

'Brother Jabez will live,' Ezrachi assured him. 'Just.'

Gideon didn't seem to hear the aged Apothecary.

'Shame begets shame,' the corpus-captain said. 'Our failure at the Feast is tied to the loss of our Chapter's sacred standard. I can feel it.'

'Your head is full of Santiarch Balshazar's sermons. I honour the primarch, but Dorn lives on through our flesh and blood, not dusty artefacts,' Ezrachi insisted. 'The loss of our standard is a mighty blow, but in truth it was but a blood-speckled banner.'

'Rogal Dorn himself entrusted his sons – our Excoriator brothers – with the standard over ten thousand years ago,' the corpus-captain said. 'It displays the Second Founding's decree and is threaded with the honours of every battle fought in our long, bloody history. It carries the distinctia of the Astartes Praeses and our service in garrisoning the Ocularis Terribus. It bears the Stigmartyr – the emblem that the Chapter adopted as its own.' Gideon turned to present his own ivory shoulder plate, adorned with the scarlet symbol to which he made reference, a gauntleted fist clenching the length of a thunderbolt-shaped scar. 'It is much more than the blood-soaked rag to which you allude and I'll have you mind your irreverence, Apothecary.'

'I meant no offence, corpus-captain,' Ezrachi replied plainly, slapping the adamantium scaffolding of his thigh. 'As you well know, there is more than a little of my own blood splashed across that standard.'

'Our brothers fight for a broken honour,' the corpus-captain continued, oblivious to Ezrachi. 'We are accursed. The Emperor's eternal fortitude, once absent in the brother that surrendered the banner, is now absent in us all. It is our collective punishment.'

'Is it not our way?' Ezrachi put to him. 'Do not the Excoriators of all Dorn's sons feel the loss of the Emperor deepest? Do not the Excoriators alone know our primarch's true grief, the agony of his redemption and the cold wrath of his renascence? Do we not purge his weakness and our own from this shared flesh through the Rites of Castigation and the Wearing of Dorn's Mantle?'

'This is beyond our inherited sin,' Gideon said miserably. 'The loss of the Honoured First Company. The near assassination of our Chapter Master. The failure and near decimation of the Fifth and now this – one hundred years of humiliation in the making, right underneath the disapproving noses of our Legionary kindred. All as spiritual censure for the loss of Dorn's gift – the very embodiment of our Adeptus Astartes honour.'

'We have lost a great symbol,' Ezrachi admitted, 'but not what the standard symbolised. That is alive and well in the hearts of every Excoriator who bears his blade in the Emperor's name. As they do here, brother, at the Feast of Blades.'

'Blades drawn in disbelief and sheathed in failure,' the corpus-captain said grimly.

'Is our standing in the Feast really so dire?'

'I'm pinning our hope on Usachar and Brother Dathan. Usachar is a squad whip and a veteran. Dathan is young but fast and has a way with a blade.'

'Some hope, then,' Ezrachi said.

'Usachar is chosen against Knud Hægstad of the Iron Knights and young Dathan has drawn Pugh's champion,' Gideon reported. 'It's never easy crossing blades with those chosen to wear the primarch's plate, but with the Imperial Fists defending their title and the Feast fought on a First Company-conquered world... I don't rate our chances. Even if they win, they'll have to face that damned Crimson Fist in the next round. It's fairly hopeless.'

'So,' Ezrachi put to the corpus-captain, 'it's time.'

'I would enter the arena myself, but for the desperation it speaks to our brethren.'

'Making your decision all the easier and more forgivable,' the Apothecary persisted. 'You have no choice. Give the order. Let me set free the Scourge.'

'I would not do that for a hundred worlds,' Gideon snarled. 'He's afflicted and has damned us all. Dorn has seen fit to punish him. The Scourge can rot for all I care. The Darkness is his to endure and I for one would not spare him his agonies.'

I am in a place… of darkness. I have never been here, yet I know it well. My mind – like my body – is in sensory overdrive. Something far beyond my genetic inheritance, beyond the rigours of Chapter indoctrination and the suprahormones roaring through my veins. This moment feels more acute, more vivid and keener than any I have formerly experienced. Every molecule of my being is devoted to it. Like the seconds have been honed to a razored edge.

Despite the intensity of this experience, the world about me is dark and indistinct. Everything, from the walls to the floor beneath my feet, is cloaked in a peripheral haze. I try to focus, but anything upon which I settle my eyes assumes the quality of screaming shadow. The howling gloom spreads like a stain, running into everything else and framing me in a vision of smeared charcoal.

I wander the labyrinthine nightmare of this place, weapon in hand. Searching. Splattered with blood that is not my own. Knowing that brothers both lost and true clash about me. There is gunfire. There is death. I can hear calls of distant anguish. I cannot make out the words but know that they are laced with venom and cold reason. The hot ringing of blades fills the air, punctuated by the crash of bolt-fire. I am on a smoke-stained battlefield. Boarding an enemy vessel. Reclaiming heretical dirt. Bringing sanity to a daemon world. I am in every battle that I have ever fought, one superimposed upon the other. Death and foes blurring. The colours of destruction smudging and blotting until all that is left is black.

My hearts hammer in unison. I am running. Fearful, but not for myself.

The dark nothingness about me saps my soul. Blood courses through my body. Battle beckons. I tremble not with dread but with expectation, the impending realisation of my genetic heritage. I am a warrior down to the last molecule of my being. I was engineered to kill for something greater than myself, to serve the

Father-of-All with blade, bolt – even my last breath, and all those preceding.

I live the lost brothers I have ended. Their bodies fallen and terrible in the murderous ruin they have committed – one upon the other and myself upon them all. Mighty brothers lie twisted and broken. Their god-flesh is still. Fratricide over. The chime of battle hangs about their corpses. Their weapons decorate the changing floor. My own joins them.

A doom, so deep, has reached me. A pain so clear and a loss so searing to my existence that it shatters my soul. Like a dread nova, erupting through histories both galactic and personal, the Darkness finds me. For a moment, there is light in the nothingness. The Emperor of Mankind is with me – here, in this hopeless place. His presence and legacy a beacon in the blackness. Withering to look upon. Impossible not to. I approach as one might his doom. Hesitant. Uncomprehending. Child-like. The moment overwhelms me and tears cascade down my blood-flecked cheeks. Then like a nova – brief, beautiful and sad in its distant diminishing – the beacon fades. I fall to my knees and I weep uncontrollably, for there is nothing left to do. No higher power to whom I can appeal.

The star has faded. The light is gone. In its place is dead space, laced with the poisonous shockwave of the aftermath, trembling through the ages. All that is left is the bottomless grief of the orphan Angel. My hearts know his immortal sorrow. Rogal Dorn. My father's loss. My loss through his. I feel what he felt, stood over the Emperor. I know the fear and misery he allowed himself. That moment of doubt and horror-stricken possibility becomes my eternity. It saturates me with its despair. I sink deep within myself and find a greater darkness there. An Imperium without an Emperor. A fatherless humanity. An eternity without direction. Dorn's Darkness.

I roar my defiance, like an infant freshly ripped from the womb. I fall to my knees. A new coldness clings to me. I quake. I know only fear and fury at an empty cosmos, devoid of answers.

But there is a figure. Something I have not seen before. There and yet not. An armoured shape that steps from the darkness into silhouette, glorious against the emptiness. Unlike the stygian surroundings or the Emperor, his presence eclipsed by his own brilliance, the figure falls into harrowing focus. Its movements are slow and deliberate, and as it walks towards me, it grows in stature and menace.

An ally? An enemy? There are no shortage of either, dead on the innumerable battlegrounds about me. I remain kneeling, as though my legs are now part of them all. My mind is overwhelmed with a grief beyond grief. I sit. I watch. I dread.

The revenant approaches. Its searing plate is of the blackest night. Each ceramite boot is wreathed in spectral flame. I look on as its incandescent steps fracture and frost-shatter the metal of the deck beneath them. The ghost-fire curls and crooks its way about the figure as one burned at the stake. It slows to an appalling stop and looks down on my kneeling form. Before me is an Angel of Death. A brother of the beyond. Devoid of Chapter markings, the armour speaks only of the grave, a rachial nightmare of rib and bone, a skeleton set within the surface of the sacred plate. Beneath, the ghastliness goes on. The faceplate of its helmet is smashed and a ceramite shard missing. The bleachwhite of a fleshless skull leers at me. The glint of a service stud. The darkness of an eye socket that burns with unnatural life. Perfect teeth that chatter horribly.

'What are you?' I manage, although it takes everything I have left to brave the utterance.

It says nothing, but reaches out with a raven gauntlet. A bone digit protrudes from the splintered ceramite fingertip. I watch it drift towards my face with horror. The thing touches me. And I scream.

CORPUS-CAPTAIN GIDEON STEPPED into the stone corridor. Closing the barbican behind him, the Excoriator rested his broad shoulders against the cool metal of the door. Beyond, Gideon could hear the crisp ring of blades rise up from the pit and through the solemn gathering of Adeptus Astartes officers stood amongst the tiered galleries.

Apothecary Ezrachi stepped out onto the long, empty corridor. He wiped blood from his hands with a surgical rag and stared down at the corpus-captain, whose head was angled to the door.

'Usachar?'

'Cut to ribbons,' the Apothecary told him, his voice bouncing around the confines of the subterranean passage. 'He'll be more stitch than flesh when I'm finished with him.'

Gideon turned his head to put his ear flat to the metal barbican. The sound of clashing blades had ceased. A sombre announcement was being made. Even muffled through the door, it was obvious to the corpus-captain that Brother Dathan had not been successful.

'Expect another for your slab,' Gideon informed the Apothecary. He turned to look at the aged Excoriator. Rubbing the red from his hands, Ezrachi returned the grim gaze.

'Corpus-captain...'

'I know,' Gideon said with slumped resignation. 'I would not do this but for the dishonour we would endure in exiting the Feast so early and the disgrace to carry back to Eschara. I promised Master Ichabod a victory to lift the Chapter and carry our brothers through these dark times. I cannot return with both empty hearts and hands. News of our failure would likely finish what the filth Alpha Legion started. I fear the disappointment alone might end him, Ezrachi.'

The Apothecary shook his battered face. 'Quesiah Ichabod is the greatest Excoriator to have ever lived. Those armoured serpents were lucky – and perhaps born so – but even they, with their lies and infernal ways, could not take him from us. Besides, he is now on Eschara with one of our best, the Chief Apothecary.'

'I can't look my Chapter Master in the eye and tell him I did everything in my power to secure victory when I did not.' Gideon seemed to come to a dismal decision. 'I'd hoped that it would not come to this. Nine Excoriators have fought for their Chapter in the Feast, yet ten were sent for such a hallowed duty. Only Dorn knows why Master Ichabod insisted upon his inclusion, but that is now the choice laid before me. Can the Scourge be made fit for anything, let alone battle?'

'I believe so. We are pure of hearts but not of blood. As

part of a former Legion and now as a Chapter, we are not alone in our experience of genetic deficiency. The Wolves and the Angels, as well as the brethren of future Foundings, carry the flaws of their blood heritage on to new generations,' the Excoriators Apothecary explained. 'When the Darkness takes one of our number, it might appear to us a wretched palsy: the slackness of the jaw, the tremor of the limb, the blankness of the eye. But those who survive it report the experience as a living nightmare, a sleeping wakefulness in which they relive the bottomless woe of Dorn's most trying time – the grievous loss of our Father-Emperor, at least as we knew him. This is both our father's genetic blessing and his curse to his sons. To know the possibility – for even a second – of an Imperium without the Emperor. To feel what Dorn felt. The profound misery of a primarch. The paralysing fear that even one as great as he experienced, for himself and for humanity, over the Emperor's shattered body. To live the Darkness.'

'Such details have little meaning for me, Apothecary,' Gideon told him. 'The Adeptus Astartes are bred for battle. They exist only to avenge the Emperor and put the enemies of humanity to the blade. I need warriors, not dreamers. Whatever the actual nature of this affliction, it does not befit one of our calling. If it were me, I'd rather my brothers ended such a vegetative existence than watch me live on in a senseless state.'

'Since the Darkness can strike any of us at any time, corpus-captain, I'll bear that in mind,' Ezrachi promised with a subversive curl of the lip. 'While we dwell on such matters, you should know that the procedure I intend is untried and that the brother in question might not survive it.'

'For the calamity he has brought down on all of us, I would lose little sleep over that.'

'I suspected as much,' the Apothecary said. 'I inform you only that it in turn might inform your strategy for our brothers in the contest. You do know it is possible that his suffering caused the loss of the Chapter standard rather than his failure being the cause of the Darkness.'

'What do I care for that?' Gideon snorted. 'He failed his primarch. He failed his Chapter Master. He failed us all. The only care I have in this is to find use for such traitorous hands. What will you do and how long do you need?'

'Santiarch Balshazar has his way of managing the afflicted,' Ezrachi replied. 'A spiritual treatment that those suffering the Darkness survive or they do not. While I respect the symbolic significance of the Santiarch's practice and the rituals specific to our Chapter cult, my method is comparatively direct.' The Apothecary indicated a point at the back of his skull, where in the fashion of the Chapter, his thinning hairline met a scarred and shaven scalp. 'The catalepsean node is located here on the brain stem. As the implant responsible for modifying the circadian rhythms – our patterns of sleep and elongated periods of consciousness – it seems possible that a malfunctioning node could be responsible for a loss of motor control and the experience of a "living nightmare". I plan to drill through the bone and insert a hypodermic lightning rod into the brain. There I shall issue a localised shock to the catalepsean node, hopefully interrupting the affliction of the Darkness and reinstating the natural function of the implant.'

'Sounds painful.'

'Undoubtedly.'

'Good,' the corpus-captain said. 'When you are finished with Usachar and Dathan, return to the *Scarifica*. The Rites of Battle begin for the next round shortly. The Feast waits for no one. Send word if your experiment meets with success. I'll also need informing if our fallen brother fails us once again.'

'How do you define failure?'

'A living-death or an actual one,' Gideon told the Apothecary as he took his leave. 'It makes very little difference to me when it comes to Zachariah Kersh.'

'I TRUST EVERYTHING is prepared?'

'Yes, my lord.'

Apothecary Ezrachi stomped down the ramp into the

cargo compartment of the frigate *Scarifica*, his leg clunking against the metal floor. His nostrils flared. They were down in the bowels of the ship. He would have preferred a more suitable location for the procedure, but his brother Excoriators would not tolerate the Scourge's presence.

Crates and bulk-canisters had been cleared in the centre of the compartment, creating an open space. There stood a decorative casket, an item transported from Santiarch Balshazar's Holy Reclusiam, buried deep within the Excoriators' fortress-monastery on distant Eschara. Beaten from dull adamantium, the box had the dimensions of a sarcophagus and the extravagant garniture to match. Its frontispiece featured a raised depiction of the Emperor-of-All; despite the casket standing upright, it represented him as prone, maimed and broken, following his confrontation with the beast Horus. Santiarch Balshazar's solution to the affliction of the Darkness. A darkness of his own. The most solitary of confinements, where no self-respecting Excoriator need look upon his weakness and invalidity.

On either side of the sarcophagus's head was a small confessional grille. On the left, Ezrachi's apothecarion aides busied themselves in ivory robes, adorned with the insignia of the prime helix. They were making adjustments to a tripod arrangement and drill, the trepan of which was pointed through the open grille. On the opposite side were the Scourge's own serfs, looking thoroughly miserable. Since the disgrace of their master they had been relegated to the cargo compartment also, bunking and toileting in the dark, down with the casket that held the fallen Kersh.

There were three. Old Enoch was the Scourge's seneschal. He sat, perpetually oiling the braided length of 'the purge' and mumbling insensibly to himself. He was caretaker of the ceremonial lash and overseer of his master's devotional mortification. Enoch's son Oren proceeded to mop the area around the sarcophagus base where a growing pool of waste was escaping the casket-base. He was the lictor. Barrel-chested, with the thick arms of a scud-wrestler, it had been Oren's solemn function to administer 'the purge' with all the devotion of which he was capable. His father supervised the ritual, his crabby eyes burning in disappointment that his own son had not been honoured with tissue compatibility for a life beyond mere humanity. Old Enoch's daughter Bethesda was the Scourge's absterge. An elfin waif of a girl – gaunt and grim – she was charged with the routine cleansing and dressing of the Adeptus Astartes' ceremonial wounds. Excoriators all took their purification across their broad, muscular backs – as part of the ritual they called 'Donning Dorn's Mantle'. Beyond basic servitude to the Scourge, the three serfs were charged – by Kersh himself above all else – to excoriate his flesh and purify him of weakness so that he might achieve endorphic communion with the primarch.

Bethesda was reading to the Scourge through the confessional grille on the other side of the casket, although it was unclear how much of the text Kersh was hearing. Whilst enthralled by the Darkness, victims couldn't speak or communicate. They couldn't feed themselves or take water and seemed feverishly insensible to everything happening about them. At the Apothecary's entrance, Kersh's servants stood or turned to present themselves. Bethesda slammed the tome shut. Ezrachi caught the title: *The Architecture of Agony* by Demetrius Katafalque. He knew it well. A treatise of devotional suffering by the former captain and first Master of the Excoriators Chapter.

'Pray, continue,' Ezrachi ordered softly. 'This will not be pleasant and I wish our convalescent every distraction.'

Bethesda returned to her reading.

'… During Terra's infancy, in which the warriors of brute nations were flogged as a test of their manhood…'

'We've broken through the lower cranium, my lord,' one of Ezrachi's aides told him, standing at the tripod-trepan like a workman at a lathe.

'All right,' Ezrachi called to his aides. 'Do your duty.'

'…Later monastic orders of the Church Katholi indulged flagellation as a form of militant pilgrimage…'

Kersh seemed unmoved by the horrific procedure, held

in place within the casket. The Scourge remained silent and still, the drill embedded in his skull and Bethesda's hon-eyed words filling the cargo compartment.

Locking off the drill, one of the aides depressed a plunger on a power cell situated between the legs of the tripod. The other wrapped himself around an underslung buttstock and trigger arrangement hanging beneath the drill.

'Charging. Six megathule range.'

'...of the Old Hundred. The Geno Seven-Sixty Spartocid fought for the Emperor in the Unification Wars and during the Great Crusade, where it was considered a genic officer's honour to match the number of strokes suffered by a stere-obreed soldier, for failure under his command...'

'Launching hypodermic rod.'

The apparatus fired and a sickening thud reverberated around the chamber. The robed aides made adjustments to their drill.

'...whereas it is practice aboard the mighty *Phalanx* to embrace a technological solution to the self-infliction of suffering, I favour my Lord Dorn's practice for my brother Excoriators. On our primarch's fosterworld of Inwit, the winters were cold and the lash was hot. Such instruction was adopted across Dorn's early empire and favoured by the Progenitor personally as a form of martial communion and as purification for the soul...'

Pressing his face into the micronocular eyepieces above the stock, the aide consulted a pict screen before announcing, 'We have achieved the catalepsean node, Apothecary.'

'What are you waiting for?' Ezrachi barked. 'Pray to Dorn and deliver the charge.'

A faint hum indicated the duration of the treatment. Bethesda closed the Scourge's copy of Demetrius Kata-falque's mighty tome and got to her feet. The chamber fell still. Ezrachi's brow began to knot with disappointment.

'Again.'

The aides repeated the procedure. All in attendance waited.

Then it began. A sound like distant fury, building within

the casket. An agonising roar that was everywhere. The rage of a woken giant.

'Fire the seals,' Ezrachi ordered Oren and Old Enoch. 'Get this thing open.'

The sarcophagus started to shake. Ezrachi pursed his age-cracked lips. Perhaps the Scourge was experiencing a variety of fit. Perhaps the procedure had caused some kind of neural damage. Perhaps the warrior simply wanted out of the casket. 'The drill!' the Apothecary remembered, prompting his aides to simultaneously begin retracting the hypodermic rod and reverse-screwing the trepan drill-bit.

As the box shuddered and the furious lament built to a horrible crescendo, the sarcophagus lid swung open. Silence reigned in the compartment once again. The depths of the casket were a foetid darkness. The trembling cabinet grew still. Inside, the laboured breathing of the Scourge could be heard. The apothecarion aides worked frantically to withdraw the deadly reach of their apparatus. With a teeth-clenched grunt, Zachariah Kersh pulled his bulk from the sarcophagus interior.

He was as naked as the day he was initiated, five hundred and fifty-two years before, and stumbled from the interior and out into the cargo compartment. His beard was scraggy and cotted, and his white tonsure overgrown and threaded with silver. The Scourge had a face to match his name, both afflicted and afflicting. He had inherited the dour mask of his Lord Dorn, behind which eyes alive with predatory intensity and accusation burned. He would pass for Demetrius Katafalque himself, if the etchings were to be believed, but for a ragged wound on his right cheek, which had long healed exposing tendons, part of the jawbone and the darkness of his mouth.

Kersh wasn't as tall as many of his Excoriator brothers but more than made up for this deficiency with muscle crafted in the desperation of battle, rather than the monastery gymnasia. His flesh was a primarch-pleasing canvas of burn marks and scar tissue, stretched across a frame broad with age and experience. He wavered before a delighted Ezrachi, reminding the Apothecary of a statue of Terran antiquity with his demigod's physique. The Scourge had emerged alive, covered in his own filth but free of the Darkness and its curse.

Bethesda came up behind him with a cream shroud and threw it across the Scourge's lash-mangled back and globed shoulders. The fabric blotched immediately with the Excoriator's blood, sweat and mess. Kersh half slipped and went down on his knees, reaching out for support and finding only the slender serf. With his great hand on her tiny shoulder he steadied himself. Reaching for the back of his skull with the other, Kersh tore out the broken drill-bit and hypodermic rod, flinging the attachment at the compartment floor where it *pranged* off the metal decking.

Ezrachi hesitated, his lips forming around a greeting. He wanted to know if his subject had survived the procedure with his faculties intact. The Scourge beat him to it.

'Stay out of my skull, Apothecary,' Zachariah Kersh growled. Shoulders dropped with relief among the gathered Chapter serfs, and Ezrachi smiled.

'You're welcome, brother…'

THE SCOURGE'S ABSTERGE crossed the benighted cargo bay and entered the bondservants' berth with a heavy water cask. It was less a berth than a dusty unguent locker used by Techmarines to store oils and bless them in readiness for use in the enginarium. The Cog Mechanicum hung above a small shrine to the Omnissiah that Old Enoch had put to good use as a counter or tabletop. The seneschal was stripped to the waist, baring a shrivelled chest, and had laid out a bowl and a shaving blade. He peered at his gaunt, empty features in a section of metal wall that he'd had Bethesda clean and polish to dull reflection. The absterge poured fresh water into the bowl, at which her father said nothing. The seneschal dipped his hand into a can of blessed oil and rubbed his bristled chin with the thin unguent. He then went to work rhythmically with the razor, scraping his slick, leathery skin and cleansing the blade in the water.

Putting down the cask, Bethesda passed her brother Oren, who had toppled one of their metal bunks and was using it to accomplish pull-ups. The lictor's meaty arms pulled his broad bulk up off the locker floor. With each rise and fall Oren gave a piggish grunt. Bethesda knelt in the corner of their berth and stacked a small collection of empty unguent cans. She produced a selection of half-spent candles and began to amuse herself with their arrangement.

'What in Katafalque's name do you think you're doing?' Oren asked between grunts, but Bethesda didn't answer. Enchanted with her simple display, she attempted to light the candles with a screw-flint. The brawny lictor came to a stop, watching his sister. 'I said, what are you doing? Answer when you're damn well spoken to.'

Bethesda looked up, smiling to herself. 'I'm just lighting some candles.'

'Where did you get them from?'

'Traded them, with one of the attendants in the chapel-reclusiam,' the serf admitted.

'What in damnation for?'

'Sundries.'

'You stupid slattern,' her brother came back savagely. 'I mean, why?'

'For the Scourge,' she answered. 'To celebrate his delivery from the Darkness.'

This time it was her father's turn to grunt. Oren put an angry boot straight through the cans and candle arrangement.

'Not in here you don't.'

Bethesda went to reclaim her smashed candles. She murmured, 'Just because he is what you can never be.'

'What did you say to me?' Oren growled, his eyes livid and cheeks flushed. He closed on her and she stood with fragile defiance. Bethesda heard her father's razor pause. Old Enoch mumbled something. Oren paused dangerously before her, his chest rising and falling with a sibling's petty anger.

'Once,' he told her through clenched teeth, 'I wanted

more than my pitiful existence to be an Emperor's Angel. More than a hundred pitiful existences to be the warrior at whose pleasure I serve – the Scourge. An Excoriator without equal. I know better now. Our master is but a false prophet. An Angel fallen. He is so deep in his brothers' blood that he might as well have slain them himself. We are punished. The Darkness has taken us all. But know this, good sister, if *I* had been Chapter Scourge, I would not have given up our Stigmartyr so easily.'

A call came from the distant cargo bay. A demigod demanding attendance. Old Enoch grumbled his garbled insistence and Oren backed away from his sister, holding her gaze as he did so. As the lictor left the locker, his father dashed his unkindly face with water before using a ragged towel to dry it off. He turned and stood, giving Bethesda a sour glare. Throwing the towel at her, he mumbled his disgust before following Oren out, leaving the absterge alone with her candles.

CHAPTER TWO
STIGMARTYR

'CEASE!'

Zachariah Kersh heard Ezrachi's command across the *Scarifica*'s penitorium and the crack of the whip. Kersh's personal serfs paused at the Apothecary's order. Oren hesitated, the stock of 'the purge' clutched in his white-knuckled fist, the bloodied lash resting in coils on the deck beside him. Old Enoch looked to his Adeptus Astartes master, whose teeth-clenching snarl fell and eyes opened. He gave the seneschal a stabbing glare. Old Enoch began babbling to his son in a savage tone that echoed the Excoriator's displeasure. His chest heaving with exertion, Oren gathered 'the purge's' sacred length before handing it to his father for cleansing and consecration.

Kersh took his palms off the numbing cold of a section of reinforced armaplas. The blast shielding was closed, but the plas of the vistaport still retained the scalding sting of the void beyond. The heat from each handprint vanished from its deep blackness. The Scourge turned to present himself to the Apothecary and his freshly mauled back-flesh to the port. Ezrachi shook his head as he took in the constellation of ugly welts on the Space Marine's body. Old scars from battles fought long ago.

'What on Eschara do you think you're doing?' Ezrachi put to him. The Apothecary's ceremonial plate was splattered with blood and he held his white helmet under one arm. 'My express instructions were for rest, not mortification.'

'I shouldn't have to learn my shame from an errant,' Kersh said, staring at the approaching Apothecary but nodding at Old Enoch. 'I heard from mortal lips how Dorn's flesh had failed them, failed their master and failed their master's master.'

Ezrachi slowed. 'I regret that,' he said finally. 'There have been pressing demands on my time. I had hoped to perform such a duty... at a suitable moment. Still, in my absence you had my orders–'

'I have fallen so far in my estimation,' Kersh seethed, 'and that of my brothers that I'm not even sure I deserve to live.'

The Apothecary jabbed a gauntleted finger at Kersh's superhuman bulk. 'Do not be casual with this divine instrument, for it belongs neither to you nor your brothers,' Ezrachi warned. 'Your soul belongs to the Emperor and your flesh to Rogal Dorn – as you have correctly observed. The death separating the two belongs only to your enemies. In the meantime an Imperium's interest resides in what may become of this crafted form before that eventuality.'

'This flesh needs purification. I must find myself and the presence of the primarch within me.'

'You have been one with the Darkness,' Ezrachi countered. 'You have walked in Dorn's plate, seen the galaxy through his eyes, known the emptiness of his grieving heart. Some may say that no living Excoriator has known his father as well.'

'Where is the Stigmartyr?' Kersh asked. 'Where is the Chapter's sacred standard now?'

'It is lost...' a voice rumbled from behind Ezrachi. 'Like you.'

Another Excoriator entered the penitorium. He was stripped to the waist, like Kersh, and accompanied by his own trio of Chapter serfs. His flesh was that of a veteran, leathery and lined from a lifetime spent in battle. His brow bore a neat row of service studs and a necklace of chainsword teeth jangled about his taut neck. 'And now… like us.'

'Tiberias,' Ezrachi warned.

As his seneschal, lictor and absterge filed past, the Space Marine turned to hang a towel from a hook set into the wall. The word *Vanguard* was tattooed across his broad shoulders, identifying him as an honoured brother of the First Company. As he turned again his baleful gaze drove the Scourge's eyes to the deck. The sting of shame kept them there for a moment, but before Kersh knew he had done it, he was staring back at the Excoriator in defiance.

'Kersh,' the Apothecary said.

'Do not spare me, brother,' the Scourge called at Tiberias. Fresh blood pitter-pattered the deck about the Space Marine, falling from the torn flesh on his back. Bethesda approached with Kersh's own towel. 'Back…' the Scourge growled, causing the absterge to drop the item where she stood and retreat. Ezrachi watched, uncertain, as Tiberias approached. Kersh took several steps also, scooping up the towel and wiping the glistening sweat from a knotted brow. 'Where is it?'

'What would you do with such information?' Tiberias teased through a sneer. 'Reclaim it?'

'I would.'

'And I would check your instruments, Apothecary,' the veteran said to Ezrachi, 'for your patient here seems still to dream.'

'You'll wish I was dreaming, brother,' Kersh told him.

'I am no brother of yours, Scourge…'

'Must I beat it out of you?'

'Desist. The both of–' Ezrachi began.

'I'll fight you for less than that,' Tiberias informed him as the two of them closed. 'The Alpha Legion has the Stigmartyr now.' The two Excoriators began to circle. 'You and the Santiarch are all that remain of the Chapter Master's inner circle. And I am all that's left of the Honoured First.'

51

Kersh looked from Ezrachi to Tiberias, then back to the Apothecary.

'Chapter Master Ichabod?'

'The Chapter Master lives,' Ezrachi confirmed, 'but the rumours are that he is waning.'

'Rumours!' Kersh spat. 'You are Ezrachi, of the Helix – what does your Lord Apothecary say?'

'My lord is dead,' Ezrachi admitted, more harshly than he intended. Taking his helmet from under his arm, he hugged it to his chestplate. 'Like Tiberias says, the circle is broken. Chapter Master Ichabod is strong, but his wounds are grievous. The Alpha Legion's assassination failed, but they employed a virulent toxin for which we have no record, nor antidote. It is only a matter of time.'

'How long?'

'Weeks. Perhaps years. In truth we do not know.'

'We must search for the source of this toxin.'

'Already begun – that is the Fourth Company's honour. They suspect it to be a naturally occurring substance, since it betrays no evidence of engineering. They have been despatched to every known death world in the segmentum. That is why I have been attached to this venture. Apothecary Absalom of the Second was due to travel with you to the Feast, but he is needed to coordinate the search and to formulate an antidote. He is Lord Apothecary now.'

'Then where are the Alpha Legion?' Kersh demanded.

'They have slithered away like the serpents they are,' Tiberias said.

'The Fourth waste their time,' Kersh said to Ezrachi. 'We must find the Traitors and recover both the banner and intelligence of the toxin's origin.'

'You think we have not all thought on that?' Tiberias goaded.

'They are everywhere and nowhere,' Ezrachi said with sadness. 'They have played with us. Even the most promising leads have thus far turned out to be no more than shadows and whispers. That was until Veiglehaven.'

'Veiglehaven?'

'The Fifth Company were lured there,' Ezrachi told the Scourge.

'Looking for the Chapter standard,' Tiberias added, jabbing a meaty finger at Kersh. 'Your standard.'

'A trap?'

The Apothecary nodded sadly.

'How many?'

'Over half the company was lost,' Tiberias said. Kersh's gaze fell to the deck. 'Brothers, sent to suffer an ignoble death, while you live and breathe before me. The Scourge? More like *a* scourge. A scourge on this Chapter. Your hearts beat only to expound your dishonour. How do you suffer the insufferable? Our blood – on your hands.'

'It's Dorn's way,' Kersh said finally, his eyes rising once again to meet his accuser's. 'We are for the Emperor, to the point of death. Devotion at any cost – even that of my soul, Brother Tiberias. We talk of your blood and its whereabouts. My understanding is that you will find it in ample quantity on the blade of the White Templar you fought in the Cage.'

The Excoriator's sneer split into an ugly snarl. His bruised fist came at Kersh with a furious desire. Tiberias was fast but his movements were those of a close combat veteran: precise, measured and committed. Predictably so. Kersh had spent a lifetime at his Chapter Master's side, fighting experienced warriors of all creeds and species. The enemy would always send their best at him and it had been the Scourge's simple honour to end them before they could end his master.

Kersh held his ground, craning and stretching. Tiberias's fists were everywhere: punching, back-handing, swinging. Each failed to find its mark – the fury of each strike lost on air. The Scourge angled his shoulders, swooping and bobbing his head just out of the veteran's considerable reach. A bare foot struck out at Kersh, forcing him to pivot. He slapped the knee aside and flung his towel into Tiberias's contorted face. The honoured brother tore it away, only to find that Kersh had pivoted back.

A gobbet of blood and teeth erupted from the veteran's mouth as his head was smashed to one side. The Excoriator's mighty body followed, his feet thrown up into the air and his tattooed shoulders hammering into the hard deck with a metallic boom.

Kersh stood with Ezrachi's helmet clutched in one hand. The Apothecary had tried to get between the two warriors in his ceremonial plate, but Kersh had snatched his bone-white helm from his hands. It sat snug in his fist as he'd spun around, like a moon in rapid orbit around a serene gas giant, until it crashed into Tiberias's face.

Ezrachi knelt down beside the felled Space Marine to check his ruined features. A broken nose and shattered jaw fountained a further spray of blood as Tiberias coughed up more teeth. Kersh looked down at the gore-smear across the white of the helm's faceplate.

'I've found more of your blood, Brother Tiberias,' the Scourge spat, prompting the veteran to shove the aged Ezrachi aside and scramble, half blood-blind to his feet.

'Come on, meat,' Kersh dared.

'Enough!' Corpus-Captain Gideon called, striding into the penitorium. 'Save it for the damned arena,' he said in disgust. 'Get him out of here. Clear the chamber.'

Chapter serfs hurried past, while Ezrachi angled the unsteady Tiberias's shoulders towards the exit. The Apothecary gave the Scourge a sullen scowl.

'I will see you planetside,' Ezrachi told him. Kersh threw Ezrachi back his besmirched helm.

The Apothecary looked back at Kersh and then left. The corpus-captain hit a vox-stud in the wall.

'This is Gideon. Open the blast shields, port-side aft.'

The penitorium shuddered as the clinker plates of armour running down the frigate's aft section began to part. As Gideon crossed the chamber, the colossal metal slats receded like blinds to admit the scene beyond. Light flooded the dim penitorium. 'With me,' the corpus-captain ordered.

Kersh hovered for a moment, just long enough for

Gideon to register his defiance, before striding across to the vistaport. The armaplas window ran the length of the penitorium. The two Excoriators stood in silence, taking in the planet below and the craft upon which the *Scarifica* held orbital station. Beside the Excoriators frigate sat the Death Strike gunfreighter *Nihilan Proxy*. Beyond that the pocket-frigate *Bellicose* rolled, bearing the Chapter insignia of the Black Templars. Several other rapid strike vessels, all belonging to different Adeptus Astartes Chapters, lay in high orbit, gathered about the battle-scarred flanks of the *Titus*, a veteran Imperial Fists cruiser.

Below them was a world the yellow of cowardice and swirl-smeared in a cloud-cover of soot and ash. The *Titus* and the attending smaller craft drifted above a blackened pole. About the fat belt of the planet's equator, Kersh could make out the lightshow of colossal impacts and explosions beneath the smog. A huge xenos craft hurtled towards the region. An obscenity of interstellar scrap, the vessel had the unmistakable graceless and clunky design of a greenskin kroozer. Flanked to starboard by Imperial Navy destroyers and a light cruiser, and on the portside by an Imperial Fists Gladius frigate, the unstoppable craft seemed to have an enemy escort. An almost continuous stream of fire existed between the Navy vessels and the monster's thick hull, however, and the Imperial Fists vessel was engaged in a desperate high-speed boarding action. Beyond the spectacle, the distant sparks of lance beams and cannon fire marked out a distant cordon, a gauntlet of Navy and Adeptus Astartes vessels through which a swarm of other greenskin attack craft were attempting to punch.

'All right,' Kersh said finally. 'Where are we?'

'Samarquand.'

'Never heard of it.'

'I'm not surprised. It has been part of the Urk Empire for two thousand years. A greenskin overlord called the Great Tusk holds the system here.'

'Some overlord, I haven't heard of him either.'

Gideon ignored Kersh's obvious insolence. 'The

Samarquand agri-worlds supplied the cluster-hives of
Coronis Agathon. Twelve verdant planets – amongst the
most productive in the Imperium – inadequately garrisoned
and consigned to doom and the infection of the xenos.
Unfortunately, the Great Tusk and its line are plagued with
an uncharacteristic lack of ambition. The fat monsters seem
content to sit here, breeding in their own squalor. Their fleet
and forces have never committed themselves out-system or
joined the invasions plaguing nearby sectors.'

'We think that this Tusk is building up to something?'

'Two thousand years is a lot of patience for a greenskin,
don't you think?' the corpus-captain returned. 'No. But a
populous xenos empire, no matter how small, cannot be
tolerated so close to Imperial shipping lanes.'

'So, destroy it,' Kersh said.

'The effort to do so continues to this day,' Gideon told
him.

'For two thousand years?'

'In turn, the Imperial Fists, the Dark Angels and the Space
Wolves all have had honoured commitments to remove the
Great Tusk and cleanse the system. Progress has been slow.'

'The xenos are dug in?'

'Nothing so sophisticated. There are just too many of
them. Reports return of coast-to-coast greenskins on the
planet surfaces: the Vostroyan Firstborn 13th Regiment, the
Moloch 132nd Rifles and the Urdeshi 27th Mechanised –
all wiped out in taking Samarquand.'

'Then Samarquand is taken.'

'Emperor be praised. Our brethren the Imperial Fists have
succeeded where the Wolves and Angels failed. Samarquand IV has rejoined the Imperium. Still, one amongst
twelve, with the enemy intent on taking it back…'

'What in Dorn's name are we doing here?' Kersh interrupted. 'What am I doing here?'

'If it were my choice, Scourge, I would not have you here
at all.'

'Have our brother-Fists requested our assistance?'

'No.'

'Then don't we have ongoing engagements of our own to honour?' Kersh pressed. 'The Alpha Legion. Chapter Master Ichabod?'

'You are here at Master Ichabod's decree and that is all your wretched ears need know.'

Kersh turned on the corpus-captain. 'I belong at my master's side.'

'You are not wanted, nor needed there,' Gideon said. 'You are to play no further role in the tragic events afflicting our Chapter. Do you hear me, Scourge? Whatever worth you have left is to be measured here.'

'Here?' the Excoriator said, jabbing a finger at the vistaport. 'I don't even know where *here* is.'

'Samarquand IV is the chosen ground for the eight hundred and sixteenth Feast of Blades.'

'We're here to compete?'

'You're here to compete.'

'With the Chapter under attack and our master's life hanging in the balance, we are here contesting?' Kersh said, his words dripping with incredulity. 'Have you gone mad?'

'The Feast is important.'

'The Feast is a distraction!'

'An important one. These are dark times, Kersh – and not just for the Excoriators. The Emperor's Angels are spread thin across the stars. Dorn's sons spread even thinner. Chapter relations must be maintained. The bonds of brotherhood strengthened and tempered through contestation.'

'We have only just concluded a Feast.'

'Tradition dictates the Feasts are centennial – at least centennial. It is the right of the reigning Chapter to call a Feast before its time. They often do.'

'Why, by Katafalque, would they do that?' Kersh sneered.

'The Feast of Blades serves its purpose,' Gideon said. 'Many pacts are created and obligations honoured among our brethren – but we are bred for victory. Reigning Chapters want to build on past triumphs, for their success to echo through eternity, to catch Dorn's approving eye or ear, wherever the Lord Primarch might be. They call the

Feast to best complement their advantage – the prowess of their champions, the perceived weakness of their opponent Chapters. Like us, they want to win. I would be surprised if the recent trials of our own Chapter hadn't been a factor in the Feast's most recent calling.'

'Could we not we request that another Chapter take our place?'

'On occasion that happens.'

'Then why didn't you make that happen?'

'A brother's love is hard won,' Gideon told him. 'The Feast of Blades is not, however, an empty exercise. Chapter relations bear fruit. Even now, the Fire Lords move in to relieve our Second Company at Celator-Primus.'

'We are Excoriators–'

'Yes, we are. You'll find our blood in the earth of Holy Terra and staining the mighty walls of the Imperial Palace. We hold our ground now as we did then, in our primarch's plate. Our very existence is a war of attrition. As a Chapter we shall not falter. Not now – not ever.'

'Agreed,' Kersh said. 'But why contest honour when we can earn it through the worthy deaths of our enemies?'

'There is a fire within you, Scourge, that even I can feel,' Gideon told him. 'Be it loyalty, shame, hunger for revenge – I know not. I care not. The Chapter is suffering its worst losses in five thousand years. These are dark times and I need that fire burning bright in every company, every squad, every Excoriator. As well as reinforcing relations with our primogenate kin, participation in the games generates Chapter pride. With Master Ichabod afflicted and the Stigmartyr lost, our brothers' hopes have turned to ash in their chests. The mere embers of faith sustain them. Ichabod hoped that some success at the Feast might stoke the fire in their hearts. That is why he sent me. That is why he sent you.'

Kersh stared out across the frozen void. 'How do we fare?' he said finally.

'The worst in our history,' the corpus-captain admitted. 'Nine of our ten champions have been beaten and are out of the contest – and the Feast is but yet at an early stage. You are the last. That is why I had Ezrachi experiment with that damned box.'

'If I fail?'

'Then we have dishonoured Dorn and our entire Chapter. In your case, again. It would strengthen the belief in our brothers that we are ruined and I don't know if Master Ichabod would survive such news.'

'But we would leave the Feast early?'

'Think not on crusades to reclaim the Stigmartyr. If winning back your honour is the prize, then that can only be achieved here. If you do not do your utmost – as every Excoriator before you – to succeed in the Feast, then I shall leave Samarquand with my ten defeated champions and take the *Scarifica* to Onassis and join the Marines Mordant on their penance crusade through Tempest Hippocrene. You will not see our home world, Eschara, for a hundred years, and when you do, it will be because the dishonour of our failure has been bled from your body. I will then select you for participation in the Feast once more. Consider this both my threat and my promise, brother.'

Kersh stood there. Angry at Gideon. Angry at himself. He watched the Imperial Fists cruiser peel away from the greenskin hulk. The Imperial Navy vessels disengaged likewise, their magnabore laser batteries silent but still glowing. The kroozer rippled with explosions. Sections broke away and the bulbous monstrosity split in two. Both sections tumbled towards Samarquand IV, wreathed in an upper-atmospheric blaze. These were followed by falling stars that had erupted from the belly of the Adeptus Astartes strike cruiser and were now thunderbolting down through the wake of the wreckage. Drop-pods laden with Imperial Fists, intent on finishing the job and cleansing the inevitable crash-site of greenskin scum.

Kersh turned to Gideon, but he had gone, leaving the Scourge in the penitorium on his own. The deck lamps were out and the cool chamber was only lit by the sickly light of the planet below. A shiver danced up the Space Marine's spine and the flesh on his forearms suddenly pimpled, telling Kersh that the temperature in the penitorium had dropped considerably. Something brushed past the tiny hairs standing erect on his thick neck, causing the Excoriator to spin around. He found nothing but empty darkness. He hocked and spat into the black.

'I spit on your childish tricks, Tiberias,' Kersh announced to the echoing chamber, 'for they proceed from a cowardly soul.'

Kersh turned back to the thick armaplas and the deeper darkness of space. He soaked up the emptiness for a moment – the totality of black loneliness offered by the void – before realising that he wasn't actually alone. The unrequested appearance of his serfs would simply have irritated the Scourge. If he had sensed Tiberias then the Excoriator's brawny arms would have flared with the sudden burn of anger and adrenaline. This was something else. The pit of his stomach curdled. He felt the coolness of his blood. Then, the chatter of teeth.

The Scourge turned his head slowly. He saw a ghostly reflection in the plas, the silhouette of an armoured figure, cutting its shape into the darkness beyond.

'No…' Kersh mouthed, his breath misting before him. His eyes widened. Before him was the revenant from his dark dreams. It didn't look at him. It merely existed. There. A horrifying reality. Its grotesque armour was the skeletal nightmare he remembered, and through a rent in its helm, Kersh caught a glimpse of something unliving, a vision of fear crafted in bone and smouldering with radiance unnatural.

Something akin to fear fluttered through the Scourge's being. He had not been built with the emotional spectrum to experience dread as mortals did, but something deep and primordial within him was reacting to the phantasm, and it was not pleasant. This alien feeling soon churned into something all the more recognisable to the Space Marine. Anger. The desire to meet a threat head on and end it. The revenant could be heralding the return of the Darkness or it could be an unknown menace that was a danger to the ship. Either way, Kersh felt that he had to act. He risked a fleeting glance about the benighted penitorium, his eyes darting for anything that might serve as a weapon. The brief search revealed nothing and within a moment, his distrusting gaze was back on the revenant. Except, it wasn't there.

Through the vistaport plas, the busy hull of the *Scarifica* became silhouetted against the sallow curvature of Samarquand IV. Amongst the aerials, crenellations and grotesques, Kersh could make out a distant, armoured figure on the exterior of the ship. The revenant. It too was in silhouette and held his attention as it worked its ghostly way up through the crowded architecture.

'Terran Throne…' Kersh murmured, his eyes almost to the armaplas. Step by spectral step he followed it with his eyes, until, with a ghoulish uncertainty plucking at his hearts, he watched it disappear around a maintenance barbican.

He felt something wet and slippery to the touch on the plas interior. Backing away, Kersh found himself staring at High Gothic scrawl written with a fingertip on the vistaport surface. Some of his own words – words he'd used in the penitorium only minutes before – quoted back to him. *In dedicato imperatum ultra articulo mortis.* 'For the Emperor beyond the point of death,' Kersh mouthed. Stunned, the Excoriator strode across the darkness of the chamber. Hitting a stud by the penitorium bulkhead, he brought the deck lamps back to life. With the lamps on, Kersh could see that the words were spelled out in blood. Blood taken from the pool Brother Tiberias had left on the floor. There were bloodied footsteps also. Armoured, broad and heavy. They led from the spot Tiberias had fallen to the High Gothic on the vistaport. They seemed to come from nowhere and they led to nothingness.

Kersh hit the stud that opened the bulkhead and found Old Enoch, Oren and Bethesda waiting obediently outside. Gideon had dismissed them but no one had given them permission to re-enter the penitorium.

'Did anyone enter after the corpus-captain left?' he put to

them. They looked to each other and began to shake their heads.

'Are you all right, my lord?' Bethesda ventured.

His eyes narrowed, then he turned back to the penitorium chamber. The pool of Tiberias's blood still decorated the floor, but the footprints were gone. The Excoriator scanned the vistaport, but all trace of the words had vanished. He approached and looked back out along the *Scarifica*'s hull for any sign of the figure, but there was none.

'My lord?' the absterge asked, stepping into the chamber.

Kersh turned and placed his scarred back and shoulders against the cool plas. He looked up at the blood-speckled ceiling of the penitorium. 'I need the Apothecary,' Kersh told her.

'He is not here, my liege.'

'Where is he?'

'On the planet surface.'

'Then that is where we will go. Prepare a transport.'

CHAPTER THREE
THE FEAST OF BLADES

'LISTEN, EZRACHI…'

Kersh followed the Apothecary down the crowded stone corridor towards the arena. In turn the Scourge was trailed by his three serfs. Ezrachi limped through a throng of mortals and dead-eyed servitors. Each was pushing its way past, fetching, carrying and attending to urgent if minor duties. A sea of different Chapter colours, they parted as the Excoriators Apothecary marched to the rhythm of his leg's hydraulic sighing.

'I tell you, I am not well. I am not myself.'

'Well, whoever you are,' Ezrachi told him, 'you're entering the Cage in about three minutes, so I suggest you get yourself ready.'

'I am suffering a spuriousness of the mind.'

'Existential anxiety is an understandable side effect of such an unusually long time spent in the Darkness.'

'Perhaps there was an error with the procedure…'

'Gideon said that you would try something like this.'

'I see the impossible.'

'Seeing is believing, Kersh. Make the impossible happen here and we might just have a chance.'

'I am still afflicted, Apothecary!'

Serfs, who usually had their eyes directed to the floor in the presence of an Adeptus Astartes, looked up at the tormented Excoriator.

Ezrachi ground to a halt and turned. 'I've reviewed the procedure and already made a thorough medical examination of your person. The procedure was a success.'

'An occulobular defect?'

'Impossible.'

'Suprahormonal imbalance.'

'Would have other symptoms.'

'Cerebral damage.'

'I was wrong, Kersh.'

'What do you mean?'

'Back on the *Scarifica*, I ordered rest and recuperation. I was wrong. All of your wounds, those sustained at the hands of the Alpha Legion and the catalepseal procedure that followed, are all but healed. We are the Emperor's Angels and we are made in his image, but we are not the same. I underestimated your powers of recovery. You are gifted, Scourge, and I need you to use that gift now. Your brothers expect this of you. It is a matter of honour and you must answer your Chapter's call. This above all other considerations. Do you hear me, Kersh? The time is now. Two minutes – or the Excoriators forfeit the contest *and* their honour.'

The Scourge's shoulders sagged. 'Then I am simply losing my sanity.'

'A mortal condition – I assure you. Follow me,' Ezrachi instructed and ducked through an archway. Inside, Kersh found a small chamber. Each Chapter had been set aside a small area close to the arena known as the Cage to use for their preparations martial, medical and spiritual. 'Assist Brother Hadrach,' Ezrachi ordered Kersh's serfs as the Scourge came to stand on a central stone bearing the Excoriators' seal. The young Techmarine Hadrach had forgone his ceremonial plate and had settled instead for forge-robes.

He worked feverishly over an adamantium anvil with an assortment of calibrated hammers, but paused long enough to give Kersh a stare of positive dislike.

'As you were, brother,' Ezrachi said, and the Techmarine returned to his work. Old Enoch and Oren started walking pieces of armour from Hadrach's workspace to their Excoriator lord. Bethesda disrobed the Scourge. As her two compatriots began decorating their master's muscular form she got to work on the belts, clips and seals that held the ceramite plates together.

'What is this?' Kersh asked looking down at the deep yellow of the battered breastplate the absterge was harnessing to his chest.

'All combatants wear the old Legion's colours in the Cage,' Ezrachi told him. He peered out of the chamber and down the corridor before turning back to the Scourge. 'A sign of symbolic unity.'

Hadrach handed Old Enoch and Oren a shoulder plate each. The first was the allegiant yellow of the Imperial Fists. The second bore the Chapter marking of the Excoriators. It had been this plate that the Techmarine had been working on. It was crumpled and badly damaged.

'That will have to do. Usachar took a real beating.'

'Ezrachi...'

'The contest had already begun when you were awoken. You therefore did not attend the opening rites.' The Apothecary peered into the corridor once more, anxious about the time. 'What do you know about the Feast of Blades?'

'I know that it's a diplomatic waste of time to have brothers fight one another when we have a galaxy of enemies more worthy of our blades.'

'The Feast of Blades commemorates our Lord Primarch's decision to break up his Legion as the Codex Astartes instructed. Dorn chose the Iron Warriors fortress known as the Eternal Fortress on Sebastus IV as the instrument upon which to break us.'

'And make us,' Kersh acknowledged. 'I know the saga of the Iron Cage.'

'We entered the Eternal Fortress as a Legion,' Ezrachi said. 'We left as a multitude of Chapters. It pained the primarch to do this, but he knew it was necessary. Dorn himself presided over the first of the centenary Feasts. He wished successor Chapters to maintain good relations and a cult brotherhood. This commitment was re-honoured following the Daedalus Crusade. Our brothers from participating progenitor Chapters were invited to attend, and many of the Feast's present rites and rituals were established. We know that Rogal Dorn broke the blade he'd used on Horus's barge, after it had failed to protect his Emperor. His second sword, the weapon to which we refer as the "Sword of Sebastus" or the Dornsblade, emerged with the primarch from the Iron Cage. It is one of our most revered artefacts, a weapon carried and used by mighty Dorn himself. The Chapter that wins the Feast has the honour of retaining the blade and the solemn duty of presenting it at the next Feast – the contest they will host, at most, one hundred years later.'

'Thanks for the history lesson. You sound like Santiarch Balshazar.'

'You should know what you are fighting for.'

Kersh watched Bethesda fasten his shoulder plates in place. 'I haven't worn carapace since I served in the Tenth Company.' Kersh wore a simple sparring arrangement. Upon a tunic and plated skirt sat an aquila-adorned chestplate, codpiece and ceramite shoulder-guards. Plated gauntlets and boots completed the armour. He wore no helmet and both his forearms and muscular thighs were exposed.

Ezrachi led Kersh from the chamber. 'The rules are simple. Each round consists of a knock-out. Two champions enter. The one that walks from the Cage is declared the winner. Contestations last as long as they have to. The Cage is a ceremonial arena but is no dusty amphitheatre. It is an architectural interpretation of the Iron Cage as far as accounts allow, but the layout is changed between and within each round.'

'Within?'

'Within.'

Ezrachi took the Scourge through a sequence of gates and drome-barbica. The iron portcullis and stone of each entrance was decorated with sculpted scenes depicting Imperial Fists at their primarch's side – a reminder to all who came to fight at the Feast that the Fists above all were Dorn's chosen. The first among equals. Those deemed worthy to wear the primarch's plate and colours. It sent a powerful message of martial and cultural superiority to other Chapter champions.

The Apothecary directed the serfs up to the tiered gallery. Old Enoch mumbled a blessing and Oren gave a moody nod of subservience.

'Fight well, my lord,' Bethesda said and lingered before disappearing after her father.

'Talk to me about weapons,' Kersh said. Ezrachi nodded. Kersh – ever the pragmatist and warrior.

'You are only permitted two weapons within the Cage,' the Apothecary told him. 'This,' he said, slapping the Scourge across the back. 'Use it as you will. The second is a gladius secreted about the Cage. There are two: one for you and one for your opponent. The tips and edges of both blades have been smeared with a powerful paralytic toxin, engineered by the Adeptus Mechanicus especially for the Feast. The more you are cut, the more likely that you will go down. Your opponent will, of course, walk away victorious.'

The pair of Excoriators stood at the gate to the Cage. A single bell chimed, indicating the beginning of the contest.

'Ezrachi?'

'Yes?'

'What if it's not the procedure? What if it's not my mind? What if it's a further manifestation of the Darkness?'

'What do you mean?'

'What if these things I'm witnessing are… real?'

The Apothecary paused. 'That would be a spiritual matter. Why don't you discuss it with a Chaplain? As fortune would have it, you're about to meet one.'

As the portcullis gate began to climb, a second bell sounded. Ezrachi brought his clenched right gauntlet to his lips and kissed it reverentially.

'*Dextera Dornami*, Zachariah Kersh,' the Apothecary said before climbing a set of steps up to the gallery. Kersh nodded and knelt before the opening gate. He formed a fist with his own gauntlet before touching his forehead with one knuckle, then his lips and then his breastplate – one heart then the other. Getting to his feet, the Excoriator entered the Cage.

It was like no amphitheatre or training dome he had experienced. The arena was large, perhaps the length of two gunships arranged nose to tail in diameter, Kersh estimated. The pit floor was uneven, an angular landscape of blocks, crafted from dark Samarquandian stone. There were square pits and perpendicular rises, steps and crenellated bulwarking. High above, through a caged dome, Kersh could make out the tiered gallery. This was no feral world gladiator pit. There were no howling onlookers or the frenzy of battle wagers that usually accompanied such contests. Rows of dark, armoured figures stood in silence, like impassive statues. The audience had the composure and still interest of those visiting a museum, with Chapter serfs, invited guests and gaunt servitors standing about the Emperor's Angels, as the demigods looked on in expectation and judgement. Kersh swiftly picked out Oren and Old Enoch gathered about the dull white sheen of Ezrachi's armour. Bethesda was at the bars, her knuckles blanched and her face a mask of fear and forced fortitude.

Kersh slowed to a standstill, looking up through the cage roof. There it was. Behind Bethesda was the horrid figure from his unending nightmare. His recent haunting. The phantasm in plate and bone. It stood amongst his brother Adeptus Astartes, watching him. As Kersh walked into the pit the sombre glow of its helm-optics followed him across the arena with dark interest.

The gate closed behind him. Kersh scanned the angularity of the Cage for any sign of a gladius. Breaking into a run, the Excoriator set off for higher ground and a better vantage point to spot a weapon. The soles of his boots scuffed the stone as he leapt lightly from block to block. His kept his shoulders low. His gaze was everywhere. His movements were athletic and economical. A predator's approach.

Kersh heard a sudden roar of exertion as his waiting enemy revealed himself. The Space Marine slammed into him from the side with the force of a freight-monitor. Slabs of muscle and shoulder plates clashed as Kersh was knocked clean off his feet and down a steep flight of steps. The Excoriator's kaleidoscopic tumble was punctuated by the harsh stone edges of the steps until finally Kersh met the grit and stone of the mezzanine level below.

Prone and vulnerable, Kersh turned. His attacker had can-nonballed him off one floor of the busy, vertiginous arena and down onto another. His objective became immediately clear. The Space Marine clambered swiftly up an angular column. Kersh heard the scrape of metal on stone. Turning to face him, his opponent held in his gauntlet one of the two gladius blades left about the chamber.

Ezrachi had been right. Kersh had been drawn against a Chaplain. A heavy amulet dangled down by his opponent's waist on a necklace of precious prayer-beads. The amu-let itself was a stylised, adamantium aquila, which Kersh recognised as the Chaplain's rosarius, deactivated for the competition, as honour dictated. His shoulder plate identi-fied him as a member of the Fire Lords Chapter, but Kersh would have known this from the Space Marine's tattoos. The Chaplain was a walking illustration – every part of his body inked to represent the swirling inferno he wished to bring to his foes. His canvas-flesh curled with flame and fury, while the blackened dome of his skull was spiky and soot-smeared, like the burned stubble of agri-world fields.

With another roar, the Fire Lords Chaplain launched himself from the top of the steps. He hungered for a swift end to the contest and closed with the distracted Excoriator. The gladius cut through the air. Kersh rolled to one side, allowing the blade to fall where he had lain, chipping the

ROB SANDERS

stone. Rolling back, the tip of Kersh's boot made contact
with the Fire Lord's jaw, sending the Chaplain off balance.
By the time Kersh was back on his feet, the Fire Lords Space
Marine was coming at him with the envenomed blade, flicking it this way and that, exploring the Excoriator's defences.
Kersh danced away on the toes of his boots. He arched and
angled his body, retracting his limbs and skipping back out
of the blade's path.

The Chaplain's style demonstrated flair and expert cho-
reography. The movement of the gladius flowed, stabbing
and slashing with a razored poetry. It reminded Kersh of
flames dancing in the darkness and was no less entrancing. The Scourge brought up his plated gauntlets, allowing
the tip of the blade to glance rhythmically off the back of
his fists. Kersh envied the warrior's grace. The Excoriators
were attrition fighters. Fluidity, timing and technique were
all subservient in Kersh's Chapter to the simple, primordial
desire to be the last man standing. Survival was everything.
Magnificence with a blade was worth little to the dead.

Kersh allowed the gladius to snake its way through his
defences. As the Fire Lord sensed an opening, he extended
his reach, allowing the Scourge to lay one of his gauntlets
on his opponent's wrist and the other around his throat.
The Fire Lord's blade danced no more as the two Space
Marines fought for the right to direct it. For a moment the
Adeptus Astartes stood in a stone embrace – immovable –
faces taut in a contest of strength and will. The Chaplain
grasped Kersh's own wrist, attempting to break the lock the
Excoriator had on his throat. He swiftly exchanged this for
a desperate grip on the Scourge's chestplate and the two
Space Marines spun around. The Chaplain ran Kersh back
into the brute architecture of a block obelisk. The surface of
the Samarquandian stone shattered and fell in pulverised
fragments. Kersh pushed back, slamming the Chaplain into
the thick iron wall of the Cage. The Fire Lord's shoulder
plate screeched against the metal as Kersh pinned his shuf-
fling opponent against the wall. The metal surface boomed
with the repeated impact of the Chaplain's gauntlet as Kersh

smashed the Fire Lord's fist and weapon into the wall. The Chaplain released his hold on the Excoriator's carapace and began slugging him in the side.

The Fire Lord's hand opened and the gladius fell to the floor of the Cage. This surprised Kersh, who hadn't expected his efforts to be rewarded so swiftly. His immediate desire to lay his own hand on the tumbled blade slackened his grip, and before he knew quite what was happening, the Chaplain had hammered the Excoriator with a skull-bouncing blow. Kersh went down with the sword. Skidding around on the grit of the Cage floor, he slapped a hand out, feeling for the gladius's hilt. The heel of the Fire Lord's boot found his grasping gauntlet first. With his hand pinned, Kersh braced himself for impact. The sole of the Chaplain's other boot hovered above him and then came crashing down again and again on the fallen Excoriator's face.

Opening one bruised and bloodied eye, Kersh realised that the abuse was over. The Fire Lord was no longer above him and he heard the scrape of the gladius being reclaimed. There were other disturbing movements. The architecture of the Cage, mirroring the nightmare of the Iron Warriors' Eternal Fortress on Sebastus IV, was moving. The section of stone upon which he lay was either rising or the floor around him falling away. Rolling off the moving block, Kersh landed messily on the Fire Lord below. The Adeptus Astartes both went down, and once again the gladius became a prize wrestled between them. Grasped with gauntlets at both hilt and blade tip, the Fire Lord and Excoriator battled for supremacy of the weapon. The Chaplain found his grimacing way on top, the inked globes of each bicep thumping with might as he attempted to force the blade down across Kersh's throat.

The Scourge gagged as the Chaplain leant in closer. The Fire Lord's breath was a chemicular wheeze. It was as though the Space Marine had been swilling promethium. The blade fell a little further and Kersh's eyes widened. Raw effort had drawn the Fire Lord's lips back in an ugly snarl. Instead of the perfect teeth of an Angel, the Scourge found himself staring at a maw of flint. The teeth had been replaced with shards of razor-sharp stone, each with the appearance of a primitive arrowhead or spear tip. Biting down, the Fire Lord's clenched jaws sparked. The Chaplain hissed through his teeth, sending a gout of flame at the Excoriator's face.

Kersh threw his head to one side, allowing the gladius to fall even further towards his throat. He felt the flesh on the side of his bulging neck roast and blister. Jerking his head in the opposite direction, Kersh felt the flames of a second searing breath burn his ear and the side of his face.

Writhing and stretching, Kersh caught a glimpse of the silent crowds above. He could feel Ezrachi's disappointment. He saw Bethesda's stricken beauty. He then caught a glimpse of the sickening apparition that haunted him still. It stood there amongst the still figures of the audience. Waiting. Watching. It seemed not to be looking at him, Kersh suddenly realised. Following the angle of the phantasm's dread helm, the Scourge cast his eyes across the brute landscape of the Cage, the mock courtyards and battlements of the Eternal Fortress in miniature. Where the stone blocks of a mezzanine platform had rumbled aside, Kersh could now see the dull glint of the second gladius on the other side of the arena.

The sword became everything to Kersh. He hungered for the solid satisfaction of its grip, the cutting sheen of its leaf-shaped blade and the blunt punch of its broad, tapering point. With one concentrated effort, the Excoriator pushed the poisoned blade away and heaved the fire-breathing Chaplain off him. The two Space Marines rolled until Kersh released his foe and threw himself across the arena floor. The Scourge stumbled to his feet as fast as he could, but felt the bite of the Fire Lord's sword-tip clip the back of his thigh and knew he had not been fast enough.

The effect of the Mechanicus-engineered toxin was almost instantaneous. Like the sting of some giant arachnid, a crippling deadness spread through the muscle of Kersh's leg. With the Chaplain still on the ground, Kersh made a dash across the Cage, but his sprint soon became a hobble and the hobble a limp. The leg became rapidly useless to him. A handicap in flesh and bone. It refused to bear weight or answer the Excoriator's desperate desire. The Excoriator flailed across the dread architecture of the arena, falling rather than dropping off blocks of black stone and crawling rather than climbing over crenellated bulwarks and barriers. As he slipped down into a depression in the Cage floor, he found himself in a shallow pool. Splashing through the dark water, he felt the breeze of sword swipes brush his skin. The Fire Lord was moments behind.

Ahead, Kersh could see a tower of blocks. It was atop the tower he'd spotted the second gladius. The stone blocks were unusual in as much as they were decorated with a neat pattern of equidistant holes. The Scourge slid down onto his palsied leg, showering water at the tower side.

The clunk of a firing mechanism reverberated through the stone. Iron spikes shot out of the holes in deadly unison. Kersh had heard of the Eternal Fortress's nightmare design, its labyrinthine layout and nests of traps. The Imperial Fists had designed their representation of the Iron Cage with peerless attention to detail.

The Scourge skidded down below the reach of the lowest spike. The Fire Lord, in his desire to acquire his enemy, had not been as fortunate. He peeled off to one side but was still gouged through his shoulder by a sharpened iron shaft. As he groaned and began the agonising process of extricating himself from the metal barb, Kersh began hauling himself up the spikes. Using them as a ladder, the Excoriator climbed gauntlet over gauntlet up the side of the block tower. His paralysed leg dangled uselessly as he pulled himself over the angular edge and up onto the flat summit. There the gladius was waiting. Crafted. Sharp. Glistening with paralytic toxin.

Looking down through the forest of spikes Kersh saw that his opponent had gone, leaving a length of bloodied iron as evidence of his difficulty. From the block tower, the Scourge commanded an excellent view of the Cage, but with blocks rising and sinking, and entire floors moving, it was almost impossible to get a fix on his enemy. His superhuman hearing and vision swam with the rumble and disorientation of the arena's motion. He had lost the use of one limb, but with the gladius in his grip, the Excoriator felt like he had gained the full use of another.

Dropping down the opposite side, Kersh faltered. His leg gave out immediately and he fell. Scrambling back to one foot he hopped about, sword held out in front of him. Dragging his paralysed leg around he slowly turned, expecting his enemy to erupt from anywhere. The Fire Lord, however, was nowhere to be seen. As he hopped full circle he came to the sinking conclusion that he had been fooled. The Fire Lord stood on top of the block tower from which Kersh had descended. He dropped in the fashion favoured by his brothers during their specialist planetary assaults, landing with the surety and barbaric grace of a drop-pod. The Fire Lord tossed his gladius from one hand to another. The puncture wound through his shoulder plate leaked blood down the side of his yellow carapace, but the Chaplain seemed unconcerned. His eyes burned into Kersh and his flint teeth ground together, flashing and sparking. The two shared a moment of calm before the Fire Lord assumed his familiar fighting stance. With both gauntlets on his sword and his leg like an anchor on his own movements, the Excoriator did likewise.

'Come on, meat,' Kersh growled.

The Iron Cage sang with the clash of fevered blades and the grunts of superhuman exertion as Kersh and the Fire Lords Chaplain did their utmost to best one another. Kersh was a killer of champions. It was his duty on the battlefield to neutralise the direst individual threats and cut down the best the enemy had to offer, freeing his Chapter Master to strategise and direct his Adeptus Astartes forces. His swordcraft was clean, brutal and, like his primarch, often demonstrated flashes of inspired invention that were difficult for his enemies to counter. The Chapters attending the Feast of Blades only sent their best, however, and his opponent was an equally gifted brute. His blade swirled and swooped like the raging of an inferno. He passed the gladius rapidly from hand to hand with ambidextrous skill and confidence. Where the blade wasn't the Chaplain's fists and boots were, and it was all Kersh could do to parry and deflect the rhythmic barrage. The Chaplain's movements were entrancing and his form, despite his grievous injury, perfect.

The Fire Lord's blade slithered through Kersh's savage defence and nicked the Scourge above the brow. A curtain of blood washed over his eye. As the paralytic seized him, Kersh felt one half of his face freeze up. The eye closed and his lip began to droop on one side. He compensated with a desperate lunge unworthy of his training or Chapter standing. The Fire Lord hissed through his flint-clenched jaws once more. This time Kersh realised that the tongue of flame was aimed at his gladius. The orange gout evaporated about the blade, leaving the metal steaming and tacky. With horror, Kersh realised that the Fire Lord had cleansed his blade of the paralytic toxin.

The assault continued and, as Kersh's sword was battered this way and that by the Fire Lord, blocks shifted and the dark landscape of the Cage changed about them. A block had descended immediately behind Kersh creating a small pit. Half-blind and hobbled, with the pit edge behind and the irresistible onslaught of the Chaplain in front, the Scourge was trapped. He felt the audience's expectation and his own desperation on the air. A seed of doubt blossomed within him, and he felt the weight of the apparition's gaze. For a moment the Darkness returned and Kersh knew a universe without hope. Perhaps his affliction had damned them all and the Excoriators were doomed to failure. To fail at the Feast. To fail as a Chapter.

Kersh became intensely aware of the limitations of his Adeptus Astartes body; what it could do and what it couldn't. He was to be bested by a brother more worthy of the Emperor's beneficence. A true son of Dorn. A master of the blade. An actual champion of champions.

The Fire Lord had found him. The Chaplain's blade struck

out with such fluid force that it not only smashed the Excoriator's plated gauntlet to pieces, but broke several bones in his hand and knocked the gladius through the air like a propeller. Both warriors watched the blade clatter to the ground nearby. The end had come. They both knew it.

The Fire Lord arched. It was to be a strike from above. Something suitably dramatic to finish the Excoriator. To cut him down and drop his beaten body into the grave that had opened up beyond. A warrior vanquished. A Chapter routed. Honour tarnished.

One side of Kersh's lip curled. His gauntlet shot up, batting the Fire Lord's arm back. Snatching up the Chaplain's rosarius, the Excoriator back-slashed the Space Marine across the face with the adamantium aquila. Gritting his teeth and holding on to the wire cord with both his gauntlet and smashed hand, Kersh leant into a centrifugal swing. Using his weight as the counter-balance, the Scourge swung his opponent about him. Dragged around, the Fire Lord fell back over Kersh's trailing leg. The two Space Marines toppled. Kersh fell to the floor, but not before he had tossed the Fire Lord into the pit behind him.

Even prone, Kersh saw the flailing Chaplain strike the edge of the opening's far side. The impact knocked the gladius from his hand and together both sword and Space Marine disappeared into the darkness. Kersh pushed himself up, balancing on one leg. He hobbled over to his own sword and scooped up the weapon with his unbroken hand. Limping back, he proceeded to half-scowl down into the depths. The Fire Lord lay on his broken back, his ragdoll form spread out across the bottom of the pit. Grasping fingertips reached out for his gladius, the weapon having fallen just out of reach.

'Yield, brother,' Kersh called down to the Fire Lord.

'Not to you,' the Chaplain finally managed, his voice just above a strangled hiss. 'Not to the dishonourable wretch they call the Scourge. Not to the unfavoured of Dorn.'

Kersh narrowed his eye. He nodded slowly.

'As is your right, brother.'

The Excoriator spun the gladius around in his gauntlet, so that he gripped the cross guard and the weapon's pommel and grip protruded between his fingers. The blade he held parallel to his wrist and forearm. Sliding down onto his chest, Kersh dropped down into the pit. He knelt on the Fire Lord's chestplate and brought back the sword hilt, ready to strike. The Chaplain's eyes said it all. He would not surrender. The gallery waited. The Fire Lord would not yield. Kersh retracted his arm, ready for the first, merciless blow.

'Kersh!' the Apothecary called down, unable to disguise his disgust – even in a single word. The Scourge turned his head slightly. Above him, at the edge of the pit, was an Imperial Fists contest arbitrator. The aged Adeptus Astartes looked down on them both. With grizzled hesitation, the arbitrator raised a solemn gauntlet at the Excoriator's gate. The Fist nodded to Ezrachi and left.

Kersh sagged. Returning his gaze to the Chaplain he found a little of the fire gone from the Space Marine's eyes. Using the sides of the pit for balance, he stood as best he could and threw the gladius down at the still body of his mauled opponent.

'It seems I was favoured by Dorn today, brother,' he announced before spitting some of his own blood at the stone wall. Kersh looked up at the domed cage ceiling and the stunned audience above. He saw Bethesda – her face unreadable – and Ezrachi, whose bleak revulsion was all too easy to read. The apparition, it seemed, had gone. With no little revulsion of his own, Kersh finally called up to the gallery.

'Who's next?'

I am not sleeping, yet even as I think this, I know this to be a kind of sleep. Within his daily regimen of training, cult devotion and litany, an Excoriator allows himself four hours of rest. The demands of a single day in the Adeptus Astartes would kill an ordinary man. Our engineered forms are biological instruments of the Emperor's will, but the mind needs rest. There is much to learn; errors to interrogate; the capabilities of an Angel's body to master. Ever since the Darkness, I have been unable to lose myself in what might be described as a natural sleep.

My body is beaten and bruised. Some of my bones are broken. My blood swims with magna-opioids and growth hormones that help repair my injuries. A punishing training schedule and the ever more punishing contestations of the Feast are followed by 'the purge' and penitorium, the ritual purification of the flesh. My body, superhuman though it might be, is exhausted, but my mind will not submit. Abatement comes only in the form of catalepsean abstractions, like the one I assume I am experiencing now. Different parts of my genetically altered brain are allowed to shut down in sequence, while I remain in a state of semi-wakefulness. I have rested this way even in the lethal environs of death world phase-forests and quakeclonic superstorms. Your survival instincts remain intact while parts of the mind are allowed to rest. It cannot replace sleep, however, and the distinction between what is an abstraction and what is real is increasingly difficult to make.

Sitting here, I did not realise that I had entered such a state. I am down in the hold of the Scarifica. *Despite my successes in the Feast of Blades, my presence on the dormitory decks and in the refectory is still not tolerated by my Excoriator brothers. Corpus-Captain Gideon has allowed me restricted use of the penitorium, chapel-reclusiam and the apothecarion – although I avoid the practise cages. Most of my preparation takes place down on the planet surface. Apart from the ceremonial presence of the Imperial Fists about the purpose-built Cage colosseum, only a garrison of the Thracian Fourth remains on Samarquand. All other resources are stationed on the cordon, keeping the Great Tusk and its greenskin invaders away. When I asked why the Fists would select such a place for the site of the Feast, Ezrachi told me that it was customary for the hosts to select the site of a recent Chapter victory for the contest location. Such choices were in line with the martial heritage of the Fists and their affiliated Chapters. With battles against greenskin blockade runners proceeding above our heads, and Imperial Guard cleanse and burn sorties decontaminating the earth for kilometres around, such a choice smacked of theme and pride. Regardless, it left me with the solitude of the ash fields and the apocalyptic ruins of a reclaimed world as my training ground.*

I am sitting on a cargo crate. I sense the Apothecary and his Helix-serfs about me. My own people also. Ezrachi's servants work solemnly on my face. Their needlework is neat and confident, and my flesh is a tessellation of stitching and stapled gashes. Between the nipping bladework of Sergeant Tenaka of the Death Strike and brutal headbutting I received from the hulking, nameless Crimson Fist I had the unfortunate honour of crossing swords with in the latter stages, my face is a mess. I know that each of these scars – these excoriations – are Katafalque's blessing and the mark of Dorn, but my skull aches and my features feel as though they have been reassembled like a child's puzzle. Ezrachi's aides do their best with what's left.

The good Apothecary works on my swordarm himself. The crate is covered with surgical foil, and Ezrachi's instruments are laid out along the strapped-down length of my forearm. My flesh is open and the inner workings of the limb exposed. In the previous round, Knud Hægstad of Brycantia thought it prudent to shatter my arm – unhappy at what it was doing with a gladius on the end of it. I had the Iron Knight pay for the injury by cleaving off his hand – gauntlet, gladius and all – with the finest overhead downcut I believe I have ever performed. Dorn demands perfection. Demetrius Katafalque writes in detail on the sound a blade should make during the successful execution of such a manoeuvre, and the sword sang like a Terran songbird. Perfection is an ideal to which I aspire, but an imperfect victory still has a great deal to recommend it.

Ezrachi informed me that such an action, although legal in tournament terms, had offended several of the participant Chapters, the Iron Knights and Imperial Fists among them. It was not my intention to invoke an insult, an echo of the primarch's own severed hand. That was how it was received by the Brycantians, however – a polemic and litigious breed, more interested in the detail of ritual law and tournament etiquette than victory itself. They petitioned my disqualification, and not for the first time. Earlier in the Feast, I left a former champion of the same

Chapter called Hervald Strom gutted and all but dead on the Cage floor. A full day's delay to the Games was called. A day for Ezrachi to attend to my wounds and Shiloh Gideon to berate me – although behind the corpus-captain's words I sensed an unmistakable pride and relief. The dishonour of conduct in battle was preferential to the dishonour of early defeat. Strom lived, tough Brycantian bastard that he is, and my advancement was allowed.

The Excoriators would not indulge in such Chapter politics. There were no appeals on the ramparts of the Imperial Palace. No petitions to be had with the Sons of Horus, degenerate World Eaters or the warsmiths of Perturabo. When Berenger of the White Templars took my eye, I did not call for the tournament official or Feast charta. I did not yap like a dog, protest or pontificate. I fought on, like I was born to do. I took the only thing that mattered from my opponent: victory. I tire of rules and regulations. I yearn for the cold simplicity of the battlefield, where enemies were at least good enough to signal defeat with their deaths.

The Apothecary attended to my eye and offered a bionic equivalent. I refused. Ezrachi and Hadrach insisted that I would see better than with the original, but I cared not. When pressed they admitted that the change in depth perception would take some getting used to. I couldn't afford the distraction this late in the contest. I opted for a simple ball-bearing to be inserted instead as a temporary measure. The matt, scratched surface of the metal revolves as I move my head. I catch others watching its motion. Ezrachi insists he'll replace it after the Feast, but I have to admit that it is growing on me. The Apothecary already has his hands full with my shattered arm. He is surgically inserting an adamantium pin and piston arrangement that runs the interior length of the limb.

My serfs make themselves busy about my sitting form. With my arm strapped, there is little in the way of blood. What there is Oren moodily massages into the deck with his mop. Old Enoch is on his knees, babbling prayers and incomprehension. Bethesda is beside me, working around Ezrachi's aides. She's applying a moistened cloth to my brow, for all the comfort it gives me. I allow this irrelevance to continue. She is young and my form more than mortal. Her reverence is only human and if such meaninglessness gives her comfort then who am I to deny such minor mercies?

Of course, my visitor is here. It indulges in what might be described as an otherworldly pacing, the inky blackness of the hold giving up its armoured form before the phantasm disappears, again one with the darkness. I catch it in the periphery of my vision. It seems always there, even when it's not. Once, in the chapel-reclusiam, I turned to find it beside me. The cleaved faceplate of its helmet radiated a chillness that turned my breath to fog. I heard its teeth chatter and, as I turned away, I caught once again the helmet interior and the fleshless face within.

It seems never not with me. On the dark and lonely passages of the lower decks I hear the distant footfalls of the revenant. On Samarquand its distant form stands atop the ruins and on the smouldering horizon, observing my progress as I run, train and fight. It is there above the Cage, always. I no longer look for its macabre presence, for I know I will find it amongst the colosseum crowds. Watching. In silent appreciation it stands, never talking, but a seeming supporter of my gladiatorial efforts.

'Wake him,' I hear a voice command. I know the voice. It is Corpus-Captain Gideon.

'I am awake.'

THE CORPUS-CAPTAIN ENTERED the gloom of the cargo compartment. His eyes flashed around the chamber. It was clear that the Excoriator had never been down in the hold before. Beside him Chaplain Dardarius glowered in his dark plate.

'Chaplain Dardarius,' Kersh greeted the Excoriator. 'The good corpus-captain has allowed me restricted visitation to the chapel-reclusiam, yet when I am there you are not. Have you come down here to hear my affirmation? To cleanse my soul of doubt with your counsel as the lash cleanses my flesh of weakness?'

The gaunt Dardarius looked from Kersh to the sarcophagus that still decorated the chamber floor and then to

Ezrachi, who busied himself with the surgery. 'Chaplain?' the Scourge pressed.

'Later,' Gideon instructed. 'The Master of the Feast has made his ruling.'

'Fortinbras came himself?' Ezrachi asked, getting up off his adamantium knee and allowing an aide to close up the surgery.

'And?' Kersh said.

'Fortinbras rules in favour of a continuance.'

Kersh looked to the Apothecary and his arm. 'Let's finish this.'

'There's a condition,' the corpus-captain said.

'Yes,' Kersh agreed with building annoyance. 'It's a little matter called victory.'

'The Fists have ruled in our favour,' Dardarius added with low contempt. 'But the corpus-captain's equivalents amongst the remaining Chapters do not recognise your legitimacy, Scourge.'

'They'll recognise my blade as it comes for them.'

'They will not honour you with sole engagement.'

'What does that mean?' Ezrachi put to the Chaplain.

'It means their cowardice prevents them from stepping into the arena with me,' Kersh barked.

'Their honour prevents it,' Dardarius corrected.

'Again,' Ezrachi asked. 'What does that mean?'

'The same honour also prevents them from claiming victory in the Feast without your besting,' Gideon said. 'Therefore, Master Fortinbras, with the primarch's wisdom, has decreed that the Feast of Blades be decided by a three-way duel.'

'A three-way duel...' Ezrachi nodded.

'The champions of the Fists and the Black Templars need not besmirch their reputations by facing you in single engagement,' Dardarius informed them, 'yet their victory will be rightful in your defeat.'

'You seem confident of their success, Lord Chaplain,' Kersh accused.

Dardarius took a moment. 'You face Alighieri of the Black

Templars. A devout Brethren of the Sword, a Castellan and veteran of the Volchis, Deltamagne and Hive Nimbus Crusades. He is half your age but has twice your conquests to his name. As for Montalbán, he is Pugh's champion and the best of the Fists – the best of all of us, perhaps.'

'I find your lack of faith inspirational, Chaplain,' Kersh told him. Dardarius simply bowed his head.

'Well, that is the situation, brothers,' Gideon said finally. He looked to Ezrachi. 'Get him planetside. Get him in his plate.'

'And what from you, corpus-captain?' Kersh asked. 'Any advice?'

Gideon pursed his lips. 'Do what you do best.' The Excoriators captain went to leave. 'Don't lose.'

MONTALBÁN. ALIGHIERI. KERSH.

The Excoriator was surprised to find the rush of combat – the mad murderous scramble of gladiatorial confrontation – absent from the Cage. There were no stealth approaches or ambush attacks. No battle calls and no furious charges. The Imperial Fist and Black Templar simply walked out into the arena and composed themselves by their barbica-entrances. It was refreshing. All the while the Cage itself seemed to dominate with the mechanical thunk of blocks and floors moving about them, with pits opening and simple towers rising from the symbolic architecture. The Cage seemed in overdrive.

Above, Kersh saw that the gallery was crowded with superhuman silhouettes. The sons of Dorn had gathered to witness the final of the Feast; to discover which Chapter would demonstrate themselves worthy of their brothers' esteem and be granted centennial custodianship of the primarch's blade. History was about to be made. The eight hundred and sixteenth Feast of Blades was to end and a champion be immortalised in memory.

Alighieri was a devout killer. Zealot. Fanatic. A devotee of victory. He knew no fear. Doubt had never known a home in his pious hearts and his belief was absolute – in his primarch, his Emperor and his Imperium. The Black Templar was already on his knees in the arena grit, indulging in a warrior's blessing. The dim light of the Cage shone off his bald crown and the bleak line of a mouth ran beneath the lustrous length of his crusader's moustache. Alighieri was all about the moment. He lived his penitence and existed in a perpetual state of judgement – both on his enemies and himself.

Montalbán, by contrast, radiated presence. He was huge, second only in size to the savage Crimson Fist Kersh had fought in the earlier round. Unlike Alighieri, Montalbán's belief grew from a place deep within his colossal chest. His faith was that of an Angel, long accustomed to the supreme capabilities of his superhuman body. He already thought of himself as a champion of champions. A symbol in flesh, sculpted in Dorn's own image, whose eyes were not the pinpoints of grim determination that belonged to his Black Templar opponent, but gleaming, grey discs of adamantium assurance. A warrior who had played through the engagement in his mind a hundred times and had won every time. The Imperial Fist went through rudimentary flexes and stretches. His throbbing arms and shoulders were like rolling foothills to the tabletop mountain of his blond hair and graven brow, and beneath these hung a stoic visage of immortal calm.

Both Adeptus Astartes looked virtually untouched by the trials of the Feast so far, a testament to their skill and the ease with which they had despatched their opponents. Kersh looked like hell in comparison and decidedly ugly in his display of stitches and scarring both old and new. With his remaining eye the Excoriator caught a glint of light off the mirrored blade of a gladius. Montalbán strode over to the weapon and picked it up in one meaty gauntlet. Looking over at Alighieri he found that the Black Templar had ascended the wall of a mock-battlement. Stepping lightly across the merlon-tops, the Castellan found the second gladius and picked it up nimbly.

Kersh felt suddenly vulnerable.

'Scourge!'

Kersh heard Montalbán call him and turned back. The mighty Imperial Fist was stood over the third sword. Kersh died a little inside. The blades had been randomly placed. It was not the kind of fortune he'd been hoping for. Hooking the tip of his gladius under one of the sword's cross guards, Montalbán scooped the weapon up into the air. It spun the distance between them before being snatched out of its flight by the Scourge. With the gladius firmly in his grip, Kersh nodded his appreciation.

'For all the good it will do you,' Montalbán announced across the animated arena. He flashed his eyes at the Excoriator in mock surprise. 'Here comes Alighieri. It begins…'

Alighieri was there. Like some feudal knight in an ogre's cave, the Black Templar launched himself at Montalbán from the battlement, gladius clutched in both hands. Kersh admired the Castellan's courage. It had been a brave opening gambit. The Imperial Fist turned on his heel and smacked the blade aside with his own, although the weapon looked comparatively short in the giant Montalbán's fist. Alighieri hit the dark stone floor of the cage, tumbled and rolled, landing back on his feet like a cat. He came straight back at the Imperial Fist with immaculate bladework, each swipe and slash a manoeuvre of cold conviction.

It became immediately apparent to Kersh that although undeniably skilled, Montalbán's fearsome reputation as Chapter Master Pugh's champion was not built upon swordplay. He was fast for one so tall, however, and the power of each strike was irresistible. For every stabbing riposte the Templar offered in the wake of the champion's broad sweeps, Alighieri suffered the reply of a hammerfall of cleaving cuts and smashes.

As blades sparked and the Black Templar was pounded back, Kersh found his grip tighten around his own gladius and his hesitant steps pick up speed. It was not fear that had slowed his advance, although the Excoriator feared it might be interpreted as such if he dallied much longer. It was opportunity. He had been unfortunate with the positioning of the gladius, but the opportunity to witness even a few seconds of his opponents at each other's throats was a welcome gift. Kersh took in the Imperial Fist's reach and his preference for scything sweeps and rapid downcutting. The Space Marine treated his blade like an extension of his arm, driving the razored edge at his opponent with brute proficiency.

Alighieri, the Scourge observed, guided his gladius. His technique betrayed a crusader's bluntness, but the Castellan had a clear respect for the weapon's balance. His wrists did much of the work, working within the counter-arcs of both pommel and fulcrum. He favoured the tip of the leaf-shaped blade, relying on its length for the demands of a hasty defence, and worked the weapon with an even speed and rhythm. Strike for strike, the Templar was the better swordsman, but round after round Montalbán had smashed the skill senseless from his opponents' hands and it appeared that Alighieri would be little different.

Within moments Kersh was among them. The Scourge was a killer rather than a fighter. He lacked both the Black Templar's deftness with the blade and the centrifugal power of Montalbán's swordarm. The Excoriator's gladius came at them both with murderous intent, however. His first few swings spoke of a squat ferocity, the first almost taking out the giant Montalbán's throat and the second flashing narrowly before Alighieri's face. The pair instantly sensed the threat and responded with a double-dealing of punishing bladework. Kersh could barely get his gladius between the Black Templar's stabbing weapon and Montalbán's bludgeoning, overhead barrage. He wouldn't have achieved that if it hadn't been for the pair's own exchanged blows.

With the impact of the Imperial Fist's weapon still ringing through his own and up through his arm and shoulder, Kersh rolled beneath a low, opportunistic swipe from Alighieri. Out from between his brothers, Kersh assumed a defensive posture at the apex of the revolving triangle the three Space Marines had created. If the sons of Dorn formed the points, the clash of blades gave the shape its scalenic sides.

As the battle roamed the Cage, the architecture of the arena transformed about the three warriors, adding the simple danger of disappearing footholds and floorspace to the evolving deathtrap of blades slicing up the air between them. The movement of the blocks in symbolic representation of the Iron Cage fortress was more than disorientating. Preoccupations with footing, falling and hazards sapped the only seconds the Space Marines had to spare between the furious onslaught of their opponents' blades. Serrated discs spun like circular saws along the gaps between floor blocks, forcing the Adeptus Astartes to sidestep and jump in their carapace.

Pummelled into the ground by Montalbán's unremitting overhead assault, Kersh was forced to roll across a quad of blocks set with vents that were flush to the stone. As the Excoriator tumbled, the vents emitted a volatile gas that was sparked and ignited about him. Burying his head in his arms, Kersh rolled shoulder over shoulder until he emerged, hair singed and armour smoking from the shallow field of flame. A pit had unexpectedly opened up beneath Montalbán and the giant had dropped down into a darkness into which Alighieri and the Scourge were forced to follow.

The Black Templar was easily the most sure-footed of the combatants, but even he could do little to avoid the clouds of thick, greasy smoke that erupted from grilles in the floor beneath the Space Marines' boots. The tacky fog smeared the skin and ceremonial carapace, as well as gunging up the eyes and enveloping the warriors in brief banks of billowing gloom. Through the smog, sword strikes lost their discipline and technique lost out to the hack and slash of open opportunity. All three of the participants' blades made contact through the smoke, but it was impossible to tell which strike belonged to which warrior.

Alighieri received a slash across his forehead, an arm and a leg, considerably hampering the Black Templar's former grace and agility. Kersh took a swordpoint in the groin – at the top of his left thigh – as well as a slice across the back of the neck running parallel with the line of his carapace.

The Excoriator felt the now familiar spider-bite numbness creep through his flesh as the paralytic took effect. His head began to droop to one side and the Scourge was forced to bunch his shoulders and tense the sinew in his neck to rawness in order to keep it upright. Montalbán emerged the worst hit, being the largest target in the greasy blindness. A razor edge had found a backstrap on his carapace, cutting it free and allowing the ceremonial armour to fall away from his broad, muscular chest. The hulking Imperial Fist was adorned with crippling nicks and slashes across his shoulders and down one leg, but seemed unconcerned. His movements were as assured as they were before, the giant simply pushing through the paralysis like a runaway train that had blown its brakes. Grabbing the chestplate, Montalbán tore it free of his perfect form and tossed it aside.

The nightmare of battle went on. Dorn and his Fists had endured weeks of torment and relentless assault at the design of Perturabo and his traitor Iron Warriors. There the battle-brothers had come to know each other's true worth as both warriors and spiritual siblings, this as part of their own primarch's design. As the crowds built and gathered in the gallery above the Cage and the spectacle of superhuman endeavour and skill continued, it became apparent that some of that same hard-won respect and the kindred bond of Dorn's spirit had been ignited between the three warriors. Too many blades had been turned aside and too many brief fantasies of triumph had been quashed for the Emperor's Angels not to feel the sting of Legion pride in their brothers' indefatigable efforts.

Neither Montalbán, Alighieri or the Scourge had any idea how long they had been fighting. It was not the weeks of their brothers' historic trials, but it was longer than all of the other rounds and contestations of the eight hundred and sixteenth Feast added together. Movement became a sluggish blur and detail of the surrounding arena ran like painting left out in the rain. The snarling faces of Montalbán and Alighieri flashed before Kersh. So furious and exhausted was the exchange that at one point the Scourge fancied he even saw his own face amongst the glint of blades.

In the background, beyond the whirlwind of the fray, Kersh sensed his ethereal stalker. In the shattered fragments of reeling moments, the Excoriator caught an impression of his private revenant – not watching from the gallery in ghastly expectation, but down in the evolving arena. It was everywhere. Different places; different moments. An armoured shade, bedecked in death, whose presence seemed to suck the life out of the very space it occupied. It watched and waited with the patience of the grave.

The living in the Cage could only measure the passage of time in the fat beads of sweat shaken from their skin, the ache and burn of their battered bodies and, if they had had the luxury of a spare moment to observe, the closing gap between the faces of their riveted audience and the bars of the domed ceiling-cage of the arena.

The spectators found the contestants closer than ever as the three Space Marines scaled a line of block-columns rising up out of the Cage floor. Bounding from the top of tower to stone tower, the Adeptus Astartes exchanged blows. In yet another fearless move, Alighieri had launched himself across the open space between the towers and landed on the one being defended by Kersh. Somehow the Black Templar had avoided being cleaved in two by the Scourge and danced in and out of the Excoriator's tiring swordplay. The two were so close that Kersh could hear the incessant stream of battle-catechisms and recitation spilling from the Black Templar's lips. The manoeuvre was even more daring than the Scourge had anticipated, as he discovered when Alighieri made it through the blaze of his blade and clipped the gladius from the fingers of Montalbán, who was swinging for all he was worth atop the tower beyond. The gladius left the Fist's gauntlet and spun through the air above a large pool. Blocks had sunk into the floor of the arena, lined by the towers between which the Space Marines had been leaping. Dirty water had rapidly seeped up through grilles in the block-bottom of the large pit and filled it to a reasonable depth.

Montalbán watched the weapon fly across the water's expanse and clatter to the ground on the other side. Instead of waiting for Alighieri to join him on his tower, the Imperial Fist dropped down the side of the column, sending a quake through the dark stone as he landed. The Black Templar wouldn't have been able to make good on his bold opening since Kersh had come back at him with a lunge that had every right to gut the Castellan. Somehow the nimble Alighieri managed to arc his palsied form about the sword's stabbing path.

The tower suddenly bucked. Kersh initially assumed that the blocks were once more on the move, but a second impact convinced him otherwise. The giant Montalbán was throwing his bulk at the tower base like a beast of the plains felling titanwoods. The third slam of superhuman shoulder against stone took out the base block and toppled the tower. As the column shook and tipped, Kersh lost his footing and went down in an ugly fashion. Striking his chest against the block edge he felt the shell of his fused ribs crack. He clawed at the smooth surface of the dark stone, allowing his gladius to tumble from his grip and into the filthy water below. The unsuccessful Scourge followed the weapon and was in turn followed and buried by the falling blocks of the collapsed tower.

The fallen column had created a shattered causeway across the pool and a path Montalbán fully intended on using to swiftly reclaim his weapon. Once again, the Black Templar's light feet and balance had proved their worth and the Imperial Fist found a dry Alighieri holding an awkward fighting stance but blocking his way across the stepping stone. The Fist's lips wrinkled in infuriation. Slapping the palms of his gauntlets on a colossal fragment of the broken base block, Montalbán heaved the slab of stone above his head and launched it at the Black Templar. As the rock flew like a meteorite along the path of the causeway, a wide-eyed Alighieri was forced to jump from the bridge and dive into the water.

As his feet found the bottom and the Castellan surfaced,

sword in hand, he found himself staring up at Montalbán's rippling chest. The giant had torn the remainder of the base-block out of the arena floor and was once again hefting the rock above the flat-top of his blond hair. Alighieri prepared himself to dive left or right out of the boulder's trajectory. At that moment, like a daemon of the deep, Kersh broke the water's surface. Coming up behind Alighieri he grabbed the Black Templar by both the wrist of his swordarm and his neck. The Castellan struggled in desperation but the Space Marine's speed and agility were no match for the Scourge's meaty arm-lock.

Kersh held Alighieri to him, holding the Black Templar in place and outstretched, resting his forehead against the back of the warrior's skull. The Castellan's face fell as he watched Montalbán hurl the rock at them both. Kersh felt the Templar's bones break as the stone shattered against Alighieri's presented form. The pair were smacked down through the water, leaving a cloud of rock dust to mark the point of dreadful impact.

Once again beneath the surface, the Scourge was slammed into the pool bottom by the weight of the broken block. The back of his head bounced off the stone and something cracked. Heaving the deadweight of the sinking rock off both himself and Alighieri's motionless body, Kersh kicked off the pool floor only to find his right leg wouldn't answer. It was broken and useless. Clawing for the surface with one hand he dragged the Templar behind him with the other.

He need not have bothered. The arena was morphing about them once again with a mechanical shuddering. Water drained about the Scourge through the grilles, and the pool bottom rose up to meet him.

All three Space Marines were now back on the same level. Alighieri was a broken and bloodied mess. Half of his chest had been caved in by the rock's impact. Kersh slithered up beside him and put his ear to the other half and then to the Black Templar's torn lips. Incredibly, he was still breathing. Barely.

Kersh heard the damp scrape of his blade on the arena

floor and craned his stiff neck around to see the giant Montalbán reclaim it from down beside the toppled tower. Swinging it experimentally about him the Imperial Fist advanced. The gallery was silent and still.

'Scourge!' Montalbán called as he strode across the arena. 'The time has come.' Like a great death world predator, the Imperial Fist broke into a run. His sword came up overhead.

Kersh turned back to Alighieri's broken body. His eyes drifted along the Black Templar's arm and to the gladius clutched in his smashed hand. In the mirror blade of the weapon the Excoriator found himself looking at a reflection of the revenant. It peered out through the ceramite shard missing in its midnight faceplate. Kersh saw its teeth rattle and otherworldly life glow from the eye socket of its bleached skull, the full horror of its form revealed through a chink in its armour. An opening. A vulnerability.

Kersh felt the hulking Fist's steps pounding through the floor. He was almost upon the prone and supplicant figure of the Excoriator. 'Are you ready, brother?' Montalbán boomed above him. Kersh began to tear feverishly at Alighieri's broken fingers. With the gladius in his own, the Scourge sat, turned and twisted. Sent catapulting over Kersh's own bleeding head, the sword shot the short distance between the Excoriator's loosened grip and Montalbán's exposed chest.

With a thud the gladius buried itself in the Imperial Fist's torso. Stumbling, the mighty Montalbán tripped over the prone forms of Alighieri and the Scourge. Crashing to the arena floor, the champion rolled across one shoulder plate before coming to rest on his back. Crawling arm over arm, Kersh dragged himself alongside the fallen giant. The Imperial Fist's eyes were stricken and wide open. He held his back off the floor and thrust his chest at the cage-dome of the arena ceiling and the spectators beyond. The toxin smeared on the tip and blade-edge of the gladius was spreading through the Space Marine's chest, paralysing his twin hearts and bringing them to a stop.

'Am I ready?' the Scourge hissed in the champion's ear, repeating his previous question. 'For anything, brother,' Kersh told him with blood dripping from his lips. 'Even you.'

The Excoriator rolled onto his own back and stared up at the gallery of silhouettes staring back at him. 'Call the Apothecaries!' he bawled finally. Above, Master Fortinbras nodded his authorisation and the drome-barbica opened. The arena grew still and silent, and figures in gleaming white plate dashed out across the dark stone. Robed serfs and servitors followed with equipment. A Black Templars Apothecary went to work straight away on Alighieri's crushed chest and collapsed lung.

The Imperial Fists Apothecary expertly withdrew the gladius Kersh had put in Montalbán's chest. His serfs went to stem the blood pooling and streaming down the side of the champion's torso. The Apothecary took a pair of hypodermic syringes from a medical crate carried by a gruesome servitor. One at a time the Apothecary stabbed them down through the muscle and black carapace of the Imperial Fist's breast. With both piercing the Space Marine's hearts the Apothecary depressed the plungers with his palms and administered the anti-paralytic. Montalbán spasmed. The needles twitched in rhythm as the Space Marine's hearts resumed their thunderous beat as the Fist gulped a deep lungful of air.

Ezrachi suddenly appeared above Kersh. The solemnity of the occasion prevented Ezrachi openly celebrating or offering congratulations, but the Apothecary was clearly having difficulty hiding his pride and pleasure behind a mask of professional concern.

'Remain still,' he told the Scourge, an unintentional grin breaking through the his usual scowl. 'You have a fractured skull, a multitude of breakages and internal bleeding.'

'I feel tired,' Kersh told him, his speech beginning to slur.

'That'll be the concussion,' Ezrachi said.

'Ezrachi?'

'Yes.'

'Is this a dream?'

The Apothecary watched the Scourge's eyes close. He looked from the prone Black Templar to the giant Imperial Fist. He recalled what it had taken for Kersh to beat them both.

'I hope not.'

CHAPTER FOUR
THE CHAINS OF COMMAND

THE CHAPEL-RECLUSIAM OF the *Scarifica* was all but empty. The Scourge knelt beneath its vaulted ceiling with his eyes cast down on the black marble of the chamber floor. The polished stone reflected a little of the stained-glass brilliance of the window beyond the altar – a tessellate representation of Demetrius Katafalque at Rogal Dorn's side during the post-Heresy crusades of penitence. Kersh brought up his gaze. Before the glorious depiction, laid out across the simple altar, was the length of a highly-wrought stasis casket. The bejewelled case hummed, the temporal suspension of its contents and interior drowned out only by a small choir of chapel servitors. Chaplain Dardarius had the drones embedded in the stone plinths which lined the chamber so that they stood like statues, perpetually engaged in a round of liturgical chants.

Kersh was dressed in full battle-plate, as honour decreed. With the Excoriators frigate well into its journey home and Kersh recovered from his arena injuries, Corpus-Captain Gideon had allowed the Scourge his suit of power armour in quiet recognition of the warrior's achievement. Kersh hadn't worn the plate since the terrible day the Darkness had taken him. The day he had lost the Stigmartyr.

The day he had allowed the filth Alpha Legion to slither past and sink their fangs into his Chapter Master's flesh. The Scourge had experienced mixed feelings upon first donning the ornate ceramite plates. It felt undeniably good to be back in both power armour and his Chapter's colours, but his chest flushed with shame at such gladness. He had come through the Darkness but had left the Chapter in a darkness of its own, bereft of its standard and afflicted with grief and doubt. He was in good health while his Chapter Master writhed in envenomed agony. He was alive when so many of his brethren had fallen. These burdens and more weighed heavily on the Excoriator, and after his daily 'Donning of Dorn's Mantle', Kersh spent time in quiet reflection in the chapel-reclusiam, searching his soul for a little of the primarch's wisdom and fortitude.

Kersh wasn't convinced that Gideon had reunited the warrior with his armour in entirely good faith. The *Scarifica*'s journey to Eschara was a circuitous one, returning battle-brother after participating battle-brother to their far-flung companies and Chapter houses across the coreward expanse of the segmentum. Each veteran of the Feast was returned to their corpus-captain in a small but significant ceremony, attended by battle-brothers of their company, senior officers, contestants and Gideon himself. As champion of the Feast of Blades, it was appropriate that Kersh appeared as such, in full battle armour. The Scourge suspected that this consideration – rather than a renewed respect and liking for Kersh – had a great deal to do with the corpus-captain's decision to return the blessed plate to him. A ceremony without a champion would have been embarrassing.

In this way Gideon had also decided to return the Scourge to his commander last. Apart from Kersh's ceremonial significance, his commanding officer was the Chapter Master himself. Since the Excoriators home world of Eschara was the final destination on the frigate's journey, it made sense to deliver the Scourge last. Still, this did little to assuage the warrior's impatience. As he had confided to both Gideon and Ezrachi, Kersh was eager to return to Eschara, beg forgiveness of Master Ichabod in person and request that Santiarch Balshazar despatch him on a penitence crusade of his own, to track down the Alpha Legion and reclaim the Excoriators Chapter's precious standard. Only through such recompense could the Scourge earn redemption in the eyes of his brothers and achieve a spiritual peace.

About the kneeling Scourge's penitent form his mortal serfs busied themselves, at once dedicated yet inconspicuous. While Techmarine Hadrach was responsible for the maintenance of the ancient plate and the suit's machine-spirit, many Chapter rituals and cult appeasements fell to Kersh's seneschal, lictor and absterge; and there was much to do. The plate was magnificent – as befitting a Scourge of the Excoriators Chapter. Every Excoriator honoured with carrying the Chapter standard or 'Ancient' had worn the suit and it was as old as it was immaculate. Like the banner itself, it displayed the venerated symbol of their brother-hood – the Stigmartyr – on the suit's loincloth. Kersh had considered himself, therefore, part of the standard, making its personal loss all the more grievous.

Seals, chains and brown leather strapping dripped from the suit, but Old Enoch and Oren occupied themselves with the plate itself. The armour was a relic and as such had been heavily modified by Adeptus Astartes artisans, but its studs and robust cabling betrayed its original mark and designation. The ceramite surface was pock-marked and scarred like the meteorite-battered surface of a moon. The ivory paint was mottled silver-grey with burns and bolt-craters from the many engagements the armour had witnessed. It had been the Scourge's honour to add to these. Equally scarred and annotated was the helm sitting on the flagstone before the Scourge. It spoke ugly belligerence with its unsmiling grille, snake-eyed optics, studs like horn buds and a short, brutal crest.

Oren's bulging arms were put to good use rubbing sacred

oils into the ancient plate of the suit's pauldrons. Each was a representation of the Stigmartyr: crafted ceramite fists, clutching Kersh's shoulders and shot through with lightning bolts that protruded both front and behind like wicked spikes. The sacred oils preserved the excoriations and provided extra spiritual protection for the plate. Bethesda stood barefoot beside him, reading benedictions of bearing and repairing from a devotional tract, her syllables a sibilant whisper amongst the servitor chanting. Old Enoch knelt beside one gleaming vambrace, a diamond-tip vibro-quill in his bony hand, annotating each nick, scar and hollow with a date and location.

Each of the seneschal's additions bore the same name: Ignis Prime. The planet on which Chapter Master Quesiah Ichabod had come to inspect the mountaintop Excoriators garrison of Kruger Ridge, only to find a slaughterhouse rather than a Chapter house, and a waiting ambush in the form of heretic Alpha Legionnaires. It was there, barricaded in the oratorium, that Zachariah Kersh had fallen to the Darkness, failing both his Master and his Chapter, and allowing the Alpha Legion's victory to become complete.

The Scourge blinked, shaking another abstraction from the mists of his mind. 'Where is the Chaplain?' he asked. He had come to the chapel-reclusiam to see Dardarius, against his better judgement. Since finding a new home for the sacred Dornsblade in his tiny temple, the Chaplain was now rarely found anywhere else. Old Enoch mumbled something unintelligible.

'The corpus-captain sent for him, my lord,' Bethesda answered, closing the tract.

Kersh's eyes narrowed. 'The engines have stopped.'

Old Enoch nodded. The faint rumble was absent from the deck. After the long haul from Samarquand, short jumps and frequent receptions had become the order of the day. As the *Scarifica* moved between the cruisers, keeps and warzones of the Excoriators Chapter, Kersh had learned that precious little progress had been made in locating an antidote for the toxin slowly eating its way through his Chapter

Master. The hazardous environs of feral hellholes and death worlds had not given up their secrets. Meanwhile, all companies were on high alert. News of Kersh's victory at the Feast of Blades had indeed lifted the hearts of his battle-brethren, but it made their duty of garrisoning the sectors bordering the Eye of Terror no easier. Servants of the Dark Gods were ever ready to test the mettle of Excoriators bastions, gauntlets and cordons, and with recent misfortunes the numbers of battle-brothers holding such precarious boundaries were dwindling.

'Enough,' Kersh commanded, scooping his helmet from the floor and rising to his full height. A sporran arrangement hung across the ceremonial loincloth, holstering an Adeptus Astartes Mark II bolt pistol. The ancient weapon was squat, fat and ugly like a guard dog, and sat within easy reach across the Excoriator's groin to allow not one but two scabbard-sheathed gladii to hug the Scourge's hip. The first bore a bulbous pommel, sculpted in the fashion of a clutched talon of the Imperial aquila. Both gladius and pistol, with the relic plate, accompanied the honour of being the Chapter Scourge.

The second sword was plain and had been with Kersh since his inception as an Adeptus Astartes Space Marine. The Excoriator used it as a functional back-up weapon. With standard held high and a Chapter Master to defend, Kersh did not want to fall to an enemy for want of weaponry, and many enemy champions were skilled in the arts of disarming and blade deprivation. In the end the Darkness had turned out to be the true master of such strategies. Gideon's ceremonies did not necessitate carrying such an arsenal aboard the ship, but traversing the dreadspace about the Eye of Terror did, with all battle-brethren on board instructed to be armed and ready for the ambushes, boarding actions and unpredictable mayhem the warp rift routinely threw at them.

The serfs lowered their eyes and retreated. The Scourge turned to his seneschal. 'Discover why our engines have stopped.' Old Enoch bowed his head and left. To Oren and

Bethesda he simply said, 'Pray, leave me.'

As the lictor and absterge repeated their father's sub-servience and exited the chapel-reclusiam, the Scourge approached the altar. The bejewelled case was closed. Look-ing furtively about him, Kersh found the chapel empty but for the blind chorus of the choir. Depressing two gleaming studs the Scourge disabled the case stasis field and opened the casket.

Within was the Dornsblade. Sheathless. Simple. Resplendent. The weapon's spartan honesty had shocked the Scourge at first. With most warriors – even amongst the Adeptus Astartes – the greater the glory of the wielder, the more extravagant the decoration of the weapon wielded. Even laid out on the ermine interior of the stasis casket, the Dornsblade rang with history. It entranced the observer with the dull gleam of honours eternally earned. It was rumoured to be unbreakable, a symbolic reminder of the unbreakable spirit of the Imperial Fists in the face of adversity, given form in the trials of the Iron Cage. It also represented Legion unity during the necessities of the Sec-ond Founding.

It was crafted from a single piece of high-grade adaman-tium and remained completely unadorned. Cross guard, hilt and pommel were all bare metal, with the heavy blade counter-balanced by a solid pentagonal prism, with angular edges and featureless faces. The hilt had been cross-hatched and scored to provide a grip, and the cross guard had been stamped with three simple numerals across its breadth: VII. The blade was razored and featureless, bar its bronzed discolouration, which was believed to be the stain of the traitor blood that had baptised the blade in Rogal Dorn's hand, during the Battle of the Iron Cage.

The blade misted. Kersh suddenly became aware that the temperature in the chapel-reclusiam had dropped. The lamps dimmed and the choir trailed off. The Scourge saw the white clouds of his breath before him.

'Only you,' Kersh announced to the temple without turn-ing. 'Phantom.' There was no reply but for the chill on the air. The Excoriator turned but the revenant was nowhere to be seen. Kersh suddenly became aware of footsteps in the corridor approaching. The lamps returned to full brightness and the coolness dissipated. Snapping shut the casket and re-engaging the stasis field, Kersh turned just in time to see Gideon enter with Chaplain Dardarius. The Chaplain's eyes narrowed and his gaunt expression soured. He made it clear he was unhappy with the Scourge's proximity to the relic blade. Apothecary Ezrachi followed and behind him two strangers entered the chapel-reclusiam.

They were Adeptus Astartes. Excoriators. The first was like Dardarius, a Chaplain, also dressed in midnight black but sporting a hood and cloak mantle in the Chapter's colours. The second wore the faded blue plate of the Librarius and a surcoat of tattered white identifying his rank as that of an Epistolary. Instead of a helm, a crafted metal hood protected the Librarian from both physical and psychic attack, and the willowy shaft of a war scythe rested in one gauntlet, the wicked blade-tip of the force weapon barely scraping the deck.

'Corpus-captain,' the Scourge acknowledged. Gideon looked uncomfortable.

'May I introduce Chaplain Shadrath and Epistolary Melmoch,' Gideon said, 'attached to the Fifth Battle Company.'

Kersh looked to Ezrachi, whose eyes failed to meet his own, and then to Chaplain Dardarius, who glowered back. Both Shadrath and Melmoch walked out before the altar and the case containing the Dornsblade. Shadrath pulled back his hood to reveal a Chaplain's helmet. From temple to jaw, the faceplate was decorated with a half-skull. He knuckled his forehead, the half-grille of his helm and then his breastplate – crossing from one heart to the other – before kneeling in front of the relic. Melmoch, whose piercing eyes and unguarded smile seemed out of place on the psyker's weather-beaten face, merely kissed his fist before joining the Chaplain on the chapel flagstones.

'No champions for the Feast were selected from the ranks of the Fifth,' Kersh stated. 'No offence intended, Chaplain.'

Shadrath said nothing, but came up off his ceramite knee and stared at the Scourge through the darkness of his helmet optics. The Epistolary looked to Kersh also, a knowing smile fixed on his odd features. 'Then this is about the Stigmartyr,' Kersh concluded. 'You have found our sacred standard?'

'We have not,' Shadrath admitted, the grille of his helm reverberating with his grave words. 'Though, we have lost over half our number in the endeavour.'

Kersh felt his face tighten. 'I...' he began.

'...don't have the words to express the loss of these brothers,' Shadrath interrupted with plain but savage honesty, 'both to their company and their Chapter.'

Kersh bridled. 'Do you have intelligence of the Stigmartyr's whereabouts or the movements of the traitors who took the standard?'

'Our reconnaissance is sketchy,' Shadrath said. 'The enemy had the benefit of a clean escape and unchallenged withdrawal.'

The Scourge stared hard at the Chaplain's half-skull helm. Without diverting his eyes, he said to Gideon, 'Corpuscaptain, we have returned the Feast's contestants to their battle-brothers. Although Chaplain Shadrath is welcome to bathe in the hard-won honour of our contest victory, the *Scarifica*'s schedule is tight and we are needed above Eschara.'

'You will not be travelling on to Eschara,' Gideon told him.

'What?' the Scourge seethed, at last turning to face the corpus-captain.

'Chaplain Dardarius and myself will see to it that the sacred Dornsblade is delivered safely to our home world. Have no fear of that.'

'I am the victor, the champion of champions. It is my right to bear the blade back to our brothers and present it to Chapter Master Ichabod.'

Gideon offered him a data-slate he held in one gauntlet.

'The Chapter Master has greater honours and greater need

for you elsewhere, Scourge. You will not return to his side or even to the decimated First Company. You have been promoted, Kersh. You are corpus-captain of your own company, with all the power and responsibility that entails.'

Zachariah Kersh couldn't believe what he was hearing. Silence intruded on the gathering.

'The Fifth...' he said finally.

'What is left of it,' Chaplain Shadrath hissed.

When Kersh didn't take the data-slate, Gideon stepped forwards and placed it in his ceramite fingertips. 'Corpus-Captain Thaddeus is dead. Long live Corpus-Captain Kersh. Your orders, corpus-captain,' Gideon said. 'From Eschara. From the Chapter Master himself.'

Kersh stared down at the slate. 'There must be some kind of mistake,' he insisted. 'An astrotelepathic error. A garbled communication. Some confusion with the message terminus or destination.'

'I was the terminus,' Epistolary Melmoch told him, the broad smile still clear on his warrior's features. 'There was no mistake. I transcribed Master Ichabod's orders personally. He was very specific, as you can read on the slate I've prepared for you.'

The Scourge's gaze was on the floor. His mind light years away.

Gideon spoke. 'I have taken the liberty of setting your personal serfs to work on packing up your... belongings and transporting them across to the *Angelica Mortis*, the strike cruiser in whose shadow the *Scarifica* currently resides. Your strike cruiser, corpus-captain. You will not be alone, either. I'm sending Ezrachi with you. Shadrath tells me the Fifth are bereft of their Apothecary as well as their commanding officer and, Emperor willing, we shall make Eschara without need of his talents.'

Kersh looked to the old Apothecary. Ezrachi raised a crabby brow. The Scourge said nothing for a while. 'Kersh,' Gideon said. 'This is a great honour.'

Kersh's face was creased with lines of fresh vexation and responsibility. 'I am corpus-captain of the Fifth...' he said.

'You are,' Chaplain Shadrath confirmed.

'Then may I have the chamber once more, to fully take on board the magnitude of such an honour and consult the Chapter Master's orders?'

Melmoch, still smiling, bowed his head and withdrew from the chamber.

'As you wish,' Shadrath hissed through his helmet half-grille and followed.

Gideon offered his gauntlet. 'I know we've had our differences,' he said, 'but what I saw you accomplish in that arena will stay with me the rest of my days. Let me be the first to congratulate you, corpus-captain.'

Kersh didn't take the offered hand. He turned to face the altar. Eventually, Gideon let it drop and nodded. It was the Scourge's way. As he left, with a sneering Dardarius at his heels, Kersh called, 'I fear you may be the last to do that.'

Gideon stopped and nodded once again.

'Kersh, to command is not to be liked, feared or even respected. It is to be followed. Every corpus-captain finds his way. Some ways are harder than others, but they are all lonely paths,' Gideon told him. 'That's why I left you Ezrachi.' With that, Gideon left the chapel-reclusiam.

Once again, silence reigned.

'This is a mistake,' Kersh said, looking up at the towering stained-glass tessellations of Katafalque and the Primarch Dorn.

'As corpus-captain you must master the art of the politician,' Ezrachi answered. 'It's never a mistake when the Chapter Master makes it.'

'I'm the Scourge,' Kersh said, not seeming to hear the Apothecary. 'I was born a warrior. I was engineered to kill.'

'You're a killer, yes. But killers need to be led, sometimes by other killers. You think yourself not worthy?'

Kersh let the question hang.

'You are the first Excoriator to win the Feast of Blades. The first of our kind to earn the primarch's sword. This promotion is just reward for your efforts at the Feast. Also, you are justly qualified for such a position. Before you were the

Master's Scourge you were a squad whip.'

'First with the Eighth, second squad. Then, like Tiberias, with the Vanguard – First Company.'

'Then I fail to see the mistake.'

'The Feast is a distraction. I am afflicted. The Chapter has lost its standard and shares that affliction. I must assume responsibility for the Stigmartyr's loss and the damage done as a result. I was a fool to think the Master would welcome my return – with or without the Dornsblade. He cannot trust me by his side. This promotion is a convenience. A way to keep me at arm's length. Like sending me to the Feast in the first place.'

'From what I know of the Chapter Master, that seems unlikely.'

'Have you fought by his side for most of your life, Ezrachi?' Kersh challenged. 'Been his blade where his could not be, bled in his stead and been the moment between his life and death?'

'No,' the Apothecary admitted.

'Then tell me not of your observations from afar. I know Quesiah Ichabod. He is a fair and honourable master, the best of us by a light year. He is more than a man, but he is still human and feels as humans do. He is dying. Slowly and in agony because he took an assassin's blade that should have been mine to turn aside or receive. I am the Scourge!'

'You are human also,' the Apothecary reminded him. 'You may think this promotion a return for some perceived failure or betrayal, but I watch as your all-too-human guilt eats away at you, corpus-captain. You punish yourself enough for both you and the Chapter Master. You view the Darkness as an affliction, but perhaps this is the primarch's wish. Like Ichabod you were spared the butchery of that dark day on Ignis Prime. You both live your pain but are meant for greater things. The Feast of Blades. Company command.'

'Command?' Kersh snorted. 'You honestly think of me as a commander? I am my brother's right hand and the blade in his blind spot, not a voice on the vox directing that blade. I am not strategist or tactician. I am an attrition fighter in the best traditions of our Chapter, but when I cross blades I little know what I am going to do next, let alone a hundred others. And of the hundred, why the Fifth? Why did it have to be the Fifth?'

'There is a poetry to the thinking,' Ezrachi admitted. 'You think that you earned the displeasure of your Excoriator brothers at the Feast? Wait until you meet the remainder of the Fifth Company. Then you will come to understand the true hatred of brother for brother.'

'Like the loathing Master Ichabod must hold for me?'

'Perhaps that is the point. Or perhaps the Master still has much to teach you and this is in turn a much needed lesson. You said it yourself, we are attrition fighters. We endure as you will endure this new responsibility and all that goes with it.'

'Does your tiresome advice go with it, Apothecary?'

Ezrachi chuckled. 'I will give you honest counsel when I can. To be corpus-captain is not to have all the answers. You will lead the way and your brethren will follow, it is as simple as that.'

'I am a poor choice.'

'But you are the choice. These are the chains of command, Kersh, and they are binding.' The Scourge nodded.

'Now, corpus-captain, if you'll excuse me I have staff and equipment to transfer to the *Angelica Mortis*.'

Kersh nodded once more and the Apothecary withdrew, leaving him alone again in the chapel-reclusiam. He approached the altar, looking up at Katafalque and Dorn. He placed his helm and the data-slate of Ichabod's orders next to the Dornsblade and knelt before the glass representations. He thought on the trials of the Second Founding. Dorn's own guilt and the agony of the Codex Astartes' decree, the division of the Legion into autonomous Chapters. He considered the noble features of Demetrius Katafalque at his primarch's side. The captain who bled with his men before the walls of the Imperial Palace, under the horrific onslaught of the Warmaster's siege. Holding out for as long as he could. Putting his body between the enemy and his

Emperor. Making them pay in blood for every treasonous step. Demetrius Katafalque, whom Rogal Dorn had designated the first Excoriator. The first Master of their Chapter. The Scourge rested his gauntlet on the pommel of his gladius. The weapon he'd received upon becoming a fully-fledged battle-brother, so many years before.

'Were you ready?' Kersh put to the stained-glass Katafalque.

THE FOUR MEN of the God-Emperor knelt before the cardinal's throne.

'You think it wise to treat the Adeptus Astartes thus?'

'How many of their calling have you encountered?' Pontifex Nazimir asked his brother ecclesiarchs across the ancient's lap. They too wore their years of faith on their faces, but where the cardinal drooled into his vestments, his sycophants still revelled in the wiles of old men.

'None,' Convocate Clemenz-Krycek admitted.

'They're solemn bastards,' Confessor Tyutchev complained bullishly. 'Much in love with their own self-importance and genic heritage.'

'Common Imperials fear them,' Nazimir said. 'They are in awe of their blood-bond with the God-Emperor – but in reality the Adeptus Astartes are little more than genestock slaves.'

'We are still right to fear them,' Clemenz-Krycek replied. 'Surely it is hubris to ensnare the Emperor's Angels and shackle them to our bidding.'

'You talk of hubris – an Angel's prerogative,' Tyutchev interrupted.

'I will, of course, be guided by your excellencies in this,' Arch-Deacon Schedonski told them. 'But I too have some misgivings about using the Adeptus Astartes in this way.'

'You would ask them politely for assistance, would you?' Nazimir teased.

'No–'

'For it would be futile. They think themselves removed from the concerns of modern men.'

'They think of themselves,' Tyutchev repeated, 'as the

giants of old, battling alien barbarians on far-flung worlds, repeating the mistakes of their failed crusade.'

'They still look outwards,' Nazimir said, 'acting on orders given ten thousand years hence, from an Emperor who was not all He would be. They do not appreciate as we do, the God-Emperor's divinity.'

'They deny it.'

'A brand of heresy in itself,' Clemenz-Krycek agreed.

'It would not be the first heretical thought an Adeptus Astartes has entertained,' Nazimir chuckled darkly, and the four priests made the sign of the aquila.

'Perhaps a deceit would be preferable,' the convocate advocated. 'A truth even, one that played to the Angel's noble inclinations.'

'There is no need for such subtlety,' Nazimir insisted. 'The Adeptus Astartes were built to fight, not to think. Obedience is wired into their cult observance and fealty to their forefather. Being a martial breed, they are at their best when issued with straight orders and instruction. Their power is ours to wield.'

'What do you know of these Excoriators?' Schedonski said.

'They descend from Dorn's blood, I think, and favour mortifications of the flesh. They are, of course, one of the Astartes Praeses and have many honours to their name, won garrisoning the Eye and battling the dark forces of the Black Crusades. Their recent history escapes me.'

'What if this does not go to plan?' Clemenz-Krycek asked. 'What if they refuse?'

Nazimir considered the question. 'The Angels Eradicant Third Company takes supplies and munitions at Port Kreel. A sizeable contingent of White Consuls approaches the subsector from victory in the Ephesia Nebula to the galactic east. Then, there is the Viper Legion on Hellionii Reticuli. We exchange one of their names for the Excoriators Chapter in the record and repeat, until some of these wayward scions finally listen to their God-Emperor's wishes from our lips.'

'What if they become unruly?' Clemenz-Krycek put to the gathering.

'The convocate has a point,' Schedonski agreed. 'We'll be exposed. Defence force troops garrison the palace – common soldiers are not traditionally tolerated within its holy chambers.'

'Worry not about our security,' Confessor Tyutchev assured them. 'Our frater brothers will not allow violence against us.'

'You are too close to the Redemptionists,' Clemenz-Krycek warned.

'To every shepherd a flock,' the thick-set confessor replied. 'Besides, we have the Sisters.'

'It is settled then,' Nazimir said and watched Tyutchev and Schedonski nod, followed finally by Clemenz-Krycek. Tyutchev took Cardinal Pontian's hand. It was thin and frail with swollen joints and skin spotted with age. On one finger the cardinal bore a ring of office bearing the holy symbol of the Adeptus Ministorum. Tyutchev bowed his head to kiss the ring. With his lips to the sacred symbol he squeezed the cardinal's hand. Crushing several bones within, the confessor prompted the dribbling ecclesiarch to momentarily break his aged insensibility and groan.

'The cardinal has spoken,' Pontifex Nazimir proclaimed. 'And through him, the God-Emperor's will is known to us...'

I am tempted to think of this as a dream, but know it to be a mere daydream of a nightmare. I lie in my private cell, with space and sparse luxury that as corpus-captain I am yet to get used to. I feel a claustrophobic anxiety crushing me into the stone slab of the berth, regardless. The weight of a responsibility that had not existed before. Ezrachi insists I will grow into it, comparing the feeling to the deadweight of plate first worn and the way in which before long the suit becomes part of the body and no more of a burden than the weight of the limb lifted to swing a gladius or aim a bolter. I am not so sure. Fifty Adeptus Astartes now live or die at my command, with a full squad of those Space

Marine Scouts from the Tenth Company, assigned to bolster our numbers. I can feel the weight of their expectations within my chest, making it difficult for me to catch my breath.

There are far worse things waiting behind the lids of my eyes, however. For days now I seem privy to a slideshow of the mind. Images stab into my consciousness without warning during purification, briefings, cage practise and moments of calm reflection in the cruiser reclusiam. Experiences of wanton violence, delivered or received, with perspectives changing between horrible visions from perpetrator to victim. There is blood always, accompanied by suffering and screams, sometimes my own. When I'm not screaming, I'm roaring my jubilant rage. The horror is there and then it is gone, leaving me an irregular beating of the hearts and the copper-tang of blood in the mouth.

At first I considered these flashes of murderous lust to be some manifestation of my existing haunting, that my phantom was to blame. Since I could not consult Chaplain Shadrath over anomalies without crumbling whatever derelict authority I had with the Fifth Company, I reported this new symptom to Ezrachi. I was surprised to find that he too had been experiencing the visions. Further investigation by the Apothecary revealed that we were not the only ones. Without a medical explanation, the haughty Chaplain in turn had to be consulted to provide a spiritual perspective.

The door rumbles aside and Bethesda enters the cell with a bowl. The bowl rattles against the plate upon which it is sitting. If I had been asleep the sound would have woken me. It is Bethesda's way of announcing her arrival. I sit up and check the time. We are in warp translation. Outside the eddies and currents of the immaterium – a sight never meant for human eyes – ripple and swirl as the Angelica Mortis slows and charges her warp engines, ready to tear her way back into reality. I must confess to an unsettled stomach. I cannot tell whether it is simply the ether-draught of different vessels or the styles of the Navigators piloting them, but this warp jump feels different. I have never had an appetite for warp travel but had just got used to the Scarifica's smooth passages and the slim frigate's knife-like dimensional shifts. The strike cruiser, by comparison, is a blunt-nosed beast that bulldozes its way through the currents of the empyrean. The Angelica Mortis's Navigator – who I have not yet had the pleasure of meeting – goes about his translation like a Land Raider ramming through a blast door. I can feel the vessel below me, smashing through the troughs and prevailing drifts rather than riding them like the Scarifica had done.

There, stood by the opening arch, is my phantom. It has been stood there in the darkness, as has become its unsettling habit, cast in the brilliance of the warp. Its black armour shines with the indescribable spectrum of light and colour flooding the cell. It is almost constantly with me now. Always somewhere, unobtrusive, providing a ghastly background. Whatever it is, it seems to be perpetually on guard, casting me in the role of either prisoner or protectee. I am either being guarded or guarded against. The revenant never speaks but is merely there and ever more so.

The bulkhead opens and my seneschal and lictor enter. They have new robes, as befitting the serfs of an Excoriators corpus-captain. I blink as they file in past the armoured apparition. They seem not to see the thing. This is new. Usually the phantom disappears in the presence of the living. This time it remains for all to see, but for the fact that my serfs seem not to see it at all – the darkness of its armoured form becoming a peripheral blind spot or clouding in the corner of the eye.

Old Enoch mumbles an officious greeting. He is carrying the freshly oiled 'purge', ready for my purification. I look to the living and the dead, stunned at how I can be seemingly inbetween. I nod and stand. A moody Oren deposits a bowl of fresh water by my berth and follows his father into my private and adjoining penitorium. Bethesda holds before her the bowl of sourdough bread and Escharan figs. I'm not hungry and give an almost imperceptible shake of the head.

'You must eat, my lord – to keep up your strength,' the absterge says. She deposits the plate on the stone of the berth. I go to refute the suggestion but the girl pops a fig into my mouth before I can. She moves to the bowl of water and wrings out a rag. The figs are sweet and more pleasant than I remember. Grumbling, I take another from the plate to settle my warp-churning stomach.

As Bethesda cleanses my flesh in readiness for my purification,

Old Enoch and Oren prepare the penitorium for my 'Donning of Dorn's Mantle'. Two misshapen servitors enter also, wheeling in the caterpillar-tracked frame upon which my helm and relic armour hangs. My eyes linger on the sheathed blades dangling on their belts from the mount.

After Dorn's Mantle I don my plate, each piece of ceramite locked and sealed in place by the serfs and servitors. Clearing and reloading my bolt pistol I slip it into my navel holster while Old Enoch and Oren belt my gladii to my hip. The only new addition to the ensemble is Corpus-Captain Thaddeus's chainsword – a Fifth Company heirloom. A Ryza-pattern rarity, the weapon is relatively short and falchion-shaped, making it perfect for use in areas with restricted space like tunnels and the meat-grinding throngs of battle. The weapon and its harness are strapped to my other thigh.

Oren carries my helm as I make my way through the dormitories, cell blocks and refectory of the strike cruiser. Everywhere I go, unsurprisingly, eyes are averted and heads bowed – a sign of passive defiance easily disguised as subservient acknowledgement. The battle-brothers of the Fifth Company have not forgotten themselves. They are the Adeptus Astartes, proud and bound by centuries of ritual and stricture. I can see through the martial routine and cult observance, however. I see tight jaws and eyes red-rimmed with defeat and loss. They feel the emptiness of the Angelica Mortis and hear the echoes of their butchered brethren. I can hear the snap of the lash with greater regularity than cult observance requires. A company punishing itself beyond the healthy parameters of its primarch's teachings. Penitoria decks awash with blood. Angels, angry with themselves, furious at me; hollow vessels filling with hate and frustration. I have lived this loathing and there is but one cure. To become honour's avenger, to right wrongs in the heat of battle; vengeance, surgically applied – the solemn duty for which we were created.

This company is one big open wound. I feel it in the halls and corridors. I feel it across the table of the tactical-oratorium. My officers are gathered here. The great and the good of the Fifth, within whom this pain finds its most intense expression. Again, I have plate, bodies and faces but no eyes. All eyes are on the table. *They will not look at me for fear I might know their abhorrence. A hatred born of the shame of my loss both of our precious Stigmartyr and my mind to the Darkness. The same hatred tempered in the fires of their own loss and failure to reclaim the Chapter standard. It is all here, as clear as the Codex Astartes on their faces. The philosopher Guilliman has no advice for me in his great book. Even our own Demetrius Katafalque composed no chapter for this in* The Architecture of Agony, *although it would have been a worthy subject for his writings.*

I sit at the head of a long stone table, a table where the seats are half empty. The absence of the heroes who would have filled those seats has already established a tone. Worse still, I find my phantom has already assumed a dead-man's seat at the far end of the table. It watches me with a shadowy stillness. The rest of the gathering seem unaware of its macabre presence. I have grown used to the grotesque being and its parlour trickery and attempt to emulate them.

Silence stings the air. Ezrachi is present. The Apothecary is satisfied with his new facilities and Helix-staff, but has found the company's welcome no warmer than my own. Next to him are the other company specialists: Melmoch, the Fifth's assigned Librarian and astrotelepathic communications officer – still smiling; Techmarine Dancred with his clockwork face; Chaplain Shadrath, hiding his cold discontent, as always, behind the leering half-skull of his helm. Sitting opposite is Corpus-Commander Bartimeus of the Angelica Mortis, *as gruff and blunt as his immaterial voidmanship. Beyond the bridge officer sit the Fifth Company's remaining squad whips: Ishmael, Joachim and the chief whip, Uriah Skase. Skase is a veteran – as the torn and mangled flesh of his face testifies. It sits on his face like an ugly, snarling mask, seemingly only held together by the staples, stitches and decorative rings that run across it. I have no reason to believe that the rest of his body isn't scarred in the same way, like some hideous resurrection experiment.*

Ezrachi has already told me that Skase is going to be a problem. More so even than Chaplain Shadrath. He is a legend within the company. An assault squad whip, he has more combat experience than the rest of his squad added together. He has walked away from the most grievous injuries and heaviest fighting of the Fifth Company's many victories and has been at the forefront of the Excoriators' efforts to reclaim the Stigmartyr from the filth Alpha Legion at Veiglehaven. He is loved by his men, who view him as an indestructible force. Ezrachi heard that he was so unrelenting on the battlefield that on the midnight plains of Menga-Dardra, a Black Legion Land Raider slammed into him with its dozer blade, ran him down and crushed him beneath its tracks, only for the mauled and buckled Skase to get back to his feet and rush back into the heart of the fighting. Worse, he had been Corpus-Captain Thaddeus's right hand and, with Shadrath, had held the company together in the wake of the atrocities at Vieglehaven. Every Excoriator in the Fifth had fully expected Uriah Skase's promotion to corpus-captain as a given. That was until Chapter Master Ichabod's intervention and my unwelcome arrival aboard the Angelica Mortis.

The surviving battle-brothers of the Fifth have been reorganised by Skase into three full squads. He has taken the first, Squad Cicatrix. The second, Squad Castigir, is led by Skase's own right hand, Squad Whip Ishmael, an Excoriator crafted of much the same unforgiving brutality as the chief whip. Brother Joachim has been recently promoted to whip of Squad Censura. Joachim is younger and fresher of face, but his devotion to Skase and his ideals is clear, assuming the form of a kind of hero worship. Together, the three whips have the allegiance of the company's fighting brotherhood locked up and the Fifth Company's detestation of my existence is universal.

The only battle-brothers not under Skase's influence are the Tenth Company Scouts under Veteran Squad Whip Keturah. Fortunately, Silas Keturah allows for no other influence upon his neophytes but his own. I have felt little warmth for my own authority from the silver-haired veteran, who has clearly not relished using his young charges to bolster the depleted numbers under my command. Whenever we speak, I feel his critical scrutiny through the visor interface built into his brow and the cyclopean burn of the sniper's single bionic lens, whirring softly to magnification.

By the time I finally speak, I have been sat there for some time

– lost in my thoughts. No doubt my brothers will think this some proud indulgence and abhor me all the more.

'CORPUS-COMMANDER BARTIMEUS, when do you expect us to make St Ethalberg?' Kersh asked across the cool stone of the table. When Bartimeus didn't immediately reply, Kersh pressed. 'Learned brother?'

The Scourge immediately regretted the derisive comment. Sarcasm was an indulgence and one not befitting the Emperor's Angels, let alone a corpus-captain. Ezrachi had warned him that it would be unwise to meet the discontent in the company head on. He advised the Scourge to think like an officer and handle his men as such. Kersh's belligerence was not so easily tamed, however, and his warrior's pride was constantly fed by the sting of the company's own mordant provocation. As Ezrachi had observed, it was fuel for the mutinous cancer already eating away at the Fifth Company's collective soul. Initially, the Space Marines – already unhappy with the choice of their new corpus-captain – had been taken aback by the Scourge's manner, but this soon settled into a morose sourness that became the hallmark of their disappointment and acceptance.

'Warp translation was successful,' the Excoriators commander mumbled with ill-disguised truculence.

'Speak up, sir!' Kersh barked. 'This is the tactical-oratorium. You're not talking to one of your bridge drones now, corpus-commander.'

Bartimeus glared at the Scourge. Raising his voice a little, he reported, 'We are approaching from the edge of the system at quarter sub-light speed.'

'Why the hesitant approach? Were not my orders to reach the cardinal world at best possible speed?'

'That is the best possible speed,' Bartimeus snapped back. 'The system is crowded with Adeptus Ministorum craft and the like on similar approaches.'

'Understood,' Kersh acknowledged. 'And what of our turbulent passage?'

'Sir?'

'I felt every bump and roll in the pit of my stomach. Did we encounter difficulties during the jump?'

'The *Angelica Mortis* is a thoroughbred cruiser, a veteran of her class...' Bartimeus began defensively.

'I don't doubt it, corpus-commander,' the Scourge replied. 'No censure was intended. I was making reference to the journey, not the vessel.'

Bartimeus's broad features dropped a little. 'Immaterial squalls and storms are common this close to the Eye. It is possible that we crossed the wake of a convoy or flotilla, just clear of their entry point.'

'Possible, corpus-commander?'

'Yes.'

'Is it possible that it was a fleet or an armada, rather than a convoy?'

'I'm sure I could not say...'

'Well let's try to be sure, shall we? Work with the Epistolary here to have your observations communicated to Cadia and Cypra Mundi. They may contribute to other intelligence. There could be a Black Crusade, for all we know, blasting its way out of the Eye of Terror.'

'I think that unlikely...' Bartimeus bit back.

'And I think we should not profess to know the polluted contents of the Despoiler's mind.'

'It's not the Despoiler,' Chaplain Shadrath announced.

'A spiritual perspective, Chaplain?' Kersh turned on him. 'I dare say the victims of previous crusades might have thought the same before their untimely deaths.'

'It is the Keeler Comet,' Shadrath hissed through his half-grille.

'Stargazer too, Chaplain?' Kersh said. 'Are there no end to your talents? Pray, tell us how this astral body might provide an impediment in the warp?'

'It's an unnatural body, my lord,' Melmoch interjected. The Librarian looked from Kersh to the Chaplain and then back to Kersh. 'Records show that it was a long-period returning body that last visited the segmentum over ten thousand years ago.'

'Was?'

'Upon its return it found the Eye of Terror in its path. Witnessing vessels claim that it has emerged… changed. A blood-red comet, with a trailing ethereal tail and an erratic and unpredictable course.'

'How can a comet have an unpredictable course?' Kersh marvelled. 'It has an orbit, it obeys the laws of gravity.'

'Not the Keeler, sir,' the Epistolary insisted. 'It seems to have a mind of its own.'

'How do you know of this?'

Melmoch told him. '*The Ancient Traveller*, sir. A pict of the original body, from antiquity, by the remembrancer Euphrati Keeler.'

'Euphrati Keeler?'

'Yes, corpus-captain. Saint Euphrati – prophet of the God-Emperor.'

'The God-Emperor?' Kersh questioned. 'You think there not enough traits to set you apart from common Adeptus Astartes, Epistolary Melmoch, that you must indulge a belief that those more than mortal find offensive?'

'I meant no offence, sir,' Melmoch stated. 'Only that the gift to which you allude is believed by some of my kind to be an expression of His divinity.'

'And by some of mine to be an aberration, good Librarian, but there we have it.'

'I am not the first Adeptus Astartes to hold such beliefs,' Melmoch said, his smile still fixed to his face.

'Well,' Kersh said, leaning his head against the palm of his gauntlet. 'We are all learning something today. To think that I was spending my time in the practise cages when I should have been in the Librarium.'

'Your travels have taken you out of the segmentum, my lord. The comet's reappearance is a relatively recent occurrence.'

The corpus-captain nodded slow thanks to the Epistolary. The Librarian would have made an able diplomat. Kersh had indeed been out of circulation for some time, but the psyker had only mentioned his duties at the far-flung Feast of Blades – and for this Kersh was grateful. He had not mentioned the time the Scourge had spent in the Darkness. Kersh allowed the index digit of his gauntlet to rest in the raw cavity in the side of his face. It had become a habit during moments of thoughtful reflection. Since losing his eye in the Feast, he had also taken to tapping the metal ball-bearing in the socket of his eye with the ceramite tip of his finger.

'And what of these visionary distractions the company has been experiencing, Chaplain Shadrath?' Kersh continued. 'The Apothecary informs me that he has checked our water, provisions and life support systems for any evidence of tampering or neglect and has found none. I put it to you that there is some other explanation, perhaps the effects of this strange comet Melmoch speaks of.'

'I believe the malign influence of the comet could be responsible,' the Chaplain told Kersh evenly, 'but I detect no signs of outward corruption or spiritual licentiousness. At present I have too little to go on to make an informed judgement.'

'I am beginning to understand how you feel, Chaplain,' Kersh retorted. 'Well, while you reach a conclusion the rest of us will go on fearing for our eternal souls.' Before Shadrath could reply the Scourge moved furiously on. 'Brother Dancred, what is the status of the company's Thunderhawks?'

The two power-towers reaching out of the back of the Techmarine's adapted armour crackled and arced with energy. Dancred's clockwork face whirred to life, the nest of Omnissiah-honouring cogs and pinions working in unison like a mask of gears.

'Two of the company's Thunderhawks are lost to us, corpus-captain,' Dancred told him. 'During the attack on Ignis Prime, the *Inwitian* was destroyed on the Chapter house landing pad. The *Flagellant* returned but has sustained too much damage to be saved. I have conducted the appropriate rites and appeased the fading spirit of the fallen machine. It will live on through the invaluable parts it will provide for ongoing repairs to the *Demetrius Katafalque III* and the venerable *Gauntlet*. The *Impunitas* did not partake in the original operation or the rescue on Ignis Prime.'

'The *Impunitas* is our only functioning gunship?'

'Yes, corpus-captain.'

'Well, Brother Dancred, that simply will not do,' Kersh said. 'The Fifth Company will need all of its weapons of war.'

'The *Gauntlet* is our oldest and most decorated Thunderhawk. Her firepower will be yours shortly, my lord.'

'Make sure it is, brother,' the Scourge said, and then a little softer, 'and know your efforts are appreciated.' The Excoriator turned to Ezrachi. 'Have you had opportunity to inspect the gene-seed?'

'Apothecary Philemon gathered the progenoids of the dead and dying at the Chapter house, as his solemn duty demanded,' Ezrachi reported. 'He lost his life to the Alpha Legion's second ambush with Corpus-Captain Thaddeus. Squad Cicatrix had the honour of driving back the Traitor Legionnaires and recovering the bodies.' The Apothecary nodded respectfully across the table at a smouldering Skase who, disarmed at such diplomacy, managed an almost imperceptible nod back. 'In doing this Chief Whip Skase and his men saved the harvested gene-seed of their fallen brothers, and the company is rightfully in their debt.'

Kersh would not be drawn into the Apothecary's placation. 'The seed itself?'

'In good condition and stored in the apothecarion frigocombs–'

'And what of the brothers to whom the seed belonged?' Skase boiled over. He stood, slamming the palms of his gauntlets into the surface of the table. 'Who knows the price of their esteem? We taketh away. When do we giveth – that's what I demand to know.'

Kersh burned into him across the stone. 'Take your seat, brother.'

'I will not.'

'What would you give them, whip?' Ezrachi cut in. 'Was not their loss lamented in ritual?'

'He does not speak of ritual,' Chaplain Shadrath hissed.

'He speaks of vengeance,' Kersh said. 'He speaks of a battle-brother's gift to his fallen brethren: avengement.'

'You have intelligence from the Angels Eradicant of Alpha Legion sightings amongst the petrified hives of Rorschach's World, yet you do nothing,' Skase accused.

'You think I hide upon this cruiser – afraid to engage our enemies?' Kersh seethed. 'Filth to whom we have both lost so much?'

Skase considered his words. 'You are the Scourge. You are victor in the Feast of Blades. You have not a cowardly bone in your body… and yet you have found one.'

Within the blink of an eye Kersh was on his feet and had kicked his chair back behind him. Both Excoriators had their gauntlets to their weapons. Kersh gripped the hilt of his chainsword; Skase had his palm on the haft of his power axe, just below the dormant blade, ready to snatch the weapon from his belt. 'Found your spine, Scourge? Going to cut me down with my corpus-captain's sword?'

Kersh's lip curled.

'I have lived your pain,' the Scourge told him honestly. 'No one wants to face the Alpha Legion more than I. They have the Stigmartyr and I am honourless without it. I have pledged on the primarch's blade that I shall reclaim it, but until I do the blood of those who lost their lives in its taking, and the attempts to reclaim it since, stains these hands.' Kersh released his weapon and presented his palms to the squad whip. 'Know that the loss of the Stigmartyr, for me, is more a punishment than you could ever devise. So be satisfied, loyal whip, for no more blood of the Fifth Company will be spilt here today – by my hand or yours. As corpus-captain, I will not permit it.'

'That's not good enough…'

'Well, it will have to be, Chief Whip Skase.'

Skase looked about him at the frozen masks of alarm and expectation around the table. Releasing his axe, the squad whip slowly presented his own open palm and took his seat. 'I have my orders,' Kersh announced to the gathering, but his eyes were still on Skase, 'and you have yours. The reason we do not make straight for Rorschach's World to act upon this intelligence is because Chapter Master Ichabod has already designated our present duty. His orders take us to St Ethalberg. These are the chains of command,' Kersh repeated from his earlier conversation with Ezrachi. 'And they are binding.' The Scourge let his words sink in. He detected faint nods about the table.

A bridge serf entered. Bowing before Kersh he delivered a whispered message to Commander Bartimeus.

'We are about to make the cardinal world system,' Bartimeus relayed gruffly.

'Oversee the warp translation,' Kersh ordered, prompting the Excoriators commander to follow the serf out of the oratorium. When the young Joachim and Squad Whip Ishmael got to their feet the Scourge turned on them. 'Remain!' he barked, causing the pair to sink moodily back to their seats. 'Damned insolence,' Kersh told them. 'You will leave when you are dismissed and not a moment before.' He turned back to Skase. 'You forget yourselves but you can be forgiven, given the poor example set by your chief whip. Therefore, after due consideration, I have decided his punishment to be a three day cessation of ritual observance. Over this time he should consider himself unfit to don the mantle of Dorn.'

Chaplain Shadrath's helm turned sharply. Ishmael and Joachim glared. Skase sat enraged but silent.

'Mortification of the flesh is every Excoriator's right,' Squad Whip Ishmael shot back.

'No, brother,' Kersh returned, 'it is not. Union with the primarch is a privilege and should be denied to those whose actions have proved unworthy of his ideals. I'm sure Chaplain Shadrath would agree.'

Shadrath said nothing.

'Then I too volunteer for punishment,' Ishmael said.

'Seconded,' Joachim echoed.

'As you wish,' Kersh told them. 'Your confessed unworthiness is noted. The Chaplain will oversee the implementation of this punishment.'

The oratorium felt the cold sting of the corpus-captain's orders. The chamber was silent. 'Dismissed, brothers.'

As the Excoriators left, Ezrachi held back.

'That could have gone... smoother,' the Apothecary said. Kersh wasn't in the mood, however.

'Why don't you devote your talents to the wounded pride of my officers?' Kersh bit back.

'I fear they are wounds that are already festering and beyond my abilities,' Ezrachi admitted.

Kersh nodded, appreciating the Apothecary's appraisal. The Apothecary went to leave.

'I want you to accompany me down to the cardinal world,' Kersh called as he reached the oratorium archway.

'As you wish, my lord,' Ezrachi said.

'I need someone who can cut through the Ecclesiarchy politics and subtlety,' Kersh admitted. 'I haven't the ears for Adeptus Ministorum guile and sermonising. I am not much of a politician.'

'I think you have already proved that today,' Ezrachi said, allowing himself a dark chuckle before disappearing through the arch. The bulkhead fell to closing and Kersh was left in the empty oratorium.

Looking down the length of the table, the Scourge found himself staring at the revenant, who had been there all the while, like a macabre ornament. The otherworldly eavesdropper sat still and said nothing.

'What are you looking at?' Kersh said irritably.

CHAPTER FIVE
SUSPIRIANA OBLIGATIO

THE THUNDERHAWK IMPUNITAS dropped out of the heavens.

St Ethalberg was a bitter, unforgiving world. As soon as the gunship broke the upper atmosphere it tumbled through a maelstrom of glass-shard gales and caustic snowstorms. Below, the planet surface was a stake trap of steeple-colossi, lofty towers and hive-shrine spires. A dark world of vertiginous devotion, reaching up into the chemical blizzard above.

Zachariah Kersh entered the cockpit. The helmscarl and his crew went to kiss their fists but the corpus-captain stopped them.

'As you were.'

Kersh stared out through the hail-dashed canopy. Ahead was their destination. Carved from the frost-shattered peaks of the Vatic Heights was St Ethalberg's administrative and episcopal capital. Here the monstrous pinnacles of the Palace Euphorica breached the clouds, the palace in turn nestling like a behemoth amongst the dark and forbidding sprawl of the grand cathedrals. It was from the daunting heights of the Palace Euphorica that the Ecclesiarchy provided spiritual guidance for the billions of pious St Ethalbergers below and for trillions more beyond the cardinal world and across the subsector. Highest of all was the bulbous tower known as the Pulpit, containing both the cardinal's throne room and an Adepta Sororitas Preceptory.

'My lord,' the co-helmscarl called. Looking out to the left and right of the Thunderhawk, Kersh saw a pair of Vendetta gunships falling into escort position.

'Identify.'

'Ethalberg Inclements, fourth reserve.'

'Defence force?'

'Aye, my lord.'

'Confirm our credentials and take us in,' Kersh commanded.

Flanked by the local military aircraft, the battle-scarred *Impunitas* made for the landing pads that sprouted from the tower minaret like a crown. With the pock-marked Thunderhawk on the deck and Vendettas hanging with ominous intent in the sky like scavenging raptors, the Excoriators disembarked. Striding out into the cruel bluster of the cardinal world stratosphere, Kersh watched Scouts from Tenth Company's Squad Contritus fan out with their silver-haired squad whip ahead.

Silas Keturah and his neophytes were all clad in their ceremonial carapace and dark, hooded cloaks, which streamed behind them in the relentless gales. They clutched slender sniper rifles to their chests. Each trailed a clutch of neat cables that disappeared beneath their mantles as well as large magnocular sights, laser guidance and long barrels terminating in a chunky muzzle, decorated with a fluttering Chapter pennant. The Scout squad took ceremonial flanking positions and walked the Excoriators party into the cardinal's palace. For his unpurged sins, Kersh had Ezrachi, Epistolary Melmoch and Chaplain Shadrath accompany him.

Above the landing pad, amongst the busy Gothic architecture of the Pulpit, Kersh spotted gun emplacements and demi-turrets mounting heavy stubbers and autocannon.

This didn't surprise the Scourge. The Palace Euphorica was not only the cardinal's seat, it was also the residence of the planetary lord. On St Ethalberg these positions were one and the same. The local defence force therefore had the responsibility of securing the palace perimeter, though they were rarely tolerated beyond its gates. Kersh looked up at a crow's nest and watched the Ethalberg Inclements shiver in their Guardsman's flak and sink down into the moth-eaten fur of their lined jackets.

The Excoriators marched, dwarfed by the gargantuan archways, naves and vaulted aisles of the cathedral palace. They were greeted by a gushing wretch of a cleric-warden, whose responsibility it was to officiate the north-west advent-archway. Due to the altitude, and like everyone else who worked within the palace, the warden wore a smeared plas altitude mask. The warden chattered inanely as he led the Space Marines inside, the warmth of his breath a continual stream of white haze escaping his mask.

Inside the monstrous dimensions of the Palace Euphorica, flocks of ancient priests and miserable novitiates moved across the polished obsidian expanse like birds, while others emerged from the myriad confessional booths and private chapels lining the chambers. Muscular fraters in sectarian skirts and conical sackcloth hoods observed the Adeptus Astartes with obvious suspicion from the darkness of ragged eyeholes. Kersh observed the Redemptionists with equal suspicion, and in particular, the slung-straps and crescent clips of grubby autoguns that were protruding from behind their bully-boy backs.

The ambulatory along which they walked was punctuated with lecterns, pulpits and altars, while statues of all-but-forgotten saints and ecclesiarchs seemed to watch the Excoriators pass beneath their stony gaze. Behind these, at intervals along their path, Kersh spotted the gleaming darkness of the revenant's plate – the deathless thing appearing much like a statue itself. The open space about the Excoriators was thick with the bass of devotional choirs and sibilant chanting, but the air itself was thin and gelid.

Through an endless succession of cavernous chambers, the Space Marines were led by the warden into the equally enormous palace throne room. Kersh snorted. A chill mustiness assailed his nostrils like the smell of bad meat in an ice-locker. The throne room itself boasted power-armoured sentinels: bolter-wielding members of the Adepta Sororitas. With their claret-coloured plate and dusty black vestments, Kersh recognised the Daughters of the Emperor as belonging to the Order of the Bloody Rose. He nodded his head at the Celestian in respect but found that his generous gesture was not returned.

Although the throne room was large, it seemed crowded, as befitting a centre of episcopal and administrative authority. A woebegone choir seemed to hold the same despondent note while a small legion of cenobite scribes scratched commandments and observances into vellum with barbed quills. Armed Redemptionists milled about the devotional throngs, while vergers lit candles and restocked globes of billowing incense that swung on extensive lengths of chain suspended from the chamber ceiling.

At the epicentre of the activity was a vaulted throne, sat atop a tall stone column. The column was situated between a nest of other stunted pillars, each displaying a fully armed Sister of Battle, standing statuesque around the throne. A rickety scaffold had been constructed about the structure to enable access to the column's summit and the frame was swarming with Sisters of various Orders Hospitaller. The throne itself was illuminated by a shaft of kaleidoscopic light falling from a circular stained-glass window situated in the ceiling. The desiccated husk who sat upon the throne was buried in a mitre and the heavy robes of his calling. A mind of mulch, within the wasted body of an ancient, Cardinal Bonifacius Pontian occasionally dribbled recitations or befuddled prayers to the gathering.

At first Kersh took Pontian to be the source of the chamber's crisp stench. The cardinal had probably been quietly rotting away on the throne for the best part of a half-millennium. But the smell was not Pontian. Casting his eyes up the wall of both sides of the throne room, the Scourge regarded what he thought at first glance to be decorative stone statues and gargoyles. Water ran from the goylespouts and down the architecture in the manner of an ornate water feature, to be collected in the fonts that lined the wall below. The water was clearly collected from the steeple architecture, after falling as caustic sleet from the bitter cardinal world sky. Upon second inspection, however, Kersh saw that the forms were not statues built into the wall but unfortunates chained from it. Heretics, witches and mutants – unbelievers all – suspended from the cathedral-palace walls. Their faces and extremities were black and frostbitten, their features dissolved in the baptism of an agonising chemical-freeze. Their slow suffering, in turn, blessed the waters of the fonts below – waters that were being collected and distributed in vials to favoured priests and devout clerics across St Ethalberg and the subsector beyond.

'Sir,' Ezrachi said, drawing the Scourge's attention back to a pack of priestly jackals who were approaching the Excoriators. The cleric-warden backed away like a beaten dog. Four ecclesiarchs presented themselves; old, wiry men, knotted with age and cunning. The first had been surrounded by Sisters of the Order of the Eternal Candle, who had parted at his brusque insistence. He limped over to the Adeptus Astartes using an ornate cane and was joined by a priestly inferior, who had fire in his eyes. Another ecclesiarch had been in deep discussion with a Guard officer and his ensign, while a thick-set third had been flanked by two brutish Redemptionists, who looked more like bodyguards than part of the priest's pious congregation. Peeling off from their retinues, the four converged on the advancing Excoriators.

'Corpus-Captain Kersh,' the first announced with a sickly smile. He jabbed his cane towards the Scourge. 'I am Nazimir, Pontifex-Urba of the Palace Euphorica. Welcome to St Ethalberg.'

Kersh cast his eyes over the pontifex at the heretics suffering on the wall. 'Thank you, pontifex, but I can think of few places in the galaxy less welcoming than this,' he told him.

Nazimir managed a sardonic laugh, passing Kersh's reply off as a joke. 'Can I introduce Convocate Clemenz-Krycek, Confessor Tyutchev and Arch-Deacon Schedonski.'

'You can,' Kersh said, 'but I'm even less interested in meeting them than I was in meeting you.'

Nazimir's smile died on his face.

'We have invited you into our–'

'No, sir,' Kersh corrected him. 'You have demanded an audience with the Emperor's Angels. You now have that audience. You have applied some mysterious pressure, through your wiles and politicking, that has meant that Quesiah Ichabod – Master of the Excoriators Chapter – has insisted I exchange words with Cardinal Pontian of St Ethalberg. I am here to do just that. No less. No more.'

'We speak for the cardinal,' Nazimir said, leaning on his cane.

'The cardinal cannot speak for himself?'

'Not for many years now.'

'Then the cardinal and I have said all that we are ever going to say,' Kersh told them and turned away. Marching for the colossal archway egress, the Scourge said into his vox, '*Impunitas*, this is Kersh. Prepare–'

'Corpus-captain!'

'Excoriator!'

'Kersh!'

Something hit the Scourge's pauldron. With blistering reflexes the corpus-captain turned and snatched the object out of the air, his face a mask of grizzled venom. In his gauntlet he held a crumpled vellum scroll. The stunted Schedonski held the other end in his gnarled claws with the length of manuscript taut between them.

'That was unwise, mortal,' Ezrachi warned.

'This is the *Suspiriana Obligatio*,' Schedonski continued. 'It details the mysterious pressure you speak of, Excoriator. It is the holy covenant that binds us and blesses our union with common purpose.'

Snatching it from the priest's grip, Kersh slapped the tattered scroll into Melmoch's chestplate. The Librarian scanned through the manuscript, feeding the length of the scroll through his gauntlets as he read. The Epistolary's eyes blazed across the complexities of Adeptus Astartes Chapter commitments, blood oaths and the resolutions of antiquity. His shoulders sagged.

'Well?' Kersh pressed, his snarling face still fixed on Schedonski.

'It's a small avocation, my lord, but it exists. The cardinal world is granted succouricance rites for their role in the prayer-suppression of the daemon Chorozramodeus. These are guaranteed through the Conclave Suspiria and the Decree Vinculum, sworn on the bones of Constantine of Alamar. These rites extend through the unhonoured obligations of the Relictors, an existing accord between Chapter Masters Bardane and Abadiah – and through Abadiah, Master Ichabod. The rights also extend through the reassignment of the Aquinas and Ptolemy subsector boundaries. This, sir, all reinforced by a solitary but significant verse from the *Mythos Angelica Mortis*.'

'The witchbreed speaks true,' Schedonski spat, ill-disguising his disgust at the presence of the psyker.

'Kersh,' Nazimir sneered as Schedonski gathered the vellum. 'You have obligations, corpus-captain. The weight of history lies on your broad shoulders. It would be a shame to see you falter and have such responsibilities pass from the penitent Relictors, through your failings, to another Chapter.'

'That is why your Chapter Master has sent you here,' Confessor Tyutchev pitched in. 'He appreciates the import of pact and decorum. Mind you do the same, Excoriator.'

'Be guided by the God-Emperor's will in this, Angel,' Convocate Clemenz-Krycek instructed.

Kersh let the ecclesiarchs' insults wash over him. He looked to Ezrachi. He had brought the Apothecary along to help him cut through such chicanery.

'You have words for these words?' Kersh asked him.

Ezrachi's face was taut with tension. The priests' conduct had irritated him as much as any Excoriator in the chamber.

'We are the Adeptus Astartes,' he replied. 'Our actions speak louder than our words.'

Kersh nodded. 'Squad Contritus, are you in position?' the Scourge said simply. His vox crackled back a short confirmation. Nazimir's hooded eyes narrowed with confusion. The priests looked about the throne room. The Excoriators' escort of Scout Marines had vanished. Only Kersh and his power-armoured brothers remained. 'Pick your targets,' Kersh said, his eyes burning into Nazimir. Red dots appeared on the hoods of armed Redemptionists about the room, causing consternation and panic in the hordes of clerics, scribes and menials about them.

'You would mount an operation within the Palace Euphorica!' the pontifex screamed incredulously.

'Execute,' Kersh commanded.

A *thud-whoosh* reverberated about the chamber. Headless bodies crashed to the cathedral floor in unison. The response was immediate. The statuesque Sisters of Battle in their crimson power armour turned to present arms – the gaping barrels of their bolters pointing at the Excoriators. The Inclement Reserves immediately went for their officer sidearms and, like the fraters who had got their chunky fingers to their secreted autoguns, were scanning the alcoves, statues and doorways to private chapels for any sign of their assailants. Squad Whip Keturah and his Scouts had all long secreted themselves, peeling off one by one unnoticed to take concealed positions about the colossal chamber. They had attached sonic-suppressors and set their rifles to non-visible wavelengths.

'What are you doing?' Convocate Clemenz-Krycek shouted.

'Again,' Kersh ordered. Spinning around, the priests watched a fresh set of frater bodies hit the throne room floor. Scribes and clerics shrieked and scattered like a flock of frightened birds. Kersh spotted the phantom at the heart of the horror and confusion. It watched and waited. The thunder of bells rang through the palace.

'My lords!' Schedonski called.

'The Angels have gone mad,' Nazimir screamed at the Adepta Sororitas, waving his cane about. 'Defend the cardinal!'

'Kill the interlopers!' Tyutchev yelled to his frater militia.

'Hit them again,' Kersh said impassively. Once more, the bodies rained to the ground.

The thick-set confessor stepped over the dead and walked fearlessly towards the Excoriators. 'Heretics in our midst, corrupted by the dark power of the Eye,' Tyutchev blurted, before finding the broad blade of a ceremonial kris come to rest beneath his wrinkled chin. A helmeted Sister Superior stood behind the confessor.

'Stop this!' the ancient Nazimir wheezed.

'The confessor is correct,' Kersh announced calmly. 'There are heretics in our midst. Do your duty, Sister.'

Nazimir, Clemenz-Krycek and Schedonski all exchanged horrified glances. The battle-sister hesitated long enough to demonstrate that the Excoriator's words were encouragement rather than instruction. Then she slit the confessor's throat, spraying Nazimir with blood, and allowed Tyutchev's body to fall with his Redemptionists. For a moment the throne room was lost for words.

'What are you doing?' Clemenz-Krycek finally repeated.

'Tell them,' Kersh ordered.

Chaplain Shadrath gave the fool ecclesiarchs the horror of his half-skull helmet. 'The Adeptus Ministorum is forbidden to keep men under arms,' he hissed, 'by order of the High Lords of Terra. You have broken the *Decree Passive* – a violation punishable by death.'

A clumsy stampede could be heard in the adjoining chamber accompanied by the echo of hastily issued orders. The bells had summoned the Ethalberg Inclement Reserves in their threadbare furs and cheap flak.

'Squad Contritus, stand by,' Kersh spoke calmly into his vox-link.

'No, no, no!' Arch-Deacon Schedonski shouted, waving his arms at the giant archway entrance to the throne room.

He was swiftly accompanied by the Guardsmen to whom he had been talking. The officer and his ensign ordered the charging defence force troops to stand down.

'We had no knowledge of the Redemptionist transgression,' Convocate Clemenz-Krycek said.

'For the love of the God-Emperor, please, I beg of you,' Nazimir pleaded. Kersh looked to Epistolary Melmoch and found the psyker's disarming smile waiting for him.

'I hear enough of this God-Emperor from my Librarian,' Kersh told them. 'The love of our Emperor?' Kersh marvelled. 'You think yourself worthy of that?' Nazimir fell to his arthritic knees. 'You think you can earn his love through your worthless words? Your hives and palaces of soulless devotion? Your veneration of an empty idea? I feel the love of my father, as he felt the love of his. This flesh – these hearts – were made to feel. His blood courses through my veins. His loss lives on behind these eyes. He is more than man, but he is not a god. It is your fear that casts him as such. You are weak and foolish, and in your billions need him to be more than he is. But you are wrong, mortal. He is more than man for not being some all-powerful deity. His deeds are his own and we aspire to his greatness – not appropriate it, mythologise it and worship it as a shield against a galaxy of petty doubt, dread and pain. For his love I would do anything. I would obliterate this palace from orbit, for example.'

'And you should,' Chaplain Shadrath hissed with masked menace.

Nazimir gagged and vomited in his altitude mask. The stringy gruel dribbled out onto the throne room floor. Kersh looked from the Chaplain to the approaching convocate.

'We ask only mercy, my lord,' Clemenz-Krycek implored him.

'But I won't,' Kersh said finally. 'I will not destroy a world on a technicality.' Shadrath turned away in silent disgust.

'An Angel's wisdom indeed,' Clemenz-Krycek gasped and kissed the Excoriator's gauntlet.

'As the Fifth Company will not shirk their responsibilities on a technicality, either,' Kersh said.

'Rorschach's World waits for us,' Shadrath insisted. 'It will not wait forever.'

'Noted, Chaplain,' the Scourge answered. 'But Chapter Master Ichabod's word has been given and we will honour it.'

'Thank you, my lord. A thousand thanks,' Clemenz-Krycek said.

'Now, mortal,' Kersh said, looking up briefly at the insensible ecclesiarch in the elevated throne above. 'What does the cardinal ask of the Excoriators? Be brief – our patience wears thin.'

Clemenz-Krycek bent down and rifled the vomit-splattered robes of his pontifex. He extracted a data-slate and handed it to the corpus-captain.

'The Keeler Comet blasts across the night skies of the subsector,' the convocate said. 'The crimson comet brings doom to all the planets on its path. This is well known. But it brings fear and madness to the region as a whole. An explosion of cultish activity. Insanity, violence, bloodshed. The statues of the Notre Dumas shrineworld bleed for the ungovernable atrocities committed there. Our sister cardinal world of St. Faustina is in uproar, with the enforcers forced to put down riot and rebellion with brutal force. The sanctuary worlds of Frau Mauro and Benedictus Secundus suffer blood cults and outbreaks of vampiric contagion. We have also lost contact with the Preceptor retreats on Caritas Minoris, Boltoph's World and VII-Solace-Sixteen. We despatched the cloister-corvette *Seraphic Dawn* to investigate these mysteries, but she too has not returned. And this is but the Ministorum worlds in the subsector. Emperor only knows what is happening on the others. We fear for what might be in store for St Ethalberg itself. We have trebled persecutions within our jurisdiction, requested more Sisters from the Convent Prioris on Terra and prayed for the intervention of the Holy Ordos.'

'We are the Astartes Praeses,' Kersh announced. 'It is the Excoriators' sacred duty to garrison damnation's borders. What you speak of is not unusual in such regions. The Eye of Terror is a storm. Its immateriology is unpredictable and cruel.'

'But the comet, my lord–' Clemenz-Krycek insisted with his eyes to the floor.

'Is a new manifestation, I grant you,' Kersh admitted. 'As you have observed yourself, however, we are the Emperor's Angels. We are not investigators. We are not charged with keeping order on Imperial worlds. I suggest you pursue the advice of the Inquisition. If the local military forces on these worlds cannot cope, then the Ordo Hereticus will use its influence with the Imperial Guard to have regiments brought in-sector and assigned to peace-keeping and security duties.'

'Corpus-captain,' the convocate said, 'there is a small planet, out in the Andronica Banks, close to Hinterspace – a cemetery world called Certus-Minor.'

'Go on,' Kersh prompted.

'Like the Preceptor retreats, we have lost contact with the cemetery world. We have stopped receiving astrotelepathic messages, and our last convoy of necrofreighters have not returned. Pontifex-Mundi Oliphant is both planetary governor and senior ecclesiarch of the cemetery world. The last few messages we did receive from him indicated that Certus-Minor was experiencing the same problems as other worlds with heretic cults. The very last, that his people had discovered a colossal monument, made of human skulls and bearing the markings of the Ruinous Powers.'

'This giant monument just appeared?' Kersh frowned. 'I find that hard to believe. Were there no witnesses to its construction?'

'I cannot answer to that. Pontifex Oliphant communicated fears that cultists operating on the planet might be trying to summon some unholy creature from the warp – that the object might be a gate or portal. He was instructed to quarantine the region around the object, establish a prayer-cordon and not interfere directly with it. He was told we were sending for assistance.'

'You want us to destroy this dread monument?' Kersh asked.

'And whatever might proceed from the infernal artefact,' Clemenz-Krycek replied. 'We have heard nothing from Oliphant since – and that was over a month ago.'

Kersh looked at Epistolary Melmoch. 'Opinion.'

'This close to the Eye, anything is possible. I echo your concerns about this portal's construction, but with the right tracts and dark knowledge a group of accomplished cultists might be able to achieve such a Ruinous wonder.'

Kersh looked to Ezrachi.

'It is the Chapter Master's wish that these obligations be honoured,' the Apothecary commented, adding with a harsh edge, 'no matter how foolishly these miserable wretches have acted in our midst. They are but mortal, after all.'

Kersh turned back to Clemenz-Krycek. 'You went to a great deal of trouble to secure our involvement. What is the significance of this cemetery world?'

'Certus-Minor is the birthplace of Umberto II – Ecclesiarch and High Lord of Terra. It is also the location of the memorial mausoleum containing his bones. It was the Ecclesiarch's dying wish that he return. Such a prestigious burial ground is secured at a premium by the great and good of our fair Imperium. It is a holy place – we cannot allow the unclean to contaminate its sacred soil.'

Kersh considered the power and influence wielded by the families of the dead, their loved ones bound for a costly grave plot on the distant Certus-Minor. It was little wonder that the Ecclesiarchy on St Ethalberg had managed to secure the Excoriators' involvement. Kersh felt a shoulder plate press against his own. It was Shadrath.

'May I speak with you?' the Chaplain hissed.

'Proceed, Chaplain. We are all friends here now.'

Shadrath held on to his words and his fury a few moments longer.

'We have intelligence of Alpha Legion activity in the Scintilla Stars,' he stated, finally. 'We have a small portal of opportunity. I suggest we take it. The Fifth Company's finest hour waits for us on Rorschach's World – not some miserable cemetery world in the lonely depths of Hinter-space. The Stigmartyr is there for the taking, but our sworn enemy will not wait.'

'Nonsense, Chaplain,' Kersh said. 'It is the Alpha Legion of which you speak. Rorschach's World is a trap and the intelligence allowed us by that most secretive of Legions is our invitation. We will be there for the taking. The trap will wait for us, Chaplain, for we have yet to spring it.'

'Corpus-captain–'

'Calm yourself, Chaplain Shadrath,' the Scourge warned. 'Before you do us both an injury.' The Chaplain shook his helmet slightly before backing away. 'Convocate. Pontifex,' Kersh addressed the priests. 'Chapter Master Ichabod's word is his bond, as is mine. My Excoriators will travel to Certus-Minor, destroy this corrupt monument and anything that has issued forth from its darkness. I pledge no less but no more. Then, I hunt Traitor Angels in the Scintilla Stars as my Chaplain advises.'

'Bless you, my lord,' Clemenz-Krycek said, kissing the Excoriator's withdrawing gauntlet once again.

'Squad Contritus, vigilance on the withdrawal. Proceed,' Kersh voxed. From alcoves, gargoylesque wall flourishes and behind statues, fonts and chained heretics, the Scout squad emerged. They stepped lightly and with caution through the throngs of throne room onlookers, their cloaks about them and the long barrels of their sniper rifles low-ered. As the Excoriators made their way from the chamber, escorted by a reforming Squad Contritus, Kersh bowed his head to the helmeted Sister Superior. 'Sister, I leave you this mess to clean up,' the Scourge told her. She stood impas-sive. He turned to leave.

At the great archway entrance the Excoriators came face to face with Arch-Deacon Schedonski and the swarm of Inclement Reserves summoned by the bells. The scrawny Guardsmen gulped and parted as the striding giants moved through their number. Among them, the armoured visi-tant stood, Kersh catching a glimpse of the darklight in one bony eye socket through the crack in the vision's helm.

Kersh stopped, looking from an uncertain Schedonski back to the bright-eyed Clemenz-Krycek and miserable Pontifex Nazimir, knelt in his own vomit.

'Pontifex – where is your Emperor now?' Kersh asked. He crossed his arms and extending a finger on each gauntlet, pointed at his twin hearts. 'He is here. We shall deliver your cemetery world. I have given your cardinal my pledge. Let me give you another. I am Adeptus Astartes, mortal. If you or your mongrel priests ever attempt to issue ultimatums to me or my brothers again, you will hear my own, issued in the thunder of my bombardment cannon, as I wipe you and your palace from the face of this world with one righteous strike.'

The ecclesiarchs nodded their dumbfounded understanding.

Kersh turned and marched from the throne room. '*Impunitas* – this is Kersh. We are inbound. Prepare for take-off.'

PART TWO

OBLIVION IS THEIR GIFT...

CHAPTER SIX
CEMETERY WORLD

THE EMPYREDROME WAS situated atop the bridge tower, commanding one of the best views the strike cruiser could offer. A large caged sphere of reinforced, psi-matrix-attuned crystal, it was known to the Adeptus Astartes and the bonded crew as the *Magna-Cubile* or 'Great Nest'. This was understandable given that it was the private immaterial observation chamber for the *Angelica Mortis*'s Navigator, Alburque Ustral-Zaragoza III. It was all the more appropriate for the fact that the Navigator housed his psyber-eagle, Arkylas, in the drome.

The huge bird was a beauty of bronzed feather. Its wicked talons gripped a sturdy perch frame and its beak was a chrome-plated nightmare. Like the House internuncia who attended upon the Navigator in their claret hoods and robes, Arkylas was blind. The seeing were not tolerated within the chamber. With the Navigator's warp eye open, exposing all in the Empyredrome to its lethal gaze, only those who had had their eyes removed were truly safe.

Zaragoza's throne was set on a labyrinth of rails that took him – with the aid of internuncia muscle – to the crystal plate of the drome, where a perimeter of lens-arrays, specula, magnocular spyglasses and telescopes decorated the perimeter. The Navigator himself was neurally plugged into the chair and sat amongst a nest of runescreens, brass pict-monitors and hololithic displays, which his freakishly long digits and fingernails seemed to perpetually dance across.

'Check me,' Zaragoza instructed three calculus logi – lobotomised internuncia. The Navigator shot a stream of warp dilation and velocidratic equations at the hooded attendants. One by one, the internuncios confirmed the Navigator's calculations as accurate. Satisfied, and not a little impressed with himself, Zaragoza settled back into his throne and clicked his spindly fingers. An internuncio came forwards with a polished metal platter and dome. Removing the dome, the servant revealed a dead rat, recovered from a trap in the vessel bilges. The Navigator picked the vermin up by its tail. With a pendular motion, Zaragoza tossed the dead meat at Arkylas.

Despite being blind, the psyber-eagle snatched the rodent out of the air with predatory grace. It never failed to give the Navigator a thrill. 'Did you see that beak?' he marvelled, pointing at the magnificent bird. The hooded vassal didn't respond. Zaragoza grunted. 'Of course you didn't,' he said to himself. He clicked his fingers to the other side of the throne and another blind servant came forwards with a tray bearing a decanter of amasec and a crystal glass.

The internuncio poured his master the drink and Zaragoza was about to take it when the deck about them began to vibrate. Trinkets and instruments fell from their racks and the servant spilt the amasec. Arkylas flapped its wings.

'My lord.' An internuncio came forwards. He wore a vox-headset arrangement around his darkened hood. 'Corpus-Commander Bartimeus for you from the bridge. He demands to know the source of this turbulence.'

'He's not the only one,' Zaragoza said absently. The Navigator screwed his eyes tight shut and opened the weeping slit of the third that sat in his forehead. The Empyredrome, like Arkylas and the internuncia, was still there – it had just faded to transparence. The Navigator drank in a vista of insanity. About him, with the strike cruiser and even the Empyredrome mere ghostly outlines, the sea of souls raged. A transdimensional medium, it appeared as a poly-chromatic ocean, viewed simultaneously from above and below. It was unrivalled in its expanse and drama, and through his third eye the Navigator could observe its deranged seascape.

In the ethereal distance Zaragoza could see the heavenly light of the Astronomican, a silvery beacon of serenity in the fermenting pandemonium of the warp. Its beatific beams reached out across the psychic universe, drawing the Navigator to them and filling his being with an angelic chorus of indescribable bliss. It was only by the good grace of the Astronomican that Zaragoza could navigate at all. Much closer, like a puce glower in the warpscape, the night-marish region of the Eye of Terror broiled and spumed its malevolence, threatening to obscure the Astronomican and swallow the heavenly beacon whole.

Zaragoza looked out beyond the strike cruiser's prow, beyond the existential static of the Geller field and the glint of warpreal entities impressing themselves on the bubble of reality enveloping the Excoriators ship. There was a psysmic tidal wave of raw immaterial energy rolling towards the Adeptus Astartes vessel for as far as the Navi-gator could see. The *Angelica Mortis* was heading bow-on for the monster with little hope of evasive course correc-tion beyond dropping out of warp space and continuing at sub-light speed – which Bartimeus would not hear of. The vessel had encountered numerous smaller displace-ments on its journey to St Ethalberg. As they had pushed on to Certus-Minor, along the ethereal equivalent of the Andronica Banks and out into Hinterspace, the immateri-ology had grown increasingly agitated and unsettled. This was not what Zaragoza had come to expect in the region, which was usually relatively free of such stormy conditions.

Strangely, it was not the wave that bothered Zaragoza. The *Angelica Mortis* had been on the etherwave's inclining approach for some time, and it was the Navigator's plan to hold course and either have the sturdy Adeptus Astartes strike cruiser ride the beast out or punch straight through the maelstrom's churning crestface. The Navigator had observed hundreds of vessels on their voyage seemingly lose their nerve and run before the gargantuan swell. Zaragoza had commented to Bartimeus, however, that such numbers and configurations appeared to him more like disbanded patterns of planetary evacuation than flotillas and convoys directed from their courses. In the presence of such evidence Zaragoza felt a little uncomfortable pressing on. He was an experienced Navigator from a House with long service record with the Adeptus Astartes. But he did not know what was causing such an immaterial phenomenon, and could have no way of knowing if an even larger wave lay behind the first.

Squinting down with one of his other eyes, Zaragoza scanned data from a runescreen detailing readings from the *Angelica Mortis*'s ethervanes.

'The Von Diemen Rip currents,' Zaragoza mumbled to himself, 'the Pherrier circumpsyclone, Wallach's Rapidity, the Cascade Borgnino, the Paracelsus Gyres...' The Navigator's face creased with confusion. 'Readings all nominal to profile.'

The Navigator frowned, lost in thought. His thin eyebrows slowly rose. Throwing a lever, Zaragoza sent the throne spinning around so that it was facing aft of the vessel. 'There you are,' he announced and held out a spindly hand. A waiting vassal pressed a pair of psyoccular magnoculars into his hand, which the Navigator proceeded to put on. At another hand motion the two other hooded servants put their backs into moving the throne along its rails and up to a large brass telescope. Through both the psyoccular and spyglass arrangement Zaragoza studied the object that had so singularly grabbed his attention.

The Navigator had seen it several times before but at much too great a distance to identify its nature, class or dimensions. It had been barely more than a fuzzy blur in the maelstrom of Chaos and could literally have been anything. It also seemed to appear and disappear, leading Zaragoza to believe it might be some colossal beast of the warp or a daemonic entity attempting to breach the inter-dimensional barriers of reality. On each of these occasions he had made a note in the translation log but had not deemed it important enough to alert Corpus-Commander Bartimeus. The Excoriator was a blunt instrument and not one for extraneous detail. With the vessel at closer range, Zaragoza knew different now.

The Navigator stared at the object in awe. The etched grid-lens gave him an idea of its true proportions. Snatching up a communications cable hanging beside the throne, Zaragoza screwed it into one of the many mind-impulse ports decorating the back of his head like craters upon a moon's surface.

'Translation log entry,' the Navigator said, prompting a blind vassal to appear beside him with a data-slate. 'Unknown vessel identified emerging from the Osphoren Flux on an identical course to our own. Vessel signature in absence, but the architecture is distinctive and, along with its size, bears the hallmarks of an ancient vessel. Dimensions are... difficult to measure with this equipment. However, I can confirm that it is the largest vessel I have ever seen and, even with these instruments and at great distance, I estimate that it must be six or seven hundred cubic kilometres. Larger than Lentigo, the largest of the Escharan moons.' The internuncio inputted the log entry.

Zaragoza shook his head. The explanation for the turbulence and agitation in the region now became obvious. The *Angelica Mortis* was caught in an immaterial confluence created by the etherwave before them and the psysmic swell being driven before the colossal vessel to their aft.

'Open a vox-channel with the bridge,' Zaragoza ordered the nearby internuncio. 'Inform Corpus-Commander Bartimeus that empyreal conditions are likely to worsen, but that I have detected the source of the turbulence. Tell him I am sending a pict-capture. Tell him that he's not going to believe it.'

* * *

CERTUS-MINOR. CEMETERY WORLD.

The venerable *Gauntlet* had made a high-velocity insertion, leaving the *Angelica Mortis* in good company with the defence monitor *Apotheon*, a fat necrofreighter and a small gathering of sprint traders. Coming in low and deep, the Thunderhawk tore up the serene surface of one of the great lakes across which it passed. Behind its tail the gunship threw up a continuous fountain of spray, but below the craft the silvery waters reflected a mirror image of the *Gauntlet's* underbelly and banking flank. Like all of the Excoriators' Thunderhawks, the *Gauntlet* retained her scars, each bolt-hole, las-blast and impact crater in her ivory plate repaired but preserved and annotated with a date and location. As the oldest of the Fifth Company gunships, the *Gauntlet* bore her battle scars with pride and distinction, even if, when pressed, the Excoriators within admitted to the knocks and rattles of her advancing age.

Lifting her nose slightly, the *Gauntlet* cleared the satin surface of the lake. Beneath the Thunderhawk extended an expanse of crafted stone. Grave markers, tombstones and statues of every crafted tradition, built almost one on top of the other, crowded the landscape with barely a scrap of precious cemetery world earth between them. Vaults, mausolea and private crypts sprouted from the sepulchrescape, dwarfed only by the ancestral tombs and necropoli of noble families. Kicking up a storm of grit and dust, the *Gauntlet* fell in line above an arterial lychway. The cemetery sectors and burial grounds were cut up by a necroplex of labyrinthine lychways that allowed access to individual plots and charnel houses. The crossroads of these stony procession ways were furnished with cenoposts and shack hamlets, housing sextons, grave fossers and hearsiers, along with their families.

Pulling up, the gunship began lowering its landing gear. Before the *Gauntlet* was the only metropol the cemetery world boasted. Grave dust and burial space existed at a premium on Certus-Minor and sprawling cities were considered a funereal waste. This was why Obsequa City had been built tight and tall. A cluster of steeples and spires betrayed the city's Ecclesiarchical purpose, with lofty cathedrals competing for sky with basilica towers, shrines and citadel-sacristia. Nestled at the heart of the devotional architecture and adorning the metropolis like a crown was the roof-dome of the Umberto II Memorial Mausoleum – the largest and tallest building in Obsequa City. The vaulted mausoleum housed the preserved bones of Umberto II, former Ecclesiarch and High Lord of Terra. Taking in the breathtaking detail of the colossal dome with a banking pass, the *Gauntlet* began to rotate and descend. The Thunderhawk dropped down into the only level and open space in the city. Crowded by requitaphs and chapel belfries, the Umberto II Memorial Space Port was little more than a small landing plaza for mortuary lighters and hump shuttles.

With its gear on the ground, the *Gauntlet*'s tactical bay ramp lowered and Squads Cicatrix and Castigir filed out with weapons drawn. They fell to immediately securing the area around the Thunderhawk. Kersh had ordered vigilance upon arrival. With knowledge of damned monuments to dark gods and cultist activity on the cemetery world, the corpus-captain wasn't taking any chances. For all the Excoriators knew, heretics could have possession of the space port and be waiting for the Space Marines in ambush. Nobody in the Fifth Company wanted a repeat of Ignis Prime and the Kruger Ridge.

Kersh stepped out onto the level rockrete. The dizzying heights of bethel towers and cathedrals surrounded the landing plaza, extending upwards on a steep incline like a miniature hive. Kersh looked back down at the pict-captures he was holding. As Ezrachi followed, the Apothecary's leg sighing in hydraulic rhythm, he too held a capture in his ceramite fingertips.

'What am I looking at?' the aged Excoriator asked.

'Psyoccular image captured from the Empyredrome,' Kersh replied as the pair of Space Marines strode across the plaza. 'Aft orientation. Censor-cropped by Chaplain

Shadrath, in the interests of spiritual licentiousness. Rendered to full magnification.'

Behind them, the Chaplain himself, Epistolary Melmoch and Techmarine Dancred followed. Ezrachi passed the pict-capture to the Librarian and took another from Kersh. From the tactical bay rumbled the tracks of a mobile weapon. The quad barrels of a Thunderfire cannon emerged, followed by the chunky brutality of its itinerant chassis. Its armour plating bore the colours, scarring and annotations of the Excoriators Chapter, the Cog Mechanicum and a name: *Punisher*. Following the Techmarine like a hunting dog, the cannon's machine-spirit drove the heavy metal beast on down the ramp. Dancred gave both it and a miserable servitor-loader an instruction in lingua-technis, prompting both drone and weapon to follow.

'This can't be a vessel – not if these reticles are anything to go by,' Ezrachi commented.

'Bartimeus's Navigator thinks it is,' Kersh said.

'Could this not be some great beast of the warp?' Melmoch asked. 'They, for example, look like wings to me.' He passed the pict-capture to Brother Dancred. The Techmarine's gearface formed a clockwork scowl and the Space Marine slowed to a stop.

'That is a vessel,' he confirmed. 'Something ancient, abominable and glorious. The Imperium hasn't made vessels of this size and design for thousands of years.'

'Again, Bartimeus's Navigator concurs. It's probably some mangled hulk that's been lost in the warp for an eternity. I've despatched the *Impunitas* to observe our translation point from a dwarf moon on the edge of the system. They will inform us of any new arrivals.'

Brother-Contego Micah moved past with heavy, purposeful steps. Micah was the Fifth Company's freshly promoted champion. His predecessor had lost his life defending Corpus-Captain Thaddeus on the Kruger Ridge. Micah was young for his position but a cool, impassive Excoriator. He was a gifted marksman and took the responsibilities of company champion seriously. Micah seemed just as unhappy about Kersh's promotion as everyone else in the Fifth, but had studied his corpus-captain's orders and their mission brief and had volunteered practical propositions regarding the company's caution and security on Certus-Minor. Like many of his brothers, he was determined that the Excoriators would not fall to the predations of the Alpha Legion again – even if that meant keeping Zachariah Kersh alive. Micah held his combat shield out in front of him, resting it on a cradle attached to the chunky barrel of the champion's boltgun. Leading the way with the gun shield and the muzzle emerging from its ceramite cleft, he assumed position on point, putting himself squarely between his corpus-captain and possible enemies.

'The hulk is not our concern,' Chaplain Shadrath hissed from behind Kersh.

'How I wish that were so, Chaplain,' Kersh said, stopping and turning. The Excoriators came to a halt on the landing plaza. 'Like you, I am eager to be on to Rorschach's World. Company protocol is clear on this, however. We are bound by reclamation treaties with the Adeptus Mechanicus and Ordo Xenos Carta Contagio. Any hulks appearing within Imperial space must be investigated.'

'There are priorities…'

'There are,' Kersh agreed with an edge, 'but I have reports of pirate attacks from the sprint trader *Avignor Star*, an astro-telepathic blackout and Alpha Legion activity in the region to consider. And that on top of the prospect of a space hulk and the taint of Chaos on this Ecclesiarchy world. Our talents are superhuman, Chaplain Shadrath – not supernatural. We cannot be everywhere at once.'

'Corpus-captain,' Brother Toralech interrupted. The Space Marine brought a ceramite finger to the side of his helm. 'The *Gauntlet* has relayed a vox-message from the *Angelica Mortis*. Corpus-Commander Bartimeus requests permission to take the cruiser out of low orbit to commence battery practise.'

'Denied,' Kersh answered simply. 'The *Angelica Mortis* will hold her position.' The Scourge glowered at Shadrath before turning and striding across the plaza. The towering Toralech relayed the response, resting the shaft of the billowing company standard against the rockrete and the long barrel of his flamer against a battle-scarred pauldron.

As the Excoriators strode across the landing plaza, hearsiers paused in their unloading of sarcophagi from mortuary lighters to watch the giants go by. A delegation of priests and their accompanying honour guard of defence force Guardsmen approached from the Memorial Space Port gate.

'Salutations, great warriors,' the priest announced, his eyes to the ground. He bowed his mitre, his vermillion robes flapping in the breeze. 'I am Vasco Ferreira, the Pallmaster General. We received word – the last in a long time – from his grace Cardinal Pontian of St Ethalberg that assistance was coming. We had not dared hope that the Emperor's Angels themselves would–'

'Pallmaster,' Kersh stopped him.

'My lord?' the priest replied fearfully.

'You have a superior?' the corpus-captain asked.

'I answer to the pontifex,' Ferreira said, 'as all God-Emperor-fearing people do on Certus-Minor.'

Kersh softened his words with a vague smile. 'Take us straight to him, please.'

'Of course, your magnificence. A thousand apologies,' Ferreira said.

With the Pallmaster General leading the way, the Excoriators were flanked by members of the Certus-Minor Charnel Guard, dressed in flak, robes and feather bonnets. They were sombre figures, all in black and carrying long, ceremonial lasfusils. The solemnity continued as the Adeptus Astartes were escorted out of the gate and up through the winding alleyways and steep steps of the cemetery world city. About them walls reached for the ivory skies and the incline became increasingly precipitous. In adjoining naveways and alleys, as well as at archways and fenestra, the Excoriators encountered gathered Certusians. The cemetery worlders looked on with sober reverence and wonder. They remained a silent sea of gaunt faces, the Ecclesiarchical baseborn: vergermen, foss-reeves and vestals. Occasional preachers punctuated the torturous route, making the sign of the aquila and offering blessings.

Across a small square, at the top of the city, the Excoriators were confronted with the colossal archway-barbican of the Umberto II Memorial Mausoleum. The pillars of the stately sepulchre were thick and tall, and the darkness of the threshold beckoned pilgrim and cleric alike. Two Sisters of Battle, garbed in the midnight-blue sheen of ceramite and hugging belt-fed heavy bolters to their breasts, flanked the entrance. Standing tall before the arch was a baroque nightmare, a penitent engine housing a wretched, emaciated repentant. Crucified across the walker, the unfortunate seemed at peace. Kersh shuddered to think of the carnage the reformite could wreak, with its caged limbs, mounted chainfists and heavy flamers.

Modest, by comparison with the mausoleum, was the Obelisk or official palace residence of the Pontifex-Mundi. The palace was positioned opposite the mausoleum, across the devotional square, and it was here that Brother Dancred had *Punisher* and his attendant servitor remain. The ecclesiarch's reception chambers were housed beneath an enormous bell in the palace belfry, and from his balcony, the pontifex could command a view not only of the domed roof of the mausoleum but also the receding steeple-skyline of Obsequa City. The palace chambers were dark and dour, and Kersh noticed the retinue of priests and affiliates haunting its shadowy recesses. Pallmaster General Ferreira peeled off and joined their ranks. Amongst their number Kersh also spotted the sickly glow of his revenant's eye, peering out from the crack in its benighted helm. The ethereal presence watched and waited with immutable patience.

Pontifex Oliphant stood in the balcony, his crooked figure cutting a silhouette into the pearly sky. Turning with half a smile, the ecclesiarch proceeded to limp with difficulty across to the entering Excoriators. As Kersh came closer he realised that the pontifex suffered from some kind of paralytic affliction. Half of Oliphant's kindly face was stricken in a mask of horror, and he dragged the dead-weight of one leg behind him like a second thought and allowed his arm to dangle uselessly by his incapacitated side. He wore only simple robes and sandals, with little of the ceremonial paraphernalia the corpus-captain had come to expect from the Ecclesiarchy. He even forwent a mitre. Instead, Kersh noted the thin hair plastered across the pontifex's forehead and the beads of sweat trembling on his brow. Even standing seemed like an ungainly effort.

'Pontifex,' Kersh said, offering an armoured gauntlet. Close up, Kersh could see that Oliphant was quite young for his position, despite his old man's carriage and obvious infirmity.

'Angel,' Oliphant said, clutching but one ceramite finger of the proffered hand with his own weak digits. Kersh felt the ecclesiarch rest against his mighty frame and saw the momentary relief on his half-frozen face. 'Our prayers have been answered. I knew you would come. The God-Emperor sends us the sons of Dorn. A true blessing.'

'Pontifex,' Kersh began, 'I am Zachariah Kersh, corpus-captain of the Fifth Company. I bring good will from Chapter Master Ichabod of the Excoriators Chapter. He has secured assistance for this cemetery world through your guarantors at St Ethalberg.'

Oliphant went to speak but wavered suddenly. Thinking the ecclesiarch was going to fall, Kersh grabbed him by the shoulders.

'The pontifex's throne,' Ferreira called and two sallow cenobites wheeled a rolling chaise to Oliphant, although it looked to Kersh more like an invalid's carriage than a throne. Depositing the pontifex in the chair, the Scourge stepped back.

'The Emperor's blessings on you both,' Oliphant said to Kersh and Ferreira.

'Pontifex,' the Excoriator continued, 'I have been brief with your deputation and with your indulgence I will be brief with you. There is but one of our calling for every world in the Imperium and Certus-Minor is currently graced with a half-company of the Adeptus Astartes.'

Oliphant attempted a twisted smile.

'We are but a tiny part of the Imperium and we wish no imposition,' the pontifex said.

'It is no imposition, pontifex,' Kersh said, 'but our enemies are legion and spread across the segmentum like a bloody smear. We would like to be of service and then be on our way.'

'Of course,' Oliphant said. 'I shall introduce my clerics to you later. Perhaps I might convince you, corpus-captain, to receive the God-Emperor's benediction with us on the morn. The suns will rise on Saint Barthes's Feastday.'

'I think that unlikely, pontifex.'

'Just a blessing then, to consecrate your efforts here and protect you and your Angels in the prosecution of the God-Emperor's will. After all, does not the God-Emperor fight on our side?'

'Our bolters protect us under such circumstances,' Kersh told the pontifex. 'And as I indicate, we are unlikely to be planetside when the sun rises. If there is an evil here then we shall not dally in its destruction. Further evils wait for our bolt-rounds and blades on other worlds, and we are not in the habit of keeping the Emperor's enemies waiting.'

'Well,' Oliphant said finally, holding on to a weak smile, 'we shall see, sir. Let me instead introduce you to three of our flock charged with cemetery world security. I think they are best placed to advise you on our problems.'

Three figures stepped forwards from the shadowy gathering around the edge of the chamber. 'May I introduce High Constable Colquhoun of the Charnel Guard, Palatine Sapphira of the Order of the August Vigil and Proctor Kraski of the enforcers.'

'Honoured to be serving beside you,' Colquhoun said crisply. He gave a grim but reverent salute to the rim of his feather bonnet before returning his black-gloved hand down beside the tapered barrel of an officer's laspistol. Palatine Sapphira, conversely, had a pout of positive dislike crafted into her uninviting features. Her slim, cobalt power armour sported two chunky Godwyn-Deaz-pattern bolt pistols at the thighs and an ermine cloak that hung from her shoulders. She compulsively fiddled with a silver aquila hanging around her neck and burrowed into the Excoriator with her dark eyes.

'The pontifex has overplayed our part, I'm afraid,' she told Kersh with a voice of steel. 'My mission here only looks to the preservation of Umberto II's remains and the security of the Memorial Mausoleum.'

Kersh had encountered the Order of the August Vigil before, on the genestealer-infected shrineworld of Alamar, where Sisters of the order had been charged with safely evacuating the bones of Saint Constantine in advance of planetary Exterminatus. Their Order Minoris specialised exclusively in the security of Ecclesiarchical relics and sites of Cult significance.

Unlike the immaculate Guard officer and Battle Sister, Kraski was a grizzled veteran. An arbitrator in the senior years of his life, he was charged with keeping order and upholding Imperial Law with a small team of enforcers on the tiny cemetery world. His ragged beard moved to the motion of his jaw working on a vile slug of chewing tobacco, while the smashed lens of a bionic eye stared back at Kersh with blind obsolescence. His enforcer carapace was scuffed and blistered, while the black fur of his great-coat was dusted with the sandy, Certusian earth. Sitting slung across one of his shoulders, however, was the gleaming barrel and pump-mechanism of an oiled and lovingly maintained combat shotgun.

'Words are for poets and priests,' Kraski told the Excoriators, pushing the plug of tobacco from one side of his mouth to the other with his tongue. 'I'll take you straight to the Exclusion Zone and there you can see the work of evil first-hand.'

The Scourge nodded. 'After you, proctor,' he said with solemn appreciation. The corpus-captain had the feeling he was going to like the arbitrator.

* * *

THE MAID MARIKA knew only her holy duties. As a vestal it was her privilege to escort the Lord High Almoner about the narrow passages and crooked stairwells of Obsequa City. The Lord High Almoner had a sacred responsibility: the redistribution of wealth. The Adeptus Ministorum taxed Certusians on the Imperium's behalf and its demands were harsh. Maid Marika very much enjoyed her role, amongst two trains of her sister vestals, accompanying the Almoner during his ceremonial act of virtue, pressing coin back into the hands of the poor and needy.

Marika gently swung her incense burner back and forth on a silver chain, allowing the fragrant mist to billow about her and behind the Lord High Almoner's train. A sweet indication of their passing that hung in the air and reminded common Imperials that the God-Emperor still had a charitable thought for them. The incense often made Marika light-headed and the virgin indulged this, walking about the sheer city streets in a dreamy daze.

As she crossed St Lanfranc's corpseway, at the rear of the train, she became enveloped in a cloud of incense and stopped by the cobbled crossroads to rub her watery eyes. As both the smoke and tearful blur cleared she was struck by a vision. Marching down the corpseway were demigods in plate, the giants of legend and antiquity, only immortal-ised for common Imperials in the stonework of cathedral architecture. Marika could not believe her smoky eyes. The Adeptus Astartes. On Certus-Minor. Her gaze fell from the scars on their immortal faces, across the scars decorating their ancient ceramite and down to their dread weaponry. The cavernous muzzles of handheld cannonry. Sheathed blades of unimaginable keenness, honed to death-dealing perfection. Thick digits. Broad hands. Housed in ceramite and throbbing with the God-Emperor's own murderous strength.

'Maid Marika!'

Fury – untold. An awakening.

The Adeptus Astartes were gone. The vestal stood alone and had done for some time.

Chancellor Gielgus ventured through the perfumed smoke that cloaked the alleyway. 'Marika, where in Terra have you been?' he scolded. 'The train is stopped. The poor are waiting. The High Almoner is furious.'

As the chancellor approached he could hear the whoosh of the incense burner swinging around at speed. Finally, he came upon the silhouette doing the swinging. 'Stop that, child,' he ordered. The Maid Marika was still but for the blazing arc of the incense burner, which was pouring out smoke. As he came closer, stroking his beard, the chancellor said, 'What has come over you?'

Something was wrong with her face. As he neared and the mist between them became thinner, he could see that the vestal's eyes were blank orbs of unseeing red. 'Marika?'

Chancellor Gielgus only heard the beginning of a wrath-fuelled screech. The silver incense burner broke its searing orbit and smashed down on the top of his skull. Brained, the old man fell to the gutter, only to have the demented vestal fall upon him again and again with bludgeoning blows from her flailing burner. His stymied calls for mercy – and then help – went unanswered, as through the smoke the blood sprayed and the Maid Marika became as one with her unnatural rage.

BRAUGHN MENZEL RESTED his boot against the blade of the shovel and forced the tool down through the sandy earth. The cutting crunch of the spade filled the fosser with a strange satisfaction. There was nothing like the sound of sharpened plasteel slicing through cemetery world earth. The gravedigger needed something to keep him going. His shoulders burned and his back ached. The grave was unfinished and he would have a hundred more to dig before the end of the week. The mortuary lighters brought an unending supply of the dead from necrofreighters down to the Certusian surface. The prestige of spending just a century in the same precious earth as Umberto II drew cadavers from light years around. Senior officers of the Guard, Imperial Navy commanders, the inbred swine of hive-world

Houses, merchants, Navigators, planetary nobility and devoted members of the Ecclesiarchy itself were all buried in Certus-Minor's sacred topsoil. On the other side of the cemetery world Braughn's opposite toiled, digging up coffins and sarcophagi for shipment back to the families following the expiry of the lease. An unending cycle of inhumation and exhumation on a planetary scale.

Tossing the dirt up and over his shoulder, Braughn came to a stop. He rested against the shovel's stalwood shaft. Sometimes Braughn allowed his sons Yann and Otakar to watch the mortuary lighters at work when they should have been digging with him. At thirteen and fifteen there was precious little excitement in their lives, and the best that they could hope for was recruitment into the Charnel Guard and the possibility of one day travelling off-world with an Imperial Guard regiment. There would be no watching for lighters today – not with word that the Emperor's Angels had come to Certus-Minor. The boys had caught a glimpse of the Space Marine gunship as it left Obsequa City and thundered overhead bound for the Great Lakes. Braughn little expected his sons' eyes to leave the sky for the rest of the day.

He reached over the side of the grave and took a plas bottle from beside the tombstone. Yann had brought mule's milk from their shack at the cenopost. His mother had corked it with a rag which Braughn proceeded to extract before squeezing the liquid into his parched mouth. He gulped down the sour milk with relish before wiping his mouth with a dusty sleeve. An odd noise grabbed his attention, a dull, metallic thud.

'Boys?' Braughn called. When no answer came, the fosser kicked a toe grip into the grave wall and grabbed the edge of the tombstone in an effort to haul himself out of the grave. Halfway out of its depths Braughn looked up to see his youngest son Yann laid out in the cemetery world grit. Braughn felt his heart drop. 'Yann!' he yelled miserably. The side of the boy's head had been caved in and his lifeblood was leaking into the earth. The fosser tried to scramble out of the grave. 'Otakar!' Braughn called with fearful urgency. Turning his head, the fosser found his eldest son stood behind the tombstone. He held his shovel above his head like an axe. His eyes were blood-blind and hollow. 'Son...'

The shovel came down and sliced the fosser's head from his shoulders. The head bounced and rolled through the dust until it came to rest beside Yann's body. Braughn's body fell back into the hole and came to rest, twitching in the depths of the grave. Looking from the butchered body of his father to that of his dying brother, Otakar Menzel radiated a hatred his heart had never known. Taking his shovel in both hands, he stomped through the dust, heading for home, where his mother would be waiting with mule's milk and a smile, and the boy's bloodlust would find new expression.

ALOYSIUS MOSCA FELT the abbot's thin staff-sceptre jab his back-flesh. Mosca had not volunteered for the prayer cordon. The chaplain of his cell-block had ordered recompense for an incident at the barracks armoury. He had been part of a team of fraters assisting in the thrice-blessing of reserve ammunition and weaponry for the Charnel Guard defence force. Every lasfusil, stubber, powerpack and individual bullet required consecration, and above the instruments of death and destruction, Mosca had found himself in a dispute with a fellow frater. The dispute had become heated in the silence of the barracks armoury and Mosca had hit out with the palm of his hand. It was not intended as a strike or an assault, but the frater who fell and gashed his head against a mortar rack did not view it that way and reported Mosca to the chaplain. Assignment to the prayer cordon had been the chaplain's idea – a part of Mosca's spiritual probation.

Like thousands of others – some probationers, some volunteers – Mosca had been marched along the Great Eternity-East lychway. When the cavalcade arrived at the bleak Fifth-Circle cenopost and the miserable hovel-hamlet of Little Pulcher, Mosca and his brothers were blindfolded and led arm on shoulder to the shores of Lake Serenity. He could hear the rhythmic drone of the drainage pumps in the distance. Turning their backs to the lake they were instructed to retain their blindfolds and link hands with one another. Mosca could only imagine they were creating an unbreakable circle of prayer around the damned artefact that had been discovered below the drained surface of the lake. There had been low whispers and tattle of such a find in the fraterhouse and in the cloisters. Gossip only to match rumours of grave robbery, diabolists and disappearances out on the lonely lychways of the necroplex and burial ground provinces beyond.

Abbots walked around the inside of the circle issuing threats and jabbing encouragement as the cordon alternated between communal prayers spoken aloud to hymnals and liturgies sung to the pearlescent skies.

'Sing, you wretch,' the Abbot behind him ordered. 'I want the God-Emperor himself to hear you.'

Mosca recognised the voice. A deep, baritone menace belonging to a fat bastard Mosca remembered from the Progenary. He also remembered the beatings he received at the pudgy hands of the priest and the rattan cane he used on the backs of the choristers' legs and hands.

Mosca's eyes moved about under his blindfold. His mouth, moments before full of bombast and lines from 'Exalted God-Emperor, the Shepherd of Souls', fell to silence. Lips curled. Nostrils flared. Teeth gnashed together on the gristle of long-forgotten hatreds. Mosca released the hands of the choristers to either side. One had crushed his palm with a pious grip; the other had been moist and slippery with some penitent shame.

Tearing the blindfold from his contorted face, Mosca revealed the blood-brimming rage of his eyes. Reaching down into the folds of his cassock robes and dust cloak, the cemetery worlder found the hot euphoria of a rough hand-grip and trigger. Backing away, Mosca brought the brute length of a heavy stubber – thrice blessed and liberated from idleness in the barracks armoury – from concealment.

Turning and hugging the flared muzzle of the brute to his body, the chorister yanked frenziedly on the trigger.

The barrel danced this way and that under the recoil and Mosca's unpractised aim, but at almost point-blank range the stubber's bullets punched through the pig-priest's back. With his white vestments blanching red, the abbot crashed to the floor. Like a rider trying to tame a bucking mule, Mosca brought the chugging weapon around and sent a hailstorm of lead into the presented backs of the choristers. As the massacre unfolded the cordon began to break up. With cemetery worlders screaming, falling and being blasted from their feet, Mosca spun around to present his death-dealer to fleeing choristers on the other side.

Roaring his hatred – his being filled with white-hot insanity – Mosca felled the running choristers, the juddering barrel of the heavy stubber showering the panic-addled crowds with bullets. Like trees before the axe they fell, before their scrambling steps could carry them to the cover of headstones and cemetery statues.

With the choristers dead and the cordon broken, Mosca turned to bathe in the hate-wrought radiance of the unholy monument he'd been securing. Through a blood-filtered gaze, he drank in the scale and magnificence of the thing. It called to him and fed his fury with its dread architecture. Pointing his weapon to the sky, Mosca fired once more. With the belt feed of the weapon dancing a diminishing jig, he sent bullets rocketing for the heavens in honour of carnage and annihilation. He didn't notice the poor marksmanship of Charnel Guardsmen flashing about him – the single bolts of their lasfusils flying past. He was lost to the moment and lost to the monument, until a lucky shot found him – burning out the back of his skull and bringing peace to a mind devoid of reason.

CHAPTER SEVEN
THE BECKONING

'GIVE ME A circle of the target,' Kersh requested.

'Affirmative.'

The *Gauntlet* banked slightly against the setting suns. At an open airlock situated in the flank of the Thunderhawk, Kersh, Melmoch and Dancred looked down on the abomination. Nobody spoke. Micah, the Scourge's new shadow, waited nearby. In the tactical bay behind them, Proctor Kraski chewed tobacco while High Constable Colquhoun relayed instructions to his Charnel Guard vox-operator and Pallmaster General Ferreira leant against the compartment wall clutching his stomach and covering his mouth. Beyond, Chief Whip Uriah Skase and Squad Cicatrix primed their weapons and offered thanks to the primarch.

Below the *Gauntlet* were the still waters of Lake Serenity. On the distant shoreline of the lake drainage plants boiled off the fresh water, releasing clouds of steam from fat funnels up into the atmosphere. The waters had receded as such from a shallower inlet, revealing a monstrous monument that had been hidden beneath the lake's crystal surface. A hideous multi-sided pyramid, the monument appeared like an eight-pointed star from above. It was a dirty cream colour impacted with silt and draped with scraps of freshwater weed. About the gargantuan artefact, Kersh could make out the thin circle that made up the prayer cordon, with temporary Charnel Guard heavy weapon emplacements situated at intervals beyond.

'Put us down beyond the cordon,' Kersh ordered.

'Affirmative, corpus-captain.'

With the gunship's landing gear scraping down between the headstones of freshly dug graves, Kersh jumped from the airlock. About him, in the drained earth reclaimed from the lake, fossers had already gone to work with their shovels and masons had put the finishing touches to the gravestones adorning the neat, rectangular pits. Peering into the nearest empty grave Kersh spotted an odd arrangement of pipes running between the headstone and the grave bottom. Wire cables ran down the side of the pipes and up into the stone of the marker.

Proctor Kraski came up behind the corpus-captain.

'What are the pipes for?' Kersh asked the enforcer.

'Mistakes happen,' Kraski informed him nonchalantly. 'Thousands of stasis caskets and sarcophagi arrive here every day from Imperial worlds across the sector: hive-worlds, cardinal worlds, garrisons and so forth. Occasionally people are interred accidentally – sometimes even on purpose.'

'Buried alive?' Kersh marvelled.

'Without power and a stasis field, dead bodies rot in the sacred earth. Those buried alive might ordinarily have an hour or two of air, screaming for their lives below the ground where no one can hear them.' Kraski turned his head and spat a stream of tobacco and saliva behind his back. 'It is cemetery world practice to fashion all headstones with a safety mechanism: an air source and wire cords leading to small bells, set by the masons in the decorative detail of the gravestones.'

'All the graves have these mechanisms?'

'It's an ancient custom.'

Marching around the Thunderhawk's nose, the Excoriators

and their guides made their way towards the prayer cordon. The choristers were blindfolded and had little idea that it had been an Adeptus Astartes gunship that had landed in their midst. They also had little idea that as abbots broke the chain and moved several choristers to one side, the Emperor's Angels walked among them.

Beyond the cordon, Kersh strode into shallows, splashing down into the emptying lake. Fresh water lapped about his armoured ankles. The cordon lined the shore but the receding waters were still reasonably deep about the abominate structure. The Excoriators strode towards the damned object, with Skase and his squad kicking up fountains as they filed forwards in a canopy formation. Kraski, Colquhoun and Ferreira made headway a great deal more difficult, especially since the Pallmaster General was retching into the shallows following his first flight by Thunderhawk.

As the Scourge approached he saw that the huge pyramid was constructed of human skulls. Each was a brick within the horrific structure, cemented together with lake silt and sand. Kersh's boot tapped against something in the water. Kneeling down, the corpus-captain grasped the object and brought it to the surface. In his gauntlet Kersh held a cracked human skull. Rolling it over in his ceramite glove he examined the dome of the cranium. A symbol or design had been daubed in red paint on the top, a cross run through with three parallel, horizontal lines. Kersh tossed the skull over to Melmoch who caught the macabre object, drawing a scowl from the Pallmaster General.

'Bodies,' Brother Micah called from a position ahead. Using the barrel of his boltgun he lifted a mesh of tangled bones and shredded clothing. The shallows closer to the monument were a mantrap carpet of twisted skeletal remains. Lifting his weapon higher, Micah angled the bones around. 'They all seem to be wearing these,' the company champion said. From his muzzle dangled a lead cloak on a chain, wrapped around the vertebrae of an unfortunate's neck. The Pallmaster General looked up from his retching and narrowed his eyes.

'How did you discover this aberration?' Kersh put to the cemetery worlders.

Colquhoun directed their attention to the funnels of the distant drainage plants. 'In order to maximise plot space and extend the burial grounds, Lake Serenity had been marked for land reclamation. As the water levels fell, the top of the structure made itself known.'

'What about the skulls?' Kersh said. He turned to Proctor Kraski. 'That's a lot of heads to go missing.'

'They're not cemetery worlders,' the arbitrator said, spitting a stream of tobacco-stained saliva into the shallows. 'The murder rates are impeccable here. Until last month, I only had four murders on my slates for last year, global total. Two, the cycle before that.'

'What about last month?' Kersh enquired.

'Thirty-seven,' Kraski said.

'There are a lot more than thirty-seven skulls here,' Dancred said. Behind him, *Punisher* had rolled down the *Gauntlet*'s opening bay ramp and trundled through the shallows to take position beside the Techmarine.

'We have occasional robberies,' Kraski said.

'Robberies?'

'Grave robberies,' the enforcer confirmed. 'Mostly fossers – having a hard time meeting Ministorum taxes. You have to catch the ghouls in the act because the cunning bastards re-bury the bodies and therefore the evidence. Did catch a couple of lost souls out here a few months back. Took a ceremonial sword from a Guard officer's casket shipped from the Kallistan garrison world. Took the officer's head, as well. After I introduced them to my power maul they confessed that looting the graves is prolific in the martial grounds…'

'Areas set aside for military burials?' Kersh queried.

'Yes,' Kraski replied, 'which is unusual, since the ghouls are more likely to make good on the trinkets of some hive-world spirestress than the casket of a Navy commander or Guard brass.'

'What of the decapitation?'

'Put in an exhumation request,' Kraski told the Excoriator before spitting. The enforcer and Pallmaster General Ferreira exchanged a hard look. 'But it was denied. We liaised with the Charnel Guard and organised extra patrols but nothing came of it.'

'Melmoch?'

The Librarian seemed lost in the monument's warped design. 'Epistolary Melmoch!' Kersh repeated.

'Eight points,' Melmoch replied. 'The dread star of the Ruinous Powers. Two pyramids, sitting one within the other, eight sides to face, eight corners to turn. Eight – the Blood God's integer.'

Kersh had fought the Blood God's servants. Crazed cultists. Berserkers. Renegade Space Marines of the Goremongers Chapter. Even princes of the Rage Lord's daemonic pantheon. They had all shared the same unrelenting desire to spill the Scourge's blood.

'What is the monument's function? Is it some dark gateway?' Kersh put to the Librarian.

'No,' Melmoch replied. 'Not a gate. A throne.'

'A throne... of skulls?'

'A throne to be taken,' Melmoch said. 'An invitation issued. A beacon beckoning.'

'A beacon for what?' Kersh asked.

'I have no idea,' Melmoch told him honestly. 'Proctor, all the surrounding remains seem to be wearing these cloaks. What are they used for?'

'It's part of an Ecclesiarchical practice,' Kraski said. 'I know little of it.'

The Excoriators turned on Ferreira.

'Lead capes,' the Pallmaster General confirmed. 'They are a form of punishment. Penitents volunteer to bear the considerable extra weight as part of their rite of atonement. They are a metaphor for the tardiness of their wearer's spiritual progress.'

Melmoch looked back at the knotted remains in the shallows. Kneeling he plunged his gauntlet into the water and retrieved a rusty blade. Scanning his eyes across the glassy surface, he found a second and a third, all simple knives, pitted and brown.

'Melmoch?' Kersh prompted. 'Opinion?'

'Corpus-captain, I think that it is entirely possible that the monument is a reasonably recent construct. These bodies probably belong to cultists devoting themselves to the Blood God and his murderous ideals. As the proctor indicates, graves are robbed and skulls are taken. The martial burial grounds are targeted because the Blood God favours the skulls of warriors for his throne. The caskets are reburied to avoid suspicion in the same way that the monument was constructed in secret on the lake bed.'

'Breathing apparatus. Heavy equipment. That is a significant undertaking,' Dancred reminded the Librarian.

'More than you know,' Melmoch said, standing upright with the knives in his gauntlet. 'The monument has been entirely constructed by hand. Each skull added to the submerged structure would be a one-way ticket for its bearer. Each cultist would wear a lead cape and take a blade with them. The lead would take them to the bottom, where they would add their grave-robbed gift to the throne. They would then slit their throats and baptise the unholy monument in the murk of their offered blood. Murder – of the self.'

Nobody said anything for a few moments.

'Macabre,' Dancred said finally.

'Committed,' Melmoch replied.

'Futile,' Kersh concluded. The Scourge bit at his mangled lower lip. He looked about the Excoriators and cemetery world significants, then took in the ghastly monument with an all-encompassing stare, from top to dreadful bottom.

'As every Excoriator knows, it is a great deal easier to destroy than it is to create,' Kersh said. 'We'll widen the exclusion zone and have the *Angelica Mortis* obliterate it from orbit.'

'Completely out of the question,' the Pallmaster General suddenly piped up. There was a new-found edge to his voice – an imperiousness that Kersh hadn't heard him use with the Excoriators before. 'The cemetery world's sacred earth will not be tainted with violence and bombardment.'

'It already seems tainted,' Kersh returned. 'That is why we're here.'

'It would cause untold damage to the surrounding plots and tombs…'

'We can calibrate the warhead,' Techmarine Dancred informed him.

'What if you miss?'

'We're the Adeptus Astartes, Pallmaster,' Kersh barked back. 'We do not miss.'

'I'm sorry, corpus-captain,' Ferreira said. 'But I cannot allow that kind of an intervention.'

'It is a Ruinous artefact,' Chief Whip Skase called across with venom. 'We do not need your authorisation to destroy it.'

'Corpus-captain,' High Constable Colquhoun interjected. 'I'm as eager to be rid of this abomination as you are, but the Lord Pontifex will not sanction an orbital attack on Certusian soil. There must be another way. Please, my lords.'

'If you don't want our assistance,' Skase threatened, 'then you can keep the damned thing. The Excoriators have duties to attend to elsewhere…'

'Skase…' Kersh said. The chief whip looked from Ferreira and Colquhoun to the corpus-captain. 'What about that?' Kersh nodded at Dancred's itinerant Thunderfire cannon. *Punisher* had rolled through the shallows to take position dutifully by the Techmarine's side. 'Could we demolish the monument rather than obliterate it?'

'Unbelievable,' Skase concluded in the background.

'The Thunderfire cannon can deploy subterranean ammunition designed to destabilise and disorientate,' Dancred said, his face whirring and clunking. 'Directional salvoes combined with strategically placed demolition charges from the Charnel Guard armouries – in prodigious amounts, of course – might topple the structure.'

'That will take days!' Skase fumed. The squad whip wanted off the cemetery world as soon as possible to continue the hunt for the Alpha Legion.

'Can it be done?' Kersh asked, looking at the sheer size of the monument.

'I can demolish the structure, but then what?' Dancred asked.

'Then we bring in the flamers and meltas,' Kersh confirmed, 'and wipe any evidence of the thing from the face of the planet.'

'The Charnel Guard could–' Colquhoun began.

'The Charnel Guard will maintain the prayer cordon until we have destroyed this thing of evil. Only Adeptus Astartes are to work within the cordon to reduce the risk of contamination.'

'As you wish, my lord.'

'Brother Dancred will oversee the monument's demolition,' Kersh instructed. 'Squad Cicatrix will provide security and destroy all remnants of the structure once it is down.'

'You would have us waste more time on this miserable little world?' Skase accused.

'Chief Whip Skase, the eradication of Chaos is not a waste of our time. It is the purest expression of the purpose for which we were bred and I'll have you not forget that,' Kersh bit back.

'You question my courage,' Skase seethed, advancing on the Scourge.

'Increasingly,' Kersh spat.

The two Excoriators splashed through the shallows at one another and their ceramite would have clashed had it not been for Brother Micah getting his bolter and combat shield between them. Shoving Skase back with the shield, Micah also put his shoulder against his corpus-captain's chestplate. Two of Skase's squad grabbed their leader by the arms and attempted to haul him back.

'It's the monument,' Melmoch called. A calm descended on the scene. Skase and the Scourge's twisted faces fell and the pair looked at the Epistolary. 'This is its dread influence. It demands blood, spilt in its name.'

Kersh looked to Skase and then nodded slowly.

'Squad Cicatrix will return with me to Obsequa City,'

the corpus-captain ordered. 'Squad Castigir will have the honour of destroying this thing of evil. Chaplain Shadrath will return with the squad to monitor the operation for corruption.' Kersh turned and began to stomp his way back through the darkening shallows towards the waiting Thunderhawk. 'Come,' he commanded. 'We are wasting time. The chief whip was at least right about that.'

I have a new-found respect for my former commanders. Squad Whip Thanial; Brother Erastus; Corpus-Captain Tobiaz, Corpus-Captain Phinehas; Chapter Master Ichabod. All were great Adeptus Astartes and I feel that I can live up to their warrior example. How any of them survived the trivialities of command, however, I know not. On the battlefield, I have seen mortals exceed the cruel limitations of their bodies. I do not hold them in contempt or exercise a prejudice for such handicap. They, however, exceed the cruel limitations of my attention and interest. They can talk for hours of nothing. You would think a short existence would breed a brevity in their number, but no.

I sit here, at the long stone table of the pontifex, with the great and the good of Certus-Minor and more food than an army could eat. Ezrachi sits at my side. Beyond Melmoch, he is the only one of our number I thought to afflict with this intolerable duty. The Librarian was acting strangely – a little absent – and with glazed eyes had requested to remain in his allocated cell. The pontifex, crippled down one half of his body, has a palace menial cut his portions and bring fork from plate to mouth. The gaggle of priests at the table devour their portions with relish and I'm sure the feast is the finest quality the Adeptus Ministorum kitchens can produce. But like the conversation, I have no stomach for it. On backwater swillholes and death worlds I have eaten things that would make a grox retch. Here, I do little more than push the fine fare around my plate and then push the plate itself to one side. All the while, Pontifex Oliphant and his clerics jabber incessantly.

Oliphant seems a good man. He doesn't make my skin crawl like the cardinal world husks we found on St Ethalberg, but I find the boundless benevolence of his devotion difficult to endure.

Every statement must be qualified with a prayer. Every act is worthy of Holy Terran grace. The pontifex showers me and my Excoriators with compliments and blessings, and prattles his priestly interpretation of the God-Emperor's will. I am glad I did not include Brother Melmoch in such company. I would be ill-disposed to such blind slanders falling from Adeptus Astartes lips.

My mood sours. I do not feel myself and I indulge my baser feelings with a mask of a face. A frozen frown of unmistakable contempt which grows with every word from the ecclesiarch's crooked mouth.

Oliphant has dragged himself to his feet. With one shoulder held higher than the other he offers a twisted toast. The menial prises the pontifex's fingers open and slips a goblet of wine into his trembling clutch.

'To our saviours, the Adeptus Astartes,' he begins, and as he does so is joined by his legion of priests. 'May the God-Emperor smile on their efforts as He does our own. Let Him look out across His holy realm and watch over them as they carry out His will. Let Him bless their endeavour with His divine favour. Let Him lend them the strength to do what is right and cleanse our sacred earth of this foul contagion. In good faith we live in expectation of success and the failure of darkness. After all, does not the God-Emperor fight on our side?'

I think of the Ruinous monument. Of the thunder of Brother Dancred's efforts on the horizon and Squad Castigir waiting with meltas and flamers to scour it from the planet surface. The throne of skulls calls to us. I can feel its malign influence in my intolerance, the flex of my muscles and the edge in my voice. It reaches out for the warrior in me like some final furious defiance. The last pollutive gasp of a proud evil about to take its fall. I think of Skase. His hatred and that of his brothers. Shadrath's scorn. The loathing of the squad whips. The bright fire of Joachim's fraternal allegiance. The cold fury in Ishmael's eyes.

This is an insufferable position for all. If I were but a squad whip in this company I would share their anger and indignation, and like Uriah Skase, I would make my displeasure known. It is my honour that hangs in the balance. My standard lost. My vendetta to prosecute with the filth Alpha Legion. I marvel that my own Excoriators cannot see the pain I share with them. As corpus-captain, however, my gaze must be broader. The Fifth Company's hearts beat to a mutinous rhythm, and like the race to the runner, our time on Certus-Minor only serves to amplify the defiant thunder in their chests. It would be easy to excuse this as some malignant influence of the Chaos artefact. I am their corpus-captain and I know better. I cannot find it in myself to thank Chapter Master Ichabod for this duty, or see the wisdom in his orders. In a galaxy overrun with mankind's enemies, I fail to see the significance of a single cemetery world. My Excoriators need to exorcise their grief through the blessings of battle. Only in the crash of their bolters and the fall of their enemies can the Fifth Company find itself once again.

Oliphant talks still but I am no longer listening. He spits his prayers and blessings to the God-Emperor through his palsied lips, but his feeble words are drowned out by my silent rage. Like the pontifex, the priests are on their feet with goblets in their hands. Their gathering dims the chamber. They feel like a curtain about me, shutting out the world. I long to be free and for a terrible moment my hand drifts for my weapons.

Then I see it. My spectre. My revenant. My madness – sat at the other end of the table. The dead thing fixes me with the unnatural life force glowing in a single eye. It stares down the table at me like a lance beam from the rent in the being's helm. Then, in an action that chills me to the core, the revenant takes up a goblet from the table and holds it up to toast me also.

My vision blurs. The deep black armour of the spectre blotches and runs into everything else. The clerics take their wine and then, depositing their cups on the tabletop, begin to clap their appreciation. A silent applause. The chamber shrinking. Their forms in shadow growing. Then, beyond them I see others. A gallery of shadows. Shapes in midnight plate. Indistinct but obviously armoured. Pauldrons. Helmets. Optics burning with otherworldly intelligence. They are everywhere. Row after row. An army of revenants. A host of darkness. Everything becomes an inky blackness, like being trapped deep under an ice-covered lake. Through an opening – distant and darkening – I see only Oliphant, deific praise still escaping his lips.

Before I know I've done it, my fists come down. The stone table jumps, the impact of my assault sending a quake down its entire length. Goblets dance. Plates and cutlery leap and rattle. Red wine spreads like blood from wounds across the table, pitter-pattering off the edge and onto the floor. I am on my feet, towering above the frozen gathering. They are simultaneously shocked and terrified. Rooted to the spot. Even Oliphant has stopped. Light has returned to the chamber. The revenant is gone and so has his company of lost souls.

'Enough,' I say. The word is mine, unlike the wave of anger upon which it rides. 'The Emperor is flesh and he is blood. He lives and breathes. His sons honoured this, as do his sons' sons. When will humanity, from whose ranks the Emperor emerged, recognise this? Priests... what do they know of the Emperor's will? Priests, who take history – the truth of deeds long done – and use it to peddle lies and expectation. Who are you to offer hope? Vague promises of sanctuary and intervention, designed to distract humanity from the misery of an Imperial existence? The Emperor is a powerful man – but he is not all-powerful. If he was, do you think he would allow his people to languish as they do under threat of torment, poverty, hunger and death? As a man he is father to us all, not some omnipotent god to feed your desire to be loved and assuage your mortal fears. As a father, he does his best – as he always has – to protect his children. He reaches out to smash, with a righteous fist, those that seek to harm you. We are that fist.'

My own fists are buried in the cracked stone of the table-top. I don't really know to whom I am talking. Oliphant? The absent Melmoch? Myself? I lean at the gawping priests, my arms straight and shoulders hunched. I turn to look at Ezrachi, seated by my side. He is more the politician than myself, but I know that as an Adeptus Astartes, the priestly prattle rankles him also. His face is hard but not cast in the kind of disapproval I have come to expect from the Apothecary. My own face falls from fury to consternation.

'The Darkness,' I mumble. It is neither statement nor question. Ezrachi's crabby brow furrows. The Apothecary is suddenly on his feet.

'Please excuse us,' Ezrachi says bowing his head. 'Pontifex, gathered dignitaries. The corpus-captain's duties demand his attention.'

The pontifex, a good-natured smile still somehow plastered across his half-paralysed face, nods reverently back, an act mimicked by the stunned priests about the table. With that, Ezrachi gets me out of the chamber.

ACCOMPANIED BY THE sibilance of his bionic leg, the Apothecary helped Kersh to the ground floor and the square before the pontifex's palace.

'It's returning. I'm sure of it,' Kersh said.

'I severely doubt that,' Ezrachi told him, 'but I'll do some tests.'

'I told you before, I'm seeing things that are not there.'

'Symptomatic of sleep deprivation. I can give you something for your sleeplessness. Even an Adeptus Astartes must sleep some time. We should not forget the monument. We have little idea of its malign influence. Melmoch tells me that it is corruptive and had a strange effect on both you and Skase. The Ruinous Powers delight in their mind tricks and we should not discount it.' Kersh nodded slowly. 'I don't think it's a good idea to alert the Chaplain just yet. I shall summon Melmoch for a second opinion.'

Outside, one of Certus-Minor's long nights had fallen. All three of the cemetery world's suns were absent from the sky. Brother Micah stood sentry on the palace door nearby a pair of Charnel Guard. He had been waiting. Upon seeing Kersh slumped against the aged Apothecary, the young champion was prompted to ask, 'What's wrong with the corpus-captain?'

'You protect him,' Ezrachi said with annoyance, 'Let me treat him, eh?'

'Brother Toralech is trying to relay an urgent message from Corpus-Commander Bartimeus, but can't get a vox-link,' Micah informed the Apothecary.

'As you can see, the corpus-captain isn't answering his vox-bead right now,' Ezrachi replied sardonically.

With Micah under one ceramite shoulder and Ezrachi the other, the pair of Excoriators took Kersh across the square in the great shadow of the Umberto II Memorial Mausoleum. The journey downhill on cobbles, with the weight of the stumbling Scourge between them, was difficult. In the darkness of an alleyway the Space Marines heard screams and the echo of running footsteps. Gunshots followed. With his free hand Micah brought up his bolter and combat shield attachment, but Ezrachi pulled both Kersh and the company champion into the deeper darkness.

'It's local business. Let the cemetery world authorities handle it,' the Apothecary insisted. 'I don't want anyone to see the corpus-captain like this.' The three Excoriators held a hidden vantage point at a corner. Silent and still the Space Marines watched a servant girl, a common drudge, run for her life past them. Micah risked a brief glance around the corner. Heavier footsteps followed and close after he saw a thick-set foss-reeve bounding up the alleyway like a man possessed. As the reeve rounded the corner, Micah stepped out and shouldered the cemetery worlder into the opposite wall. Striking the masonry, the reeve hit his head and then tumbled to the cobbles, rolling shoulder over shoulder down the alleyway until he came to rest in a gutter. Ezrachi's lip curled.

'He didn't see anything,' Micah said before leading the two of them back down the alley.

It was the company champion's responsibility to protect the corpus-captain at all times and even Ezrachi had to admit that the young Excoriator had done an excellent job of memorising the steep maze of lanes, passageways and alleys back down towards the Umberto II Memorial Space Port. The path was an escape route from the palace to the hermitage Ezrachi and Chaplain Shadrath had arranged for the Excoriators to use as a planetside dormitory.

As the Adeptus Astartes passed a dirge-cloister, they observed members of the Charnel Guard and a pair of Kraski's enforcers gathered outside an emporium. The Excoriators with their superhuman hearing could hear stifled screams and growls of intimidation from within. The enforcers kicked in a flimsy door and entered with their shotguns raised. The Charnel Guard followed in their ceremonial gear and with their long lasfusils. There was a sudden rush and a cacophony of threats, followed by the inevitable bark of the enforcers' weapons. The flash of lasfusils filled the narrow casements.

'What on Terra is going on?' Micah posed.

'Come on!' Ezrachi urged and the Excoriators pushed on along the final few alleyways. About them, against the backdrop of night, the city seemed alive with anger, shrieks of alarm and the occasional crack of stub-fire.

'Shouldn't we alert the Chaplain?' Micah asked as they approached the hermitage.

'Not the Chaplain,' Ezrachi insisted.

'Who then?' Micah pushed. 'Bartimeus? The chief whip? This is why we have a command structure.'

Micah stopped. Ezrachi didn't wait for him. Taking the full weight of the barely conscious Kersh onto one shoulder, the Apothecary dragged the Scourge with him along the cobbles.

'You can debate the directives for command with me later,' Ezrachi called behind him. 'For now, help me get your actual commanding officer inside.'

'Apothecary.'

'What?' Ezrachi barked. When Micah didn't appear beside him or even reply, the Apothecary stopped and made an ungainly one-hundred-and-eighty degree turn. Micah stood in the middle of the alleyway, his boltgun slack in his grip. The Excoriator was staring up past the belfries, spires and steeples of the city and into the open night sky. Ezrachi did the same. There, hanging above the cemetery world like a drop of blood, was the bulb-head of a comet. A crimson comet, whose tail trickled after it, smearing the heavens with gore. Ezrachi had heard of the crimson comet. The worst of omens, it brought death in its wake to entire worlds, for along its pilgrim path blazed the Blood God's servants, unimaginable in number, with an unquenchable thirst for slaughter. The Cholercaust had come to Certus-Minor and with it had come inescapable doom.

CHAPTER EIGHT
FALLEN STAR

LORD HAVLOC NESTLED in his command throne – an object that had become as much part of him as he had the Traitor battle-barge *Rancour*. Pincering a strip of ancient flesh between a pair of black talons, Havloc peeled it from his grotesque shoulder. His infernal face – a mangled snout of sabre-tusk and red, reptilian scale – twisted with repugnant hate. The lord of the *Rancour* had long felt disgust for his previous, weakling form. He let the strip dangle and drop beside the flesh-throne before examining the bone-scabrous daemonhide beneath.

About the creature the darkened bridge of the battle-barge extended, a nightmare of brasswork and chain. Gouts of flame routinely erupted from the grille floor, beneath which a gladiatorial slave-pit extended for Havloc's pleasure. The roar of murderous intention and resulting death-shrieks that rose from the pit competed with the excruciating struggle of the *Rancour*'s ancient engines. Catwalks and elevated gangways led from the throne pulpit across the open space to the banks of rancid cogitators and runescreens, manned by half-mad emaciates and wretched captives that had proven themselves in the pit. The blood-smeared slaves were manacled to their stations and sat in their rags, staring glaze-eyed at their stations, reliving some past horror aboard the *Rancour*.

Dominating the far end of the bridge were the gargantuan lancet windows, cracked and misted with old blood. Through them the deep darkness of space was visible. One celestial object dominated, however. In the main lancet screen, perpetually held in a set of cross hairs by the mechanical course corrections of brass automatons, was the gory miasma of the Keeler Comet's tail. With ancient orders and angelic masks, the automatons maintained the *Rancour*'s course heading, its torpid pursuit of the crimson comet across the stars.

Behind the mangled blasphemy of the battle-barge's stately dimensions a colossal fleet extended. Like a growing stain on the empty void, the Cholercaust continued to grow. Daily, vessels of all descriptions joined the Ruinous armada. Some were warships, eager to join the Blood Crusade and prove themselves worthy of Khorne's favour. Others had been led there under the command of killers and champions, whose carnage-clouded visions had revealed to them a slaughter without end, a patron-pleasing brotherhood of the barbarous. Others still were captured freighters, traders and heavy transports, swarming with the surrendered slave-stock of sundered worlds, Imperial innocents whose fate now lay in the Blood God's claws and whose depraved treatment aboard the seized vessels led them down Khorne's doomed path.

Silhouetted in the comet's tailsmear, a Traitor Astartes stood before the lancet screen in the studded extravagance of archaic Tactical Dreadnought armour. The figure was a vision of red and brass, spiked like an undersea urchin and draped in skull and chain. His helm was a sculpted representation of monstrous jaws swallowing a bronze globe whole. Held beside the ceramite hulk, one in each gauntlet, were a pair of ugly chainaxes. The Traitor Terminator rested their shafts on the mesh-decking and allowed their chunky belligerence and barbed outline to hang over his grotesque helmet. Lord Havloc might have been commander of the *Rancour* and leader of the crusader fleet, but Umbragg of the Brazen Flesh – World Eater and Skull Champion of the Blood God – led the Cholercaust once the berserker armies of Khorne stepped out onto the soon-to-be blood-drenched earth of Imperial worlds. He stood like a statue, unmoved in his silent fury, watching the Keeler Comet's haemorrhaging bulb bleed out across the cosmos, leading the Blood Crusade fleet across the stars to its next planetary victim.

On the bridge the air was thick with rage, heat and the haze of blood, pierced only by the Blood God-honouring screams of the dying. Devil-mutants and fang-faced bestials armed with serrated flails drove a chained train of fresh captives out onto the pulpit-mezzanine. There, before the horror of Havloc's daemon form, the slaves shrieked their terror, emptied their bladders and begged for a mercy that would never come. With an imperceptible narrowing of his yellow, serpentine eyes, Lord Havloc gave successive orders for execution.

Like his glorious deity, Havloc the Cold-Blooded had a special loathing for the meek and yielding. The Blood God drank deep in the fury of the sword's swing, the thunder of flesh-pulping gunfire delivered at point-blank range and the seething malice of murderous thoughts. These the Chaos entity drew upon, whether carried out by the depraved champions of his hateful cause or enemies, worthy in their violent desires and bloody intent.

A monstrous hulk lumbered forth, an obscene fusion of what had been a man and machine. Weapons protruded awkwardly from stone-hard flesh which had in turn grown cancerous and rampant across the thing's armour and helmet. Two holes had been punctured in the tissue of the mask to allow the thing to see, and the eyeholes continually bled and crusted.

Released from his bonds, a fat slave threw himself down before Havloc's feet – cloven hooves that had long been fused to the base of the throne. The hulk snatched up the pleading captive by the head with an embedded power claw. Its other arm was a flesh-cradle for the broad disc of a spinning buzzsaw, which with an effortless swipe, cut the slave's screeching head and shoulders from the rest of his thrashing carcass. Lord Havloc and his followers were baptised in the blood of the slaughtered. Depositing the decapitated head in a net of rotting skulls hanging off the hulk's back, the brute kicked the rest of the butchered corpse off the side of the pulpit-mezzanine. The body tumbled into a crowded den of flesh-hounds below, initiating a short-lived daemonic frenzy. This the hulk repeated with two further submissives until before Havloc came a spitting whirlwind of a girl. Her chains jangled and her feet flew as she attempted to thrash her way out of imprisonment. The Chaos lord licked his lips with a thick, forked tongue. He nodded and a bestial released her from her bonds.

From the back of the throne, Havloc spread a large pair of black, leathery wings. The girl spat at the *Rancour*'s commander and, free of her shackles, came straight at the beast. Havloc relished her mindless fury – her lack of fear and desire to kill. Flapping his wings in front of him, Havloc sent a wall of foetid air at the girl. Running and kicking, the spirited slave was blown from the grille of the pulpit-mezzanine. She tumbled with a half-caught scream before hitting the floor with a sickening crack. The scream came fully-formed this time. The slave was squirming around on the blood-slick floor of the gladiatorial arena below. A shattered tibia had sheared up through her knee.

'That should slow her down a bit,' Lord Havloc hissed, emerging from behind his retracting wings. Howls of furious delight rose from the audience as another slave was freed from a holding cage. Snatching a crude flensing blade from a hook on the rusting pit wall, the gore-speckled defending champion swept down on the girl.

The howls and shrieks of the berserkers on the bridge suddenly seemed to combine into one horrific roar. Flames thrashed to greater heights and the corroded metal of the deck began to vibrate, causing fragments of grit and shattered skull to dance, and blood to steam from its agitated surface. Umbragg took to one ceramite knee. The damned all spoke as one.

'Havloc...'

Even the Chaos lord bowed his head and lowered his wings, as though the voice was everywhere and its owner looking down on him from above.

'My lord,' Havloc grizzled, with fear and fire fighting within him. 'Great Pilgrim, the Right Claw of Khorne, Chosen of the Brazen-Fleshed. What is thy bidding, my merciless master?'

'I lead,' the cacophony of spite continued, 'the Cholercaust follows. To what part of the doomed Imperium does the crimson comet – the physical embodiment of the Blood God's will – take us next?'

'Under your ruthless leadership, Great Pilgrim – back to Terra, to the crumbling walls of the corpse-Emperor's palace and the Eternity Gate. For your murderous amusement, the War-Given-Form has blessed your path with a faith world. A planet of the dead, where the corpse-Emperor's cultcubines minister to the galaxy's silent majority.'

'A planet of the dead, indeed,' the Pilgrim boomed through the mouths of the mob. 'Hone your blades, my slaughterkin, for shortly they shall taste priest-flesh...'

I dream.

For the longest time I have lived a nightmare. My eyes have been half open to events unfolding about me while behind them a macabre puppet show has played. To be neither awake nor asleep. A mind-breaking combination of both. It is custom to pinch oneself – to test if one is awake. I need no such test to know I am finally asleep. To know I am in the cradle of the unconscious. The world about me has that punch-drunk quality, the distant resonance of the unreal.

I walk the surface of the cemetery world. The sandy Certusian earth crunches beneath my boots. Through my helmet optics I zoom in on a crenulated horizon. A sea of gravestones and masonry markers extends before me. Above, the ivory sky broils and bubbles in the distance. Then, like an atomic explosion, a mushroom cloud vomits forth from the heavens and billows thunderously for the surface. There is no sound – only doom. The creamy cloud spumes and rages, swirling black, then red and gold as a swirling wall of flame overreaches the blast wave and the inferno hits the ground.

I turn and run. Armoured footfalls pulverise the grit beneath my boots as stride for stride my plated form attempts to outrun the conflagration. As the firewall of destruction billows furiously across the necroscape behind me, I feel my progress slowing. Even in full battle-plate I could make the horizon, but it is not the distance, nor the extra weight of ceramite that impedes me. I hurdle gravestones and will myself on, but as the flames engulf the world behind me, my boots sink deeper and deeper into the grave dirt. The soil has lost its consistency and I have run myself down into a quagmire. The earth – black, sodden and heavy – pulls me down into the ground itself. It oozes up my greaves, splatters plate and swallows cabling. With my legs and arms churning the morass, I see shattered bones, earth-stained skulls and rotten remains in the mire about me. Even a smashed stasis casket surfaces for a moment, like a sinking ship, before disappearing back into the depths.

With every movement my ceramite sinks further, and within moments I am up to my helm in cemetery world dirt. I turn to see the bank of flame – an unstoppable inferno of fire and fury that has scorched the Certusian surface clean – erupting upon my position. The most primal of instincts takes over, and before I know it, I have dived down below the quagmire and into an underworld of darkness, grit and death. My optics turn black. I desist in my armoured struggles and allow the cemetery world to take me down, while above the earth hardens, as the inferno bakes the ground with the heat of its righteous fury.

Kersh opened his eyes. The vague recollection of a dream misted his mind like a taste water wouldn't wash away. He felt smothered yet calm and took a moment to savour several deep breaths. He allowed his head to roll to one side.

A form sat by his bunk crystallised into focus. Bethesda, his personal serf and absterge, was watching him. Her mask of tension broke with relief and she smiled. The curl of her lip was simple and sweet, and Kersh found that he was actually quite glad to see her.

She turned and called 'lord' lightly at the dormitory door. It opened slightly and Kersh saw Micah's face in the crack. His expression became a grin.

'It's good to see you, sir. I'll send for your Apothecary, plate and bondsmen.'

Kersh nodded and went to sit up. The hermitage slab made a harsh bunk, but the Scourge had known worse. He had been stripped of his warrior's plate and lay in his clean but blood-stained robes, bearing the venerated symbol of the Stigmartyr. As was custom, the cream of the garment was fresh but the spiritual work of 'the purge' was forever allowed to stain the material.

Putting the soles of his feet on the cold stone of the hermitage floor, Kersh felt something fall from his chest. On the flags beneath him, the Excoriator found a liquid-crystal wafer. He picked it up. It bore an illustration: a single eye, unflinching, open and glinting with predatory intention. The Space Marine felt some unease looking at the disturbing image. It was as though the card itself was watching him. Below the illustration, inscribed in High Gothic, was the title *Magnus Occularis*. The Scourge's brow creased with confusion.

'Did Melmoch leave this?' Kersh asked. Bethesda shook her head.

'Your armour, sir?' Micah said as Kersh strode past and out into the dark hermitage thoroughfare. The company champion's thoughts were always centred on his commander's safety. The dim light of struggling candles illuminated the glower on the Scourge's face.

'The plate can wait,' Kersh murmured, advancing up the cloister past the heavy doors of private dorms and hermitories. The corpus-captain came to a silent halt outside one. The ferruswood door was slightly ajar. Beyond, Kersh and Micah could hear the savage crack of a 'purge' at work. Kersh recognised the knotty face of Chief Whip Skase's lictor. The serf himself was stripped to the waist and his body slick with the effort of mortification. Edging around, Kersh could also see the pool of blood gathering around the purged. Dorn's Mantle had not been so much donned as spread across the floor. Both Skase's seneschal and absterge were employed with mops and buckets, attempting to stem the flood. Against the wall stood the chief whip himself, stoic and immovable – like a statue – his mangled back cut to ribbons.

Pain and endurance were their genetic heritage and through the spilling of blood, Demetrius Katafalque had taught them that spiritual communion with the primarch could be achieved. In the cold remove achieved by Excoriators during the hot agony of purgation, Rogal Dorn had answers for each of them. Kersh had seen Excoriators punish themselves as such before. He had done so, cloaked in the shame of losing the Chapter Stigmartyr and failure to protect his Chapter Master. It led to a dark place. The long journey from Samarquand had taught him that his flesh had a greater purpose in Dorn's eyes; that beyond the spiritual unity of the Mantle lay only a labyrinth of needless suffering in which to lose oneself forever.

Kersh was so struck by the spectacle – the simultaneous sadness for and anger towards the hurting Skase – that he did not even acknowledge Ezrachi's hydraulic approach. Others in the dormitory had, however, and a figure behind him promptly closed the hermitory door.

'Have Toralech relay a message to the Chaplain,' Ezrachi ordered Brother Micah. 'Inform him that the corpus-captain is conscious and demands a report.'

Micah nodded and peeled off into the shadows.

'I ordered a cessation of ritual observance,' Kersh growled at the ferruswood door.

'And Chaplain Shadrath enforced it,' said the Apothecary. 'You've been out a few days.' Ezrachi turned the Scourge's face towards him before dazzling the Excoriator with some medical instrument that sent a flickering beam between his eyes. Since the dull, scratched surface of a ball bearing sat in one socket, Ezrachi focused his attention on the corpus-captain's remaining eye.

'Days,' Kersh marvelled. 'The company...'

'Shadrath will make his report. Be still.'

Kersh allowed the Apothecary his rudimentary medical tests.

'It's not healthy,' Kersh said looking back to the door, but the Apothecary brought his attention back to the beam.

'I've spoken to Skase,' Ezrachi said. 'Right now I'm more worried about you.'

'Was it a relapse of the Darkness?'

'No,' Ezrachi said with some certainty. 'I just don't think you were sleeping. Even an Adeptus Astartes must sleep some time. I can give you something for that. You must tell me if you begin suffering the delusions you spoke of.'

'You think I'm hallucinating?'

'I should have listened. My apologies, corpus-captain. We must accept the possibility that the catalepsean node is still malfunctioning. It might require further surgery. It is certainly more evidence for the likelihood of the Darkness having a genetic rather than spiritual cause.'

'Well, thrilled as I am to help you solve a medical mystery,' Kersh told him, 'just fix it, will you?'

'I need the surgical bay in the apothecarion – on board the *Angelica Mortis*. I'm happy, however, to submit a report indicating that you're fit for duty.'

'I suppose this recent incapacitation has further cemented ill-will towards my command amongst the Fifth.'

'The rank and file hate you with a passion,' Ezrachi told him with brutal honesty. 'Nothing has changed there. Events, however, have overreached us.'

'Explain.'

'Follow me.'

The Apothecary led Kersh up a spiral staircase of stone and dust. In the awkwardness of full plate, Ezrachi found that he had to angle his pauldrons to ascend, while the globes of the Scourge's muscular shoulders merely brushed the staircase walls. A door at the top of the twisting steps opened out into a narrow balcony. Below them the tiled roofs of the hermitage extended; above, a small bell tower reached for the darkness of the cemetery world sky. Stars glimmered in the heavens, and on the horizon, the Eye of Terror's distant, heliotropic haze besmirched the depths of the void. It was not the warp storm's horror that held the corpus-captain's attention.

'Katafalque's blood,' Kersh said, the oath carried off on the light breeze. Above Certus-Minor, the sky had been cleaved in two, a gore smear trailed across the starry firmament – like that a wounded soldier might make, crawling for his life. Instead of a soldier, the haemorrhaging bulb of a crimson comet blazed the bloody path. 'The Keeler Comet...'

'Destruction follows in the wake of the comet,' Ezrachi told him. 'It is more than just an omen. If the crimson comet appears in a sky then the world to which that sky belongs is doomed to fall.'

'Stop talking like a prophet and give me specifics. Specifics I can kill.'

'We've been out of segmentum, but Shadrath claims intelligence is patchy. The comet leaves no witnesses to its passing,' the Apothecary said.

'No survivors?'

'Some claim the comet eats worlds whole,' Ezrachi replied, 'others that it is responsible for some kind of rift or daemonic incursion. The Imperial Navy reports sightings of an armada trailing its tail, a Blood Crusade called the Cholercaust. The Exorcists, the Grey Knights and our cousins the Fists are rumoured to man a cordon at Vanaheim – to prevent a crusader advance on Segmentum Solar.'

Kersh's eyes drifted down to the planet surface. Beyond the city, the necroplex of grave markers, statues and mausolea extended before being swallowed by the darkness.

'How long until dawn?'

'Two, perhaps three hundred hours standard. The cemetery worlders call it the Long Night.'

'We've got to send word to Vanaheim,' Kersh said. 'We need to alert the Viper Legion on Hellionii Reticuli. The Cadians…'

'This world's problems have already begun,' Ezrachi said, pointing behind the corpus-captain. Turning, Kersh took in the rising spires and towers of Obsequa City with the dome of the Umberto II Memorial Mausoleum topping the cathedralscape like a crown. Smoke streamed from various fires across the city while tiny sparks of las-fire could be seen flashing across the streets below. Amongst the chaos, Kersh could make out large crowds in the streets. A mortuary lighter made an unsteady take-off and blasted past the belfry at full throttle. Kersh could imagine the panic and pure havoc created on the cemetery world at the appearance of the crimson comet. Kersh made for the stairs.

'I presume an evacuation has begun,' the Scourge called behind him.

'With necrofreighter captains auctioning space in their empty holds to the highest bidders,' Ezrachi said with obvious disappointment. 'The ruling classes and many of the priests simply abandoned world. There was little in the way of haggling – speed being of the essence.'

'The pontifex…'

'Remains,' Ezrachi said. 'He claims he won't leave his people or sacred Certusian soil. There are, of course, many thousands of scribes and labourers without the coin to secure a passage off-world.'

'What about the Sisters?'

'Umberto II's remains are too fragile to transport,' the Apothecary explained. 'With or without the pontifex, the Order of the August Vigil have orders to protect the Ecclesiarch's bones. I think we can rely upon them to do that, but little else.'

Kersh stormed out of the stairwell and out onto the hermitage thoroughfare.

'My battle-plate,' he roared up the cloister at his serfs. 'Do you know anything about this?' Kersh asked, holding out the crystalline wafer he'd been holding. Ezrachi took it. 'It was placed with me as I slept.'

'From the Emperor's Tarot. Members of the Librarius use them,' the Apothecary told him. Ezrachi squinted at the card. 'The Great Eye,' he read.

'Give it back to Melmoch,' Kersh ordered.

'It wasn't Melmoch,' Ezrachi said. As the Scourge continued marching up the cloister, the Apothecary stopped. He opened a nearby door and called, 'Kersh!'

Scowling, the Scourge returned and looked in through the open door. It was the small sanctuary chamber Ezrachi had converted to a temporary apothecarion. Epistolary Melmoch lay upon a hermit's slab, arms across his chest.

'Is he...'

'No,' Ezrachi interjected as the two Excoriators entered the room. 'But he is out cold. He breathes but fails to respond to drugs or stimuli.'

'What happened?' Kersh asked as Bethesda and Old Enoch began running in pieces of plate from the rack outside.

'He was found like this,' Ezrachi replied. 'I believe it might have something to do with this,' the Apothecary said, picking up a small, ornately decorated urn from a dormitory shelf. He handed it to the Scourge who examined it with interest. 'It was reported stolen from the Memorial Mausoleum by the Sisters but found here with Melmoch.'

'What is it?'

'The Palatine was short on detail but I gather it is used in an annual, ceremonial capacity to dust the Ecclesiarch's shrine. The material inside the urn is formulated from a by-product of the Emperor's metabolism, if you believe that. The dust particles are impregnated with negative psychic energy, so I'm told. For all I know there could be bread crumbs inside, but for the fact that the Palatine and her Sisters were almost on the verge of charging down the hermitage door to recover it and the effect exposure has had on Melmoch here.'

'Why would he do that to himself?' Kersh asked as his serfs worked fast about him.

'This is nothing. Ever since the comet appeared, witchbreeds have been dying,' Ezrachi told the corpus-captain.

'What do you mean?'

'Astropaths hanging from cloisters, Navigators stepping unsuited into airlocks. All kinds of insanity.'

'What about the *Angelica Mortis*?'

'Zaragoza's dead. That bird of his went mad and tore his throat out,' the Apothecary said.

'Something wrong with the pet?'

'Or with Zaragoza,' Ezrachi said. 'Who knows? Shadrath recalled the *Angelica Mortis* back to the cemetery world. She has the sprint trader *Avignor Star* under her guns. The captain wishes to leave with the last of the great and good, but the trader carries the only remaining Navigator. Commander Bartimeus is under orders to destroy her if she attempts to leave. With the pontifex's chief astropath, Melmoch and this Navigator are the only psykers left on or around the planet.'

'Chaplain Shadrath has been in command?' the Scourge asked.

Ezrachi nodded. 'He charged me with your care and completed the destruction of the Ruinous monument.'

'The monument,' the corpus-commander repeated, looking down at the Librarian. 'Melmoch said it was a beacon.'

'Well, now we know what it was beckoning,' the Apothecary said.

'Why didn't Shadrath just leave?' Kersh asked. 'That's what he wanted.'

'He had no orders to leave,' Ezrachi insisted. 'I told him your symptoms were likely to be short-term. He restricted his commands to the execution of your wishes and precautionary measures. The *Gauntlet* sits on the rockrete, fuelled and ready to go. The strike cruiser awaits your order to leave. We are leaving, aren't we?'

Kersh's mind seemed elsewhere. He was looking down at the small urn.

'We should return this…'

'Kersh!' Ezrachi said. 'We're leaving, yes?'

'You would have me abandon one of the Emperor's worlds at the sight of an omen in the sky?' Kersh grizzled.

'Whatever is ending worlds in the wake of the Keeler Comet, I fear we are too few a number to dissuade it from taking this tiny planet of the dead,' Ezrachi barked back. 'We have a ship. We have a Navigator. We should alert the cordon at Vanaheim. There – shoulder to shoulder with our brothers – we can make our stand.'

'We have an astropath – you said it yourself,' the corpus-captain persisted. 'And we have a message for him to send. The Viper Legion are nearest.'

'There is an astrotelepathic blackout for light years around,' Ezrachi shot back.

'Then he shall have to double his efforts!'

'Kersh, don't do this.'

'Do what, Ezrachi? Carry out my Chapter Master's orders?'

'Our purpose here is fulfilled. Events are unfolding on a larger canvas. We must make a run for Vanaheim–'

'We are Excoriators,' Kersh seethed. 'Attrition fighters. Our gene-kindred fought before the walls of the Imperial Palace. We are not heralds and harbingers. We are Excoriators and this is the Imperium beneath our feet. We stand our ground and we fight, whatever the odds. As though this were the palace itself. I have failed my Chapter Master. I will not fail my Emperor.' The two Space Marines burned into each other with searing eyes as Kersh's serfs pressurised his seals and attached his weapons to his belt. 'And neither will you.'

Ezrachi looked away as Brother Micah appeared at the doorway. The champion looked unsure of himself amongst the heated exchange. The corpus-captain turned to the young Excoriator. 'Have word sent to Chaplain Shadrath. Tell the Chaplain I need him and Brother Toralech at the pontifex's palace, immediately. We shall meet them there.' Micah nodded. 'You too,' Kersh added before looking back at the livid Apothecary. 'And you.' Ezrachi looked down and nodded gently. 'We have words and deeds for Pontifex Oliphant and his chief astropath.'

CHAPTER NINE
HARBINGER

BEFORE THE OBELISK Ecclesiarchical palace – which served Erasmus Oliphant as both pontifex and planetary governor – two groups of Excoriators marched out of the darkness towards one another. Kersh was flanked by his Apothecary and Brother Micah, who walked a little out front with his bolter and combat shield attachment held out before him. Chaplain Shadrath had with him the Fifth Company's standard bearer, Brother Toralech, holding his banner proudly above them. A little way behind them, Second Squad Whip Ishmael and Brother Levi – from Squad Castigir – marched across the cobbles. The two Excoriators were helmetless and scorn was etched into their sour faces.

'I won't offer my gauntlet, brother, for fear you would not take it – and that would only shame us both,' Kersh opened aggressively, 'but I thank you for the care you have given to the Fifth in my absence and my existing orders.'

Shadrath came to a halt. His half-skull helm remained fixed on the corpus-captain but did little to acknowledge the appreciation.

'I did no less than Katafalque expected,' Shadrath said finally.

'And no more,' Kersh admitted.

'What are we doing here?' Ishmael spat, the veteran's face contorting itself around the expression of disgust.

'Our duty, Brother Ishmael,' the Scourge informed him. 'Which I am not about to debate here. The Adeptus Astartes is not a democratic institution. Neither is the Emperor's Imperium – I'll have you remember that. You and your Excoriators will do as you're damn well ordered.'

Ishmael and Levi exchanged dark glances.

Twin columns of Charnel Guard jogged across the plaza carrying the lengths of their lasfusils and in the full sobriety of ceremonial dress. A helmetless lieutenant led them across to the palace doors, replacing the powerpack in his taper-barrelled pistol.

'What is it, lieutenant?' the Scourge demanded to know.

'We've been summoned by the High Constable, my lord,' the dour officer replied.

'Go,' Kersh ordered his Excoriators, who had little trouble reaching the palace doors before the Guardsmen. With Ishmael and Toralech flanking the archway, Brothers Micah and Levi kicked aside the heavy doors and led the group into the small palace and up through the Obelisk's stairwells. Before the reception chambers and beneath the great belfry, the Space Marines found High Constable Colquhoun barking orders to a gathering of his Guardsmen. Some were stationed at the bronze doors of the pontifex's reception chambers, calling through the thick metal. Others had the long barrels of their lasfusils pointed at the aperture, while a small group had toppled a masonry statue at the High Constable's instruction and were trying to batter the doors down.

'Thank the God-Emperor,' Colquhoun said at the appearance of the Adeptus Astartes.

'What's happening?'

'The pontifex has been in there for many hours. We thought he was at prayer,' the High Constable confessed.

'When planetary business necessitated a disturbance I tried to enter myself.'

'Locked?'

'There is no lock. They must be blocked from the other side.'

'Anyone in there, beside the pontifex?' Kersh asked.

'Only his chief astropath,' Colquhoun confirmed. The Scourge pursed his grizzled lips.

'Toralech, Ishmael,' the corpus-captain ordered.

As the Charnel Guard and their improvised ram retreated, the squad whip and the hulking standard bearer put their ceramite shoulders to the bronze. As the Space Marines pushed against the metal with superhuman might, the doors began to give. With a screech they parted slightly, at which Ishmael put his eye to the crack. 'Barricaded with masonry,' he reported.

'What?' the High Constable exclaimed.

A sulphurous tang stung the Scourge's nostrils.

'Do you smell that?' he asked. As he snorted he detected the otherworldly odours of ozone and scalded reality. The same reek he experienced on the battlefield when the witchbreeds of the Librarius brought the full force of their warp-drawn powers down on the Emperor's enemies.

'Warpstench...' Shadrath snarled.

'Pontifex!' Ezrachi boomed through the gap in the bronze. When no sound returned, Kersh stabbed a finger at Brother Micah and then at the stone wall.

'Shoot it out!'

Pulling the bolter into his shoulder, the company champion hammered the masonry with diamantine-tip precision. As the dust cleared, a ragged circle in the wall was revealed, as well as a peppering of holes that had broken up the masonry within. Like a torpedo, Kersh launched himself at the wall. Punching through the crumbling stone, he dived through the opening. Rolling across a pauldron and the curvature of his pack, the Scourge landed back on his feet. With dust cascading off his armour, he unclipped his chainsword and brought the short, falchion-shaped weapon out in front of him. Gunning the Ryza-pattern blade to life, he waved it from left to right like a flaming torch in the darkness of a cave. Beyond, the throne room appeared in a state of considerable disarray.

Rolling into a covering position, both Micah and Levi followed their corpus-captain through, bolters up and scanning the chamber.

'Oliphant!' Kersh called above the chug of the company heirloom.

Shadrath and Ezrachi stepped through the wall with Squad Whip Ishmael bringing up the rear. Toralech waited by the opening with the standard in hand and his bolter pointed through the hole. 'Spread out,' the corpus-captain called, prompting the Excoriators to advance through the pontifex's reception chambers and throne room.

'Kersh,' the Apothecary called, drawing the Scourge's attention to the small mountain of masonry that had been ripped out of the walls and ceiling and piled before the bronze doors.

Sweeping through the wreckage of the darkened chamber, the Excoriators moved in on the throne room. As Kersh led the way with the idling chainsword, flanked by the gaping muzzles of Micah and Levi's bolters, the Space Marines found a robed form slumped in the ecclesiarch's throne.

'Pontifex?' Kersh called. When the figure didn't reply, the corpus-captain shouted, 'Ezrachi!'

The Apothecary moved up behind the group as they advanced on the throne. The remaining Excoriators gathered at the door, ready to provide cover fire. Levi moved in and pulled the figure's head back. Slipping the hood off, the Excoriators found themselves looking into the empty sockets of the pontifex's chief astropath. Ezrachi moved in.

'Unconscious,' the Apothecary confirmed. 'Like Melmoch.'

'Listen!' Kersh said, shutting off the chainsword's brutal motor. The remaining Excoriators, who had been moving through the expanse of the throne room, froze. As they scanned the chamber, they heard a distant murmur.

'It's coming from outside,' Ishmael said. Kersh joined him

on the pontifex's balcony, squinting through the darkness. A narrow ledge ran along the four sides of the Obelisk, running under the balcony, a decorative rather than a practical structure. Peering through the murk along it, the Excoriators caught a glimpse of fingers, clasping the corner of the building with bone-white desperation. A figure was somehow situated out on the ledge. As a fearful face edged around the corner, peering at the Excoriators, the figure released a howl of relief and urgency.

'Oliphant!' Kersh cried. 'Ishmael–'

But the squad whip was already over the balcony balustrade and stepping down onto the narrow ledge. 'Ezrachi,' the corpus-captain called, as he craned his head back around into the reception chamber. The Apothecary left Brother Levi with the comatose astropath and made his way up the steps.

'He's coming around,' the Excoriator announced as the astropath's head came up. Instead of empty sockets, a pair of dark orbs – black as midnight and sizzling with blank hatred – rolled over in the psyker's skull. Momentarily transfixed, Brother Levi watched as twisted horns of charred bone sliced their way out of the man-puppet's gaunt flesh.

'Daemo–' Levi began, but the thing before him exploded in a bloodstorm of shattered skull and brain. An elongated cranium blasted out of the back of the astropath's head, while daemonfangs burst through his forehead and neck, swallowing his face whole. In its place a visage of infernal flesh appeared: primordial, bestial and depraved. Willowy, lurid limbs and talons erupted from the palms and soles of the astropath's own and the daemon grew, wearing the puppet's body like a garment over its horrific and emaciated torso. Pinpricks of immaterial life, like keyholes into a furnace, burned through the inky incomprehension in the monster's eyes. In one savage motion, the daemon seized Brother Levi by his pauldrons and enveloped the Excoriator's head with the cage of its jaws. Snapping down, the beast sheared Levi's head from his neck and swallowed, leaving the Space Marine's power armour to fountain gore from the neckbrace.

With his attention split between the throne room and the ledge, Kersh was slow to react. The first he truly understood of the danger was the sight of his Excoriators lifting their weapons at the far end of the throne room. The Scourge felt a shockwave of rage and hatred spread through the chamber like a red mist that could be felt but not seen. All Kersh saw was the cavernous muzzle of Shadrath's bolt pistol thrust at him and the Chaplain lean into a firing position.

Kersh snatched his own Mark II piece from his holster only to see Brother Micah slam the Chaplain's arms aside with his shoulder.

'The corpus-captain!' he yelled.

Before the Scourge could take aim a florid blur shot across the entrance to the balcony. The corpus-captain got the impression of something spindly and daemonic, all horns, claws and blasphemous flesh. Kersh thrust a palm back at Ishmael on the ledge, the squad whip having the exhausted pontifex under one arm. By the time he turned back, the creature had bounded halfway down the chamber on its gangly legs. Both Micah and Chaplain Shadrath's gunfire had now been unleashed, blasting its way up the precious Ecclesiarchical relics that adorned the throne room wall. Kersh brought his own to bear, trapping the beast between two converging arcs of .75 calibre hell.

Clawing a foothold in the masonry, the daemon vaulted up through the beams of the chamber ceiling and into the great belfry above. The *clangs* of its ungainly movements could be heard against the metal of the Obelisk's bell. As the Chaplain indulged a slick reload of his pistol, Brother Micah sidestepped across the chamber towards his corpus-captain, dribbling bolt-rounds at the ceiling beams. These were joined by the judicious crash of the Apothecary's pistol and the fully automatic hurricane of fire from Toralech. The standard bearer had been drawn in by the sound of gunfire and held his banner upright like some religious artefact, ready to repel the infernal beast with faith alone.

'Hold your fire!' Kersh ordered, bringing even Toralech's chattering bolter to a halt. The Excoriators listened to the ring and scrape of the thing's talons on the bell. Kersh's eyes widened as the potential calamity of the situation crystallised in his mind. 'Fall back!' the corpus-captain roared, but by then the calamity was already in play.

The Obelisk's Great Bell crashed down through the ceiling beams from the belfry above. The colossal instrument descended on a furious cloud of masonry dust and debris, clanging and pealing its thunderous way down through the throne room floor. Kersh watched in horror as Chaplain Shadrath, Toralech and Brother Micah all disappeared, carried down with the bell as it made its cacophonous descent through the different floors of the Obelisk. Once again, Kersh was treated to the hazy impression of the daemon, clinging to the bell crown and riding the instrument down through its path of destruction.

Ezrachi had been fortunate not to have been caught in the path of the object, but now with the demolished throne room floor collapsing under him, the Apothecary had little choice but to make a clumsy bound for the balcony. The Excoriator's hydraulic leg wouldn't entertain the speed such a manoeuvre entailed and Kersh watched the marble floor fall away beneath the Apothecary.

Dropping both pistol and chainsword, Kersh threw himself down and half over the crumbling floorspace. Marble disappeared beneath his chest also, leaving only his legs and armoured midriff spread awkwardly across the balcony. With one of the Scourge's gauntlets clutching for a handhold, the other shot for the falling Ezrachi. His ceramite fingertips clawed their way around the edge of the reductor adorning the Apothecary's armoured wrist. Ordinarily, Ezrachi would use the sacred tool to extract gene-seed from fallen Excoriators. As the Apothecary dangled from his corpus-captain's grasp it became clear that the instrument had saved him from falling. Holstering his pistol and getting his gauntlet to the Scourge's arm, Ezrachi gave Kersh a glare of crabby exertion before hauling himself up the ceramite plating of his arm and shoulder. Swinging his bionic leg up and onto the balcony edge, the Apothecary used his powerful hydraulics to do the last of the heavy lifting.

As the two Excoriators lay on their chestplates looking down through the devastation the bell had punched through the different levels of the palace, they heard Colquhoun's Charnel Guard hit the stairs and make their way down towards the ground floor.

'The casualties...' Ezrachi began, getting to his feet. Kersh snatched up his pistol and chainsword.

'Let me at least kill it first,' the Scourge shouted as he gunned the chainblade to serrated life. 'Call for the *Gauntlet*,' Kersh ordered, 'and get the pontifex off that ledge.'

With that, Kersh turned and dropped off the side of the balcony. As the Great Bell had fallen, taking out floor after floor, it had left behind a narrow rim of masonry on each level, keystones and structural girder-stumps protruding from the exterior wall. Bounding from one to the other, dropping whole floors and spiralling his way down through the wreckage, Kersh went after the daemon.

A thick cloud of dust rose to meet him about halfway down, indicating that the bell had finally reached the ground floor of the palace. With the powdered masonry and final resonance of the instrument hanging in the air it became increasingly difficult to make the footholds out. When what looked like a snapped support strut turned out to be nothing, the Scourge fell the remaining three floors. Hitting the uneven floor of debris and stone carnage, Kersh felt the hydraulics of his power armour groan and protest. Springing back and rolling, he assumed a combat stance in the miasma of dust. Kersh could make out little but the ghostly outline of the toppled bell and mess of ropes, cords and pulleys left by the falling instrument, hanging in the haze like vines in a jungle mist.

'Shadrath... Micah... Toralech. Respond.' The vox-link fed back only static.

The beast was suddenly upon him.

Launching itself over the bell, with a shattered length of girder clutched within its infernal talons, the daemon howled its inhuman desire to end the Scourge. The potent length of a slack, bestial tongue swung from the creature's maw. The chainsword raged in Kersh's hand.

The corpus-captain followed the savage motion of the girder with his sword. Kersh ducked the first swing – a manoeuvre that had every right to take his head from his shoulders. A second and a third danced in an arc of pure wrath, flying for the Excoriator time and again. Attempting to keep his focus and composure amid the supernatural speed of the strikes and the primeval roaring and hissing of the thing, Kersh sidestepped across the uneven ground. He leant back out of the path of the shattered end of the girder as it descended, his throat a hair's breadth from the razor tip of the metal support strut. A roll to the left took him away from the improvised weapon, and the daemon had to content itself with the lump of palace masonry it pulverised instead. A sudden backslash, riding on a crest of spite, found the Scourge, smacking his backpack and slamming the Excoriator into the wall.

Kersh swung straight back with the raging teeth of his chainsword, clipping the tip off the retracting girder. Clasping the weapon like a lance, the daemon charged at the Excoriator. Kersh batted the metal away with the flat of his sword, allowing the girder to skewer the stone of the wall right beside him. The Scourge accelerated the chain on his weapon to an insane screech before cutting down through the girder's thickness. Again the creature retracted the strut only to have Kersh follow, pressing his advantage. The beast rewarded its opponent with a series of strikes designed to cut the Adeptus Astartes in two, but each one met with the Scourge's serrated blade and the immovable arms of the Excoriator behind it. The girder's length was cut down again and again, forcing the creature to step back up the bell. With just a stump remaining of the daemon's weapon, Kersh brought up his pistol. By the time the Mark II delivered its death-dealing blast, however, the monster had flipped back behind the bell, leaving the girder to fall to the uneven floor and fat bolt-holes in the metal of the bell.

Fuelled by the creature's retreat, Kersh stormed across the demolished architecture. A lightshow cast ghostly patterns through the swirls and eddies in the dust. The Scourge immediately recognised the semi-automatic *whoosh* of the Charnel Guard's lasfusils and the High Constable's calm and routine instruction. The beast had retreated straight into the fearful Guardsmen, waiting in formation at the bottom of the stairs.

Kersh would have stormed into the hail of las-bolts himself if it hadn't been for the company standard, resting in the rubble. Toralech's hand was still clenched around the banner pole, despite the fact that the hulking standard bearer's body was a twisted mess of bone and ceramite, half buried in the wreckage. Kersh spat and swore. Suddenly a gauntlet snatched at his boot. Spinning around, Kersh saw a partially buried Excoriator. Looking from the lightshow to the gauntlet, the corpus-captain slammed his Mark II and his chainsword down in the rubble. Heaving pieces of stone off the Space Marine, Kersh found himself looking down at the cracked, half-skull face of Shadrath's helm. The Chaplain had been buried in masonry and the rim of the Great Bell rested across the smashed ceramite of his chest.

'Hold on,' Kersh told the Chaplain and rested his pack against the metal of the bell. Hooking his fingers around the rim, the Scourge pushed with his legs.

From the stairwell beyond, Kersh could hear the disciplined fire of the lasfusils break up and the screams of Guardsmen echo about the ruins of the palace. Heaving upwards, the corpus-captain lifted the colossal weight of the bell slightly, allowing the rim to clear the buckled chestplate of the Chaplain. Kersh heard Shadrath take a laboured breath, then the sounds of slaughter. The beast was among the Guardsmen, tearing and gutting its way through the Charnel Guard with hateful ease.

Within moments the thing was back. Down on all fours, the daemon charged at Kersh. It smouldered with the scorch tracks of las-bolts that had found their mark, and steamed with the blood of the Guardsmen it had butchered. Kersh held his ground as Chaplain Shadrath squirmed his way out from under the Great Bell. At the last moment, Kersh released his grip. The bell came back down on the Chaplain's pauldron, trapping his arm and causing the Excoriator to grunt in pain and exertion. The daemon hit the metal of the instrument with the dome of its elongated cranium – its twisted horns ringing against the surface. Snatching the relic-gladius from his belt, the Scourge allowed the weight of its bulbous pommel to carry the blade around with centrifugal certainty before slashing down through the beast's willowy arm.

Kersh's stroke took off the limb at the elbow. But though such a loss might have given most enemies pause for thought, the daemon seemed oblivious. It spat its gall and fed its rage with a blinding counter. Using the dribbling stump of the same limb, the monster smacked the gladius out of the Scourge's grip with bone-ringing force. Pushing itself off the bell with its hind-talons, the daemon blazed at the Excoriator. Slamming the length of its skull against his chest and midriff, the beast ran the corpus-captain into the opposite wall. Stone crumbled and masonry fell as the creature butted the Space Marine repeatedly into the unforgiving surface. Kersh tried to reach for the hilt of his remaining gladius – the only weapon he had left – but was forced to grab on to the monster's horns in order to prepare himself for the next brutal impact.

Twisting the hydraulic sinew of his armoured wrist, Kersh broke off a length of the fiend's horn and thrust it into the thing's hideous visage. The reaction was immediate. Its head came up and its jaws flashed open, wider than the Scourge thought possible. Gagging under the creature's gorebreath, Kersh once again grabbed the torturous cage of horn that protruded from the daemon's skull, forcing it back. As the Excoriator fought to force the monster back, the slack length of bloodlustful tongue suddenly became solid and sharp, like a speartip. Kersh intuitively craned his head out of harm's way, as the tongue shot out like a slaughterhouse groxgun. Puncturing the wall, the repellent tongue retracted. The Scourge threw his head the other way, only to have the devilish tip nick the side of his head and impale the brickwork.

Out of nowhere Kersh heard the familiar crack of a bolt pistol. The beast seemed to arch and screech its vexation before rocketing away, allowing several rounds to pluck at the stone about the Scourge. Falling to a crouch, Kersh saw that Chaplain Shadrath – his shoulder still trapped beneath the Great Bell – had got his other gauntlet to the corpus-captain's Mark II pistol. The daemon was back down on all fours, bounding this way and that, causing each of the Chaplain's unsteady shots to narrowly miss. Leaping up onto the side of the bell once more, it forced the instrument down with its infernal weight, causing the Chaplain to gasp and drop the weapon. Pinning his wrist to the floor with one wicked hind-talon, the beast reared its other above Shadrath's cracked helm in readiness for the kill.

The ruins were suddenly filled with the clamour of bolt-fire. Brother Micah, masonry dust still cascading from his plate, took several determined – if shaky – steps around the Great Bell. His combat shield attachment was buckled but his bolter raged fully-automatic fury at the beast. The creature let loose an inhuman wail as the bolt-rounds plucked at its daemonflesh. With its stump and talons held out as an instinctive shield, and its digits and claws blasted off by the barrage, the monster backed away from the advancing champion.

As Micah's half-spent magazine ran dry, the mauled beast turned to find the Scourge standing behind it. The Excoriator stood tall and held a large chunk of ruined masonry above his head. His face was a strained mask of fury and physical effort. Smashing the small boulder down on the creature's long head, Kersh watched the daemon stagger back. Shaking dust, grit and rock fragments from its hellish form, the beast seemed momentarily dazed. Fearless and foolish, the Scourge ran at the monster, wrapping his arm around its neck, grabbing it by its repulsive tongue and clutching its head to his armoured side. He felt the spirit of his plate protest against such close proximity to the Chaos daemon. Kersh was beyond caring, however. Holding the beast in an armlock, the Scourge pummelled the beast with his other fist.

Kersh felt his being expand to accommodate the pure rage coursing through him. A natural gene-bred hatred of the Emperor's enemies, growing into something unnatural and monstrous. Fighting the warp-sired thing had given rise to something ugly and uncompromising within the Scourge, a primal thing beyond his Adeptus Astartes training and the cool conduct of battle. A feeling that superseded strategic frustration and a Space Marine's bottomless desire to win. Anger, indiscipline, anarchy. A lack of control that could only be described as bloodlust. Kersh became a ceramite chalice, spilling over with hot, mindless fury.

Spitting curses and oaths, beating and punching the monster, Kersh's actions were no longer his own. His eyes remained fixed on the rubble through which his boots and the monster's hind-talons stumbled. An image flashed before the Scourge's eyes. A momentary flicker. A memory, seared into the Space Marine's unconscious.

The crystalline wafer he'd found on his chest. The Emperor's Tarot card. The *Magnus Occularis*. The single, unflinching eye, its doom-laden orb staring through the Scourge and filling him with the chill sensation of a feeling equally unnatural in an Excoriator. Fear. Kersh remembered the Darkness. Dorn's gift. Dorn's curse. A galaxy undone. A future alone. Kersh could not see the revenant but he sensed he was there. Just like he had been in the living nightmare of the Darkness. The Scourge felt his heart freeze within his chest. A benumbing emptiness that extinguished the fires of wanton wrath gutting him like a burning building.

At once, Kersh was himself again. The fury gone. The spite steaming away before a Space Marine's singular purpose. The Scourge became aware once more of the monster in his grasp. The threat. The need to act. Kersh dragged the daemon over to the knotted carnage of the Great Bell's pulley system. Snatching a length of bell cord, the Scourge looped the thick rope around the daemon's macabre skull. As he released the beast he felt furious life return to its blasted limbs. Two remaining talons scraped across the ceramite of his shoulder plate before Kersh got to a second rope and began pulling arm-over-arm for his life. The daemon flew skywards, its legs swinging back and forth like a doll's, its neck and bulbous head snug in the improvised noose. It gagged, spat and hissed its brute vehemence. The Scourge held the beast there for a moment, taking no little satisfaction in the monster's spasmodic thrashing.

'Kersh!' came a call from above. The corpus-captain began an almost torturous return to his senses. It was Ezra-chi. Kersh felt a tremble on the air. The welcome quake of a Thunderhawk's engines.

Two figures approached through the dust and mist. In one hand Brother Micah trained his reloaded boltgun on the snared beast. With his other he held up Chaplain Shadrath, freshly extricated from beneath the bell's crushing weight. Shadrath held the company standard in his fierce grip. They too stood entranced by the monster's jigging and twitching. Patting the Chaplain's plate, the company champion allowed Shadrath to lean against the battered standard and brought his weapon into his shoulder. Micah angled the sights of his bolter up at the daemon. Kersh saw the fire in the champion's eyes.

'Save it,' the corpus-captain commanded, before adjusting his vox-channel. '*Gauntlet*, this is Kersh.' The Scourge returned to his ropework, hauling the beast up through the rock dust and gloom. 'Target lock, palace interior.'

The three Excoriators watched the daemon disappear above them. Kersh feverishly worked the bell cord, feeling the creature's livid desperation through the length of rope. The line suddenly went slack. Simultaneously the roar of heavy bolters echoed through the ruins and the haze above flickered with a steady stream of firepower.

A mangled form tumbled through the murk, striking the Great Bell and sending a thunderous death knell reverberating through the palace. The Excoriators looked down at the smoking remains of the daemon at the foot of the instrument. Whatever murderous, immaterial life had flowed through the daemonflesh had now left it. The corpse was black and shredded, punched through with bolt-rounds and mauled beyond grisly recognition.

'Are you wounded?' Micah put to his corpus-captain.

'No, but you are.'

'Are you all right?' the champion pressed.

'I am now,' Kersh told him, stepping over the infernal remains. Walking across the rubble, Kersh reclaimed his weapons.

'What do you want me to do with it?' Shadrath hissed.

Before leaving the chamber Kersh stopped and turned, taking one final look at the smouldering daemon. It was already beginning to lose its tenuous grip on reality, the red flesh bubbling and spitting. A bronze steam rose from the infernal corpse – its corporeal presence beginning to ebb away – threading through the smoke and slaughter. The Scourge would take no chances.

'Burn it,' Kersh told the Chaplain and left.

CHAPTER TEN
NECROPLEX

Brother Omar gunned the bike's throttle. The vehicle bucked with obedience, its machine-spirit hungry for the road. As a neophyte, Omar's flesh had yet to be worthy of the lash, and no dents, rents or craters marked his carapace – his armour bearing the ignoble sheen of battle virginity. With the fat tyres of the bike tearing up the grit of the lychway and his dark robes flowing behind him, Omar surged up along the column cavalcade.

With the appearance of the blood comet in the Certusian skies, cemetery world society collapsed. The wealthy and educated fled. Merchants sold their stock. Scribes and scriveners left their quills in their ink. Priests abandoned their flocks. Anyone with ears and coin had packed what they could carry and joined the crowds gathered about the mortuary lighters and hump shuttles on Memorial Space Port rockrete. Their ears were ringing with tales of the Keeler Comet and the death of worlds that followed in its wake. Their purses were soon emptied by greedy freighter captains whose crammed vessels hung in low orbit like last chances.

Such fear felt alien and craven to Omar – as it did to all Excoriators. As a Scout and brother of the Tenth Company, he was young enough to remember the doubts and uncertainties of childhood. Back beyond his years of psychosurgical enhancement and cult instruction. A time when fathers ruled and a mother's embrace was everything. A time of nightmares, when darkness felt full of dread and danger.

Brother Omar remembered and he felt for the cemetery worlders left behind. Like children, the remaining Certusians seemed haunted by their ignorance. Their existence had been the Emperor's word, delivered daily through priestly lips and the reassuring drudgery of a hard day's labour with teat or shovel. Now they had neither. Newborns went unfed and the dead unburied. There was only blind panic. Infrastructure had swiftly broken down and early fears for basic requirements such as food and safety found expression in petty tyranny, violence and murders of seeming necessity.

It was for this reason that Corpus-Captain Kersh gave Squad Whip Keturah and his Scouts orders to ride out. To blast along the lychways and crow roads of the necroplex, across the sea of grave markers and stone sculpture, and through cenopost communities. In the absence of the Emperor's words, the corpus-captain thought it important that common Imperials had the example of the Emperor's flesh to comfort them. Even in such dark times, the sight of a hulking Adeptus Astartes – even a Scout – drew eyes and minds. Demigods walked among them.

Partly to escape the violence, raiding and looting that had swiftly engulfed the hamlets and foss-parishes, and partly because they knew no better, cemetery worlders began to move in ragged convoys on Obsequa City. Herd instinct had led the Certusians to do this, and as lychways intersected, the crowds and pilgrim processions grew larger and longer. This too had been encouraged by Corpus-Captain Kersh, who had too few Excoriators and Charnel Guardsmen at his disposal to defend a world from what might follow in the blood comet's wake.

Omar, like his brother neophytes, had been instructed to ride across the tiny world, stopping briefly in each cenopost hamlet he rode through to order Certusians to move on to the capital. Obsequa City was designated a planetary hold-point, to be further fortified by honoured members of the Fifth Company, and like a rescue vessel, the city took in as many as needed shelter – crowding the cells and domiciles of those who had escaped off-world and creating a tent shanty on the open and now empty expanse of the Memorial Space Port. It had taken Omar several days to reach the grave-lined shores of Lake Sanctity on the far side of the planet, and from there onwards he found that he was riding along the teeming lychways with the cavalcades rather than against the current of cemetery worlders. Omar had ridden amongst them all, vergermen and their families, gravediggers, foss-reeves, pallbearers and vestals, attending to the old, the sick and orphaned. Shabby masses, their rags covered with grave dust, pulling carts and carrying all they owned in the world.

The strategy was not popular amongst the members of the Tenth. Brother Kush had been briefly seconded to Squad Cicatrix during training rites on board the *Angelica Mortis*. There he had been exposed to the full hatred the Excoriators First Squad felt for their new commanding officer. Kush, in turn, had brought these opinions to his brother neophytes, who had swiftly begun to revel in similar derision of the unfavoured Scourge, his loss of the Chapter Stigmartyr and his affliction with the Darkness. The Scout dormitory had soon became a forum for a kind of hollow boasting and scorn that Omar tried his best to avoid. When Squad Whip Keturah had delivered orders to break out the bikes and take to the lychways, Omar had been secretly relieved. After Keturah had left, Kush and several other Scouts had questioned the wisdom of the Scourge's strategy. Omar had listened but said nothing. Kush claimed Kersh's seem-ing concern for mere mortals was further weakness in the flawed commander – labelling it hesitation and cowardice when faced with the prospect of actual battle on the Vana-heim Cordon or Rorschach's World.

As Kush and his brothers went to leave the dormitory they had found the squad whip standing in the corridor. Keturah had run a hand through his silver mane and fixed them all with the cyclopean intensity of his bionic eye. Omar had withered under his gaze, but again opted for silence.

'I know there are mixed feelings about the corpus-captain amongst the Fifth Company,' Keturah finally said in steely syllables. 'No such confusion exists in this company. Do you understand? When you are corpus-captain, you can debate deployment and strategy. Until then you will follow orders without discussion. Is that clear? Zachariah Kersh has had more broken bones than you have bones all together. He's spilled more blood than entire companies have ever seen and has recent scars older than you. For Throne's sake, he won the Feast of Blades. He has wielded the sacred Sword of Sebastus – the primarch's own weapon. Above all, he's your commanding officer. And mine. Show some respect.'

'But, whip…' Kush had began.

'Brother Kush,' Keturah had said calmly, 'you will take a vow of silence in regards to this matter or I will have the Apothecary sew your mouth shut for the duration of this mission. Do we have an understanding?'

Kush nodded. 'Yes, squad whip.'

'Until I say otherwise,' Keturah had told Kush, 'you are forbidden from donning your shoulder carapace and gauntlets. Shed your field smock and cloak also. Cuirass and faulds only. I want your brothers to see the shame of your unspoilt flesh, to see your lack of battle scars and, by extension, your lack of judgement in this matter.'

'Yes, squad whip.'

After Keturah had left, Kush honoured his word to the squad whip. His lips said nothing. But they didn't have to. His eyes –· burning with defiance and meaning – did the talking.

On the lychway before him a throng had gathered, making it difficult for Omar to ride. There was light ahead and some isolated screams, prompting some Certusians to turn around and start pushing their way back through the oncoming crowd. Clutching at the brakes, the Scout brought his machine to a gravel-crunching halt. Turning, Omar took the bike out along a narrow walkway, leading between gravestones and statues, alongside a crypt belonging to some hive-world House or family. The swarm of cemetery worlders on the lychway seemed to have come to a stop at a cenopost ahead, and Omar gunned the bike down a slender pallbearer's track, riding up several burial mounds and clearing a line of gravestones in order to reach another track. This brought him out at the cenopost, a small collection of shacks and permanent hovels. These were built around the necroplex crosslyches and intersections dominated by a simple block cenotaph, carved in the semblance of the Adeptus Ministorum's symbol and inscribed with prayers and blessings. It also bore the hamlet's name. Little Amasec.

Immediately, Brother Omar saw the reason for the cavalcade's halting. The ground about the bike's chunky tyres was mushy and both bodies and body parts lay strewn across the crossroads in pools and puddles of blood. Several hovels were on fire, while a tiny market and a nearby brewhouse were beginning to take, streaming with smoke and filling the air with a murky haze. Omar rode around and between the bodies. Beyond the cenotaph the slaughter continued, and as the Scout idled the bike up to the far end of the hamlet he could see the lychway beyond littered with bodies. Cemetery worlders pounced upon, beaten, torn, bitten and ripped apart. A cavalcade just like the one Omar was riding along.

Parking the bike, Omar dismounted. Taking several squelchy steps out onto the lychway, cloaked in haze, the Scout squinted through the darkness. Something was moving up ahead. A dark shape making its way along the road towards Little Amasec. A man in rags. He slipped and stumbled amongst the bodies, several times having to pick himself up.

'What happened here?' Omar called, demanding an

211

answer. The man did not reply, though. The dark shape's head seemed to suddenly angle. He looked up at the Excoriators Scout, framed in the burning village, before breaking into a run.

The neophyte's brow furrowed. 'Answer me, Certusian,' he ordered. The man ran on. He was unarmed but something in the cemetery worlder's gait told the Scout that he was not running to him but at him. As the figure closed and the cenopost flames flushed his features, Omar saw the madness in his face. Mindless, animal fury. With teeth bared like a snarling mongrel and sunken, bloodshot eyes, the cemetery worlder came at him.

'Halt!' Omar ordered, but the boom of his voice did nothing to the wretch. He came straight at him, leaping at the Excoriator as one might scale a statue. Omar's boot came out in a simple but brutal front kick. The Certusian's face cracked and he flew back towards the floor. With his shoulders striking flat into the grit, the man slid a little way through the gore before coming to a chest-heaving stop. Omar spun around and put the heel of his other boot across the madman's neck, positioning his toe-tip against his chin.

The Certusian's nose was now but a bloody crater in his face. Omar knew such a kick could have killed the mortal and should at least have knocked consciousness from him. There he was, however, spitting up teeth and gobbets of tongue that he'd bitten off. Something primal within the wretch would not let go, and before the Scout knew it, the lunatic was scratching and tearing at his boot like a rabid dog.

Brother Omar had heard of unfortunates afflicted with xenos infections and the infamous Zombie Plague, but the wretch seemed to demonstrate no evidence of alien contamination or living death. Inside his scrawny ribcage a lean heart beat with rage; blood boiled through his veins; his eyes crackled with single-minded, murderous desire. Nor was the cemetery worlder enthralled or possessed by some denizen of the warp. His wrath was all his own. Omar could only reason that the Keeler Comet, blazing its bloody path through the Certusian skies, had some part to play in the strange phenomenon.

Looking up, Omar's enhanced vision detected further movement in the darkness. Smoke swirls and shadow overlapping shadow that betrayed the presence of more figures in the gloom. A horde of maniacs, blank and spent, wandering about the grave stones and cemetery fields, spleen-fired to instant rage by the sight of the Excoriator. He heard the unintelligible, glottal rasp of bestial intention and watched the first of the psychotics break ranks. They streamed towards him through the smoke – one, then two; ten, twenty, many more. The lychway was suddenly swamped with the running wretches, accompanied by others, scrambling across the gravestones, statues and stone sarcophagi of the burial grounds.

Omar snorted. Words would be of little use here. Twisting his foot, he broke the neck of the wretch beneath his boot. The man's limbs suddenly spasmed and then fell. Satisfied that the maniac was dead and not some necromantic puppet, the Scout stomped back to his bike. Slipping his combat shotgun from its holster on the bike subframe, Omar worked the pump action. The weapon was a work of squat inelegance. From the brute curves of its stock, through the angularity of its breech and barrel and the yawning darkness of its muzzle, the shotgun was a monster. Bringing the stock to his shoulder, the Scout brought the weapon up to face the oncoming horde.

The first wretched specimen, a gaunt-faced fosser, simply vanished in the path of the blast – turning into a bloody smear on the darkness. This did not dissuade a feral vestal, who surged past the gruel before Omar took her legs out from beneath her with a second shot. A hearsier lost his head to the shotgun, followed by three further cemetery worlders cut to ribbons by fat pellets of scattershot. Brother Omar worked the pump-action on his weapon, calmly hammering the front line of the fast-advancing mob. As the shotgun clunked its emptiness, Omar brought his eye out from behind its sights to watch the second wave of maniacs run through the remains of the first and fly at him. From over his shoulder the Scout heard screams. These were not the shrieks of shock members of the cavalcade had made upon discovering the carnage at Little Amasec. The cavalcade was under attack.

Thumbing shells into the breech of the shotgun, Brother Omar backed towards his squat-set vehicle and re-mounted. Thumbing the gimbal lock on the handlebars, the Scout pulled the triggers on both grips. The belt-fed boltguns mounted on the front of the bike jerked to rhythmic life.

Omar swept the next line of gall-fevered crazies, aiming low and chopping through knees and groins with his automatic fire. The wretches tumbled and fell, creating a hurdle upon which much of the next wave faltered, falling themselves. Omar swept back across the line. The maniac cemetery worlders had looked up at the Excoriator with red eyes and hatred as they scrambled to pick themselves up. The Scout replied with bolt-rounds to the head as one by one, along the line of the prone and fallen, he split skulls and blew off faces. A verger, still wearing his cocked-hat and smashed spectacles, cleared the corpse mound with a half-naked hearsier close behind. Twisting the handlebars, Omar cut the pair in two with a savage stream of bolt-fire.

With the first few waves of maniacs put down and the darkness beyond giving birth to an unending horde of murderous unfortunates, Brother Omar secured the gimbal lock on his handlebars and revved the bike's heavy engine. Wheel-spinning around and spraying the livid masses with blood and grit, the Scout tore back across the crossroad at the source of the screaming. A curtain of sodden cemetery world earth followed the bike as Omar shot across Little Amasec, swerving shacks and hovels before blasting through the black and burning remains of the cenopost's tiny market. With flames licking at his wheels, Omar hit the crowded lychway.

The cavalcade of Certusians were fleeing. Some were heading into the deserted hamlet but most were climbing for their lives across headstones and graven sculptures. Like a spooked herd they had bolted off the lychway together, away from a roaring horde of degenerates who were scrabbling across the crowded cemetery architecture on the other side of the road like animals. Several fossers tried to stand their ground with picks and shovels, but went down under sheer savagery and weight of numbers. With the fossers having their eyes gouged and throats torn out by their fellow Certusians, Omar resolved to give the escaping cavalcade every chance to get away from the berserk and blood-crazed.

As the cemetery worlders he was escorting were melting into the burial grounds, Omar had the luxury of the lychway largely to himself. Clutching at the triggers and with muzzles flashing, the Excoriator cut down the degenerates throwing themselves mindlessly across the road at the fleeing cavalcade. Bodies and body parts bounced off the Scout and the front of the bike as he surged through the bloody mist he was creating. Slamming home the brakes, Omar turned and skidded around, taking the legs out from two more crazies. As the bike came to a stop, he slid his shotgun from its side-holster and began blowing growling wretches from the prone forms of the felled fossers. The neophyte was too late to save the gravediggers, however, the fevered degenerates having already ripped their victims' bodies to shreds.

Holstering the emptied combat shotgun, Omar surged up the lychway at the hordes spilling out onto the grit. Once again the Excoriator let rip with his twin boltguns, cutting a gory path through the mob and providing a barrier of explosive firepower behind which members of the cavalcade could flee for their lives. The neophyte thought about voxing for assistance. One of his brother Scouts could not be more than an hour's ride away. He also considered calling for one of the Fifth's Thunderhawks to provide air support and an evacuation for the fleeing cavalcade of cemetery worlders. He discounted the thoughts almost immediately. He would not be a burden to his squad, his whip or his company. The cavalcade's safety had fallen to the Scout and the Scout alone. The wretches about him were mindless savages; they were great in number but only mortal, and they were his enemy to vanquish.

Rather than the Certusians, the seething rabble were now very much intent on venting their quenchless wrath on the Space Marine. A whippet-like child leapt from an angelic statue with thoughtless abandon, landing on the Excoriator's shoulders and clawing into his carapace and face with her sharp nails. The momentum almost unbalanced the Scout who took to snatching at his back with one hand. This cut his firepower in half. Although the single, mounted boltgun continued to acquit itself in ploughing through the lean bodies of the savages, it failed to stop a stonecutter who dashed his head with the opportunistic swing of a recovered shovel or a pair of madmen running an abandoned cart into the path of the oncoming bike.

The bike's front wheel began to waver, and with only one hand on the handlebars and blood streaming down into his eyes from the gash on his forehead, Brother Omar strayed onto the burial ground verge. The bike smashed through two headstones before striking a sarcophagal monument at high speed. Omar flew off the bike and over the stone architecture. He felt his legs pass over his shoulders and the back of his head smack through the top of another grave marker. The Scout finally struck the base of a saint's statue with a bone-quaking jolt before coming to rest, upside down – his head askew and shoulders on the ground, while his back and legs rested against the side of the plinth.

Taking a few moments for himself, Brother Omar blinked sense back into his being. He could see the broken body of the crazed child nearby. She had not survived the crash. Shapes were moving in the darkness about him. Blood-mental savages, intent on slaughter. Within seconds the Excoriator was buried in pummelling fists, eye-scratching claws and stamping boots. There were lank bodies everywhere. The horde – like a school of predatory fish or a flock of raptors, redirecting their path – were upon him.

The frenzy continued. Rolling around and getting his boots firmly on the ground, Omar pushed for the sky. Degenerates rained about him, tumbling from the blood-furious mound they had formed. Shaking a ragged usher from his shoulder, Omar brought up his bolt pistol – freshly drawn from his belt. Single bolts thudded through the foreheads and faces of the savages. He spun around, felling the mob gathered about him. As a chorister scrambled to right himself, the Scout shot his jaw off before turning and grabbing the usher – who had flown back at the Excoriator with his bad teeth bared – burying the bolt pistol in his stomach and sending the last of the bolts through the unfortunate.

The pistol was empty, but it had bought him a few moments. In the distance, Brother Omar could hear fresh screams of the dying. The screeches and calls for help were coming from the cavalcade, who had escaped the horde that had come down on him but had seemingly ran into another, prowling the necroscape and moving in like wolves on the commotion at the cenopost. Omar couldn't imagine how many groups of cemetery world refugees had wandered into the bloodbath trap that was Little Amasec.

There were degenerate Certusians everywhere, in front and behind. Omar had stirred up a nest of stingwings in announcing his bombastic resistance with the shotgun and bike. Wretches from both the burial grounds and the crossroads were coming at him. All Omar knew was the gnashing of blood-stained teeth and the thuggish barrage of fists and feet that the mob threw at him. The savages even came from above, with maniacs so desperate for a piece of the Scout that they climbed up the backs of their compatriots and leapt at him. Taller than all of them, Omar commanded a view of his enemy, a sea of madmen and mayhem as far as he could see into the darkness. Omar was angry at himself. He'd underestimated the mortals' numbers.

He had no time to reload the pistol; besides, he needed a weapon that took life at a faster pace and didn't rely on ammunition. Brother Omar unsheathed his combat knife. Neophytes trained with the honourable gladius but were not deemed worthy of an Adeptus Astartes blade until they attained the rank of Space Marine. With its clip point, cross guard, machete-length and cleaver-like cutting blade, a 'Scout's-only-friend' – as Squad Whip Keturah called them – was still a graceful taker of lives.

Brother Omar slashed and hacked through the wall of rabid flesh. He clipped heads and limbs from torsos; he cut blades from shovels and improvised clubs in half; he sliced, speared and stabbed, gutted and butchered his way through the horde. His cloak was heavy with gorespill and the ivory sheen of his Scout carapace was stained claret-red with the sheer volume of blood gushing, spraying and spurting about him. Wiping blood from his eyes all he could see were further faces, screwed up with malice presenting eyes that glinted murder.

Omar's blade suddenly hit something solid. Something that didn't slice like flesh or merely tug at the blade like cleaved bone. The Scout had swung with all his superhuman might and struck stone. The combat blade had cut into the corner of a gargoyle-encrusted vault, a small building in the shadow of which the melee had raged. Surrounded as he was, the ringing up his arm was the first the neophyte had known of the crypt entrance. When a flick of the wrist failed to retract the broadness of the blade, Omar tugged on the hilt with both hands. The stone refused to surrender the blade, however, and once again the degenerates closed in. Teeth sank through his field smock and into the flesh of his arm, while his carapace back presented the savages with an irresistible opportunity. The Scout soon felt the weight of scores of the maniacs on him, and looking up, watched more scrawny shadows tumble down to join them from the vault roof.

Releasing the blade, Omar snatched at the wretches and tossed them away. Others he brained with his fists and tore limb from limb. Stumbling about like a hunchback under the sheer weight of crazies with their teeth and nails in him, the Scout began to buckle. A wretched specimen bit into his ear and ripped it off, prompting the Space Marine to clench his head in one fist. Omar took the degenerate's skull and hammered it into the crypt wall, pounding it until it shattered, crumbled and spilled its insides like an egg. The masses moved this way and that about him, each blood-mental savage wanting Adeptus Astartes blood on their hands.

Omar suddenly lost his footing, the ground seeming to disappear beneath him. Falling onto his back with literally hundreds of squirming and thrashing degenerates, the Scout came to the conclusion that he had tumbled into a hole. A freshly dug grave. A common enough sight on the cemetery world. There, with teeth in his thigh-flesh, arms and bloody face – with murderous hands around his neck, tearing at and under his shredding carapace – Brother Omar, Scout Marine and Excoriator, realised his fate. To be buried alive in mortal flesh and to be slowly clawed and mauled to his death.

CHAPTER ELEVEN
BY THE BLADE

ZACHARIAH KERSH STOOD atop the tower-steeple of the Basilica of Our Lady of the Sepulchre. It was much higher than the tiny hermitage tower of the Excoriators' dormitory. It had the second tallest spire and the best vantage point in the city. The tallest – the Obelisk – had suffered too much structural damage during the Scourge's battle with the daemon, and Pontifex Oliphant had given the order for his Ecclesiarchical palace to be carefully demolished. The colossal dome of the Umberto II Memorial Mausoleum commanded the best view in the city, but Palatine Sapphira of the Order of the August Vigil had forbidden use of the sacred site as a strategic consideration, the building and the remains of the Ecclesiarch and High Lord of Terra within rendering the ground holy. It wouldn't have taken Kersh much to countermand the Sister and force his agenda, but he needed the Adepta Sororitas onside and so allowed the Palatine the illusion of a refusal.

From a maintenance portico, with a pair of magnoculars to his one useful eye, Kersh surveyed the declining roof-line of domes, cupolas, spires, monuments and bell-gables that gave Obsequa City its distinct Ecclesiarchical character. Kersh looked out across the darkness, dialling through the optical spectra of the device. A thermographic representation of the city bleared into view. There were fires everywhere. Running battles between psychotic mobs and the Certusian Charnel Guard could be seen in the streets, the telltale glares of las-fire revealing the true scale of the problem. Kersh could hear the bark of enforcer shotguns even in the streets nearby and imagined Kraski's men putting down fellow Certusians with scattershot and bitterness.

Out across the expanse of Necroplex-South, Kersh could see the throngs of cemetery worlders, with simple lanterns and flaming torches dotted through their numbers, pouring into the city along arterial lychways. Kersh had sanctioned the strategy but that wouldn't have mattered. With the reports he was receiving regarding the nightmarish barbarism afflicting the burial ground communities, the corpus-captain had fully expected common Certusians to flock to the seeming safety of the planetary capital. Whether this was due to the spiritual sanctity they expected the relic-remains of the Ecclesiarch to provide, or the simple security offered by stone walls and thick narthex doors, was unclear. They had arrived in their thousands, and continued to do so. Much of the Charnel Guard were engaged in urban pacification and hastily organised 'Misery Squads' – so called for their unhappy duty of hunting and putting out of their misery cemetery worlders who had succumbed to the gall-fever and become a danger to themselves and other citizens. This left few ceremonial Guardsmen to man the city Lych Gates and process the stream of Certusian refugees. In response Kersh had despatched the Fifth Company's serfs and bondsmen – including his own – to take charge of the admittance and temporary housing of the masses in the crowded city.

Kersh tracked the powerful lamps of a Scout bike surging up along the columns of cemetery worlders towards the city. Lifting the magnoculars at the roar of engines overhead, he watched the Thunderhawk *Impunitas* pass above the city and bank. With all three of the company's remaining gunships now repaired and at his disposal, Kersh had ordered one standing by on the rockrete of the Memorial Space Port, one to remain with the *Angelica Mortis* in orbit and one to maintain constant airborne patrols of Obsequa City and the surrounding necroplex.

Lowering the magnoculars, Kersh turned his head. Beneath his boots he could feel the supernatural cooling of the stone. He heard it cracking and blistering. Behind him stood the revenant in its ghoulish black plate, rippling with the rachidian contours of rib and bone. It waited like a thing eternal, as though it had all the time in the universe.

'Ready?' the Scourge said finally and disappeared through the maintenance arch followed by his solemn and silent haunter.

Down in the basilica nave, surrounded by pillars crafted in the baroque likeness of Imperial saints, and under the stained-glass gloom of the God-Emperor sat upon the Golden Throne in lead-lined representation, the corpus-captain had called a gathering. Kersh walked past Erasmus Oliphant, the young pontifex holding his crippled side awkwardly in the simple throne his frater menials had brought in for his comfort. Palatine Sapphira stood by his side, flanking the throne with two of her cobalt-plated Sisters, each armed with their distinctive Godwyn-Deaz-pattern bolters. Behind them huddled a small group of confessors, priests and deacons who were either too loyal to their pontifex to flee, or had been too late to arrange passage off-world with their Adeptus Ministorum colleagues. Kersh heard the hurried scuff of boots on the polished marble floor of the basilica, noting a shabby and tired-looking Proctor Kraski and Colquhoun's replacement, Lord Lieutenant Laszlongia, enter the chamber via a side-arch.

With the mortals to his back, the corpus-captain stepped out before his Excoriator brothers. Kersh had assembled the significants of the Fifth Company, as well as the silver-haired squad whip of the Tenth Company Scouts, Silas Keturah. The whips of Squads Cicatrix, Castigir and Censura all stood in assembly, with squad second whips standing behind them. Uriah Skase held himself with unusual stiffness, his shoulders reclined, chestplate thrust forwards and fingers interlaced behind his back. Kersh wasn't fooled by the chief whip's seeming respect and attention. The Scourge had seen the stance before and had indeed indulged in it himself. It came from a rawness and sensitivity of the back, where flesh itself had been flayed during the worst of 'the purge's' attentions. As Kersh suspected, Skase had continued to punish himself – pushing ritual observance beyond its primarch-communing function and into the dark realms of a shame-cycle and flagellation for flagellation's sake. Whips Ishmael and Joachim demonstrated no such deference, pretend or otherwise, and instead busied themselves with furtive glances and conspiratorial mutterings between themselves and the second whips.

Kersh stood, anger slowly building in the tautness of his scarred face as he waited for the squad whips to present themselves to their corpus-captain. While they did, with insolent tardiness, the Scourge's eye fell across Ezrachi and the skull-helmed Chaplain Shadrath on the opposite side of the nave. Keturah was with them. Last in line was Techmarine Dancred with his Thunderfire cannon, *Punisher*, which seemed to follow him everywhere. Only the Librarian, Melmoch, was missing. Brother Micah, the company champion's young face a nest of cuts, stitches and bruising, took his position at his corpus-captain's side. Beside him was Brother Novah, Brother Toralech's hasty replacement as company standard bearer. Young, like Micah, but quiet and uncertain, Novah held the battered and tattered standard of the Excoriators Fifth Company in one hand. Micah had assured Kersh that he was a first class warrior, and having originally fought in the same squad as the champion, was one of the few brothers he could trust. In the darkness of the aisle, the armoured revenant melted into the shadows.

'Brothers,' the corpus-captain began, 'I have gathered you here to share my resolutions, so that we may commit to a course of action and see it through.'

'Rumour has it,' Skase interrupted, his voice echoing about the basilica's columns, 'that we are abandoning our pursuit of the renegade Alpha Legion and pointlessly garrisoning this pile of grave dust.' Murmurs of assent proceeded from the Excoriators about him.

Kersh would not be drawn.

'Chief whip, I have called members of this company to order and you will respect that.'

'I only–'

'Hold your tongue, damn it!' Kersh roared at him. 'When I want your insights I will be sure to ask for them. In the meantime you will act in accordance with your rank and responsibility, sir.'

The chief whip tensed and bridled, but Kersh saw Ishmael grab at his wrist. Skase shook free of the squad whip's grasp but remained silent, his jaw rigid with anger and eyes glistening.

With similar difficulty, the corpus-captain continued.

'The *Angelica Mortis* confirms that the Keeler Comet has passed Certus-Minor. I think we can assume that the comet's infernal influence is responsible for the mayhem and bloodshed on the planet surface. The cemetery world will pass through the comet's tail in the next eighteen hours, however, and only the Emperor knows what might happen then. Long range sensors and pict-scans confirm that an enemy armada has reached the outskirts of the system, trailing the comet at sub-light speed. We can assume this to be the Cholercaust Blood Crusade. We have little intelligence to go on in respect of the armada's numbers or composition. I won't lie to you. No world has survived the Cholercaust's attentions. The dead tell no tales. Estimates vary wildly from fifty to a thousand vessels. The Imperial Navy has verified sightings of cruisers belonging to the World Eaters...' Kersh allowed confirmation of their dread enemy to sink in before continuing. 'So we can assume Traitor Legionaries to be at the head of their numbers.'

The clockwork whir of Brother Dancred's face preceded

the Techmarine's contribution. 'You intend the Fifth Company to remain on Certus-Minor?'

Kersh paused.

'I do, brother.'

A ripple of discontent washed through the squad whips and their seconds. 'Corpus-Commander Bartimeus's estimates place the Keeler Comet on a trajectory for the Segmentum Solar. We cannot afford the Blood Crusade's further progression, nor allow its strength to grow by another conquered world. Not with Ancient Terra as a possible future target.'

'What about the Vanaheim Cordon?' Squad Whip Joachim ventured, his young eyes boring into the corpus-captain.

'Be under no illusion,' Kersh told them all, 'the decision to stay is mine and mine alone. I will not surrender this part of the Emperor's Imperium, no matter how small, to the Ruinous Powers – nor will I abandon the Emperor's subjects, those who we were bred to protect, to torment and certain slaughter. This is, of course, largely academic. We have no astropath to call for reinforcement and without a Navigator, we cannot reinforce the Vanaheim Cordon with our own numbers.'

'The *Avignor Star*?' Ezrachi asked.

'Their Navigator is dead,' Kersh informed the Apothecary. 'He inexplicably started bleeding from his mouth, his ears and his eyes. The ship's surgeon tried his best but the Navigator could not be saved.'

'The *Angelica Mortis* could make short-range jumps,' Dancred said.

'Yes,' Kersh agreed. 'And I have spoken with Corpus-Commander Bartimeus on the matter, but I have another destination for the strike cruiser. In the meantime, we have to face the reality of an imminent attack. With our number we can only afford to hold one strategic location and the city is our only real option. Pontifex Oliphant and I have arranged the recall of all Certusians from burial grounds and communities across the planet surface. They have made and continue to make their way here under the instruction of the Tenth Company Scouts. Whip Keturah, I believe you still have a number of your contingent outstanding.'

Silas Keturah fixed his corpus-captain with his single bionic eye.

'Brothers Taanach, Omar and Iscarion are still outstanding,' Keturah reported. He nodded his acknowledgement to the Techmarine beside him. 'Brother Iscarion reported issues with the vitality of his vehicle's machine-spirit.'

'I will apply the necessary oils and benedictions,' Dancred assured the squad whip.

'Taanach and Omar have made no vox contact,' Keturah informed the Scourge. 'Which is unusual.'

Kersh nodded his agreement. 'Go out with the *Impunitas*. Find them, Silas. We will need every brother in the dark hours to come.'

'You have a battle plan?' Ezrachi asked.

'One that was good enough to serve our ancestral brothers and parent Legion at the walls of the Imperial Palace,' Kersh told him. 'Brother Dancred will oversee the demolition of all buildings on the city exterior.' The Scourge paused, turned and looked at the young pontifex. He expected the ecclesiarch to offer some objection regarding the ancient lineage of the buildings or the holiness of the ground upon which they were to be collapsed. Oliphant hesitated and then nodded. The pontifex had seen up close the monstrous enemy that the Excoriators would be facing. 'We'll assume that an attack could come from any and all directions. The necroplex itself will impede large vehicles and slow the progress of mass charges on the city. There our bolters will do their worst.'

Several Excoriators nodded in grim appreciation. 'Rubble mounds from the collapsed architecture will provide cover and elevation for our shooters, but more importantly an unbroken perimeter obstacle for our assailants should we have to fall back to the next line of buildings.'

'What about the remaining citizenry?' Oliphant asked through one side of his mouth.

Kersh hesitated. 'The city is small but we simply do not

have enough Excoriators, Charnel Guard and Adepta Sororitas to hold the line alone,' he said.

'You don't have any Adepta Sororitas,' Palatine Sapphira informed him with cool conviction. 'My Sisters and I will be in the vault below the Memorial Mausoleum with the relic remains of his Reverence, Umberto II.'

'I need your bolters on that perimeter.'

'You can't have them. I'm sorry.'

The Excoriator and Sister looked hard at each other.

'You will be when we're overrun by the enemy.'

'You have your orders, corpus-captain, and I have mine.'

'My orders invariably focus on saving the living.'

'I'm afraid mine don't,' Sapphira told him harshly. 'That many might fall today is regrettable, but nothing compared to the comfort and spiritual fortitude Umberto II's sacred bones will give to future billions. See, corpus-captain – you must worry about the living but I must look to the yet to live.'

Kersh's lip curled. He would get nowhere with the Sisters of the August Vigil.

'The cemetery worlders will have to provide the extra coverage,' Kersh said with regret.

'And how do you propose they do that?' Palatine Sapphira came back at him. Her voice was cold and cautious.

'We will arm them from the city auxiliary armouries,' the corpus-captain returned.

'Impossible, that's–' Oliphant piped up, half out of his throne and tripping over his words.

'Heresy,' said Sister Sapphira, supplying the word for him. 'That would break the *Decree Passive*. Should we survive the oncoming Cholercaust, we would all simply be executed for treason of faith.'

Kersh nodded, recalling his time at St Ethalberg.

'Which is why Laszlongia would recruit them as Charnel Guard conscripts. They would be probitors, whiteshields – under the command of the lord lieutenant and the pontifex only in his role as planetary governor.'

'I don't like it,' Sapphira said after a short pause. 'It still smacks of insidiousness.'

'I'm not asking you to like it,' Kersh bit back. 'And I'd simply call it expedience.' He looked to the freshly promoted leader of the Certusian Charnel Guard.

'My lord, you want to draft the citizenry into the ceremonial defence force?'

'No,' Kersh told him. 'That's what I want you to do. I'm sure under the severity of the circumstances, the Departmento Munitorum would hypothetically approve such measures.'

Proctor Kraski seemed to consider the proposal. The grizzled arbitrator finally said, 'These here cemetery worlders are mainly diggers and labourers. Many can't read and write anything beyond the most basic prayers. You've got a lot of women and children. None of the men have any combat experience.'

'Would they know which end of a lasfusil was the most dangerous?' Kersh put to the enforcer.

'I expect so,' Kraski said, chewing on his tobacco.

'Well as long as they point that end in the general direction of the enemy, I'll be happy.' The Scourge looked from Kraski and the lord lieutenant to Oliphant. 'The women and children can form a prayer cordon inside the perimeter.'

Pontifex Oliphant's gaze moved about the floor. The ecclesiarch looked deeply unhappy and as though he were going to vomit on the basilica floor.

'The Sister is right. The *Decree Passive* is not an obstacle to be circumvented. It is the God-Emperor's law.'

'Whether you designate them so or not,' Kersh told him, 'the Certusian people are your defence force. When the enemy attacks, they will have to fight for their lives. All I'm asking is that they also fight for everyone else's. Pontifex, does not the God-Emperor fight on their side?'

The pontifex searched his soul and looked up at the dull stained-glass window above them. 'Yes,' he said tightly and left it at that.

'These backwater wretches against the damned berserkers of the XIIth Legion?' Skase said with ill-disguised scorn. 'You might as well offer them up on an altar to the Blood God yourself.'

'There is another consideration,' Ezrachi said, eager to take Kersh's attention off the provocative Skase.

'Apothecary?'

'With so many losing their minds to this gall-fever, is it wise to indiscriminately arm the population?'

'Do we know anything more of this madness?' the corpus-captain asked.

'Only that it isn't physiological,' the Apothecary replied. 'And it doesn't seem transmissible like a virus or infection. It is a malady of the mind. Men are no more susceptible than women, young no more than the old. All we do know is that the mental transformation from Certusian to savage is unpredictable, swift and that the first symptom is usually murderous bloodshed. I suspect it is some psychological condition brought on by the comet, but that is not for me as Apothecary to say.'

'The lord lieutenant here is simply going to have to exercise his judgement. I suppose a cure is too much to hope for?'

Ezrachi grunted. 'The same as for life, a bolt-round, administered to the heart or brain.'

'What about our number?' Kersh asked.

'Beyond reports of brief visions and disturbed sleep, we seem unaffected. This is probably due to cult observance and psychoindoctrination, but again, I can't know. I can run further tests.'

'That won't be necessary,' the corpus-captain said. 'I have a different duty for you to perform.'

'Sir?'

'Without delay I want you to begin extraction rites and harvest mature progenoid glands from all Excoriators with at least ten years' service to the Chapter,' the Scourge said gravely. The announcement was met with an immediate wall of shock, discontent and objection from the company whips and their seconds.

'Kersh?' Ezrachi said, falling out of formality.

'We are facing an enemy infamous for its intolerance of survivors.'

'You prepare for our failure,' Squad Whip Joachim accused.

'We are attrition fighters. We battle with the best but prepare for the worst. If we are faced with failure – and by Katafalque's blood, I hope that we are not – then we should meet our doom knowing that our legacy lives on through the genetic heritage we bequeath. We do this in the best interests of the Chapter and not ourselves. I do not ask this of you, Dorn does – so that the Imperium's future, as well as its present, might be secure.'

'How would we do this?' Ezrachi asked bleakly.

'You would transport the collected gene-seed to the *Angelica Mortis* and oversee its safe storage and containment. The sacred seed would then travel on to the forge-world of Aetna Phall.'

'Aetna Phall?'

'It's nearby,' Kersh explained, 'and reachable through the series of short warp jumps Brother Dancred alluded to.'

'That will take months, this close to the Eye,' the Apothecary informed him.

'Yes,' Kersh agreed. 'But the Adeptus Mechanicus will appreciate the importance of the cargo and have the resources to see it on to Eschara. You would, of course, be there to impress such necessity upon them.'

'You want me to accompany the seed?'

'Our only Apothecary?' Ishmael scathed. 'And the company strike cruiser? This is madness.'

'It is time you fully appreciated the nature of the foe you face,' the corpus-captain told the squad whips gravely. 'The Blood God's servants do not orchestrate and strategise. They have no knowledge of failure – only success or the eternal darkness. They do not wound and incapacitate, attack and withdraw. Victory, both personal and galactic, is everything to them. They live for the death of their enemies and think on nothing but their blades steaming with warrior blood. There will be little for Apothecary Ezrachi to do here, once the fighting begins a-proper. As for the *Angelica Mortis* – what do you think the Cholercaust will do with her? The Chaos armada will crush the cruiser like a ration can. Which is why Corpus-Commander Bartimeus and the good Apothecary will see our future safely to the Mechanicus forge-world.'

'I have heard enough,' Chief Whip Skase told the Scourge. 'It seems like you have our decimation pretty well planned out – from your decision that we should remain on this deadrock, to trapping us here without orbital support or transportation.'

'My lord, the Adeptus Ministorum monitor *Apotheon* and several system ships remain,' Pontifex Oliphant reminded the Excoriator, but Skase ignored the ecclesiarch.

'Does this strike anyone else as particularly suicidal?' the chief whip continued. 'Is this the quality of tactical advice you gave to the Chapter Master on Ignis Prime? Haven't the Alpha Legion made us pay deeply enough for your failures? Was Ichabod and the loss of the Stigmartyr not enough for you?'

'He's corpus-captain,' Silas Keturah called coldly from the other side of the nave, 'by Ichabod's order.'

'And was not Horus made Warmaster by the Emperor's?'

The basilica fell to silence before the heretical suggestion of the chief whip's statement.

'You stand here,' Kersh rumbled, stepping forth, 'in this holy place, casting aspersions, feeding your fury and sowing the seed of discord in this company…'

'If the Fifth had been mine, we would already have your lost Stigmartyr back in our possession and our plate would be speckled with traitor blood.'

'And I think that you'd either be standing on Rorschach's World scratching your head or in a pool of your own blood after walking into what even a child could see to be an obvious trap,' Kersh bawled at him. 'The Alpha Legion are serpents. They only allow you to know what they want you to know. You cannot trust such intelligence. It is either an ambush or a ruse to draw us away from our true duty.'

'This is not our duty!' Skase growled.

'Yes, it is,' the Apothecary interjected. 'You were not there on St Ethalberg. We are bound by ancient pacts and promises, as was our Chapter Master. We serve Quesiah Ichabod and must honour his word, as you must honour your corpus-captain's.'

'Words...' Skase marvelled. 'You talk about words and dusty tracts. I'm talking about our Chapter's honour and the blood of our enemies on our blades.'

'Make no mistake,' Kersh told the chief whip. 'They are one and the same. What we fought in the palace was our enemy. Some kind of daemonic harbinger, heralding the bloodshed to come. You would have us run from that? Flee to safety, leaving mere mortals to face the servants of the Dark Gods alone? What would that do for our Chapter's honour?'

'You twist my words, Kersh – for you have no honest ones of your own. I will not take lessons in my Chapter's honour from the likes of you. The Scourge, who failed his Chapter Master, who surrendered our beloved Stigmartyr to the enemy and routinely surrenders himself to his shameful affliction. And while Dorn himself curses you with his Darkness, Chaplain Shadrath runs the company by proxy.'

'You go too far, Uriah,' the Chaplain hissed.

'We have not gone far enough,' Skase insisted vehemently. 'We need leadership. Not the fatalistic fantasies of a coward, unworthy to wear Katafalque's symbol and colours. A failure, who wishes to sacrifice this company on the altar of his guilt and bring the taint of the Darkness to us all.'

'Skase–' Shadrath began.

'I think that the last time I allow you to question my courage,' Kersh told him through gritted teeth.

'Well think on, Scourge,' Skase shot back, taking a step towards the corpus-captain. 'I demand Trial by the Blade.'

The vaulted chamber echoed with Skase's challenge.

'The corpus-captain has more than proved himself in the Feast,' Ezrachi shouted.

'Not to me,' the chief whip said, slapping his boltgun against Ishmael's chestplate to take. 'And not to this company – who were denied representation due to our commitments on Vieglehaven – clearing up the Scourge's mess. Perhaps the other attendant Chapters were easier to impress.'

Brother Micah stepped forwards to present himself, the company champion's eyes fixed on Skase and hungry for battle.

'Micah, no,' Kersh said softly, laying a gauntlet on his shoulder.

'This Excoriator has forgotten himself and his proper station,' the young Micah replied, not taking his eyes off the chief whip. 'Let me put him in his place.'

Kersh shook his head.

'This is an act of sedition,' Ezrachi warned. 'A mutinous revolt against the authority of your corpus-captain.'

'I plot no more insurrection than the Warmaster's lieutenants did when they refused to join his ranks and fought for their distant Emperor,' Skase told the Apothecary. 'Besides, I encourage nothing more than company fealty in my squad. This is a personal grievance. As such, I have the right – as Excoriators and Dorn's Fists before me – to settle such disputes through the solemn contestation of a duel. My face will attest to the honour I have taken – and in my youth given – in such rituals.'

'You would do this now, with the arch-enemy at our gates?' Kersh said, shaking his head.

'And now so would you,' Skase told him, unsheathing his bolt pistol and handing it to his second whip. 'For I see my accusations hit home. It would be a dishonour to bear them, Scourge. You must fight me.'

Chaplain Shadrath turned his half-skull face to Kersh, who slowly nodded without looking at him.

'This is insane,' Ezrachi erupted.

'I must send for the blades,' the Chaplain hissed. Such duels were usually fought with ceremonial weapons retained in the company chapel-reclusiam. Kersh drew his Mark II pistol and unhooked his chainsword, giving them to the Apothecary and Brother Micah.

'No need,' the Scourge said walking forwards. 'We'll contend with what we have.'

Skase nodded his approval and drew his oiled gladius.

'My lords,' Oliphant called, getting to his feet. 'You cannot shed blood in the–' but Proctor Kraski put a hand on his shoulder and shook his grizzled head.

'The Rite has been invoked and it has been answered,' Chaplain Shadrath said, moving down the nave as Excoriators backed between pillars to give the combatants more room. From the shadows, the revenant watched with patient interest. 'Trial by the Blade. As all Excoriators are equal in Dorn's image, first blood goes to the victor, when blood is drawn from that image. Brothers will indicate their understanding.'

Kersh drew his relic-blade, taking several practise swings with the gladius. Both corpus-captain and chief whip acknowledged the Chaplain by kissing their right gauntlets.

'Begin,' Shadrath told them.

Skase was an ivory blur as he leapt at the Scourge with sword held high. As the blade came down, Kersh feigned a parry, only to slip out from under the cleaving motion. As Skase's gladius chipped the stone of the basilica floor, Kersh slapped the back of his head with the flat of his relic blade.

'You will have to do better than that, brother,' Kersh told him.

The needling comment had its desired effect. Skase came back at him, his gladius glinting its arcs and curves in the candlelit gloom of the basilica. Kersh remained poised, deflecting the blade's optimistic dance and arching his neck left and right to avoid the venomous stabbing motions the chief whip used to punctuate his spite-driven attacks. Indulging a towering parry, Kersh held the seething Skase at full stretch. Bringing up his left fist, he hammered his chief whip across the jaw before slashing back across his cheekbone with the knuckles of his gauntlet. Skase was battered back, sword in hand, but immediately brought his own fingertips to his face. Stepping closer, Chaplain Shadrath leant in to check for any evidence of blood, but there was none.

'Proceed,' the Chaplain barked, backing away once more. Kersh brought his blade in low, but the chief whip battered it aside with an angry grunt. The assault gained in furiousness and before long Skase's bladework began to lose its discipline. His lip wrinkled into a dogged, hate-fuelled snarl, and his gladius chopped and swept – demonstrating little interest in its target, the Scourge's duel-scarred face.

'Come on, meat!' Kersh called.

Backing from the onslaught, his relic blade barely managing to turn his opponent's aside, Kersh crashed through iron candelabra and shouldered a stone saint from his pedestal, sending him smashing simultaneously to Oliphant's horror and the floor. Rounding a column, the Excoriators committed further blasphemies on the pillar-representation of Saint Proulx. Razored edges sparked off crafted stone as the two Space Marines fought for the advantage. Eventually the rhythmic slashing broke and the Scourge's blade smacked Skase's into the pillar, pinning the weapon. Kersh's ceramite boot found the chief whip's exposed side. The bone-shuddering impact took Skase off the ground, his gauntlet slipping free of his sword hilt and his armoured body clattering across the flags of the nave.

The Scourge ran down on the unarmed Excoriator, eager to end the needless conflict. As the whip shook his head and lifted his face in momentary confusion, Kersh swept in to deliver a duelling scar that Skase would never forget.

Further clattering distracted the Scourge. Before him, gliding across the polished basilica floor, clinked Ishmael's blade. Squad Castigir's whip had drawn and slid his own gladius to his battle-brother, and before Kersh knew it the metal of the blade was scraping his ribs. Skase's thrust from the floor, combined with the force of Kersh running down on the blade had created force enough to slip the sword tip between two ceramite plates and puncture up through the Excoriator's black carapace. The clash had barely begun, however. Kersh instinctively wrapped a fist around the blade, preventing it from penetrating further. Skase was now on his feet, his face contorted with loathing and the physical effort required to drive the sword home. The whip had little trouble wrapping his gauntlet about Kersh's fist, which in turn had gone momentarily limp around the grip of his gladius. The two held each other in a feverish grip, paralysed like the statues about them, with their brothers looking on.

His craggy face creased with concern, Ezrachi moved in, but the Scourge shook his head stiffly, bringing the Apothecary to a pause. Skase's eyes burned with the knowledge that he held the advantage, and Kersh saw the satisfaction ripple across his features as he tried to twist his blade within the Scourge. The gladius screeched against the ceramite of Kersh's artificer armour. The corpus-captain fought the compulsion to cry out as the blade's length tore through his black carapace.

'Sir!' Brother Micah implored.

'No!' Kersh croaked with brutal defiance.

The Scourge's arm came once more to life, surprising Skase and wrapping around the chief whip's neck like a constricting serpent. The two fell in a messy embrace, Skase still holding on to both the Scourge's clutched sword and the weapon buried in his corpus-captain's midriff. The Excoriators rolled, roaring like animals, their plate clashing and the vaulted chamber filling with intermittent gasps of pain and exertion. They were soon tumbling back and forth, with plate and limb slapping through a gathering pool of the Scourge's blood. The desperate struggle painted carnage across the basilica floor, with Kersh's hold finally slipping on his own gore and off Skase's armour.

The pair rolled, Skase's blade turning inside the corpus-captain's torso. Kersh went over the chief whip and ended up with his back resting against the foot of one of the nave's many columns. Skase sat astride the bleeding Scourge, the corpus-captain's relic blade held between them. The chief whip's other hand still held its feverish grip on the gladius gutting his corpus-captain. Only Kersh's own pulverising hold on the blade prevented further tragedy. Skase snarled and pushed, forcing Kersh's own blade towards him. Leaning back against the pillar and into his pack, the Scourge quickly ran out of room to manoeuvre and could only watch the oiled length of the weapon edge towards him with cut-throat keenness.

'Chaplain!' Ezrachi called out.

'The conventions are clear,' Shadrath hissed, both Excoriators closing in with the rest of the gathering. 'First blood from the face.'

Skase's face quaked with the furious desire to win. He knew he had the Scourge and couldn't help a maniacal grin spreading across his ugly features.

'Do it, Uriah!' Squad Whip Ishmael roared from beside the column. He was joined in similar encouragement by Joachim and the squad seconds.

Skase's eyes flashed between Ishmael and Kersh; between his friend and his enemy. Unthinking, Skase leant into the thrust, putting his weight and hatred behind it. The blade shrieked through the corpus-captain's fingers. Kersh grunted as the gladius cross guard struck plate and the blade punched through his body and out his armoured back.

With his eyes wide open and his hand free, the Scourge grabbed the back of Skase's head. Ishmael and the seconds feasted on their corpus-captain's silent suffering and took the manoeuvre to be a death-grasp, a spasm of desperation.

'Let me take him,' Brother Micah called desperately – like a loyal hound, straining at his chain. Blinking and straining, Kersh shook his head.

Looking down on the gutted Scourge, Skase's mask began to fall. He hated Kersh, with every ounce of his being. He wanted to fight him. He wanted to best him. He didn't want to kill him. His knees resting in Kersh's blood, with a sword buried in his corpus-captain's flank – that was what he seemed to have done.

Skase suddenly felt his head thrust forwards. Kersh's relic blade glimmered between them, still clutched by the pair. With the Scourge's gauntlet grasping the back of his skull, Skase felt an irresistible pull forwards. Releasing the hilt of the gladius he reached out to stop himself, only to slip as his bloody gauntlet failed to find purchase. He finally slapped his palm against the stone column and pushed back, but it was too late. Kersh's blade remained rigid between them, held in their desperate hands. The Scourge's lip came up, showing bloodied teeth as he forced the chief whip's face towards the relic blade's edge. As they stared across the mirrored surface of the blade, spitting hatred at one another, the Scourge twisted Skase's head, the back of his tonsured scalp firmly in the corpus-captain's grip.

Kersh suddenly relented, allowing Skase to pull his head back a little. The chief whip's own natural inclination to relax followed a millisecond after, as the Scourge knew it would. Pulling Skase's head to the side, instead of forwards, the Scourge ran the Excoriator's already disfigured face along the blade's razored edge. The sword sliced through flesh, muscle, cartilage and scored bone. Kersh flung him to one side, this time Skase rolling through some of his own gore.

The Excoriators looked on in stunned silence. Oliphant and the other mortals present gawped in fear and horror. Leaning against the pillar, Kersh tried to kick against the blood-slick floor. He was trying to get on his feet and when he failed, settled for simply angling the point of his relic blade at the squad seconds, Joachim and Ishmael – whose own blade still impaled the corpus-captain.

Ezrachi slapped the Chaplain on the pauldron and advanced on Kersh, but wild-eyed and skewered, the Scourge turned the tip of the gladius towards the Apothecary. Prompted by Ezrachi, Shadrath hissed at the Fifth Company Excoriators.

'Stand down!'

After a moment's hesitation, their stabbing glares fell to the floor. 'The Trial is at an end. Honour has been both given and taken. First blood to the corpus-captain. Let it be recorded that at this time and in this place, he was the victor. To the bested, we honour his scars as he now honours his opponent with vindication.'

Silas Keturah was down on his knees, his carapace speckled with Skase's blood. The silver-haired Scout squad whip had torn Skase's loincloth from his belt and used it like a rag to staunch the bleeding. Kersh had cut the chief whip's face in half and the blood loss was considerable. The gathering looked to the prone Skase, with a bloody cloth to his face, to respond as the trial dictated. Keturah whispered proceedings into the chief whip's gore-blocked ear. Skase tensed. His gauntlets became fists. He squirmed before finally becoming still. Keturah put his ear to the sodden cloth. Finally, the faint murmurs of the smothered Skase could be heard. Silas Keturah raised his head. His cheek was bloody.

'The chief whip renounces his claims,' the Scout announced.

All eyes came back to the skewered Kersh. The Scourge had managed to get to his feet and clutched at the weapon imbedded in his side. Still leaning against the pillar he jabbed the tip of his own relic blade at the surrounding Excoriators.

'You think this a game?' he bawled. 'Is it not enough that there are thousands of degenerate maniacs at the system's edge, baying for Imperial blood? Must we spill each other's?'

The Scourge's harsh words echoed around the basilica. 'The fight is out there! This might be a pile of grave dust, but it is the Imperium, beneath our feet. I for one will not allow the Ruinous Powers principality here. They must take the air from my lungs, the blood from my body and the steel from my heart first. Now you will renounce your weakness – as your chief whip has. You will do as your corpus-captain has asked – as your Chapter Master has asked. You will fight here as though it were our Escharan home world or Ancient Terra beneath your boots. For if you don't, it very soon might need to be. You will give up your gene-seed or I will cut it out of you myself, that Excoriators more worthy than yourselves might take your place in the coming storm. Do you understand me, brothers?'

Kersh held their gaze before slipping and faltering slightly. Ezrachi dared wait no more.

'Kersh, you're bleeding to death,' Ezrachi said, sweeping in. He pushed the relic blade to one side and began attending to the grievous wound in the Scourge's side. The corpus-captain winced as the Apothecary manipulated the blade that sat snug in his flesh. The Scourge still held his own towards the gathered Adeptus Astartes.

'You want to see blood?' he told them finally. 'Well, you've come to the right place. You will see plenty of your own and each other's, if you continue as you are. The World Eaters will see to that. Make no mistake, they will ensure it.'

Kersh glared at his Excoriators. 'Dismissed'.

CHAPTER TWELVE
WOUND WITHIN A WOUND

WITH BROTHER MICAH under one arm and the Apothecary under the other, Kersh was helped to a tablet bunk in the hermitage. Ezrachi had set up one of the sanctuary chambers as a temporary apothecarion.

'I'm all right,' the corpus-captain had insisted moodily.

'You're bleeding like a stuck pig,' Ezrachi had carped back. Sat on the stone tablet, with Ezrachi and one of his Helixserfs exploring the wound and gathering instruments, the Scourge looked over to the only other occupied bunk in the apothecarion. The Epistolary, Melmoch, lay unconscious on the tablet, his chest rising and falling rhythmically. Bethesda entered the chamber, light on her toes, with concern and urgency in her eyes. 'Steel yourself, it's going to hurt.'

In one practised motion, the Apothecary withdrew the gladius skewering the Scourge's side. Kersh winced but remained silent. 'Probably not as much as when it went in though, eh?' Ezrachi chuckled, handing the bloody sword to Micah.

'My lord?' Bethesda said, but the Scourge was lost in thought.

'He'll live. As usual,' the Apothecary reassured her. 'Now make yourself useful, child, and get your master out of his sacred plate.'

This the absterge fell to immediately. Brother Micah turned the gore-smeared blade over in his hand.

'Don't you have anywhere else to be?' Ezrachi said with irritation. 'You could return that to Ishmael. I'm sure he'll be needing it again soon enough.' When Micah didn't answer, the Apothecary added, 'You think on the Trial? You think you would have done any better?'

'The corpus-captain won the duel. How could I do any better than that?' Micah said unhappily.

'Good answer,' Ezrachi replied, busy at work on the gushing wound.

'He's angry I didn't let him champion my cause,' Kersh said absently, still looking at Melmoch.

'I *am* your champion,' Micah said.

Kersh winced again. 'You can take the next blade destined for my belly. How's that? For now, I need you to find Brother Novah. Send him to me. I have orders to distribute. I need you out there. Ensure my orders are being followed. Oversee the beginning of the demolition. Work with the lord lieutenant and the Charnel Guard. I want recruits processed and armed. Establish emplacements, fire arcs and kill zones around the city perimeter. I want this city ready to defend itself. That is the cause – the company's cause – that I wish you to champion.'

'What of our number?'

'The Fifth Company's tactics will be more fluid and responsive to the nature, number and orientation of the threat presented. We need to expect anything. Go do your duty.'

'Yes, corpus-captain,' Micah replied. The champion stabbed the bloody gladius into a hermitage bench. 'Brother Ishmael can collect this himself,' he said with distaste, adopted his helmet and left.

As Bethesda stripped the Scourge of his plate, Ezrachi worked and his serfs stitched and stapled Kersh's insides back into some sense of order. The puncture in the black carapace, which fused his ribs together like a chestplate beneath his flesh, was harder to remedy. As the Apothecary completed the brief surgery and closed up the wound with a corkscrew needle, he gave the Scourge his report.

'I've administered growth hormone and applied a bonding agent – a surgical resin – to prevent further tearing along the carapace. The pain will fade over time. The resin will take an hour or so to set, so do your best to remain still.'

Bethesda held up the abdominal plate of ceramite through which the gladius had punched. 'Take that to Brother Dancred,' Ezrachi instructed.

'He has better things to do,' Kersh said suddenly. 'As do you, Apothecary.' Bethesda hesitated.

'Ask him for a temporary patch,' Ezrachi said. 'As I have performed on its wearer. The detail and artistry can wait – as indeed it does on the corpus-captain himself.'

'Where's Skase?' the Scourge demanded.

Ezrachi raised an eyebrow. 'Is he to be punished?'

'No,' Kersh said.

'He stabbed his commanding officer during a duel, an act it would not be unreasonable to characterise as treasonous or even an assassination attempt. He has dishonoured himself…'

'Then that will be punishment enough,' the Scourge shot back. 'That and a duty on this doomed world. Dishonoured or not, I can't spare a chief whip.'

'But I am to be spared such a duty?'

'Answer me. Where is Uriah Skase?'

'Being just as stubborn as you,' the Apothecary said. 'He probably has one of his squad stitching him up right now. You know how Excoriators are about their duelling scars. They're probably making a right grox's ear of it. You did, of course, almost cut his entire face off, so perhaps I'd better go check on him.'

'Fine,' the Scourge said. 'Begin with Skase and Squad Cicatrix. I want this company's gene-seed harvested and you off-world in the next five hours.'

Staring hard at the Scourge as his serf collected his instruments, Ezrachi nodded silently and then made for the exit. At the door he turned.

'You know, Kersh. Just because you got me into this mess, doesn't mean you're obliged to provide me a way out. Getting the seed to safety is a noble pursuit, but so is sharing the risk here and keeping it alive and well in you and your brothers.'

The Scourge turned to him. 'Aetna Phall. Then, Eschara. You leave with this company's legacy in five hours, Apothecary. I suggest you begin.'

Ezrachi's crabby lips curled in a weak smile and the Apothecary left.

Kersh sat there for a while in the peace and quiet of the hermitage sanctuary. His side ached. His mind whirled. Was this what the Emperor wanted for him and his Excoriators? Was this his duty? Or was he needlessly damning the brothers under his command to certain slaughter? He thought of the worlds on the Keeler Comet's path, and the Space Marines who must have been caught up in the trap sprung by its malign influence. The decision to run or fight. Was he fighting simply to avoid further accusations of cowardice or weakness? Was the Cholercaust his self-inflicted punishment – as Uriah Skase indulged the guilt of failure on Veiglehaven and the loss of his brothers, was he too castigating himself? As Skase had made himself live the excesses of the lash, was Kersh dooming himself and his brothers to a battle they certainly could not win? Or was he so desperate to win back his Master's love and trust after the affliction of the Darkness that he saw the Blood God's disciples as a test to be passed? Not the falsehood of games and trials, represented through the Feast of Blades or an honour duel. Would Kersh only be worthy to stand by his Chapter Master's side when he had faced the War-Given-Form and enough enemy blood had been spilt?

Holding his torso and slipping down from the tablet, Kersh took several steps and stretched his side a little. Perhaps real Adeptus Astartes captains knew nothing of the questions he'd asked himself. Perhaps in them, doubt was a distant memory of the past. He had presented a mask of confidence to his men; seemed sure in his orders – even in the face of their questioning; tried to earn his corpus-captaincy in word and deed. Yet, Zachariah Kersh felt the crushing uncertainty of fate spinning on a coin about him. Events were unfolding, irrespective of his unseemly doubts and out of his control. The mortals called them demigods, but in the harsh silence of that lonely moment, Kersh felt the emptiness of insignificance – deep like the darkness of space, a vast oblivion in which his fighting spirit guttered like a candle flame and unimportance was complete. Kersh felt cold and alone.

Standing as he was, he noticed for the first time an object on Melmoch's chest. Like that the Scourge had woken to find upon himself, the object was a card – a crystalline tarot wafer used by witchbreeds to present portents, divine futures and shed light on facets of the Emperor's will. Standing over the comatose Epistolary, Kersh picked up the card and turned it over in his fingers. On it was the representation of a colossal, rune-inscribed bell tower, imposing and ancient, with the dilapidated majesty of Terran hives stretching out beyond. The words *Campana Spiritus-Perditus* underscribed the illustration, but Kersh knew the image well. Every Adeptus Astartes did. It was the Bell of Lost Souls on Ancient Terra, housed in the Tower of Heroes, known to toll its doom-laden lament only at the death of true heroes of the Imperium.

Kersh felt cold. The unnatural absence of heat in the air. Looking up he saw the revenant, standing on the other side of the tablet, looking down at the psyker. With a sickening pause, the being looked up at the corpus-captain. Its teeth chattered in its macabre maw, and through the rent in its helm, the Scourge felt the attention of an eye within the bald socket of the thing's skull, glowing an otherworldly red.

'So this is you,' Kersh said, presenting the tarot wafer. The horror merely stared back, never speaking, never acknowledging its hauntee with word or deed. 'What does this mean?' the Scourge demanded. The revenant merely stared at the Excoriator. 'I want to know what this means, you sorry-looking, good-for-nothing fiend.' Again, the phantom did not respond. It simply watched the fury building within the corpus-captain with grotesque fascination and icy patience. Kersh turned away. He looked at the card and then back at the revenant. He half expected it to be gone as was its frustrating habit, melting into the ether of reality. It remained, however, standing over the unconscious Librarian.

'False prophet,' Kersh told it with growing bitterness. 'At first I thought you a bad dream – a resonance of the Darkness. Something I'd brought back. Then some manifestation of surgical error, a hallucination or insanity earned through drill and scalpel. For a moment I allowed myself the comfort of thinking you had answers. That you were ghosting me for a reason I would come to understand. Some sign of a greater scheme. Surely, proof that I truly have lost my mind. Now I just think I'm damned. Come to the notice of some pollutive entity or spirit that delights in tormenting me with its dark attentions. Do my struggles entertain you, wraith?'

The being looked down on Melmoch with ghoulish serenity before staring back at the seething Scourge. It reached out with a single, bony digit – protruding from a broken ceramite fingertip – and pointed to the tarot card in the Excoriator's hand. Colour began to bleed from the wafer, until atom by atom the card disintegrated before Kersh's eye, streaming away on some perverse, immaterial breeze.

'More dark riddles? Could you be any more cryptic, you bastard thing?'

The hand that had been holding the card became a fist and the raw tension in the Scourge's arm, a blow. Several stitches snapped in Kersh's side as the Excoriator launched his attack, throwing a punch at the being. As the fist flew, Kersh winded himself against Melmoch's stone tablet. His knuckles met no resistance, however. Instead of ceramite and bone, the Scourge's fist hit agitated nothingness, the spit and crackle of soul-static and shadow. What horrified the corpus-captain more was the fact that the armoured phantom actually seemed to be there and it was his own fist and arm that had assumed a ghostly translucence. Instinctively withdrawing his hand and clutching it to his chest, the Excoriator was relieved to find that it had re-assumed its corporeality. It was flesh and blood once more.

The candles about the chamber suddenly died to glowing wick-tips. The sanctuary became thick with a darkness that even the Space Marine's enhanced vision struggled to pierce. Even the revenant in his midnight plate could not be seen. Then, like a targeter, the wraith's lurid red eye cut through the murk, fixed on the Excoriator. Before the Scourge, appeared an unnatural light. The phantasmic outline of the legionnaire flickered and danced with the auric flame of ethereal damnation. Kersh watched, entranced by this being of the beyond. Not noticing that the very darkness itself had been set alight, but the mere offending presence of the thing. The gilded flames took and spread, swamping the corpus-captain in an immaterial inferno. The soulfire blazed to brightness, enveloping the revenant in light and immersing the Scourge in cool, blinding brilliance.

When Kersh opened his eye the chamber had returned to blackness. The candle wicks reassumed their glow before igniting once more. The temporary apothecarion, including the still form of Melmoch, seemed untouched by the ethereal firestorm, but the ghoulish revenant was gone. The Scourge stumbled across to his bunk and leant against the stone tablet, probing his stitches with fat fingers.

The sanctuary door opened and Ishmael entered. The squad whip met Kersh's blank gaze before walking over to the hermitage bench, his face dark like a burgeoning storm. Standing next to Melmoch, Ishmael grasped the hilt of his blood-smeared sword and plucked it from the ferruswood surface of the bench. He seemed to stare at the gladius for a moment.

'Thinking about finishing what your blade started, Squad

Whip Ishmael?' the Scourge called over his shoulder, his words barbed and accusatory. After a short hesitation, Ishmael looked around at the Scourge. A decision was made.

'Melmoch's awake,' the squad whip replied.

'What?' Kersh said, still with an edge to his voice. The whip's response had caught him off guard.

'Brother Melmoch,' Ishmael told him, his eyes still slits of insolence, 'is conscious.' Kersh approached the stone tablet. Indeed, the Librarian's eyes were fluttering open and staring glaze-eyed at the ceiling. 'Corpus-captain,' Ishmael acknowledged in a low voice before slipping out of the sanctuary.

'Melmoch,' Kersh greeted the Epistolary as he stood over him.

The Librarian sat up, leaning back on his arms. He licked his lips.

'I'm thirsty,' he said. It was a statement, but Kersh, still clutching his side, poured a small bowl of water from a ceramic pitcher and offered it to the psyker. Taking the bowl, Melmoch drank deeply, allowing rivulets of water to stream down from the corners of his mouth. 'The apothecarion?' he asked. Kersh nodded.

'You've been out a while, brother.'

'I heard voices,' Melmoch said. Kersh felt himself tense.

'Brother Ishmael was here…'

'Whooh,' Melmoch said, dropping the empty bowl and reaching for his head.

Crunching through the shattered ceramic, Kersh put a hand on the psyker's shoulder. 'What is it? Is it your gift?'

'Yes,' Melmoch moaned.

'Is it compromised?'

'Quite the opposite,' the psyker told him, his face crisscrossed with lines of pain and tension.

'You have the skill?'

Melmoch's eyes opened wide and bright, and he spoke. His gaze was piercing to the point of discomfort and his words echoed around the inside of Kersh's mind.

'There is pain here like you would not believe. Not in

this body but in the very fabric of existence. The dull agony of our savagery is a galactic affliction. The hot blood of ill will and the mindless brutality of our species sustaining its insatiable desire. Our kind were bred to trade in such currency. With each bolt and blow we feed the beast. Here and now…' The Librarian trailed off. His eyes momentarily glazed before searing back to focus. 'Here and now – this time and this place is a wound within a wound. An injury internal, like a bottomless pit discovered in the deepest trench.'

'You speak of the Cholercaust.'

'The screams,' Melmoch marvelled. 'The never-ending shrieks of slaughterlust, fear and rage, layered, echoing, bleeding into one another like a spiritual static. The starvation of reason – food for a god.'

'Melmoch, I don't–'

'It speaks through me, but to us all. You can hear it in the drawing of a blade and the *clunk* of a firing mechanism. You can feel it in your face and fingers – in the snarl and the fists you make when you want to end an existence. It's there – in the back of your mind, finding expression in the necessity of violence. It calls to you, shredding your nerve and urging the wanton abandon that every being craves – building, bubbling, brimming. Threatening to spill over into glorious reality where both power and blood flow.'

'The gall-fever,' Kersh agreed.

'The futility of fighting fire with fire. A spiral of degeneration. The War-Given-Form. It will stop at nothing until we have all become the instruments of its boundless wrath. So much hate.'

'Is that why you took this from the Ecclesiarch's shrine?' Kersh asked, dipping his hand into a belt pouch and extracting the small urn the psyker had used to put himself out. The Librarian immediately flinched in its presence. 'All of the witchbreeds are dead. Navigators, astropaths – everyone.'

'The Skull Taker knows we're here,' the Epistolary said, not taking his eyes off the orb container with its agonising contents: the God-Emperor's psi-negative essence, dust of the divine. 'It knows our gorestink, the copper tang of our blood. We are candles in the darkness to such an entity, flaring every time we lay our lands on a weapon or indulge our spite. It hates the witch most of all. A loathing beyond your all-too-human unease and disgust. The witch's soul burns bright. The witch is a coward who shuns the unthinking urgency of the hand and whose agency is the warp. That is why the witch dies first at the Blood God's hand. I needed to douse that flame, to retreat into the darkness and gather my strength – or, Adeptus Astartes or not, I would have shared the same fate as the unfortunates of whom you spoke.'

'Melmoch,' Kersh said, trying to get the psyker to focus. 'I need to know if you can reach beyond the screaming – beyond the influence of the Cholercaust and this cursed comet.'

'You wish me to send an astrotelepathic message?'

'Yes. Several. Can you do that?'

Melmoch got down from the stone tablet and steadied himself. 'I can try.'

'We need to appraise the Vanaheim Cordon of our status,' Kersh said, 'and the Terran-bound trajectory of the Keeler Comet. Their contingents must hold station. We cannot afford the Cholercaust to slip by into Segmentum Solar.'

'And the others?'

'Long range, narrow-band requests for reinforcement to the Viper Legion on Hellionii Reticuli,' the corpus-captain instructed. 'The Novamarines at Belis Quora and the Angels Eradicant stationed at Port Kreel.' Melmoch went to interrupt but Kersh had more for him. 'And a subsector, wide-band appeal for assistance. There were rumours the White Consuls were moving out of the Ephesia Nebula. We could get lucky.'

Melmoch looked hard at the Scourge.

'Of course, I will do all that you ask. You must know – the magnitude of the enemy force we are facing…' The Librarian didn't have the words. 'Even if we were reinforced, the time it would take for another contingent to reach us – the Cholercaust will be gone and our corpses will have been long stamped into the grave dust.'

'A little optimism too much to expect?' Kersh said.

'Optimism's a little hard to come by,' Melmoch said. 'I'm only being realistic about our chances.'

'Does not the God-Emperor fight on our side?' Kersh asked. Melmoch's brow furrowed, surprised at such a reference from the corpus-captain.

'He does,' the Epistolary replied suspiciously.

'Then I suppose you had better take it up with him.'

PART THREE
FOR WHOM THE BELL TOLLS...

CHAPTER THIRTEEN
HEAVENFALL

BROTHER OMAR STUMBLED through the mist. It was as though the clouds were too tired to take their own weight and had settled like ephemeral behemoths on the necroscape. Thick and noxious, the miasma stank of evil, threaded through as it was with a dull spectrum of unnatural colour, like oil spreading through water. Above the Excoriators Scout, the overcast sky – all but indistinguishable from the burial ground-hugging mist – glowed with atmospheric agitation. It was as though the heavens were alight. It was a bad sign. Certus-Minor was passing through the tail of the comet, Omar presumed.

The neophyte was a mess. His carapace was but a feral worlder's loincloth, shredded and hanging in tatters about his waist. His muscular torso glistened with his own blood, decorated all over as it was with nicks, bites and slices. A ragged strip from his long-abandoned cloak served as a bandana to keep the gore from his eyes, and his recovered combat blade dangled loosely from his exhausted grip like a machete. With only a primordial will to live sustaining the Excoriator, Omar had crawled up through the bodies, breaking bones and crushing skulls with his bare hands. With the roaring masses swarming about him, the Scout's combat blade had been knocked free. Too much of a temptation to the bloodthirsty wretches, the razor-sharp weapon had been picked up and used on the Scout, slashing him feebly across the shoulder. Back in the Excoriator's possession the weapon did its worst, however. Recalling training exercises on Cretacia, the Scout cut through bodies like death world jungle. For hours Omar had hacked back and forth, putting one foot in front of the other, leaving a trail of slaughter through the howling crowds. This, in turn, fuelled the frenzy further as maniacs descended upon the twitching corpses of the decapitated and limbless, finishing them off with god-pleasing ferocity.

Eventually, Omar reached the periphery of the horde. Continuing to cut a path to freedom, he staggered into the fog and left the screams of fury and death behind him. Mind-numb and blood-drenched, the Scout tried to orientate himself, settling on a seemingly arterial lychway in the assumed direction of Obsequa City. The neophyte was fairly sure that it was the same road upon which he had ridden out; but in the swirling fogbank, and surrounded by grave markers, statues and mausolea that all looked the same, he could have been walking in entirely the wrong direction.

A rumble and a quake beneath his feet brought the Excoriator back to his weary senses. Lifting his head and squinting, Omar could make out little. Through the murk of the mist he saw momentary streaks of fire giving the impression of something falling from the heavens. This was soon lost in the obscurity, until the Scout felt the further tremor of impacts through the soles of his gore-splattered boots.

Lifting the combat blade with one muscle-torn arm, and his knees in an attempt to galvanise his sluggish legs into a run, Omar advanced in the direction of the sound and sensation. Through the fog Omar began to make out a glow, then the flicker of small fires. Before long he found himself at the edge of a small crater, the impact zone a site of incandescent earth and destruction. Gravestones and the coffins that had been buried beneath them had been churned up and lay smashed amongst the debris of shattered bone and masonry. Moving on, the Scout encountered several more glowing craters, the undoubted sites of meteoric impact, rock, ice and ancient metals falling away from the comet and raining to the Certusian surface from its streaming tail.

Something did not seem quite right to the Excoriators Scout. Each of the impact craters was strewn with remains and coffin fragments. At the centre of each lay a single casket. They were untouched by the crash and steaming quietly in the night. Some were all but buried, while others lay across the bottoms of the craters. Climbing down into a hot trench, Omar inspected the fourth such object he had encountered. Unlike the flimsy stasis caskets used in the Certusian burial services, it was tall, broad and baroque. It stuck upright out of the ground at the bottom of the crater and was crafted from some dark, adamantine alloy. It was decorated with fretwork and ornamental art; Omar could make out some kind of bird, embroiled in flame.

Working his way around the object – which despite being surrounded by glowing, razed earth, was strangely cool to the touch – the Scout discovered Chapter designations and battle honours. Damage to the metal sarcophagus had obscured the name of the Chapter but did reveal its Founding as the unfortunate Twenty-First. Its honour roll was one a First Founding Legion would be proud of, including the Apostatic Wars, the Great Malagantine Purge, the Golgotha Castigations, the Battle of Lycanthos Drift, the Second Scouring of the Black Myriad and the Badabian Tyranicide.

Nestling the tip of his combat blade between lid and sarcophagus, Brother Omar twisted the weapon and broke the pressure seal. The object gave a loud moan of relief and the Scout proceeded to prise open the top half of the lid. Swinging open, the lid bounced on its chunky hinge, presenting a dark interior. An empty interior. Looking deep inside, Omar found nothing. No remains of the Adeptus Astartes battle-brother he expected to find within. On the inside of the lid the Scout discovered a simple plaque identifying a gene-code in symbol and number, a name, rank and company dictum. Brother-Sergeant Attica Centurius, Honoured First Company: *In dedicato imperatum ultra articulo mortis.* 'For the Emperor beyond the point of death.'

Something screamed overhead. Closing the lid and crouching, Omar looked up at the hazy sky. There were more streaks blazing across the firmament. Many more. It was as if the filthy heavens had opened and fire was falling to the cemetery world surface. The Scout felt the first impact through the floor and the cool alloy of the sarcophagus. Then a second and a third. They were close and getting closer. Soon they were almost continuous, with objects rocketing down from the sky and thunderbolting into the burial grounds. At first Omar had thought it a meteor storm, the full wrath of the comet brought to bear on the planet surface. He had even considered the barrage a further heavenfall of the mysterious sarcophagi. The Scout didn't relish being beneath either as they rained from the sky at searing speed.

Then he heard it. Something indescribably horrible announcing its arrival through the fog. Not a meteorite or an empty sarcophagus. The Excoriator climbed out of the crater and began a low walk to the lychway. There were other sounds now. An ungainly flapping overhead. The gargle-hiss of something hatching to the neophyte's right. The tremble of footfalls, colossal and closing from behind. A screech close by that went straight through the Scout and caused his eyes to bleed. Omar's stealthy advance turned into a march, and the march into a run. He no longer felt the agony in his arms and the weight in his legs. Horrors were raining about him, things infernal and impossible. Brother Omar ran into the darkness, crunching along the gravel track that he hoped to the Emperor would lead him to Obsequa City, his battle-brothers and a loaded boltgun.

The Scourge stood atop the masonry scarp. Techmarine Dancred admitted to having little trouble demolishing the exterior walls, chapels and habitations – ancient and already crumbling as they were. Now these buildings were a perimeter of steep stone wreckage, providing Obsequa City's defenders with protection, elevated fire arcs and a workable, if ramshackle, battlement upon which to station heavy weapon emplacements and themselves. Conversely, it presented an assaulting enemy with a tiring and time-consuming climb, hopefully giving the Charnel Guard and their recent recruits opportunity to riddle their attackers with las-bolts.

Kersh had instructed the Techmarine to demolish a second row of buildings and a third in concentric circles around the exterior of the city. In the two interior masonry mounds, the corpus-captain had ordered narrow rat-runs excavated by hand at intervals along the impromptu battlement. These in turn were imbedded with the last of the armoury demolition charges, with screw-lever detonators situated at the rat-run end. Kersh fully expected to order strategic retreats and planned on the rat-runs giving the Certusians and Excoriators the ability to pull back to a waiting secondary and tertiary palisade if overwhelmed. The demolitions would then collapse the runs after use, preventing enemy troops following and forcing them to embark on another las-slashing climb, giving the fleeing cemetery worlders and Charnel Guard time to set up carried weaponry in new emplacements.

The shattered-stone parapet swarmed with fearful Certusians, men, mostly, who had been selected by the lord lieutenant to bolster the ceremonial numbers of the Charnel Guardsmen on the perimeter. Some had been armed with auxiliary lasfusils from the defence force armouries, while others had to contend with scuffed and dusty remnants from storage – autoguns and stub-service carbines. Rough emplacements boasted heavy stubbers, battered incinerator units, mortars and the occasional autocannon. Where firearms weren't available, improvised weaponry in the form of picks and shovels were carried in the sweaty palms of grave fossers and hearsiers.

Punctuating the line of cemetery worlders were the Charnel Guard themselves. The dour Guardsmen were dressed in dusty black flak, swathed in sable cloaks and aiming their single-shot lasfusils over the rubble palisade. Their ceremonial duties had ill-prepared the Guardsmen for the kind of meat-grinding battle ahead, the Certusian soldiers better versed in the rites of death than the art of dealing it to the Emperor's enemies. Kersh bit at his mangled bottom lip and watched a lance-lieutenant straighten a Guardsman's cloak and dust off his shoulder when he should have been modulating the beam-focus on his lasfusil.

In a rough gun emplacement nearby, Kersh spotted his personal serfs. Amongst the rubble, Oren was leaning into the stock of a brute autocannon. Old Enoch was stacking ammunition crates behind the weapon, while Bethesda spoke to several unarmed Certusians whose duty it was to run further ammunition to the emplacement. When the assault began, a good deal would rest on the ability of the heavy weapons to keep firing. That was why in the main Kersh had ordered Chapter serfs to take responsibility for the emplacements. They were more likely to hold their nerve in the face of the enemy and do their duty. As the absterge turned she pointed out the Scourge to the cemetery worlders she was addressing – no doubt to bolster their faith and confidence. She risked a brief smile at her master which Kersh saw but didn't acknowledge. As she turned back he saw the powerpack, looped cable and chunky las-pistol attached to the belt of her robes. It was Bethesda's job to keep the supply line running. An emplacement without ammunition was an invitation to disaster.

The night air was still and an evil-smelling fog bank was rolling in across the burial grounds, reducing visibility and range. Peering along the battlement with the keen sight of his remaining eye, Kersh saw Brother Micah. The company champion had not been happy about being away from the Scourge's side, but the corpus-captain had insisted he needed a spread of experience and loyalty around the perimeter. Micah had had to settle for the next section along, barely a sprint away along the ruin palisade. He brought up a fist to the sky and then kissed it, which Kersh proceeded to mimic.

The city was strangely quiet. Along Kersh's section of the perimeter there was tension and dread etched into the face of every Certusian the corpus-captain settled his eye on. Women, children and a sparse sprinkling of remaining preachers ran back and forth between the city centre and the perimeter line, up and down the vertiginous, cobbled cuttingways and alleys with water, food and ammunition.

The thousands not employed in such service were gathered in the cramped cloisters, quads and plazas about the Memorial Mausoleum, holding a candlelight vigil with Pontifex Oliphant and creating a prayer cordon around the resting place of Umberto II. The Memorial Mausoleum's vault – where the ancient remains of the former High Lord of Terra and Ecclesiarch resided – was deep enough, it was said, to survive an apocalyptic strike by an asteroid. It was there, the safest place on the planet, that Kersh had intended Oliphant to hide.

This, after the corpus-captain had argued at length with Palatine Sapphira and, with grave reservation, that the Sister of the August Vigil had consented to allow a small number of significants to occupy the sacred chamber. She had been worried about body heat elevating the tiny vault's temperature above a preservative optimum. Oliphant had undone the corpus-captain's hard work with the Sister, however, insisting that he share the same fate as his people. Kersh had been angry at first, but had been secretly impressed with the cripple; he had never observed such concern in a priest or planetary governor before. The Excoriator was at least a little reassured that the pontifex had chosen the Memorial Mausoleum as the site of his flock's gathering, under the dispassionate gaze of the Sisters of Battle, stationed about the mausoleum with their primed boltguns.

The city between the limits and the heights was all but empty. Citizens ran supplies down blood-splattered streets as Proctor Kraski and his enforcers herded the last of the city-based hordes and fire-lighting crazies into tight alleys and cul-de-sacs. There they went to work with their combat shotguns, putting the mobs out of their degenerate misery. Kersh could hear the howls and screams of rage and death echoing about the city's lofty walls, tunnels and winding stairwells. In the tallest towers and the busy architecture of the most elevated rooftops, Scout Whip Keturah was stationed with Squad Contritus, watching and waiting – the empty streets below and the misty necroplex beyond the perimeter line falling under the constant sweep of their magnocular scopes.

Keturah had returned early from his search. Two of his Scouts were still missing, but when fireballs started tumbling out of the unnatural sky and thundering into the burial grounds, the Scout whip had abandoned the sweep – unwilling to risk the Thunderhawk *Impunitas* in the hellstorm. Kersh had ordered the remainder of his Scouts stationed about the perimeter with the other Excoriators, in small groups. At ease, the corpus-captain expected the sight of the Angels and aspirants to reinforce the nerves of the Guardsmen and cemetery world militia. In battle he expected them to remain loose and flexible – holding ground but clustering as the rapidly-changing circumstances of battle changed. Where the line was breached – and the Scourge was confident that it would be – he needed his Adeptus Astartes to swiftly move in, destroy the threat and repel the enemy advance.

Standing with him on the palisade was Squad Whip Ishmael and a member of Squad Castigir, Brother Kale. The Excoriators whip paced up and down, barking the impetuous orders of a tyrant down on the line. Under the eyes of the Adeptus Astartes the Certusians hurried to meet his booming expectations, but they little understood what the Excoriator was talking about. Kale looked on, his flamer resting in his grip, his eyes on the ominous bank of mist that hung in the night air like a curtain of dread. Beyond was the darkness and the graveyard expanse. There was something new out there in the burial grounds. Something weird and unnatural. They all knew this because they could hear strange noises rolling out of the still obscurity. Kersh listened to the enemy, the approach of the host. He could hear wet rasping, the chitinous clickety-click of movement, the horrible cracking of metamorphosis, chuntering, hissing, shrieking and what sounded like the song of some dying ocean behemoth layered over everything else. There were muffled voices, too, close yet distant, speaking to no one and everyone in a dark tongue that was neither human nor xenos but otherworldly and entrancing.

When *Impunitas* had returned with reports of orbital bombardment further south, beyond the Great Lakes, Kersh feared the worst. Obsequa City would not survive a pounding from the void and Kersh's meagre defences had not been designed with such remote engagement in mind. The Scourge thought he could rely on the Blood God's servants to meet them blade to blade. They were not known for their prosecution, or even tolerance, of such long-range warfare. Kersh's experience of the berserker factions had taught him that beyond the ancient warships of the Traitor Legions, the War-Given-Form favoured simple cultships. The Cholercaust armada would likely be made up of armed freighters, fat transports and plundered system ships, loaded to piratical proportions – ready to disgorge their savage cargos of human detritus in a swarm of battered lighters, barges, haulage brigs, tugs and hump shuttles, all reinforced and outfitted as simple drop-ships.

Corpus-Commander Bartimeus, in his last vox-transmission from the departing *Angelica Mortis*, confirmed the Cholercaust's approach from the system's edge. No one vessel, however – not even the bastardised sprint traders and void-clippers ahead of the armada, straining at the leash and burning out their sub-light engines with bloodthirsty impatience – had reached the system core. Kersh had urged the strike cruiser on with its precious cargo of gene-seed and intelligence, instructing Bartimeus to assume an escape vector towards the cemetery world's bleak sun, hopefully masking the vessel's signature in the stellar static.

The Scourge thought on Ezrachi and the brusque

corpus-commander. He had felt the Apothecary's absence immediately, having come to value if not always appreciate the grizzled veteran's advice. Kersh knew that the Excoriators of the Fifth would also miss the *Angelica Mortis*, the strike cruiser being their only hope of exodus. A lifeline cut. Their home, gone. The corpus-captain knew that the thought of the warship carrying the company's genetic future to safety would console some of the Space Marines, but for some the sore loss of the *Angelica Mortis* would only be drowned in the hot distraction of battle. For that reason, Kersh willed their enemy on.

It was Melmoch who had provided the answer to Kersh's questions. What was the nature of the orbital bombardment? If not the Cholercaust, then what was out on the burial grounds, haunting the mist and chilling Certusians to the bone with its weirdness, wailing and nonsensical whispers? The Librarian told him that the Keeler Comet was no ordinary astral body. It was no longer a simple amalgam of ice, rock and metal plummeting through the void, enslaved to an orbit and the long chain of gravity. It had punched through the Eye of Terror and had changed, its nature abnormal, its purpose warped. Like a claw, tearing at the very fabric of reality, the blood comet had opened rents in time and space, tainting the darkness and creating an immaterial breach through which the raw essence of the warp could bleed. The Epistolary told Kersh, pointing up at the unnatural flux of the sky, that he suspected the comet's tail was such a rift, and that the unfiltered insanity of the warp was pouring out into the void before falling towards Certus-Minor with gravitational certainty to streak down through the cemetery world's atmosphere. Trying to reassure the Scourge, the psyker hypothesised that weak entities and warpforms might burn up on descent, and that the grip other such creatures had on reality might be weakened by such a scorching. What horrified Kersh further was Melmoch's belief that anything resilient enough to survive planetfall and impact would be suitably difficult to kill.

'Anything?' Kersh asked.

'Nothing,' Kale replied. He held an auspex out before him, scanning the thick murk. 'No movement, no heat signature, no emissions.'

'Well, there's clearly something out there,' Ishmael bit back. The squad whip was wearing his lightning claws and watching searing energy arc between the polished surfaces of his talons.

Minutes passed. Kale continued to sweep the necroplex but detected nothing. Ishmael took out his impatience on the already terrified mortals on the battlement. Then Kersh heard it. In the distance. Along the perimeter. Amongst the sibilant cacophony emanating from the mist. The rhythmic chatter of a heavy stubber.

'Corpus-captain,' Kersh's vox-bead crackled. 'Enemy contacts.' It was Brother Novah. Kersh had stationed the newly-promoted standard bearer with Chaplain Shadrath some way to the east. The chug of the stubber could be heard much clearer over the vox-channel, and the corpus-captain also detected the ragged *whoosh* of lasfusils and the Emperor-pleasing crash of boltguns through the static. 'The chief whip, Brother Dancred and the lord lieutenant – all reporting enemy contact, sir.'

Kersh visualised the tiny city, tinier still since Brother Dancred's demolitions. He considered the relative locations of the reports. It seemed initial assaults were coming in from the north and east.

'What about Joachim, the Epistolary, Second Whip Scarioch?'

'Nothing, my lord.'

Then Kersh heard the isolated reports of nervous trigger fingers. Behind a collapsed cloister-pillar two Charnel Guardsmen had punched several holes in the fog bank with their lasfusils. The single bolts faded into the mist and the lance-lieutenant fell on the two soldiers with harsh and equally nervous words. The Charnel Guard officer was cut off in mid-stream by the *chudder* of a stub-carbine and the deeper crash of Oren's autocannon. Vague suggestions became shadows and shadows rapidly became horrific threats coming out of the mist at the battlement. The night sizzled to life as a hail of poorly aimed las-bolts lanced the miasma. The autocannon and a heavy stubber further up the palisade gave better accounts of themselves – the cannon in particular chewing up the advancing forms before they had even had a chance to make themselves known.

Kersh unclipped his chainsword and held the barbed tip of the silent weapon out beside Ishmael. He'd hoped the squad whip might return the battle-brotherly gesture and tap the back of his lightning claw against the weapon. Ishmael just gave the Scourge a look of sour disgust, slapped on his helmet and started advancing.

'Sir,' Kale called. Kersh didn't know if the Excoriator had seen his squad whip's snub. The Space Marine held up the auspex. 'I've got nothing.'

Kersh grunted. Enemies that eluded the scanners were not good news for the Excoriators.

'If you can see it and it moves, burn it,' Kersh told Kale. Re-attaching the auspex to his belt and adopting his helmet, the Excoriator ran up the perimeter, adjusting the nozzle aperture on his weapon for a blanket burn.

Firing the chainsword to life, the Scourge gunned the weapon to shrieking lethality. Slipping his own helm over his head and firing the pressure seals, he watched monstrous forms swoop, bound and scuttle from the fog. As the warp-spawned swarm grew, more of the immaterial creatures made it through the gauntlet of the las-fire. Kersh watched the autocannon and heavy stubber continue to do good work, ripping up etherforms and blowing what appeared to be limbs and appendages from the fearless horrors. The storm of las-fire that had greeted the first appearance of the entities immediately began to thin, causing Kersh to march forwards. It was as he feared. As more of the myriad monstrosities revealed themselves, common Certusians had shifted from panic-stricken trigger pumping to mind-scalding horror. The cemetery worlders and a number of Charnel Guard proceeded to gawp at the spectacle, their fragile minds overwhelmed by the impossible vision unfolding before their eyes. Some recoiled and slammed their backs to the battlement ruins, refusing to believe what they were seeing. Others fell to weeping and vomiting. Many simply could not take their eyes of the gut-curdling sight of the warp-spewed nightmares and froze up, clutching their silent weapons uselessly to their chests.

Several flying beasts corkscrewed their haphazard way through the streams of heavy weapons fire and dissipating curtain of las-bolts. Their repugnance even stirred deep-buried feelings of disgust in Kersh, looking as they did like giant insects that had been turned inside out. They swooped in low over the battlement on deformed multi-wings. Ishmael ran at the monsters, leaping off a shattered arch and reaching for the open night sky with his lightning claws. The talons crackled and steamed as the first beast flew straight into them. The creature sliced into an ugly mess on the rubble behind the squad whip before raining skywards in a shower of immaterial dissipation. Ishmael landed and, risking a swift look over his shoulder, brought up his bolt pistol and hammered several rounds into a second oncoming glider.

A third fiend rolled into a spin with its ragged wings, bypassing Ishmael and coming at Kersh. The Scourge feinted right and then turned back, sweeping down with the angry teeth of the chainsword. The weapon chugged through a large wing and tore a rent down the monster's flank, causing it to stream entrails across the crumbling masonry and smash its remaining wings in a crash-landing. The corpus-captain watched the mess stream into a cyclonic scattering of dark emotion and wastage. Bethesda ran forwards from her position protecting the ammunition supply line. Holding the chunky laspistol in both hands like a carbine, cable trailing to the humming powerpack on her belt, the absterge lanced the downed entity with automatic las-fire.

Following Ishmael to the palisade, Kersh saw the squad whip roar savagely down the line of militia and Charnel Guardsmen. As encouragement to keep firing, the Excoriator stepped up onto the parapet and blasted single bolts from his pistol down the steep rubble of the battlement, plugging the swollen abdomens of obscene scuttlers.

'Fire, you worthless wretches!' Ishmael bawled, stabbing the talon-tips of a lightning claw down the line in accusation. 'Fire or I'll make you wish you had, you merelings! I'll feed you to these beasts to give the rest something to aim at!'

A wall of insanity came at the battlement. Spindle-limbed arachnid-maws that jumped from gravestone to gravestone. Fleshy urchin-like beings that rolled across the ground on pneumatic spines, spearing all in their path. Osseous shafts growing out of the mist and impaling Guardsmen, before violently projecting hydric stalks of cartilage into the bodies of nearby victims to create a reticulated network of skewered bodies. Conical torsos, twitching with single-clawed stumps and slimy mouths that stream-vomited corrosive bile all about them. Blooms of floating cephalogeists, draping their victims in manes of life-sapping tentacles. Voracious, protoplasmic absorbers. Beasts that were claws and nothing else. Cancroid growths that spread across the ground, rocky surfaces and living tissue with sickening speed. A carpet of larval horrors that escaped the worst of the suppression fire and wriggled up through the loose rubble. Kersh saw cemetery worlders tearing at their own faces as the glassy elvers slithered into ears, mouths and eyes before writhing and exploding in a bloody, reproductive shower of empyreal birth.

Kersh fought through the spray of ichor and gobbets of warpflesh. He sawed through bestial nightmares and chopped limb-things from corporeal entities that simply grew back. He took the head from a Khymeric carnivore before cleaving the helical tusk from a screamer that swooped at him on triangular, pectoral wings. The Scourge booted aside a spongy mass of stubby eye-stalks before stamping down on the disappearing tail of a slinking gorgopede. He cut a fat, serpentine fluke from the lance-lieutenant's back only to find that it had already eaten his head and had been pushing down into his body. The air was thick with death. The battlement was swamped with horror. Immaterial entities – hungry for souls – were everywhere, and the Scourge was enveloped in a whirlwind of blade-banished dissipation as monstrosities about him died and departed reality.

The Scourge didn't know how long he had been fighting. The sea of spawn had just kept coming – monsters buzzing above, crawling over and slithering through the flesh-mounds of the slain. He had barely been allowed a moment's independent thought. His superhuman body had been enslaved to necessity – arching, reaching, barging and slamming his way through the havoc. The chainsword shimmered in his grip, so hot was the weapon in its constant state of carnage. Over the vox-bead he'd heard a similar story from around the entirety of the perimeter. He thought he'd heard reports of cemetery worlders and Charnel Guard abandoning their posts in mind-numbing terror. He'd heard of Second Whip Azareth and Brother Lemuel's sections pushed back to the second perimeter battlement and Techmarine Dancred's completely overrun.

Suddenly the path ahead of Kersh was clear. Misshapen entities became even more so as they dissolved into a blur of cannon-blasted mess. The corpus-captain thought of Oren, the moody serf proving himself behind the stock of the heavy weapon, feverishly twisting the autocannon's length this way and that on its squat tripod, mulching otherworldly miscreations in tight, controlled sweeps. Through ichor-spattered optics Kersh could see Kale doing his worst with his flamer. The Excoriator was holding part of the palisade all by himself, indulging in broad burns that sanitised the tainted rubble and roasted a labyrinthine network of bodies, shot through with the explorative shafts of a bone monster – gargling, corrupted Guardsmen and all. Brother Micah was working his way down to him, sweeping a swarm of spindly spider-creatures from his path with conservative bolter blasts while bludgeoning his way through the spiny legs of a larger chitinid with his barrel and combat shield attachment.

From what the Scourge could see, the autocannon emplacement with Brothers Micah and Kale were the only contingent holding the battlement. The cemetery worlders had fled through the rat-run, back towards the city. Some of the Charnel Guard had held their ground but had been overwhelmed by warp entities that stripped their flesh and picked their bones. Spinning around, Kersh ducked beneath the legs of a fang-faced strider. The thing had been charging at him and had snapped at the corpus-captain with an elongated jaw, malformed and twisted with surplus teeth. The Scourge heard who he thought was Micah over the vox, but couldn't make out what the company champion was saying. Kersh flicked out his wrist and brought the raging tip of the chainsword up, shearing off one of the strider's gangly legs.

Peering through the mist, the corpus-captain spotted Ishmael down amongst the gravestones of the necroplex. The squad whip was fighting like a cornered cat, his lightning claws flashing through warpflesh, slicing and stabbing.

'Ishmael!' Kersh yelled, but the Excoriator was too far out. Looking along his faltering section of the battlement and then down at the struggling squad whip, Kersh came to a decision. 'Pull back!' he yelled across the thunder of the autocannon. Riddling ground-hugging abominations with automatic las-fire, Bethesda covered the retreat as Oren and Old Enoch began separating the cannon from its mount and running the length of the white-hot weapon down the rat-run. Kale provided a wall of flame behind him and started to back towards the evacuation route.

The Scourge clambered up onto the parapet and cut his way through a conjoined monstrosity of legs and torsos. With every skidding step down the flesh-littered scarp his chainsword took an existence. A gossamer-winged whiptail landed on his helmet from behind and proceeded to dig at the ceramite with its slender pincers. Snatching the thing by the tail, Kersh threw it into the rubble-strewn floor and crunched it underfoot. With a tiny etherquake, the thing became scraps of ash and nothingness. Through the throng of mayhem the Scourge watched the squad whip fight deeper and deeper into the immaterial ranks. The flood of malformed horror continued to roll in from the darkness of the burial grounds, washing up with mindless, soul-ravenous insanity against the rocky battlement. With unreal forms dying about them, the Excoriators were enveloped in curtains of warp essence that streamed for the night sky in torrents of instability.

'Ishmael!' Kersh managed as he sheared off limbs and plunged the shredding tip of the chainsword through warp-sculpted bodies. As the corpus-captain pushed deeper through the ranks, so did Ishmael. The Excoriator wouldn't be stopped. He seemed only to exist for the killing. He responded to no entreaties – vox-transmitted or otherwise – and seemed completely unaware of his tactical vulnerability, leading a one-warrior spearhead through the ether-swarm. His lightning claws were an electrical storm sweeping through the plague of madness. His motions were decimate yet disturbing in their automotronic fervour – like the Excoriator was killing for the sake of it and had little idea of where he was.

'Squad Whip Ishmael, respond!' Kersh called across the vox-channel but only heard a continuous, guttural growl across the channel in response. Already, the swathe of destruction the squad whip had cut through the chaos was closing up. He saw the arc of a lightning claw blaze in the distance. Like a swimmer forced down below the waves, the Scourge was suddenly swamped by warp effluence. There was monstrosity everywhere. Things were on his back. His boot was held fast in the mantrap jaws of some scuttling beast. Claws and jaws of abominate designs and dimensions snapped at his armoured form, and he was forced to hold up an outstretched gauntlet to block a stream of bile jetting at his faceplate and obscuring his optics. In his ears he heard Brother Micah over the vox, but he couldn't tell if the champion was talking to him.

Kersh found himself faltering. There were beasts all around and the sheer weight of creatures climbing upon his shoulders – and the weight of the entities crawling up onto their backs – forced the Scourge down onto his armoured knees. His hands hit the ichorial mire that was the cemetery world earth, and for the first time in hours the raging shriek of the chainsword chugged to a full stop. In amongst the forest of bestial legs, lying across a carpet of half-slain freakery, was a form Kersh recognised. Splattered from head to foot with blood, both black and fresh, and with carapace tatters decorating his stabbed and sliced flesh, one of Keturah's neophytes was slowly crawling across the landscape of carcasses. Half dead already and all but indistinguishable from the dissipating cadaverscape, an Excoriators Scout had made it back through the horror of the immaterial incursion.

'Excoriator!' the corpus-captain called, but the only response the Scout could make was to crane his head upwards and roll over onto his back. Kersh saw for the first time the full extent of his injuries. Four cavernous puncture wounds decorated his stomach – equidistant and gushing with the Scout's own blood. The unmistakable wound of a lightning claw. In his battle-blindness, Ishmael had gutted a brother Excoriator and slashed him down the face with a disfiguring swipe of his sword before moving on to his next victim. The squad whip had not even halted in realisation. He was lost to the kill.

Through his mauled face the Scout looked up at his corpus-captain. 'S-s-sir...'

'Save it,' Kersh told the neophyte. 'I'm getting you back to the city.'

Roaring with exertion the Scourge got back to his feet. Abominations fell from his shoulders and the sickening mass of soul-sucking aberration about him instinctively backed away. It was not enough to save them from the monomolecular fury of Kersh's chainsword as he whirled around, tearing through bodies in a three-hundred-and-sixty degree arc of serrated savagery. This alone, however, was not enough to save the Scourge. He had fought too far into the maelstrom and had been claimed by the current of interdimensional madness. Etherspawn were everywhere and it was all Kersh could do to decapitate, disembowel and clip appendages from the twisted screechers about him and the fallen Scout.

Bodies began to fall about him. Things that looked like heads and pulsing abdomens began opening up in sizzling *plunks* of light and ethereal fluids. The curtains of insanity parted and Brother Micah appeared, protecting himself from a warp-stew-spitting cluster-bud with his steaming shield attachment before hammering back with a mulching burst of bolter-fire. Bizarre forms reaching out for the champion thudded and dropped as covering fire from the nearest of the city belfries and tower tops cut a fresh path through the army of confusion. All about him, the monstrous dead lost their forms and shot for the heavens in bursts of twisting ephemera. Kersh could imagine Squad Contritus on their bellies, their sniper rifles resting in the cradles of bipods, their eyes to their magnocular scopes, dropping abomination after abomination, working their way through to the corpus-captain. The Scourge had little doubt that their orders came from the company champion.

'Micah!' Kersh called, grabbing one of the Scout's outstretched hands. Cutting through the long neck of an oncoming freak thing with a bolter blast, Micah rested the weapon in one arm and took the Scout's other bloodied palm with his free gauntlet.

'We've got to go – now!' Micah roared. A sudden tremor beneath the corpus-captain's boots convinced him not to question the champion's wisdom. It was followed by a second, third and fourth. As the two Excoriators ran, dragging the moaning Scout behind them through the morass of bodies, Kersh got the impression of something above them. Something unnatural in form and colossal in size was striding towards the city on impossibly spindly legs. Every time one of the behemoth's cloven feet hit cemetery world soil, the ground beneath the Excoriators bounced and quaked.

'Go-go-go!' Micah urged as the Space Marines stormed across the carnage of the necroplex and up the scree-slope of the rubble battlement. About them enemies closed in and dropped, heads and bodies lanced through with sniping las-bolts. Those monstrosities making it through had an introductory blast from Micah's boltgun or a flesh-shearing swipe of the corpus-captain's chainsword to greet them.

Kersh heard the staccato of gunfire. Squinting up through the ethereal mist, the corpus-captain saw the twin twinkles of heavy bolters in the sky. Their sound was drowned out by the air-shuddering moan of the gargantuan entity above them.

'It's the *Gauntlet*,' Micah called between strides and bolt-blasts, indicating that he had called the Thunderhawk in. The Space Marines ran on, dragging the wounded Scout. Kersh heard the familiar crash of the Thunderhawk's battle-cannon. Both the Scourge and his champion involuntarily ducked their helmets as the gunship swept in low and over their heads. Peering up Kersh could see the after-inferno of the explosive shell that had ripped into the flank of the beast above. Watching the *Gauntlet*'s engine triplex blaze away, Kersh felt the heavens rumble with otherworldly agony. The colossal aberrant had taken the shot like some megafaunic giant of the plains, only to totter on its willowy legs and fall similarly so to the side. As the mist began to churn and rush about them, the Scourge slowed and slid down onto his knee, prompting Micah to do the same. The mist suddenly changed direction and came back at them as the monster's dimensions pounded into the necroplex. Kersh was almost knocked from his crouch by the impact as a sea of bestial screams erupted and were suddenly silenced by the pulverising weight of the colossus. The etherquake was palpable, the hideous wash of unreality rolling about them as so many creatures died.

Kersh and Micah were back on their feet, hauling the Scout up and over the battlement. Above them the abomination's spindly leg quivered. It terminated in a webbed hoof that seemed to point to the dome of the Memorial Mausoleum like an instruction to its warp spawn kindred. On the parapet the Excoriators could see that the freakish invaders had taken the perimeter as their own. Only a rent-armoured Kale stood at the entrance to the rat-run, his flamer blazing billows of promethium about the approach – roasting anything that made a scuttle or arachnoid stride for the bolt-hole.

Along the palisade Kersh could see the indescribable horror of the behemoth's head. Its malformed skull had hit the battlement and pounded straight through the masonry and shattered rockcrete. As Kersh and Micah closed on the flame-streaming Kale, he heard the bark of Oren's autocannon reassume its flesh-mangling orison. The serfs had successfully fallen back to the second perimeter and the heavy weapon was even joined by the optimistic flash of the occasional lasfusil, fired blindly from the parapet. Kersh was glad of the autocannon's accompaniment. Below the second concentric battlement the Scout sniper cover fire couldn't reach them. The gibbering hordes had made effective use of the dying behemoth's fall, however, crawling up behind and over their warped cousin and giving the heavy weapon little open ground to acquire the advancing insanity.

Something Brother Micah assumed to be dead suddenly erupted in tentacles. The champion sidestepped the elastic reach of the first few, but dragging the injured Scout gave little room for manoeuvre and one of the thin appendages wound itself viciously around his leg. Pulling away from the horror, Micah plugged at it with single shots from his bolter, but a second grappler wrapped itself around the weapon. The tentacle around the champion's leg bled some kind of caustic revenge from the feeler's hook-suckers and the ceramite began to sizzle and smoulder. Micah yelled out in frustration and it took the gnashing teeth of Kersh's chainsword to slice the tentacles from their beast-host. As Micah ripped the remainder of the appendage from his leg and bolter, the Scourge buried the tip of his sword in the creature's thorax, gunning the barbed chain to full shredding majesty and despatching the monster.

The Excoriators ran. The horde closed.

Bolting down through the rat-run, the steep sides of

the second battlement threatening to cascade down upon them, Kersh and Micah pounded on – the Scout Marine's blood-drenched and ragdoll body pulled behind them. Kale backed into the gap after them, the flamer's incessant inferno even more devastating and concentrated within the rat-run's narrow dimensions. Charred skeletal obscenities propelled themselves through the wall of flame only to end up on the carpet of scorched and sky-streaming remains that other freak creatures sprang through to get to the Space Marines.

The Excoriator's flamer chugged dry, and Kale threw the deadweight of the weapon at the nearest rawbone gangle-fiend. The Excoriator's bolt pistol cleared his belt holster. Still backing away, Brother Kale blasted furiously at the onrushing abominations. An absorber gushed its gelatinous way up the rat-run – it too enhanced by the bolt-hole's funnelling narrowness. The amorphous spume-form soaked up the pistol's defiance before swallowing Brother Kale whole.

Kersh and Micah ran on, forcing their armour's spirits to greater feats of fibre-bundled athleticism. The rat-run exit beckoned. Kersh saw Bethesda at the opening, the screw-handle detonator in her slender hands. The Excoriators heard an appalling roar of agony but could not stop. As the Adeptus Astartes exploded out of the rat-run, the Scourge's absterge twisted the detonator. Strategically planted demolition charges along the length of the bolt-hole fired, demolishing the gap and collapsing the run. Tonnes of rubble and fragmented masonry cascaded down, blocking off the escape route and burying the freakish abominations chasing the Excoriators.

As the dust cloud settled, with the autocannon hammering above them, Kersh surveyed the scene. Everyone, from the limping Micah to Bethesda to the Charnel Guardsman hiding down behind the remnant of a shattered spire, looked aghast. Turning, Kersh looked down on the miserable Scout he'd pulled out of the horror of the necroplex. He was glaze-eyed, twitching and mumbling to himself. Also, half of him was missing.

The absorber's clotted immateriality had gushed up behind them and had swamped the Space Marine Scout's legs and abdomen. Digesting them like it had Kale, the creature had left half an Excoriator. For a few moments that seemed like an eternity, nobody spoke.

'Find something you can use as a stretcher,' the Scourge said to Bethesda, 'then have a team of runners take him up to his Tenth Company brothers.'

The absterge bolted off to carry out her master's orders. Kersh's eyes fell on the terrified Guardsman. 'You,' the Scourge said in a tone that blistered with fury and disappointment. 'Get on that perimeter, now…'

The Charnel Guardsman snatched up his lasfusil in numb dread and ran back up the palisade to take his position on the battlement.

Hobbling around whilst slapping a chunky magazine into his boltgun, Brother Micah turned to the Scourge. The company champion kissed his fist in honour of Dorn.

'You ready?'

'No,' Kersh answered honestly, but followed the Excoriator up towards the autocannon emplacement, leaving behind the neophyte in his pain, shock and mumbling torment.

CHAPTER FOURTEEN
SYZYGY

I wish this were a dream.

The horror of the warp was visited upon Certus-Minor. The cemetery world was flash-fried in the insanity of battle as the planet's unfortunate orbit passed through the tail of the Keeler Comet. The unfiltered dross of Chaos – gathered like scum at stagnant borders between our reality and its own – pouring through the rift and raining down on this tiny part of the Imperium.

We fought for twenty hours straight, knee-deep in abomination, holding our nerve and retaining our sanity amongst the madness of raw havoc taken form. The Fifth Company held its ground and earned great honour in the field of battle. If the shoreline of dead flesh is anything to go by, decorating the city perimeter, the odds were appalling. For twenty hours the heavenfallen swept down on us, drawn unthinking to Obsequa City like a lighthouse of soulfire, hungry for our humanity. We fought like we had never done before, our superhuman bodies pushed to their limit. Hearts thundered blood around our bodies. Reactions crackled like lightning. Eyes only saw enemies. Arms burned numb defiance – living extensions of our blessed blades and bolters. We took life without strategy. Technique and the art of battle were mere memories. We killed through necessity, for behind every enemy entity lay another and another, and it was all we could do to survive.

In the twentieth hour of bloodshed the aberrations stopped. Numbers of the warped began to dwindle. The masses thinned and our efforts became easier. We pushed the monsters back to the first perimeter, and on the lost battlement we decimated their remaining number. This was no battle tactic. The beasts had simply spent themselves in mindlessly assaulting the city. There were no more to kill because we had killed them all.

Although the Fifth Company has achieved a great victory over Chaos, it was not without cost. Brothers Ebenezar, Tycharias, Moliath, Ashkelon and Techmarine Dancred have lost their lives to the horde. Their bodies are laid out as custom dictates, with all the horror of their battle wounds on display. Tycharias particularly is a mess. Dancred is a butchered carcass of Adeptus Astartes flesh and twisted, claw-mauled hydraulics, electrical systems and bionic framing. The Techmarine fought bravely, but his position on the line was overrun and the abominations pushed on into the city. Members of Squad Contritus were instrumental in holding the invasion back – their sniping talents put to the test as the steep streets of the Saint Bartolomé-East district became wall-to-wall Chaotics. The Excoriators Scouts thinned out the misshapen mass with precision fire, giving Skase and several of his Squad Cicatrix brethren time to redeploy and push the monsters back. It took several bombing runs by the Thunderhawk Impunitas to fully sanitise the vicinity of hellspawn and their taint, however, leaving the district a derelict waste.

Whereas my Excoriators have upheld their proud tradition of attrition, I must accept responsibility for the failure of almost everyone else. I ask too much of the cemetery world's common humanity. Without the weakness of Imperial citizenry there would be no need for the Adeptus Astartes, and nothing has made this clearer than the manner of the Certusian retreat. History records the accomplishments of all-too-ordinary men: the war for Armageddon, the Euphrassic Massacres and the numerous Black Crusade honours of battle-hardened Cadians. Our species can be strong and our spirit beyond measure. This is what is celebrated in the myth and legend of song and saga. But for every Imperial citizen who has ever held their ground in the face of the xenos invader, the heretical traitor or Chaos marauder, a thousand have fled. It is in the fear and dread of those thousand that the Imperium's doom is written. Men, women and children in whose trembling hands weapons turn to water. The faint-hearted majority who run for their lives in the expectation that others will save them. Perhaps the Adeptus Astartes are to blame for this. The Imperium's strength is its weakness. The existence of demigods turns common men into bystanders. They catch a glimpse of the divine and consider themselves beyond the calculus of fate. The Emperor's Angels will save them. They are witnesses to the clash of good and evil in the galaxy, failing to recognise that it is upon their collective shoulders that the destiny of an empire resides.

For all my gene-bred superiority and Angel's arrogance, I find it hard to blame them. I am more than human and yet, on the dark fringes of my understanding – lapping against the bedrock of my warrior heritage, my training and experience – I feel it too. The vertiginous, ice-water plunge of fear, simple and pure. The irrational and almost irresistible desire to run, to take one-self away from the source of danger and disgust. How common humanity manages to steel itself for such a storm of chemistry and emotion is an everyday miracle in itself. That most fly when I need them to fight is regrettable. Unlike Skase and Joachim, spitting their curses and bawling remonstration at fear-wrought statues of Certusian cowardice, I cannot find it in myself to hate these mortals. My sacrifice is my own. I do it for the Emperor and not for them. In truth, I feel nothing for their survival. We share nothing like a brotherly bond – although amongst the Fifth that too has been sadly lacking. Should they survive, neither they nor their progeny will go on to change the Imperium. Their continued existence means only one thing to me: the denial of enemy victory. I suspect that the gall-fever and the madness of an immaterial incursion are simply intended to soften us for the body blow. The Cholercaust is coming. The Ruinous Powers wish to take this world and its people from me. They will be denied. They will fail. I will ensure it.

With Brother Novah I stalk the smouldering ruins of Saint Bartolomé-East. A crater and fireball-ravaged remnants are all that remain. With the Fifth Company battle standard held high, Novah crunches through the scorched rubble. He scans the battered landscape for any signs of corruption with his boltgun while relaying orders back and forth over the vox-channels.

'Second Whip Scarioch has been confirmed as missing.'

I nod. Novah continues. 'Second Whip Etham repeats his request to go out and search for Brother Ishmael.'

'Denied,' I snap back. 'Ishmael is lost. Tell Etham that Squad Castigir is his responsibility now and he needs to start acting like it.'

'Brother Simeon is up at the Memorial Mausoleum as instructed. He reports burning bodies in the plaza. It looks like the Sisters opened fire on the crowd.'

'The Sisters?'

I stop and consider Palatine Sapphira. It would be hard to imagine the stoic Sister succumbing to the frenzy and torching Certusians for sport.

'They claim they were attacked.'

'By ether-filth?' It seemed unlikely that rift forms had penetrated that far into the city, even from Saint Bartolomé-East.

'Cemetery worlders,' Novah replies.

The gall-fever. The city churning. I shake my head. The influence of Chaos within and without the perimeter. In the wake of the initial assault, abandoned by many of the cemetery worlders and up to my helmet in immaterial filth, I had little time to consider the consequence of mass desertion. While I was fighting for my life and the lives of others, hundreds upon hundreds of wild-eyed Certusians were running uphill towards the spiritual safety of the Memorial Mausoleum. Out of their minds with fear, militiamen, members of ammunition supply chains and terrified Charnel Guardsmen fled screaming from the unleashed horror of the warp and the desperate gunfire barely keeping it at bay. For some – their minds broken – the screams would have turned to howls and anguish, and then anger. The line between fear and fury is one easy to cross in the fragile, erratic mind of a mere mortal. With the gall-fever firmly taken root, the cemetery worlders would have torn into the thousands at prayer about the walls of the great Mausoleum, some deserters still with weapons in hand.

Faced with unreasoning mobs of murderers – men intent on slaughtering all, even their own friends and families – I can imagine that Palatine Sapphira had little choice but to order her flamer-wielding Sisters to torch the rabid interlopers.

'Have Brother Simeon set his serfs to organising labour parties from the cemetery worlders,' I order Novah. 'I need them to move bodies – they should be good at that.'

As we search through the charred remains of cloisters and chapels, I outline to the standard bearer how I want the bodies of dead defenders and penetrating spawn moved from the battlements and dumped outside the perimeter. I order the last of the city's promethium barrels tipped out across the cadaver mounds of the fallen – a fuel-soaked hillock of flesh, both Certusian and immaterial – surrounding the perimeter.

The orders keep coming. Command structure and a sense of purpose nourish the aftermath of battle. Having stood amongst the killing fields of innumerable conflicts, I know that disbelief, shock and a sense of fatalism are soon to set in, combated only by leadership and labour. Without hard work the mind is allowed to dwell – on horrors experienced, the odds of survival and the futility of resistance.

I instruct Lord Lieutenant Laszlongia to reorganise his Charnel Guardsmen. I am now only interested in men who have proved their worth. Men of strong mind and spirit who held the line. Men who now know what they are facing and have the resolve to kill it. I order Laszlongia to recover weapons and ammunition and, with my Excoriators, re-establish themselves on the exterior perimeter. The blood-splattered battlements are ours again. For how long I cannot know.

The *Impunitas* hovers above the desolation and I feel the sights of her heavy bolters watching over me and the company standard. The Gauntlet I have despatched off across the necroplex to ensure that deadly pockets of auspex-defying entities do not haunt the mist. A second wave of abominations at this point would be tactically unlikely, based upon their presented behaviour, but prematurely devastating to corpse trains and combat-unprepared perimeters.

'What of the Cholercaust – estimated time of planetfall?' I put to the standard bearer. As we approach a seemingly resilient structure amongst the shattered and soot-stained landscape of destruction he achieves vox contact with the only vessel remaining in orbit around Certus-Minor. All other system ships departed under the protective wing of the Angelica Mortis with only the Adeptus Ministorum defence monitor Apotheon left behind.

'The Apotheon confirms the first of the armada's vessels breaching the asteroid field and entering the system core.'

'How long?'

'At present speed the advance vessels should reach Certus-Minor in a little under eight hours standard,' Novah tells me. I imagine the lonely defence monitor holding station above the cemetery world with her tiny engines, the reinforced shielding of her bulbous Voss prow, her grim batteries of fat cannon and the underslung length of her powerful lance quad, nestling beneath the vessel's armoured keel.

'My compliments to the commander and cleric,' I say, and mean it. The Apotheon has the best view of the Cholercaust in the system. They know what is coming. To hold position and charge weapons ready for engagement in the face of such suicidal odds is nothing short of adamantium nerve. 'Tell him to ignore the cultships and freighters. Any damage his vessel can visit upon Traitor Astartes cruisers, frigates and gunships on the approach is most welcome.'

I think about wishing the captain luck but the words die on my lips. The Apotheon will be a boarder-ravaged wreck soon and the captain will shortly be dead. Since he knows this, it seems ridiculous to extend even the vaguest of optimistic wishes.

Novah spots something charred and leathery flapping in a depression nearby and moves off to plug the surviving thing with bolt-rounds. I advance up the smoking steps of the building before me – the only one in the immediate area not to have fallen in the bomb blast. Its exterior is cracked and scorched, but symbols in the stonework above the iron doors identify the building as the precinct house of the enforcers.

Putting a boot to the metal doors I enter cautiously. The inside of the building is untouched, protected by the thick walls of the precinct exterior. A perfect place for some otherworldly horror to hide from the Impunitas's bombing run. The armoury is empty and a breeze from the open door disturbs vellum pages on the desks in the scriptoria. They float to the floor where they promptly begin to blotch and soak up blood recently spilt there. Several enforcers lie there also, one without a head and two others with ragged holes blown through their carapace and chests. Moving through the deserted precinct house, past the chastenoria, a booth-verispex and the provostery, I move down into the dungeon. An empty combat shotgun lies abandoned on the stairs. Here the cells are empty, bar one.

Sitting on a bench, behind thick adamantine alloy bars, is Proctor Kraski. The enforcer's scuffed armour is ripped and blasted, while his head leans to one side and his mouth is open. Tobacco juice dribbles from the corner of his mouth and down through his beard, pitter-pattering on the polished cell floor. Something crunches under my boot and lifting it I find a key, clearly thrown out of the cell by Kraski after he locked himself in.

'Proctor,' I call, my voice bouncing unsettlingly around the cell block. Clutching the bars with my gauntlet, one power-armoured tug forces the simple lock and I step inside the cage. Grabbing Kraski by his shaggy hair I lift his head up. 'Proctor,' I call at him again. His eyes have rolled over white but seem to quiver a little as though he is fitting. Suddenly I find out why.

In the open mouth I see something horrible looking back out at me. Several spindly legs erupt from between the enforcer's tobacco-stained teeth. An arachnoid being slips its tiny abdomen out of the opening and runs along my arm and across my armoured chest. All legs, the beast had crammed itself inside Kraski's skull and devoured the contents.

Recoiling with revulsion, my pack slams into the bars of the cell. I knock the monstrosity onto the floor where it clearly considers scrabbling back at me. Dipping my hand into my holster I soon dissuade it with several floor-pulverising blasts from my bolt pistol. The horror scuttles across the floor and up the stairs before I'm even out of the cell. Holding the Mark II in both hands I smack my pauldrons into walls, aiming around corners – expecting the thing to jump at my face. The ground floor of the precinct house confronts me with a fresh nightmare of hiding places, but a swift staccato of bolt-rounds outside persuades me that the beast has fled the building.

Shouldering my way through the iron doors I see Brother Novah waving me to follow with the battle standard as he jumps from one piece of smouldering rubble to the next. I catch up with him at the boundary of destruction, where even a chapel-cryptia had weathered the bomb blast.

'In here,' Novah hisses, angling his bolter at a hole in the wall. Advancing through the brick-blasted opening, bolt pistol held before me, I creep into the darkness of the chapel-cryptia. Lowering the battle standard to get it inside, Novah follows. The interior – usually lit by candles – is a nest of shadows. A stained-glass portal above admits only gloom, and the centre of the chamber is dominated by a sunken stone stairwell down into a crypt. About the chapel are plinths bearing coffins of weathered stone, the brittle lids of which bear raised representations of minor Imperial saints. One is ajar.

Jabbing my Mark II over at the coffin, Novah and I move quietly through the chamber. We both freeze as our sensitive hearing picks up on a scuffling within the coffin. With Novah's bolter aimed at the stone box, I count us down with ceramite fingers from three to one. Tearing off the lid with one hand I thrust my pistol into the darkness with the other.

There is a scream, which neither of us expect, and my finger twitches against the Mark II's trigger. There is a young girl inside – alive and terrified; a dirty-faced cemetery worlder, hiding in the coffin. I hold my gauntlet up, as much an indication to her that we are no threat as an order to Brother Novah not to shoot. The foundling lets rip again with another shrill scream.

Following her eyes I see that she is looking at the battle standard and the rift-spider running down its shaft. Novah's response is immediate. He smacks the banner against the floor, propelling the thing down into the darkness of the crypt.

'Down!' I yell at the shrieking child, prompting her to duck back into the stone coffin. Aiming my pistol down the steps I thumb the weapon to automatic and illuminate the thick darkness with a stabbing stream of firepower. The monster vaults straight back at me from the murk of the crypt, forcing me to drop the weapon. With my gauntlets out in front of me I hold the warp-strong thing at bay as it scrabbles for my face. 'Novah!'

'Do it!' the standard bearer shouts.

Grasping one of the creature's legs I swing it around, smacking its thrashing body against the chapel wall before hooking its obscene form back around and smashing through the stone torso of a nearby statue. Knocked senseless but still very intent on crawling into my skull, the thing spasms in my grip. I toss it into the air above the crypt where Brother Novah shreds the abomination with a precision burst of bolter-fire. With a reality-searing pop the creature vanishes and a light shimmer twirls for the roof. After a moment or two of silence, Novah says, 'Are you all right, sir?'

I nod in response and walk over to the stupefied child. She looks up at me with blank, fearful eyes. Plucking her delicately from her hiding place in the coffin, I hand her to Novah who holds her in the crook of his elbow, beneath the Fifth Company's battle standard. Pushing open the ferruswood chapel-cryptia door with the muzzle of his bolter, I hear him call in the end of our sweep of the demolished district.

I recover my pistol and re-holster the weapon. I find myself staring at the open stone coffin, its frail lid now shattered pieces on the floor. I think of the girl hiding within – the surreal nature of the moment we discovered her. Peering inside I can see something in the bare bottom of the coffin and I pick it out. It's a crystalline wafer, a card from the Emperor's Tarot. I look about, searching the shadows for the revenant, but he is nowhere to be seen.

I turn the card over in my fingertips. The wafer bears the image of a stellar eclipse – a moon covering all but the coronal ring of a distant sun – as viewed from an aligned planetoid. Under the representation is a single word: Umbra.

I feel the ghostly flutter of inspiration pass through the pit of my stomach – a sensation usually reserved for moments of inventive daring in combat, seconds before I wrong-foot my opponent with an unexpected slice of the blade or wholeheartedly commit to some bold and unpredictable manoeuvre. A sensation that has saved my life many times and taken the lives of my enemies many more. I am held there in the moment, stunned witness to the birth of an idea so audacious that it brings an involuntary smile to my mauled lips.

I am there, smiling grimly at the wafer, long enough for Brother Novah to return. He has vox-messages.

'Corpus-captain,' he says, still holding the mortal child. 'Squad Whip Joachim for you, sir. He requests that you and Epistolary Melmoch meet him in the Sepulchre Square. He says it's important.'

'Fine,' I reply. Then add, 'Vox back Brother Simeon. Inform him that I am on my way up to the Memorial Mausoleum. Tell him I want to see the pontifex. Tell him…' I hesitate. 'Tell him it's important.'

CHAPTER FIFTEEN
CESSATION

HIS NAME HAD been Scarioch. He had been a brother Excoriator, a member of Squad Censura and a squad second whip. Hours before, it had been enough for him to serve his squad whip, to honour his company and fight for his Emperor. Katafalque's words had been his guide and Dorn's deeds his example. He had been an Adeptus Astartes – an Angel of the Imperium.

All this was nothing to him now.

He-Who-Had-Been-Scarioch now only thought in shades of red. He felt only a feral injustice – a hatred for everything he had been, for order and discipline, for honour and instruction, for spiteful subservience. For the first time the Space Marine felt the full potential of his superhuman form. He enjoyed the torrent of unbridled strength coursing through his bulging veins, brawn pumped to slabs of stone, the senses of a death world predator and the thunder of hearts in his chest.

The Space Marine felt only the beginning of the end. He had become something else, something new and powerful, something that lived only for the end of others. The crack of skulls. The whisper of razored edges through soft flesh. The thud of blades buried in bodies. The spurt of sliced jugulars. The snapping of necks and spines. The sighs and gasps of the dying. The splash of footsteps in pools of spilt blood. All this He-Who-Had-Been-Scarioch could feel just beyond his aching fingertips. He desired nothing more than to make these murderous fantasies fact and his inability to enact the blood-lush nightmare only fuelled his building rage further.

They had done this to him, his so-called brothers. The killing, the slaughter – it had to continue. The craven Angels of the corpse-Emperor failed to see this. Dastards all, they had mobbed him like cowards, holding him down and prising the steaming sword from his hand. Not before the Scarioch-Thing had broken a few more jaws and noses with his brow and flailing knuckles. When he would not soothe to the lullaby of their weakling words and fraternal entreaties, they cut the cable-fibres of his armour and stripped him of his pack power-plant. They stretched his arms behind him and bound his wrists behind a cloister-pillar, using the bent length of a nearby railing bar.

The berserker thrashed against the deadweight of his plate. The pillar groaned. The metal of his bindings squealed and contorted. The raging Angel strained and struggled against his captivity. His teeth clenched and his gums oozed blood. The whites of his eyes were thread-shattered and deep red while his Adeptus Astartes flesh ruptured with the mosaic distension of bruising and exertion.

About him, forgotten brothers paced and stared, infuriatingly out of reach. Some clutched boltguns and pistols – cowards shrinking behind their killing machines. The Scarioch-Thing thought he could smell their fear. Their weakness appalled him and fed the fires of his hatred. They looked down on him with an apoplexy-stirring mixture of superiority and sadness. Their pity gunned the engines of wrath booming inside his chest. More intolerable weakness. Blood stormed through his veins – the sacramental essence of the War-Given-Form. He no longer had words.

His mouth opened and serpentine hatred leaked from his spoiling soul.

The Emperor's meek-seed had plenty to say, but their words seemed distant, almost unintelligible. He-Who-Had-Been-Scarioch detested them all.

Joachim – but a battle-virgin compared to him – who had been elevated to whip. Melmoch the mutant with his witch-ways. Brother Boaz, who had bested him once in the practise cages and had never allowed him to forget it. The disgraced chief whip, Uriah Skase, who had failed so completely when demanding Trial by the Blade. And Zachariah Kersh, Scourge of the Fifth Company, the warrior who failed his Chapter Master, surrendered his standard and dropped his blade. Him, the Scarioch-Thing hated the most.

The Excoriators looked at Scarioch.

'He is taken,' Melmoch said. 'The gall-fever has him.'

'You seem awfully eager to write him off, witchbreed,' Joachim shot back. 'Perhaps you suffer the fever, too.'

'His soul is but a plaything for the Ruinous Powers now,' Melmoch replied.

'Like yours?'

Melmoch let the goading insult wash over him. 'Is that what you would want for your brother?'

'Skase?' Joachim urged.

'Can't we just keep him secure?' Brother Boaz offered.

'Like a caged animal?' Melmoch asked.

'Until the fever passes...'

'This will not pass,' the Epistolary told him. 'He is the Blood God's now. The first of our kind to fall to his hunger.'

'He's not the first,' the Scourge said with regret. 'Ishmael is lost to us, also.'

'We don't know that,' Skase growled back.

'You know what must be done,' Kersh said.

'Skase...' Joachim pleaded.

He-Who-Had-Been-Scarioch seared into the chief whip with his bloody, anathemic eyes. The words exchanged around him boiled his blood with their meaninglessness.

Uriah Skase brought up his bolt pistol. The damned

Excoriator looked up the length of its chunky barrel at his chief whip.

'I'm sorry, brother.'

The Scarioch-Thing snarled.

Skase fired.

KERSH ENTERED THE square. There were people everywhere. All of the small plazas, dirge-cloisters and devotional quads were swamped with cemetery worlders. The throngs parted for him, Adeptus Astartes as he was, even though the Certusians had precious little space and what little they had they had devoted to blankets, shroud tents and tiny shrines. Like pilgrims, the Certusians had gathered in the shadow of the Umberto II Memorial Mausoleum, thousands of them. Despite their need and number, the distribution of water and food was orderly and the atmosphere dour and reverent. Many of the cemetery worlders were at prayer and those who weren't bowed their heads respectfully as the corpus-captain moved through the parting crowds.

With Excoriators and the remaining Charnel Guard holding the city perimeter, and Squad Whip Keturah's Scouts haunting the towers and belfries of Obsequa City, creating a city-maze of kill zones, common Certusians had been forced to make do with the harsh stone of the squares and the cobbles of the tight esplanades for beds. Kersh walked through them all: women and children, the old, the sick, Oliphant's remaining priests and the droves of newly arrived menfolk – those who could not cope with the horror of the front line and had fled their stations on the perimeter during the initial assaults. The Excoriator saw what exposure to the madness of the warp did to ordinary mortals. Some men rocked like infants, others couldn't stop weeping while others had gone mute. Some were babblers, incessantly speaking of the horrors they had seen, while others had simply crawled under a blanket and had not come out.

'The pontifex?' Kersh put to a preacher carrying a water-satchel and distributing drinking water.

The priest directed him to the next plaza where the scene was altogether different. Kersh nodded to a Sister of Battle in full armour and hefting the bulk of a heavy flamer. He couldn't help wondering what havoc the scorched nozzles of the weapon might wreak on the city perimeter. Beyond, Kersh began to get an idea. The plaza was stained with soot. Smoke drifted from blast marks, and macabre cages of incinerated bodies decorated the blackened stone where the roasted bones of tightly-packed mobs had melted and warped into giant works of demented art. Amongst these scenes of charred horror, parents attempted to comfort their children, and cemetery worlders tried to concentrate on their devotions.

Framed in the imposing architecture of the Memorial Mausoleum, Kersh found Pontifex Oliphant hobbling between the still smouldering remains, administering last rites to the dead. Several soot-smeared labourers with picks and saws had the unenviable duty of separating the merged forms while stone-faced vestals carried coffins across the plaza and tried their best to fit the twisted skeletons inside. Kersh noted that the Sisters of the August Vigil had stationed themselves about the crowds as well as on the nearby porch-barbican. A meltagun-wielding shadow in cobalt power armour watched the proceedings impassively from nearby.

'Corpus-captain,' Oliphant greeted him, the ghost of a smile on his slanted lips.

'How are you coping, pontifex?' Kersh asked.

Dragging his slack leg and shoulder, the ecclesiarch turned. 'Don't worry about me, corpus-captain. I have my life, which is more than I can say for these unfortunate souls here.'

Kersh bit at his bottom lip. 'Pontifex,' the Excoriator began uncomfortably. 'I want to apologise for your losses here–'

'Corpus-captain, please...'

'No,' Kersh pressed. 'The strategy was mine and it failed. Certusians abandoned their posts and fled back through the city where my Scouts had no orders to fire upon them.'

'You could have had no idea…'

'I could have and I should have. It takes a particular breed of man to face the arch-enemy, to hold his nerve and keep his mind. There are sights men in their multitude were not meant to see. Evils that should remain unknown. Horrors to which humanity should not be subjected. Beings in whose presence mortals succumb to madness.'

'What of those that are more than mortal? Are you immune to such experiences?'

'No, pontifex, we are not,' Kersh told him honestly. 'But it is the purpose for which we have been bred and we do not shirk from it.'

Oliphant watched two vestals carry away the black, encrusted remains of a heat-warped skeleton. Kersh saw him lift one young woman's face with one of his grim smiles.

'I was conducting the prayer vigil. The people, patient and in great number, gathered in the open spaces around the Mausoleum. We gave thanks to the great Umberto II – whose spirit watches over us on this darkest of nights – and the God-Emperor, whose servants are never far away.' Oliphant gave the Excoriator a meaningful stare, confirming to the corpus-captain that he was referring to the Adeptus Astartes. 'We were engaged in our prayer cordon when our number were surprised by shouting from the streets beyond. For-give me, corpus-captain, but at first we thought the enemy might have bypassed your insufficient number. When wives saw their husbands, and children their fathers, the crowd rejoiced. Until the killing started. I will not describe the bit-ter spectacle – not in the presence of the dead for whom we would wish nothing but an eternal peace. Many died, and in the mayhem it was impossible to tell murderer from vic-tim. In the end, Palatine Sapphira ordered her Sisters to take blunt but decisive action to put an end to the atrocity. They cleansed the afflicted crowds with holy flame and…' the pontifex struggled, seeming not to have further words for the description, '…that was an end to it.'

'Pontifex,' Kersh said, seeing the pain on the man's face: his physical infirmity, the grief he felt for his people, and the spiritual agony he suffered at having such carnage taint the sacred earth of his cemetery world. The Excoriator felt it only fair to prepare the ecclesiarch for the truth that more was coming. 'Let me speak plainly, as a warrior. What you have seen is but the beginning. The comet's malign influence has turned your people against themselves and further bolstered the enemy's number. My Epistolary suspects that the horrors we have witnessed thus far are merely immaterial overspill, the detritus of the warp, bleeding through into our existence. The Cholercaust is yet even to arrive. When it does, it will make what we have seen so far seem like nothing. An invasion made up of countless cultists, the Blood God's daemonkin and, worst of all, our Traitor brothers – the World Eaters. They are Angels insatiable in their thirst for slaughter, unparalleled in their desire for wanton carnage. They were and unfortunately still are amongst the best the immortals have to offer on the battlefield. They head a Blood Crusade that has never known defeat – that has sundered hundreds of Imperial worlds – and they will kill everything on the surface of this planet.'

The ecclesiarch's half-smile began to fall.

'You are saying that defeat is certain. That you can't protect us…'

'I'm not sure anyone can,' Kersh told him honestly.

'But, I heard you tell your Angels–'

'They are warriors,' Kersh said, shaking his head. 'They need to hear that. We are sustained by our faith.'

'Faith in yourselves…'

'Yes,' Kersh nodded. 'But to you I offer solemn truths. We are few in the face of legion. My men and I will fight for you. We will fight with the last of our strength, with but a single breath in our lungs and a single drop of blood left in our bodies. But when we fall – and we will, for the equations of battle are cold and certain – your people will be put to the blade.'

Oliphant's head began to bob gently with dark

understanding. Then he looked at the Excoriator with warm eyes and his simple smile.

'You have your faith,' he told Kersh, 'and I have mine. You remember, when we first met, I said that I knew you would come?'

'I do.'

'He came to me, corpus-captain.'

'He?'

'The God-Emperor…'

'Pontifex, with respect, you would not be the first cleric to claim to have experienced a divine visitation,' Kersh said softly.

'I know not whether I were dreaming or awake,' Oliphant continued, staring off into the distance. 'The God-Emperor came to me. Glorious in His corpse-lord's plate – black as the depths of space – yet impossible to look upon, like a sun or the fierce glare of some bright star.'

Kersh couldn't believe what he was hearing.

'You have seen this?'

'Many times,' Oliphant confirmed, his gaze still fixed some way distant. 'Before you arrived. And since. It is how I knew His Angels were coming. That help was on its way. That we were destined for the Adeptus Astartes' protection.'

'You see him still?'

'From time to time,' Oliphant smiled. 'He walks among us. He is in the corner of the eye, in the shadows, waiting to reveal His true purpose. It is His mysterious way.'

'I don't know what that is,' Kersh told him honestly. 'But I don't think it is your God-Emperor.'

'We shall see, sir,' the pontifex said. 'He will reveal Himself to you in due course.' Kersh grunted. 'The God-Emperor fights on our side, Angel. Have faith in that.'

Kersh thought of the Emperor – now all but a corpse on his sarcophagus-throne.

'Pontifex,' the Scourge said. 'The Adeptus Astartes live for victory and the Great Dorn has shown us that there are many kinds. Stood amongst the corpses in the Imperial Palace, with the Emperor – all but dead – returned to the safety of its thick walls, the primarch would have felt little desire to celebrate victory. Walking from the deathtrap of the Eternal Fortress – a survivor of Iron Warriors ingenuity and the Iron Cage – Dorn would have felt no jubilation. These were not victories in a traditional sense – those to which mortals aspire when they see demigods crafted in stone and bronze, and hear of the exploits of heroes. Demetrius Katafalque, in the *Architecture of Agony* teaches us that these were victories, that frustration of the arch-enemy's desires and the impediment of evil is a kind of victory. That in a galaxy perpetually at war – in an existence of continuous slaughter – survival is victory.'

'What are you saying?' Oliphant mumbled, entranced by the Excoriator's words.

'Do you trust me, pontifex?'

'I do, Angel.'

'And do your people trust you? Will they do as you ask – no matter how strange and daunting the road you ask them to take?'

'They are my flock. I am their shepherd. The God-Emperor shows me the path that I might lead and they follow.'

Kersh looked around at the crowds of cemetery worlders. He imagined the Certusians in their thousands and thousands, huddled about the Memorial Mausoleum. He took a deep breath and nodded slowly to himself.

'Gather your flock, pontifex,' the Scourge told him finally, 'and as many shovels as you can lay your hands on. Your people take the crow road tonight...'

SISTER SAPPHIRA ROSE from the baptismal waters of the communal font. Rivulets of holy water cascaded down and around the curves of her purified flesh. Droplets splashed against the surface of the pool and then spattered the cool floor of the chancery as the palatine stepped out into the towels and attentions of her Sisters.

She stood there in silence as members of her mission proceeded to dry her and dash her with consecrated ash from an itinerant stoup. All the while, incense burned from globes suspended from the ceiling and prayers were whispered by the attending women. As Sapphira's limbs, torso and bust were bound with sackcloth ribbon, Sister Klaudia – wearing her cornette and ceremonial robes – read from Saint Severa's *Articles of Faith and Flame* and offered blessings to her palatine and superior.

Sapphira felt the sting of the baptismal bath, replaced by the chill of the chancery air, in turn replaced by the raw irritation of the sackcloth. The chamber-candles flickered, allowing the shadows to momentarily encroach. About the chancery pillars and devotional stonework of the entrance-archway, the palatine thought she saw movement. The Sister's spine became host to an irrepressible shiver and her bare flesh pimpled. Her nightmare had returned. A giant in midnight plate. An emissary of death. A vision of nether-world insanity.

It had haunted her. She could feel its presence, like a predator stalking its prey. A thing of the beyond, come to test her faith. She had sensed it while at devotion, during lonely sentinel duty and down in the consecrated vault, where she attended upon the sacred bones of Umberto II and her obligations of protection and preservation. She had even awoken to the nightmare watching her sleep in her private cell. From the darkness Sapphira saw the glow of unnatural life, the radiance of an eye watching her through the rent of a battle-smashed helm. It was the horrid attention of that eye and visions of the ghostly warrior that drove Sapphira to hope that her own eyes deceived her. She prayed to Saint Severa and Umberto II for guidance, and had almost begged confession of Pontifex Oliphant. She could not bring herself to confide in her Sisterhood – especially at a time of such uncertainty. With the discovery of the Ruinous monument and the arrival of the Adeptus Astartes, there never seemed to be an appropriate time to admit her affliction, and Sister Sapphira had taken refuge in the regularity of baptismal baths, consecrational dustings and blessings.

The light of the all-seeing eye dimmed as two Sisters in the slender, cobalt plate of their calling entered the chancery.

It had been the breeze accompanying the Sisters' entry to the mission-house that had initially guttered the candles. The first cradled a heavy flamer while the second held a meltagun to her breast. Presenting themselves before their palatine, the pair of dominiate Sisters placed their weapons on the floor and rose, taking off their helmets. Sister Klaudia concluded her blessings and stepped aside to acknowledge Sister Lemora and Sister Casiope.

'Sisters,' Klaudia acknowledged. 'With what justification do you disturb the palatine?'

'The Adeptus Astartes have visited the pontifex,' Casiope reported, nodding first to Klaudia before addressing her superior.

'And?' Sapphira prompted.

'The cemetery worlders are being moved from the city centre and out onto the necroplex,' Sister Lemora confirmed.

'The necroplex?' the palatine marvelled. 'Out beyond the perimeter?'

'Yes, my lady.'

'Insanity.'

'Yes, my lady.'

'Palatine,' Sister Klaudia said. 'I fear the Excoriators are not to be trusted.'

'They are the Emperor's Angels, Sister,' Sapphira reminded her. 'You think them corrupted?'

'I think they're Dorn's savages,' Klaudia told her honestly. 'They fight like dogs amongst themselves and this Scourge that leads them is detested and distrusted even amongst his own kind.'

'What do you think?' Sapphira put to the other two Sisters.

'They are gene-breeds, engineered for battle,' Lemora said. 'I think they've probably settled on using the Certusians as cannon fodder.'

'You?'

'The cemetery worlders are not my concern,' Casiope told her. 'We are the Sisters of the August Vigil. Our first duty must be to Umberto II's sacred remains. The Cholercaust is here. Planetfall is imminent. It's time to withdraw to the vault.'

Sapphira remained silent for a moment, her eyes searching the darkness. She turned to Sister Klaudia.

'Begin preparations to garrison the vault,' the palatine told her. Klaudia nodded in satisfaction. 'Back to your posts,' she said to Lemora and Casiope. 'I will see the Scourge and determine the Adeptus Astartes' intentions. My armour!' she called, and the Sisters surrounding her peeled away to recover their palatine's plate.

CHAPTER SIXTEEN
THE APOTHEON

'COMMANDER!'

Lieutenant Heiss knocked again briskly on the cabin door. She looked at the matt reflection of herself in the scuffed metal. Even in such a surface she could see her auburn curls and freckled face. 'Commander,' she called again. 'We've had a vox from the surface. New orders from the Adeptus Astartes.'

Heiss had been on the bridge of the Adeptus Ministorum defence monitor *Apotheon* when the message had been received. She had never spoken to an Emperor's Angel before and would have been more anxious but for the vision of approaching destruction that dominated the lancet viewscreen.

Below the thick-set monitor, the cemetery world of Certus-Minor turned slowly. With cloud-cover the colour of soured milk and a surface mostly made up of graven stone, the small planet looked vulnerable and alone in the depths of the cosmos. *Apotheon* held station above a glassy lake near the north pole, watching over the Ecclesiarchy world like a pugnacious watchdog. The monitor had been the only vessel to remain, with the necrofreighters and transports long gone and even the system ships fled. But dread and the crushing weight of responsibility only really settled on the lieutenant when the Adeptus Astartes strike cruiser *Angelica Mortis* departed on a course for the Adeptus Mechanicus forge-world of Aetna Phall.

The *Apotheon* had remained on station, a silent observer as the Keeler Comet had approached. Heiss had then witnessed the second strangest thing she had ever seen in her relatively sheltered life. Above Certus-Minor the comet changed course. It was as though the blood-red ball of ice, rock and metal had simply changed its mind and turned, heading away from the planet on a different trajectory. When Commander Vanderberg asked her to calculate a new destination, the cogitator had offered the Vulcanis system as the most likely heading, with Ultrageddon and Voss Prime possibilities. One thing the cogitator was certain about, however, was that the Keeler Comet's present course would take it into Segmentum Solar and on towards Holy Terra.

The strangest thing Heiss had ever seen had been the tail following the comet, a sanguine stream of dust and gas, the middle of which was a glimmering fracture. It appeared to Heiss like the comet nucleus was a zipper, opening a breach in the unstable fabric of reality behind it. She had watched as swarms of otherworldly beings bled through the haemorrhage, before being pulled towards the nearby cemetery world by the planet's gravitational field. She had taken some solace in the way the distant beasts seem to streak towards the planet, burning up like meteorites on a fiery entry, but vox-casts from Obsequa City reported heavy fighting, confirming that much of the daemonkin swarm had found its way to the surface to test the defenders.

'Commander Vanderberg!' Heiss called. When again she heard nothing behind the cabin door, she pulled the plunger beside it. The bulkhead gave a hydraulic wheeze and the heavy door yawned open. 'Sir, forgive my trespassing, but we have orders from the Adeptus Astartes... Sir?'

Heiss took a brief look around the cabin. The commander's

bunk was empty, as was his private chartroom. The first the lieutenant knew of Vanderberg was the sound of her boot in the commander's blood. Vanderberg was sat at his fer- ruswood writing desk. The *Apotheon*'s log sat on the desk surface next to a data-slate bearing a message to the com- mander's sister on Scintilla. He had got no further than, 'My Dearest Greta...'

'Commander...' Heiss mouthed as she edged around. Vanderberg's eyes had rolled over but his face was just as baggy and kindly as ever. His arms had fallen down by the side of the ferruswood chair, and both wrists still dribbled with the captain's life. Stepping forwards into the pool of blood, Heiss kicked the surgical kris Vanderberg had used across the floor. The lieutenant reasoned the commander had probably taken it from the ship's small infirmary. Plac- ing her fingers against his neck, she failed to find a pulse.

Heiss stood there for a moment, uncertain. Then, slowly she turned and walked out of the cabin, leaving bloody footprints behind her. As her strides took her towards the bridge they became quicker and more determined. There was very little to do about the situation. The commander was dead. She was the only other commissioned officer on board the ship and the Adeptus Astartes had issued orders.

Walking onto the bridge, she found Midshipman Randt where she had left him, looking stricken and uncomfortable in command of the bridge under such dire circumstances. Padre Gnarls stood by the captain's throne in his preacher's robes, the gangly priest looking like a gargoyle thanks to his bald head and hooked nose. All Adeptus Ministorum vessels carried a padre as a requirement, and although Gnarls could be uppity and meddlesome, Heiss was glad to see him on the bridge where he was a calming influence. Beyond were a number of the monitor's bridge staff and ghoulish servitors.

'Thank the God-Emperor,' Randt blurted as Heiss entered. 'The Adeptus Astartes still await the commander's confirmation.'

'Confirm the order,' Heiss called across the bridge with

confidence, before sitting down in the commander's throne.

Gnarls frowned and stood behind the throne before leaning in close.

'Where's the commander?' he asked with his hooked nose over her shoulder. Heiss looked over at Randt, who was busy confirming the Excoriators' orders with the planet surface.

'Vanderberg's dead,' Heiss told him simply, without looking at the priest. 'By his own hand.'

Gnarls started to say something, but stopped himself and nodded slowly. He moved around to the other side of the throne, pulling his vestments about him.

'Obsequa City confirms,' Randt announced. 'We are no longer to observe. The *Apotheon* is ordered to disrupt the enemy approach and landing. We are to favour cruisers and gunships over freighters and cultships.'

'Acknowledge the order,' Heiss said to him. 'And wish them luck. Send our regards to the pontifex. Inform him that the Adeptus Ministorum defence monitor *Apotheon* will do the God-Emperor's work in the heavens and that we shall remain on this vox-frequency for as long as we can. *Apotheon* out.'

Heiss looked up at Gnarls, who gave her another, unhappy nod.

'It's down to you now,' he told her simply, which was probably the nicest thing he'd ever said to her.

'Helm, set an equatorial intercept course and accelerate to ramming speed.'

'Aye.'

'Mister Randt, open channels with the portside and starboard gun-decks, as well as the keel lance section. Have the enginseer informed that the lance is about to fire.'

'Yes, lieutenant.'

'Padre Gnarls…'

'Yes, lieutenant?'

'Would you be so good as to join the boatswain and help organise the repelling parties. I will keep *Apotheon* out of the enemy's grasp, but should they grapple us I would like all airlocks and exterior bulkheads welded shut and barricaded from the inside. If they want in, let's at least force them to cut their way in.'

'I would be happy to represent your interests amongst the repelling parties, lieutenant. May the God-Emperor be with you.'

'And with you, padre.'

With that the preacher left the bridge to seek out a weapon and the boatswain.

As the defence monitor's reinforced Voss prow dropped, the approaching Cholercaust fleet filled the lancet screen. It was colossal, larger than any Imperial fleet Heiss had seen gathered, and she had seen a few, having served on a Navy cutter above Ultrageddon as a young ensign. It held no tactical configuration, with vessels spread far and wide like an ugly smear across the darkness of space. Smaller vessels didn't bother to keep station on their larger counterparts and cruisers held no formation at all. The armada's shape and organisation was merely a result of the fastest vessels, and most fervid, engine-overloading captains, streaking out in front, while the swarm of fat freighters, berserker-laden giga-tankers, renegade Guard transports and Traitor Astartes vessels formed a miasma of frustration, hatred and rage behind. About the fleet swarmed sub-light gunships, brigs, tugs and small system ships, each carrying their own blood-crazed crews and killers. Behind the armada trailed a tail of wrecks and burn-outs: damaged, crippled and engine-cored vessels that still burst at the bulkheads with murderous hordes but were forced to either limp on behind the main fleet or be towed by other craft.

The Cholercaust had arrived and it was ready to disgorge the insane, the bloodthirsty and the daemonic on the tiny cemetery world that was its prey. The defence monitor's feeble engines pushed the heavily-armoured vessel towards ramming speed; Heiss had the *Apotheon* come at the tip of the approaching fleet from the pole.

'W-w-where's the commander?' Randt put to Heiss. The midshipman expected to see his captain on the bridge during such a serious engagement.

'The commander is indisposed,' the lieutenant called back. 'Now, ready lance!'

'Lance charging,' the midshipman answered.

'Find me a target, Mister Randt,' Heiss ordered, and watched as the defence monitor's runebank spat out a list of trajectories. Heiss couldn't imagine what the monstrous Chaos captains called their vessels now, but the list of missing, stolen, surrendered, mutinous and captured merchantmen that made up the Cholercaust's vanguard streamed across the screen. 'Magnify,' Heiss called. A lancet screen blinked before closing on the approaching rush of vessels. The flanks of the ships displayed faded names and designations: the *Aurigan*, *Coquette*, the *Trazior Franchise*, *Sunpiper*.

'Cultships, Mister Randt,' Heiss told him. 'Seized freighters packed with Chaotics and volunteer degenerates, no doubt.'

'I have a target, commander,' Randt told her. 'A positive identification. Frigate, *Spite*, Goremongers Space Marine Chapter.'

'That's more like it. Target that renegade Adeptus Astartes escort.'

'Enginarium reports lance charged. Awaiting your order.'

'Mister Randt?'

'Target lock: thorax and batteries.'

Heiss stared at the Traitor Angel vessel. She tried to imagine the superhuman mayhem and chaos on board. Beings who if before her on the battlefield would be twice her size, brimming with the insatiable desire to kill; who would mindlessly end her in the space of a blink. She clutched the arms of the captain's throne.

'Fire.'

The lancet screen flashed retina-scorching white. The *Apotheon*'s mighty lance, underslung along the length of the defence monitor's keel, answered the call. A thick beam of pure energy erupted from the Adeptus Ministorum vessel, crossing the vanguard of the colossal fleet like a cannonball across the bow. As Heiss and the bridge crew looked on with wide eyes and hope in their hearts, the beam seared straight through the traitor frigate. Their aim was perfect. The thorax section of the vessel vaporised and, as the sizzling beam of energy flickered and died, both the command decks and swollen engine column of the Adeptus Astartes vessel fell away in different, void-tormented sections.

A cheer exploded across the bridge, and even Heiss found herself on her feet.

'All right,' she called. 'Focus. Mister Randt, have the lance charged for a second target.'

Heiss felt the *Apotheon* follow the path of the beam, on a collision course for the enemy armada. Her second target was a portly Imperial Guard transport, the traitor vessel decorated with feral world petroglyphs and indigenous art. Her third, a monstrous vessel that appeared a mind-scalding fusion of metal hull and red daemonflesh. The horror-ship took the *Apotheon*'s fury straight in its bloated abdomen of an engine column. Instead of disintegrating like the Goremongers frigate, or exploding like the traitor transport, the possessed vessel began to ripple, tremble and spume – like a wounded wild animal suffering violent death-throes. When the lance beam punched straight through the mutant-ship, the thing started vomiting globule-clouds of zero-gravity blood. It snatched out with hooks, claws and tentacular appendages, entangling nearby cultships, before tearing them apart in void-drowning fury.

With the Adeptus Ministorum defence monitor plunging down the cemetery world's ivory curvature and cutting pack leaders in two with its brutal lance, Heiss and her crew were making themselves known to the Cholercaust fleet. Tempted by the prospect of first blood, bastardised raiders and the cannibal crews of piratical marauders surged towards the *Apotheon*. Heiss pushed the monitor's feeble engines to their limit. The vessel crossed the blood-thirsty bows of the enemy ships and presented the gaping muzzles of its waiting battery of cannon.

'Fire as you bear!' Lieutenant Heiss commanded. At Midshipman Randt's relaying of the order the starboard battery began a ragged, punishing barrage. Laser blasts thundered down the lengths of Chaos raiders and slaughtermen. Light and fire blazed its way through the oncoming vessels, torching warrior-cramped compartments from their prows to their sterns. 'Give the order to fire at will,' Heiss told Randt as the *Apotheon* completed its first broadside. The bridge crew watched a myriad of vandalised brigs, gunships and cutters punch through the debris field of spearhead derelicts and wreckage. Streaking out from them were a swarm of smaller vessels still – hump shuttles, fortified life-rafts, launches and assault boats, all packed with homicidal thugs, honed blades and hull-cutting equipment.

'Lieutenant…'

'Give Padre Gnarls and the boatswain the order, prepare to repel boarders,' Heiss said tightly.

'Lieutenant!' Randt shouted. Heiss saw it. A Khornate cultship. A heavy transport – wall-to-wall with the Blood God's murderous acolytes – passing across their own Voss prow section. It was all happening so fast. The lance. The continuous, crashing gunfire of the battery. The impending boarding action. The armada without end, Chaos vessels passing behind and about the lone defence monitor. The ships would be on an unswerving course for Certus-Minor – where from low orbit the Cholercaust fleet would launch an apocalyptic landing, its Thunderhawks, drop-ships, pods, lighters, barges, carriers, haulage skiffs and junkers numerous enough to black out the stars. From this nightmare ramshackle of craft a vast army of insane blood-crusaders would spill. Cultists, Chaotics, daemons and Traitor Angels. Uncountable. Unstoppable.

The lieutenant's lip curled. 'Are we at ramming speed?'

The young Randt looked at her grimly.

'Almost, lieutenant.'

'I want to hit her amidships, do you understand, Mister Randt?' Heiss said. The midshipman nodded. Heiss stared at the fat transport towards which they were streaking with the queasy certainty of a torpedo. Heiss licked her lips. 'I want to break her back…'

CHAPTER SEVENTEEN
UNTO DUST

THE SHOVEL BIT into the cemetery world grit. Woodes Sprenger had been a grave fosser his whole life. Under his sweat-soaked shirt and dust-coat he was tough and lean; he handled his spade with speed and a working man's determination. Tossing earth up out of the grave with hypnotic rhythm, the fosser's blade finally hit metal. Scraping off the rusty surface of the stasis casket, Woodes kicked footholds into the side of the grave and used the tip of the shovel to prise open the coffin.

The stench of stale death rose to meet the Certusian. He coughed and covered his mouth. Reaching up for his gaslamp by the graveside, Woodes brought it down to explore the coffin's contents. This was borderline sacrilege for the grave fosser, whose job – like thousands of others – was to bury the dead sent to reside in the sacred cemetery world earth and dig up caskets whose tenure had expired to make way for further cadaver arrivals. Only the wealthy and advantaged could afford a plot on Certus-Minor. They were buried, the stasis-field generators on their sarcophagi deactivated and removed, and the dead allowed to rot in

peace – as cemetery world custom dictated. Common fossers never went into the coffins – only grave robbers ever
did. In this way, breaking the seals and prising open the
casket went against every fibre of Woodes's spiritual being,
and he would not have been doing so – even given the dire
circumstances on Certus-Minor – unless the pontifex himself and the Emperor's Angels had given the order.

Inside the casket Woodes found the remains of a woman.
A desiccated skeleton buried in the copious material of an
extravagant grave gown. Woodes expected that she was
spire nobility from some distant hive-world. The bones of
her fingers were adorned with the precious metal and stone
of rings, and the vertebrae of her neck were a tangled nest of
priceless jewellery. The empty sockets of her skull leered up
at the grave fosser and Woodes coughed again. Leaning in
close, Woodes checked the system of wires running down
the depth of the grave between the sculpted tombstone and
the casket. Pulling the wire cord, Woodes set off the mourn-
ful peal of the bell positioned in the decorative detail of the
marker.

Against the tombstone Woodes saw his weapon, the
autorifle he'd been issued – with the scuff-scratched stock,
crescent clips and long barrel shroud. The noisy weapon
that had saved his life and those of others during the first
battlement assaults. With Donalbain he'd held his ground,
despite wanting to run from the terror and madness with
his fellow fossers and Certusians.

Climbing out of the grave in a well-practised motion,
Woodes picked up a small stone from the surrounding soil
and posted it through the mouth of a cherubim crafted in
the stone. He heard the tinny clatter of the stone as it fell
down through the metal pipe connecting the tombstone to
the casket and providing it with an air source.

Checking such safety mechanisms was usually the verger's
duty. Personally, Woodes had only been present at one pre-
mature exhumation. It had been in the Asphodel-East field
close to where Woodes had lived. He had been summoned
from his shack by Father Deodat, a passing preacher who had

heard a bell from the lychway. Father Deodat, Woodes, Donalbain and several other fossers from the cenopost searched for the marker and sent for shovels before proceeding to dig up the grave on the preacher's orders. The bell rang incessantly, and within the casket the cemetery worlders found an Imperial Guard officer – a dragoon in full dress uniform – who had been buried with his plumed helmet and gleaming sabre. The officer had been confused, claustrophobic and out of his mind with fear. In the darkness of the sarcophagus his frantic fingers had found the wire cord, and after an experimental pull had produced the chime of the bell, the Guardsman had proceeded to ring it in the hope that someone would discover him.

Woodes never saw the Imperial Guard officer again. Father Deodat informed the fosser, however, that the officer had told him that he'd been part of an eradication force sent to the jungle world of Yasargil to exterminate the k'nib infestation there. The last thing the officer recalled was being stung by a hanging creeper and reporting to the camp infirmary. Deodat hypothesised that his subsequent paralysis was taken for death, and that the colonel's body had been stasis-shipped from Yasargil to Pyra and from his home world to Certus-Minor. As the alien toxin wore off, the dragoon found himself confronted with the horror of being buried alive.

Nearby, Woodes heard the spade of his brother-in-law Donalbain crunch through the earth. Shovelfuls of dirt flew up out of a grave and landed in a neat pile next to the crisply cut hole. Donalbain was a fosser like Woodes and lived in the same cenopost hamlet.

'This is insane...' Woodes said to himself. He looked about him in the darkness. Nearby, cemetery worlders were dragging carts bearing barrels of promethium through the mounds of bodies that surrounded the city perimeter like a hillock or new battlement. The miserable teams pulled their carts through the corpse-piles of daemon insanity, pumping plungers and spraying the fallen nightmares with precious fuel.

'It's what the pontifex ordered,' Donalbain said. Woodes hadn't noticed the silence of the fosser's shovel. Donalbain was taller than his brother-in-law and portlier around the belly; he'd worked up a significant sweat digging the grave so quickly. The Certusian noticed an Excoriators Space Marine stood upon the perimeter battlement, Obsequa City reaching up behind him. The Adeptus Astartes warrior watched them from the continuous mountain of rubble, casting his helmeted gaze up and down the line at other cemetery worlders hard at work clearing the dead and warped flesh of immaterial entities, and digging up graves. Donalbain shuddered. He had no idea how effective the Space Marine's enhanced vision was in the darkness or, indeed, how good his hearing was. 'The Angels ordered it also, so get back to work.'

Woodes thought of the thousands of graves being dug around the battlement perimeter. Graves that were situated where the necroplex met the city limits. Graves that had witnessed the worst of the fighting so far and been hidden beneath the daemon creatures storming the city as heavy gun emplacements and the blessed weapons of the Emperor's Angels had ripped through them. 'Insanity,' he said again.

He watched two figures approach, picking their steps carefully through the gravestones, ichor-soaked earth and mangled bodies of the spawn-monstrosities. The first was his wife, Goody, dressed in her bonnet, shawl and fleece boots. Her face was soot-stained, tight and grim, but in that moment, with the grave at his feet and the shovel in his hand, she had never looked better to him. Goody had her arm around their daughter, Nyzette, and her delicate hand over the young girl's eyes. She did not want the child to see the horror of the warped bodies through which they trudged. The child clutched a home-made rag doll of Saint Astrid to her. Woodes's chest ached for the both of them. As they got closer, he walked to them, embracing both in his sinewy arms.

'Papa!' Nyzette said as she felt his lips against her forehead. He kissed Goody, holding both her and the child close to him – feeling a fearful passion for his wife that he hadn't felt for a number of years.

'Woodes…' she said.

He shook his head. 'It's going to be all right,' he told her. 'You will be safe and you'll be together. That's the important thing.'

'Papa, stay with us,' the young girl chided.

'I can't, my little blessing.'

'No, papa…'

'You must be strong and stay with your mother. You will hide and be safe, but papa must fight – you know, like he did before, when you and mama stayed with Aunt Merelda up near Great Umberto's tomb.'

'Papa!'

'Peace, child. I will be with him,' Donalbain said, smiling as he came up behind them. Goody moved from her husband's embrace to her brother-in-law. The large fosser looked down at her. 'Where's your sister?'

'Merelda's on her way down with the boys,' Goody replied before returning to the arms of her husband.

'Have you got everything?' Woodes asked her as Donalbain picked up Nyzette.

'Everything the pontifex instructed us to take,' Goody replied, taking a sling bag from her shoulder. She pulled a roll of blankets from the bag and as she did caught a glimpse of the open grave behind Woodes, the open coffin and the skeletal woman within. 'Oh, Holy Throne,' she exclaimed, clasping her mouth with her hand.

'Don't look at it,' Woodes said, taking one of the blankets and covering the desiccated cadaver.

'Can't we remove it?' Goody said, horrified.

'Not without arousing suspicion,' Donalbain said, angling the child's head away. 'Besides, disturbing the grave is desecration enough. Removing the body before the end of tenure? That's sacrilege. The pontifex would not hear of it.'

'What else have you got there?'

Goody opened the bag to show her husband the meagre rations of food she'd managed to collect and the water satchel she'd filled from one of the city's holy fountains.

She also had a small, pack-powered handlamp and a bunch of black lilies. The flowers grew along the Certusian lakeshores and were used for decorative arrangements during burial ceremonies. Goody aimed to use them to mask the musty grave-stench of the coffin. Woodes caught sight of a small knife. A stiletto shearing-blade, hidden amongst the death-blooms. He caught Goody's eye and nodded bleakly. If events did not unfold according to plan, with silence from above and provisions spent, the blade would become the most essential of her gathered items.

Woodes looked at his wife, her gaunt but beautiful face. He took her again in a tight embrace. Over her shoulder he saw Donalbain nod. Woodes's eyes drifted skywards to the darkness, knowing that they had little time, that the enemy would not wait. Looking down he saw that there were now several Excoriators stood on the rubble battlement looking down at them. The Emperor's Angels were still like statues in their scarred plate, impassive and beyond the concerns of mortal men.

'All right,' the fosser said finally, feeling Goody's slender body against his own. 'Quickly, into the casket.' Helping his wife down into the grave and taking his child from her uncle, Woodes kissed Nyzette and passed the terrified child down to his wife stood in the coffin. Goody smiled – a gesture, under the circumstances, so telling in its strength and generosity that it brought tears that streaked the fosser's gravedust-smeared cheeks. The mother and child curled up around one another in the space allowed by the sarcophagus occupant. Using the slingbag as a pillow and a second blanket for warmth, the terrified pair looked up at Woodes and Donalbain. 'Remember,' Woodes began, 'only ring the bell when you hear others. Wait as long as you can. You cannot alert the enemy to your presence.' His wife nodded.

'You stay alive,' Goody told them. 'Both of you.'

'I will see you soon,' Woodes promised. And he meant it.

Moving around to the other side of the grave, Donalbain used his shovel to close the lid. Resting the tip of the blade against the rusty lid he pressed down and re-sealed the casket. Woodes tapped on the top of the coffin with his own shovel and was rewarded with a knock in return.

With Donalbain looking for Merelda and his own young ones, the two cemetery worlders began tossing sacred Certusian earth down onto the casket and into the hole. With each disbelieving shovelful, Woodes shook his head. He could not fully reconcile in his mind the fact that he had just buried his own wife and daughter alive. That all about him, fathers, husbands, brothers and sons were doing the same for their loved ones.

The only thing that kept his arms moving and the shovel blade slicing through the mound of soil was the knowledge that they would all be safer below ground than above it when the Cholercaust arrived. That they would hopefully be spared the wanton butchery of the Chaos degenerates. With their families as safe as they could make them, the disturbed earth patted down and the promethium-soaked, misshapen daemon-forms dragged back over the burial site, Woodes snatched up his autorifle. Making the sign of the aquila, he knelt down in front of the grave marker. It bore the name *Erzsebet Dorota Catallus*. He would not forget it. An ice-water determination built in the pit of his stomach. A cold fury he held in reserve for the bastard invaders who were bringing death and destruction to his tiny part of the Imperium. Carrying their weapons and shovels, the cemetery worlders began to make their way back up towards the battlement, to take their positions and ready themselves for the carnage ahead.

I have been watching for a while. This is what it is to lead. A moment's inspiration, the hot quake of an idea or strategy in the privacy of the mind. Abstraction given form through word and order, followed by the rapid shift of men's hearts. Even Angels, who need to be led no less. Loyalty. Pride. Trust. Action. Before your eyes, command becomes reality. What you saw in the orderly, bloodless theatre of the mind unfolds in the drawing of blades and the priming of firing mechanisms. It rapidly devolves into a nightmarish version of your imaginings, replete with deadly, unseen movements, fears that find their form. That's what it is to lead, to dip the toe of one's boot into the calm, crystal waters of possibility, but to march on as you find yourself up to your helmet in the raging torrent of your brothers' blood.

Standing atop the perimeter battlement, I survey the killing fields. A sea of obscene bodies swallowing up the graven architecture of mausolea, tombstones and statues. Out there, amongst the past chaos of battle, are the cemetery worlders. Those it is clear I am here to protect. The duty I was bred to perform. A little of the Emperor's burden taken on my shoulders. What had been the silent insanity of a strategy in my mind is now consigned to history. I told Pontifex Oliphant and for his sins the ecclesiarch lent his words to my own. Thousands of cemetery worlders, ordered to bury their Certusian kin alive. The brief spark of mortal existence, burning brightly under the ground, where blood-soaked minds would not think to look for them.

For a moment I think my revenant returned. I have not seen his ghastly form in a little while. Where he haunted the shadows, there is now but empty darkness. His bale eye gazes upon some other unfortunate, for it no longer looks upon me. I should feel reassured. While I had grown accustomed to the being's attentions and fell presence, it was either the manifestation of an unnatural existence or some symptom of a fractured mind. Neither were particularly attractive prospects and I should feel relieved at the thing's absence. Still, I find myself looking. In the gloom of the Long Night; in the reflection of glass darkly; in the corner of my eye.

I feel brother Excoriators about me. They, I know are there. Immortals on the rubble palisade. Like me, come to watch what common men will do at the word of an Angel. With the slice and cut of shovels through gritty earth on the air, we watch – silently impressed. It can't be easy to dig a grave for your loved ones. Less easy still to fill one containing them.

'Anything?' I ask.

Melmoch is beside me.

'No astrotelepathic communication,' the Epistolary answers. 'Nothing from the hosts and destinations to whom I appealed. I can only reason that the comet's malign influence is too much of a barrier for my skill.'

I nod. 'Thank you for trying,' I say as we watch the cemetery worlders go about their solemn task. 'You think the dust will mask them?'

The Epistolary considers the question.

'This place is saturated with death,' the Librarian concludes. 'The earth is sacred and overpowering in its purpose. We see what we expect to see. The enemy will see a cemetery. He will taste loss. He will smell the stench of death. The Blood God's servants are warriors all. Their unthinking art is murder. Their weapon of choice is carnage – not the shovel. I think our charges safe.'

I nod my acknowledgement and appreciation of the Epistolary's support.

'What if no one survives?' Chief Whip Skase asks grimly, his mind soaked with bloody thoughts.

'Then we lose,' I answer – a statement of the obvious. 'We get to rot above the ground while those we sought to protect – the Emperor's subjects – are left to do so below us. That is why we must fight. Fight and survive. The Blood God's disciples have come here to battle, and we will give them one. In doing so we shall take their eyes off the prize – their intended slaughter of innocents and through this the sundering of this world. We fight to win, but if we lose, I want to go to my death knowing that our enemy will leave sated and swiftly move on. Like a poor marksman, the Blood God will have missed his target and his followers would have failed him. Certus-Minor will not be some deadrock, bathed in slaughter and left behind by the Cholercaust like a cautionary tale. The cemetery worlders will live and the Imperium shall know it. The continued beating of mortal hearts shall give other worlds hope. They shall know that the Cholercaust can be beaten. It will put fire in their bellies and belief in their hearts. Perhaps we will not stop the Blood Crusade here. Perhaps we will not survive. But if we fail, we do so in the hope that others – both mortal and immortal – will succeed. Let that be our legacy.'

Brother Micah comes up behind us with the Fifth Company's Chaplain. Shadrath gives me the dread gaze of his half-skull helm.

'Brother Novah has word from the commander of the Apotheon. The defence monitor has engaged the enemy. She reports a vast Chaos fleet – vessels without number. The Blood God's warriors and

319

minions. *Their landing is under way. The Cholercaust is here.'*

'The pontifex?' I ask.

Micah and Chaplain Shadrath part. Behind them is a Sister of Battle in cobalt plate, a boltgun in her slender gauntlets and a pair of bolt pistols at her hip. Palatine Sapphira of the Order of the August Vigil.

'Pontifex Oliphant is safe,' Sapphira tells me. 'He is down in Umberto II's vault with as many of his remaining priests and attendants as we could accommodate.'

'A kindness,' I return.

'The pontifex told me of your plan,' the Sister reveals. 'A kindness on your own part, corpus-captain – if a macabre one. My Sisters thought your interest in the Certusians lay only in feeding them as fodder to the enemy.'

'I'm happy to disappoint them.'

'The vault door is thick and crafted from adamantium. It should resist all but the most determined assault. I have garrisoned the vault with a squad of my Sisters, under a trustworthy subordinate. I offer myself and the rest of my mission in defence of the city, where the holy work of the God-Emperor might be done.'

I hold out my gauntlet and take her own.

'You are most welcome, Sister,' I tell her. 'We are honoured to share the burden with you.'

Shadrath steps forwards, looking up into the sky.

'Chaplain?'

Carefully, he takes off his half-skull helmet, revealing his face. It is the first time I have gazed upon his features. The shock of white hair, the unsmiling mouth and the implacable lines of almost elemental determination are the primarch's own. Like Demetrius Katafalque before him, Shadrath had been blessed with the features of the Emperor's truest Angel. I follow his gaze to see the flash of gunfire in the sky overhead, the searing burn of the Apotheon's mighty lance.

'Let's to our posts,' Chaplain Shadrath rumbles, his eyes still on the deep expanse of the heavens above. 'Rogal Dorn waits for us at the Eternity Gate.'

We nod and walk slowly away, with the Chaplain's words still ringing in our ears. We are silent, for we have no words to better them.

PART FOUR
DEUS EX DAMNATION...

CHAPTER EIGHTEEN
CHOLERCAUST

ROARING.

The distant darkness gave up the rage-fuelled cacophony of murderous intention. The Blood God's disciples honoured him with their bombast. The stomach-curdling din of barbarism and animal fury. The Cholercaust had arrived and it wanted the cemetery world to know. A deafening barrage of ferocity, made up of personal, if mindless, expressions of individual hatred. Unsettling, in sheer volume alone.

In a demonstration of steadfastness – the kind Kersh reasoned the Charnel Guard and remaining Certusians would need to see – the Scourge stood atop the ichor-splattered battlement. Once again the Imperial forces would try to hold the rubble-mound perimeter, falling back concentrically as the need arose. With the cemetery worlders – vulnerable men, women and children – buried beneath the bordering necroplex, the narrow alleys, stairs and cloisters of the city could play their part if needed. And, if it came to it, the imposing architecture of the Umberto II Memorial Mausoleum had been established as a final fall-back position. Kersh couldn't hope to win against the Blood God's unstoppable host, but the Excoriator planned on putting off the eventuality for as long as possible. The Fifth Company would sell their lives dearly and fight for as long as they could.

There was still a dim possibility that Epistolary Melmoch's appeal had reached out across the stars to a brother-Chapter. The Scourge rested his gauntlet on the angular edges of his gladius pommel. He had not entirely given up on the slim possibility that their kin could arrive to turn the tide. He hadn't burdened his Fifth Company brothers with such damning hope, though suspected it already beat in the hearts of each and every one. Regardless of such mortal folly, the howling tsunami of hate surging across the burial grounds at them was theirs alone.

The dread expectation was palpable. With his enhanced hearing the Scourge could hear the creak of Certusian fingers against triggers, the rapid beating of hearts in serf-manned gun emplacements, and the deep and determined breathing of Excoriators in their battle-helms. Then he saw it. The first offerings of the darkness. Chaos martyrs. The Cholercaust meat shield. Bodies moved through the necroplex, racing towards Obsequa City, the battlement perimeter and certain death.

The Scourge swore. He recognised them immediately. Blood-crazed cemetery worlders. Victims of the gall-fever that had swept the planet in the wake of the Keeler Comet. Husbands, mothers, children. Certusians all. Drawn to Obsequa City like a plague of moths irresistibly summoned to a flame. Kersh felt their urge to kill across the graves. He felt the Charnel Guard and surviving members of the hastily created Certusian militia tighten at the sight of their kindred: neighbours, friends, family. He felt the bile rising within him, his hatred for the servants of darkness and their barbarous tactics. Over the vox-channel, the corpus-captain heard similar confirmations from along the line. The Thunderhawk *Impunitas*, circling high above the city, also reported incoming targets. Peering up into the sky, the corpus-captain watched the stars blink. He got the impression of an ungainly daemon-flock, thunderbolting above them on leathery wings.

Kersh looked back down at the havoc storming its way across the burial grounds towards them. He hated himself for the order he was about to give. He could not afford to waste their hardest-hitting ammunition on such cannon-fodder, yet couldn't allow the masses to swamp the battlement in expectation of hand-to-hand combat alone.

'All battle-brothers and Sisters on the perimeter to hold fire,' he commanded across the channel. 'Heavy weapons to hold fire. Guardsmen and militia to fire at will.'

Shots were hesitant at first, sporadic bolts of light flung across the expanse followed by brief chatters of auto- and stub-fire. The busy landscape of the necroscape impeded the advance of the blood-mental Certusians in a way that it hadn't done so with the many-limbed spawn-swarm of the immaterial incursion. Crazies and cemetery world killers found it difficult to charge at the front line when hampered by the expanse of tombstones, statues and funeral architecture that was the necroplex. This made the howling madmen easier targets, even for the ceremonial Charnel Guard and ill-trained militia, and before long the perimeter lit up the night with a streaming lightshow of near-continuous las-fire. Auto-fire ripped through bodies clambering over grave markers and graven obstacles. Stub-round-riddled torsos lay draped over decorative stone sarcophagi, and lunatics joined the corpse-carpet of warp-spewed forms from the earlier assault.

Above him, Kersh could hear the *whoosh* of sniper fire punctuating the distant hammering of the *Impunitas*'s heavy bolters. Over the vox, estimations of the aerial assault had jumped. Both the *Impunitas* and venerable *Gauntlet* were preoccupied with shredding their way through storm fronts of red daemonflesh, while Whip Keturah and Squad Contritus reported the ragged, broken bodies of winged daemon-predators raining from the heavens. Keturah's Scouts were doing their best to support the Thunderhawks with sizzling sniper fire that cut through the beastforms as they swooped through the narrow spaces between the city towers, spires and belfries.

A blood-freezing shriek erupted from the Imperial line as a shotgun-armed verger left his post and started tearing up the rubble with wild blasts of scattershot. As nearby Guardsmen and cemetery worlders scrambled for cover, the Scourge dipped his hand into his holster. Within a blink the Mark II bolt pistol was out. Without taking his eyes from the chaos of the necroplex, Kersh gunned down the gall-fevered unfortunate. Before the maniac hit crumbled masonry the Mark II was sat back snug in its sporran. The afflicted were no longer a threat to innocent Certusians, but Kersh had made it clear that such infections and defections could still disrupt the integrity of the line and should be dealt with decisively.

Before the battlement, the corpus-captain witnessed a massacre. Every time a bolt from a lasfusil seared through a rabid, unarmed Certusian, another took their place. And another. And another. The stink of fresh death seemed only to send the following fossers, shack-wives and deranged hearsiers into a further frenzy, causing them to double their already fevered efforts to reach the perimeter and wreak havoc.

Others began to emerge through the death and thinning cemetery world gall-thralls. Kersh saw the glint of starlight in unsheathed blades, the flash of optimistic small-arms fire and the macabre flesh desecration of the Blood God's soul-pledged. He saw wires, chains and pins, plucked through faces; knife-crafted tattoos of obscene Khornate symbols, inked in darkness; eyes that were bile-yellow with spite, teeth that were blood-clenched, and skin that was withered with the burden of diabolic patronage. The Regna-Rouge. The Anarchan Razorbacks. The Hellion Dawn. The Krugarian Turncoats. The blade-venerate Gornan Venals. The Attilan Traitor 32nd. The Frater Vulgariate. The Necromundan 'Crazy' Eights. Clan Gamibal of the feared Vessorine Janissaries. The Deathfest. The Bloodsaken. Thousands besides: butcher-baptised slave-soldiers from a myriad of conquered worlds, traitor Guardsmen, heretic militia, mutants, fallen mercenaries, piratical raiders, bestial abhumans, Chaos cultists. All Kersh had fought before on battlefields bordering the Eye of Terror. All had gone down under the Excoriators' blades. Never before, however, had Kersh seen so much Ruinous detritus gathered in one place.

'Open fire!' the Scourge roared.

The bolters of the Sisters of Battle and his brother-Excoriators joined the barrage of las-bolts and lesser weaponry from the battlement, which in turn competed with the dissonant thunder of heavy stubber and autocannon gun emplacements. The collective force of such a release annihilated the remaining rows of cannon-fodder Certusians and knocked the advancing mobs of cultist killers from their feet. As they gunned back furiously from behind crumbling gravestones, other skulltakers barged past. Some simply could not restrain themselves, like mad dogs off their leashes. Others were forced forwards by the sheer weight of numbers behind them, desperate to get into battle and honour the War-Given-Form through deed and death. They too met their end in a torso-punching, head-blasting, limb-shearing broadside of bolts, bullets, light and devastation.

Kersh stood atop the rubble with his bolt pistol clutched in both gauntlets. Those cultist minions who did stumble successfully through the leadstorm to start crunching up the scree-side of the battlement were introduced to the corpus-captain's merciless marksmanship. One by one, Kersh dropped oncoming Guardsmen, self-mutilated acolytes and hideous mutants. They all hungered for his end, but instead had to settle for a bolt-round to the head.

As the Scourge plugged away, with the blood-crazed masses a wall of feverish flesh pushing ever closer through the blizzard of suppression fire, he felt a gauntlet on his pauldron. It was Brother Micah, the company champion's combat shield and boltgun combination resting on his armoured hip.

'Down!' was all Kersh heard.

Micah pushed him to one side with savage insistence. Off balance, the corpus-captain fell faceplate-first into the rubble, turning behind him just in time to see an unfolding disaster. It was the *Impunitas*.

The Thunderhawk had fallen from the sky. It clipped the spiretops of several steeples before ploughing straight through a tower-monolith and cleaving the tiered minaret roof from a pilgrim almshouse. The gunship was swarming with daemonic furies, and its cockpit canopy was splattered with gore. For a moment everything became a maelstrom as the *Impunitas* struck the ground with her blunt nose, bulldozed through the perimeter defences and smashed through the improvised battlement. Reeling from the force of the impact still quaking through the ground and his plate, Kersh felt the slipstream of a wing pass over the back of his pack.

Scrambling to his feet in the unfolding aftermath of the crash, Kersh watched the shattered Thunderhawk plunge straight through the ranks of the lost, smearing cultists into the sacred Certusian earth. The gunship listed and its smashed tail began to skid around, shearing gravestones off at their foundations. The *Impunitas* finally came to rest in the burial ground, leaning the fractured edge of its surviving wing against a single-storey sepulchre. Her graceful form was a crash-mangled mess and her thick plate buckled and rent. Smoke poured from her smashed-open troop compartment, and a single engine still raged in futile determination.

The corpus-captain's raw frustration and anger could not find expression in words. Throwing a clenched fist out at the floor he snarled within his helmet. Beyond the catastrophic loss of the Thunderhawk, his section of the perimeter had been reduced to ruins. Gun emplacements lay toppled and silent; Excoriators and Sisters of Battle were missing; Charnel Guardsmen lay broken and screaming; and there was a gaping hole knocked clean through at least two of the concentric battlements.

As Kersh stomped through the obliteration, hands

reached out for him. Certusian fighters and Guardsmen had been crushed and rolled beneath the Thunderhawk's hull. Nearby, the Scourge saw the half-sheared corpse of Old Enoch, his seneschal – his fragile body crumpled like an insect by the falling gunship. Mumbling a blessing, Kersh took the coiled length of 'the purge' from the serf's belt and dropped the looped lash over the hilts of his swords. Bethesda and Oren he found dazed but alive a little way distant. The absterge had been fortunate, bearing only cuts and savage bruises from head to foot. The lictor had broken his ritual arm and winced as Kersh got him to his feet.

'Get on the cannon,' the Scourge ordered, indicating the languishing autocannon and the boxes of ammunition strewn across the pulverised rubble. As surviving Charnel Guardsmen emerged from the gaps and crevices into which they had pressed themselves, they began to search for their abandoned lasfusils. As Sister Casiope and Battle-Brother Nebuzar of Squad Castigir ran down the perimeter towards him, Kersh bawled, 'Regroup and hold the line!'

The pair nodded, which was Kersh's sign to bolt off along the ugly scar the Thunderhawk had carved into the battlement. 'Micah!' Kersh called, 'Micah!', but the champion answered neither across the vox nor in person. There were bodies everywhere, Certusians and Guardsmen who could have little imagined that their deaths would have stalked up behind them. Brothers Salamis and Benzoheth were with them also, their ancient plate crushed like ration cans. Benzoheth's boltgun was buckled and smashed, but his brother's had escaped the worst of the Thunderhawk's attentions. Scooping up the weapon, Kersh let it dangle in his hand. As he came across the broken bodies of furies still trying to flap their useless wings, the Scourge stamped down on their daemon spines or put single bolts through the skulls of the hellish monstrosities. The corpus-captain strode on with the etherquakes of the fiends' bodies detonating behind him. Twisters of flame raged for the heavens as their daemon-essence returned to the warp.

Out beyond the battlement it was pure carnage. Cultists

had miserably lost their argument with the *Impunitas* and had been compacted into the floor and each other.

Kersh found Brother Micah near the tail of the Thunderhawk. Above, a single gunship engine continued to cycle, firing up with blazing brilliance and roasting the air before dying down to an idle chug – then building up once again to fruitless ignition. The champion's distinctive boltgun lay abandoned nearby, pointing towards the armoured boots of a body blanketed in the caped wings of a daemon fury. As the corpus-captain watched the sharp vertebrae and shoulder blades of the thing move beneath its infernal flesh with sickening fascination, he shattered its outstretched wing with a burst of fire from the bolter. The beast turned with spite and snapped like a crocodilian as it crawled across the bodies towards the Scourge. A soul-hunger raged in its horrid eyes.

'Back, warp-sired thing!' Kersh roared, blowing a ragged hole in the other wing before plucking at the monster's daemonhide with single rounds. The creature backed away, hissing and sniping. The corpus-captain stepped forwards to where the beast had been, hovering over Micah like a vampiric bat. Kersh's lip wrinkled. The champion's earnest features had gone – along with most of the contents of his skull. Kersh turned on the creature that had been feeding on him. It had used the moments the Scourge had chosen to look upon the fallen champion well, creeping swiftly up through the crash wreckage. By the time he had set his eye upon it again the monster was almost upon him. Blasting through the beast's ribcage and up into its repugnant head, the Scourge pivoted and put the remaining rounds of the magazine into further winged monstrosities that were slipping out from the Thunderhawk's interior through great gashes in the *Impunitas*'s hull. With every infernal ending, a corkscrew of hate-spitting flame wound its way towards the stars. Kersh could only imagine what the furies had done to the gunship's crew.

The devastation caused by the crash had only momentarily pushed back the enemy ranks. Already the cult armies of the Cholercaust were swallowing up the vacuum, stamping the unfortunates that had been ahead of them into the dirt and running down on the perimeter's weakened defences with hellish glee – hatefully delighted to get an opportunity to honour their bloody master. Looking back at his section of the line, where the Thunderhawk had demolished its way through his forces and the battlements upon which they were standing, Kersh found only the barest indication of a defence in evidence. The blood cultists were closing, and would march straight through the opening and into the city.

Tossing the empty boltgun away, Kersh slipped his Scourge's gladius from its sheath on his belt. He moved out towards the Thunderhawk's creaking wing, which was balanced upon the roof of a single-storey sepulchre. Cultist warriors were already there with him, the nearest, fastest and most desperate of their kind. Kersh had never seen such fearlessness in mere mortals before. They came at him – an Adeptus Astartes – without dread or doubt. A Krugarian Turncoat jumped down from the wing, his bald head gore-spattered and his filthy trench coat flapping behind him. He dappled Kersh's chestplate with rapid fire from his lascarbine before the Excoriator batted the weapon to the floor with the flat of his blade and gutted the traitor. Incredibly, a Vessorine Janissary came at him with a knife, and even more incredibly got it to the Scourge's plate. Watching the puny blade score paint, Kersh seized the clansman by his carapace and flung him into the *Impunitas*'s side, shattering every bone in his body.

A butcher-priest of the Frater Vulgariate came next with a bellow and a rusty chainsword. Knocking the blur of brain-speckled teeth aside with his cross guard, Kersh turned his power armoured bulk into the priest's reach. Slipping the gladius between his arms, the Scourge cut through the dark ecclesiarch's wrists. The chainsword dropped and died. The frater fell back, waving his gore-spouting stumps. Two slave converts died swiftly on the tip of Kersh's blade, as he slammed it through the both of them. The mongrel-faced mutant that came up behind as he administered such mercy had to settle for the blade's aquila pommel, caving its way through his snaggle-toothed face.

Hordes were already racing past the Excoriator, intent on flooding the gap in the line. With their backs to him were armoured Volscani Cataphracts, death cult assassins from 'The Covenant' and a cannibal ogryn from the Bad Moons of Goethe. Hanging from the ruined wing by a single hydraulic pintle and belt feed was one of the *Impunitas*'s twin-linked heavy bolters. Cutting through the gunship impulse cabling with his blade and shearing away the tensioned piston-trigger, Kersh sank his gauntlets into the firing mechanism, clutching at rods, pins and levers. Pulling at a robust lever, the Scourge was rewarded with a kick from the right-hand heavy bolter. The round blasted up into the wing's armour plating. Angling the bolters around on their hydraulic pintle and clutching both levers like the brakes on a bike, Kersh unleashed the devastating weapon on the storming mob.

The twin-linked heavy bolters bucked like beasts of burden reined in and under control. The barrels breathed flash-fires from their gaping muzzles, and two streams of blistering, brute-calibre firepower reached across the battlefield for the enemy. As Kersh angled the monstrous weapons around, lines of cultists disappeared in a bloodspittle haze of sweeping death. Assassins of 'The Covenant', so lithe and barbarically graceful, were mercilessly turned to chum before the gunship-mounted weapon. The Volscani Cataphracts' armour was nothing to Kersh's firepower and droves of the traitor Guardsmen were cut down in a furore of clot-splashing eruptions. The feral ogryn, Kersh simply cut down to size by scything straight through the thick muscle and bone of his legs and watching the limbless giant crash to the ground.

Through gritted teeth the Scourge continued his diamantine-tipped decontamination of the necroplex. The heads of mutants and already mindless spawn were popped off like ripe pustules. The Deathfest lived up to their name as Kersh and his heavy bolters turned several of their foetid number into a celebratory display of gore-spritz and screams. The Regna-Rouge became a dying commemoration of their colours in the Excoriator's leadstorm, their unblooded blades and torturer's instruments falling uselessly from bolt-severed hands. It was carnage.

The fallen *Impunitas* continued to feed ammunition. The weapon blazed with impunity. Kersh killed everything in his feverish fire-arc. Soon the area before his decimated section of the line was a twitching field of corpses and bloody smog. With satisfaction, he heard Oren and Bethesda's autocannon strike up its murderous orison. He saw Brother Nebuzar standing on the battlement, directing hastily regrouped Charnel Guard and cemetery world volunteers to new hold points. Lasfusils had once again started to lance the burial ground with searing bolts of light, and the nozzles of Sister Casiope's heavy flamer were turning the crash-dozed gap in the rubble battlement into a blazing inferno of light and flesh-melting heat.

He heard him first. Fortunately for the Scourge, the Blood God's disciples honoured their deity on the battlefield rather than in the temple, and with war cries rather than prayers. The deep boom of a boorish roar behind Kersh drowned out even the heavy bolters. The Scourge threw the twin-linked weapon around on its hydraulic mount. Before him was a Traitor Astartes, a rust-armoured warrior of the Goremongers renegade Chapter, with a crackling battleaxe swinging about his head.

'Blood for the Blood Go–'

Kersh yanked on the levers as the pintle completed its spasmodic rotation. The Goremonger disappeared in a blur of point-blank bolt fury. Through the miasma of shredded flesh and ceramite fragments, the corpus-captain turned the heavy bolters on the renegade Angel's warband, a blood cult mob of degenerate killers and acolytes who had seen the Goremonger's heresy and leadership as a divine expression of the Blood God's power and legitimacy. How could an Angel of the Emperor be wrong? The warband found out as the Scourge mashed through them with his belt-fed monstrosity.

Beyond, Kersh could see an ocean of human detritus. An unending army of ruthless killers. The Cholercaust's slaughterkin, united in common purpose: to work through the private deviancy of their murderous inclination while simultaneously feeding their faith and daemon deity with acts of wanton annihilation. The cult invaders just kept coming, birthed by darkness, and beyond the gloom, Kersh could hear the savage howls of maniacs-in-waiting.

Amongst the slave-soldiers, traitors and Chaos cultists, Kersh picked out increasing numbers of Adeptus Astartes, false prophets for the ravaging masses, and Ruinous warbands of blood-brothers who had embraced heresy together. Lost Angels who had fallen to the Blood God's predatory temptations and indulged their base desire to kill over the Emperor's need for them to do so. Space Marines who had forgotten themselves. Those who had regressed. Those who were now no more than agonising expressions of the savagery from which they were originally crafted. The Scourge favoured these with the Thunderhawk's remaining wrath. With 1.00 calibre mercy, the Scourge ended their torment and that of their followers. The Goremongers. The Sanguine Sons. The mad Angels of the Thunder Barons. The renegade Red Heralds. The Cleaved. The Angels Apocrypha. The Brazen Guard. The bone-dusted Skulltakers.

They came at him undaunted. Furious at his mere existence. He was a warrior to be defeated. An Adeptus Astartes. A son of Dorn. One after another they tried to rush him, cleavering aside cultists, spawn and traitor soldiers to get to him. To earn his skull for the War-Given-Form. Kersh kept killing. The ivory of his armour became a blood-misted red. The heavy bolter muzzles glowed with the heat of incessant usage. A gene-bred monstrosity – some aborted, primogenerated abomination – charged at Kersh with self-loathing and fury. The bastard-breed wore scraps of armour and the colours of the Sanguine Sons, but was a half-botched attempt at demigodhood. Malformed, insane and unfeeling – the sorry creature soaked up the heavy bolters' punishment and bounded on. The head shot that should have ended the beast was stopped by armour plating welded to its deformed skull, and it took everything the weapon had to punch through both metal and thick bone to reach what little brain the monster had.

As the abominate dropped and skidded past Kersh, the Scourge realised that the distraction had cost him. Three Angels Apocrypha had worked their way around the crashed Thunderhawk to surprise him from the other side. Helmless and sporting long hair and rapier-like blades that crackled with a dark energy, the Chaos Space Marines looked identical. Their skin was deathly pale against the sable blood-filth of their patched and studded plate. The renegades hissed and swept in with vampiric speed and appetite. Kersh barely had time to release his finger-cramping grip on the heavy bolters and slap a palm on his gladius hilt.

The first died without the blade having to clear its scabbard. There was a flash from the side of the first Angel's head. He fell to one side and struck the gunship's wing before falling and sitting in the grave dust. Half of his head had been burned out by a precision sniper shot. About the Scourge were the corpses of killers and cultists that Kersh couldn't remember slaying. They too had the telltale head craters of Adeptus Astartes marksmanship. Up in the towers and steeples of the cemetery world city, a member of Squad Contritus had the Scourge in his sights and was watching his corpus-captain's back.

The Angels were so fast that Kersh's blade was still not free of its sheath as the second sped past his falling compatriot. He was met with an ugly kick from the Scourge. Reeling from the Excoriator's boot against his chestplate, the Traitor stumbled some distance back. Throughout the body-piling carnage of the Scourge's resistance, the *Impunitas*'s remaining engine had gone through the wretched and repetitive cycle of firing up and dying down. As the heretic Angel stumbled back into the rocket's wake, the intense heat of the rhythmic burn set alight his hair and scoured the paint from his ceramite. His pallid skin melted from his skull, and as the engine built up to full intensity, sending a tremble through the crashed Thunderhawk, the renegade was lost in the air-scorching heat of the afterburner.

Kersh felt sudden and excruciating pain lance through his midriff. The third Angel Apocrypha had leant into a savage thrust, skewering his power blade through the Scourge's stomach plate and though his side. As the Chaos Space Marine withdrew his rapier, Kersh let out a half-stifled howl of agony. The heretic seemed to enjoy the Excoriator's suffering, until the Scourge drew his gladius out of its scabbard and the blade up across the Traitor's face, wiping the spiteful satisfaction from it. With blood streaming into his eyes from the vicious gash, the Angel Apocrypha also failed to see the Scourge's fist fly at him, the pommel of the sword held within it breaking the warrior's jaw. The rapier vaulted for the Scourge again, but blood-blind the Angel struck wide.

Grabbing the Chaos Space Marine by the wrist and holding the crackling blade away from him, Kersh twisted the gladius around in his other hand before plunging it down through a ceramite patch on the Blood Crusader's chestplate. The blade squealed through the weak spot, punctured reinforced ribcage and slid down into the Chaos Space Marine's chest. Squirming the hilt around like an aircraft joystick, Kersh watched the Angel Apocrypha experience the blade twisting through his innards. Black blood gushed up and out of the sides of the doomed warrior's mouth. Releasing him, Kersh allowed the weight of the warrior's plate to carry him to a gasping death on the cemetery world earth and free his blade.

A grunt from the Anarchan Razorbacks was suddenly beside him, attempting to beat him with the stock of a shotgun, while a stitch-faced pirate raider – with her mouth sliced into a frown – started blasting away wildly with a pair of autopistols. Clutching his side, Kersh despatched her with shearing economy and speed. He took a step towards the twin-linked heavy bolter but found himself distracted by the bodies being tossed into the air above the advancing mob before him. A cloven-hoofed beast of living plate was thundering through the cultist throng at high speed, its brazen bulk a seemingly unstoppable force. The quadruped's long head sported a thick brass horn, sharpened to a cruel spike, while its eyes were windows to a volcanic fury. Its broad body was a clinker-built nightmare of layered bronze plate and shredded octagon-mail. The infernal beast cared for nothing, trampling slave-soldiers, gore-swiping Blood-saken berserkers and barging aside armoured Red Herald Chaos Space Marines with its heavy metal heft.

Snatching his bolt pistol from its sporran, Kersh thrashed the trigger, sending round after round at the daemon beast. It was the definition of an easy target and getting easier with every cloven stride, but the rounds simply glanced pathetically off the living bronze hide. With the infernal engine just steps away, Kersh threw himself painfully to one side. The beast continued its relentless charge, furiously goring the underplate of the Thunderhawk's wing, before surging on and smashing straight through the twin-linked heavy bolters. The metal monster cannonaded past. On the ground, Kersh watched the beast weather a hail of las-bolts from Charnel Guard fusils, stubgun and auto-fire, as well as the slash of Scout sniper rifle blasts from the towers and belfries. An advancing wall of metal and sparks, the beast continued along its juggernaut path towards the break in the battlement.

Kersh felt a tremble through his plate. The ground was quaking again. As he got to his boots, the corpus-captain watched hate-jubilant cultists roaring the hellsteed on, before they were struck and impaled from behind – left broken-backed and crucified across the horned heads of newly arrived beasts. The Scourge shook his head in silent disbelief, witness to a diabolic stampede. Soon there were more armoured chargers than Kersh could count, and the Excoriator found himself backing towards the doomed front line.

Unclipping a krak grenade, the Scourge took several

further steps backwards. As well as the living metal beasts – in the absence of the heavy bolter's relentless murder – renegade Angels, berserkers and the Blood God's champions were leading the cult armies of the Cholercaust back at Kersh's decimated section of the perimeter. With grim resolve, the Scourge tossed the unprimed grenade into the silent booster exhaust of the cycling engine. As he ran back towards Obsequa City he heard the grenade bounce and rattle around the inside of the jet mechanism. He heard the engine begin its final, fruitless attempt to re-launch the downed Thunderhawk.

As Kersh reached the havoc of the destroyed battlement and the mess the unstoppable metal monster had made of his remaining sentinels, the corpus-captain looked back. The Thunderhawk's remaining booster had built to a strangled screech. The engine fired. The grenade exploded. The wreck of the *Impunitas* shuddered. A staggered detonation rippled through the derelict craft: the engine, the fuel compartments, the ammunition stores. The gunship became a radiating blastwave of force, flame and armour-plate frag. Cultist soldiers were shredded where they stood. Renegade Angels and Chaos champions were cooked within their plate, and even stampeding daemon beaststeeds were knocked from their fleet footing and onto their clinker-constructed backs, where they remained, kicking out helplessly in a steam-snorting effort to right themselves.

Kersh found Brother Nebuzar dead – gored straight through by the rampaging bronze monitor train. The beast had ignored the irritation of las-bolts dancing off its hide and bypassed the remainder of the Charnel Guard, instead storming straight at the cemetery world city. As the brazen mount careened through the walls of chapels, hermitages and cloisters, bulldozing its frenzied way through foundations and keystones, towers began to topple and steeples fell in on themselves.

Looking back at the benighted battlefield, Kersh saw the Thunderhawk's explosion die back to a flame-swathed wreck. The promethium-soaked mound of cadavers and daemonflesh upon which the crashed gunship had come to rest caught, and the Scourge watched the inferno race away in both directions. Within minutes Obsequa City would be surrounded by a furious ring of light and fire.

Along his section of the perimeter, the corpus-captain saw cultists and slave-soldiers thrashing in the flames. He saw a hammer-wielding Thunder Baron stride through the blaze in scorched plate as though it were nothing. The renegade Angel was followed by several lesser berserkers, who burst from the wall of flame at a sprint, flak and furs alight with the flesh melting from their cruel bones. They didn't get far, the demented warriors succumbing to the firestorms they had become long before they reached the ruined battlement. The daemonherd would not, and could not, be stopped. Those monsters not caught in the initial blast had thundered on, shaking the ground upon which they stomped, shielded from the worst of the pyremound by their hide plating.

The corpus-captain had no idea how other sections of the perimeter had fared. They could have already fallen or – without crashing gunships and a daemon drove to worry about – have held against the Cholercaust's murderous masses and madness. All he did know was that his vox had been a constant stream of messages and reports that he could barely hear above the rapid-fire cacophony of the twin-linked heavy bolters and Khornate battle-cries. Regardless of how his brothers elsewhere had fared, their first line of defence was about to fall. With the promethium holding the worst of the cultist furore back, but the daemon charge an uncontainable certainty, Kersh decided grimly that the battle wouldn't afford him a better time to retreat. He set his vox to an open channel.

'Fifth Company, this is the Scourge. The perimeter is breached. Prepare for close-quarters assault. Fall back to the city. Do it now.'

CHAPTER NINETEEN
WORLD EATERS

THE ABBEY BELL tower of the Black Ministry shook with the force of some distant calamity. Brother Omar of the Tenth Company watched dust fall from the belfry rafters. The Scout had been leant against a balistraria pillar near to the great wheels of the abbey bell. Omar followed the dust descending to the floor and settled his eyes on the empty space where his legs should have been. The incredible thing was that he could still feel them: the twitch of every muscle, the stretch of every tendon and the creak of thick joints and bones.

It had been deemed all but a miracle that he had made it back to Obsequa City through the immaterial incursion. He remembered little of his entry, but had been told the Scourge himself had dragged his bruised and bloody body to safety – well, most of it. The Scout didn't recall the agonies associated with the loss of his legs, which he considered a small blessing. He was currently benefiting from morphia and augmetics left behind by Apothecary Ezrachi, with drips, lines and transfusion satchels trailing from the cauterised stump of his lower torso. The Scout still wore his battle-battered carapace vest and pauldrons, and rather than languish in some hermitage or with the Sisters in the Mausoleum vault, he had volunteered for any useful duty he could perform. With no little admiration and the assurance that he would make a fine Excoriators battle-brother, Silas Keturah gave Omar a pair of magnoculars and his own bolt pistol. The Scout was charged with spotting and vox-relaying observations from the bell tower straight to the squad whip himself. The reports had made grim listening.

'Take that, you ugly son of a whore...'

Omar heard the *whoosh* of Scout Kush's sniper rifle as the weapon spat out another skull-emptying bolt. Omar grunted. Kush was a despicable neophyte and a disgrace to the name of Demetrius Katafalque, but he had the eyes of a hawk and the murderous desire to see every shot go home. Omar had even spotted for the Scout with his magnoculars, drawing the sniper fire down on a warband of helmless screamers from the renegade Brazen Guard, and assorted degenerates attempting to rush Corpus-Captain Kersh in the wake of the *Impunitas*'s crash. Mostly, Kush had rested the sniper rifle's long barrel against a balistraria pillar and plugged incessantly away, his eye to the magnoscope and a neat pile of powerpacks stacked beside his knee. 'Come on, you Ruinous filth – stick your head out,' the Scout murmured absently to himself. Kush fired. With a smirk of satisfaction and without taking his eye from the lens, the Scout ejected another spent pack and slipped another into the rifle's breech from the pile.

Omar brought the magnoculars back to his eyes and surveyed the carnage on the city perimeter, which was no less horrifying in night-vision. Even from the bell tower's vantage, the Scout only had a view of Necroplex-South and East. From the belfry it became obvious what the Excoriators' problem would be. Sheer numbers. Wave after wave of slaves and cultist soldiers stormed from the distant darkness. They never seemed to stop, and ran full speed at the city along the lychways and clambered across funereal architecture of the burial grounds with contorted face of fury and frustration. Spread through their colossal number were armoured champions and renegade Angels sporting blades of wicked design and obscene dimensions. Omar had also spotted daemonkin and monstrous beasts from hellish planes of existence to bolster the Cholercaust's already formidable assault capabilities.

On the south and east perimeters, at least, the Excoriators had fared reasonably well against the Blood Crusaders, flak and fevered flesh being no match for the Angels' boltguns. The Charnel Guard and hastily recruited Certusian militia did their part also, the kill zones before the battlements a hailstorm of light, lead and gun emplacement fire. The Blood God's warped champions and renegade Adeptus Astartes – using slave-soldiers as meat shields – closed the gap and created havoc for the perimeter. Their deity-pleasing antics and the brutal insanity of their assaults tested the nerve of the Guardsmen and cemetery worlders, and where Skulltaker Space Marines and berserkers breached the line and scrambled up through the firepower onto the scree battlement, massacres unfolded. The real problem, as Omar could see from the bell tower, were the daemon monstrosities the Blood God had bequeathed the Cholercaust, blessed manifestations of Ruinous destruction and murderous power crafted in corporeal form.

On the Necroplex-East perimeter, Omar had watched Brothers Damaris and Judah hacked to pieces by a small horde of bloodletting arch-fiends with hell-red hides and smouldering blades. Daemon engines of dark metal and diabolic soulfire sliced and pounded their defective way up through the defences and Epistolary Melmoch's Charnel Guardsmen. A charging herd of armoured steeds had smashed through the Scourge's section like a spooked drove of grox, scattering his sentinels and forcing them to abandon their posts and emplacements. Omar had spotted a possessed Salamander – bearing the mark and scale of the renegade Dragon Warriors on his warp-tormented form – cut through the Sisters of Battle supporting Brother Simeon, and just about everything else on the southern perimeter.

Worst of all, the Scout had witnessed the merciless decimation of Second Whip Azareth's section by what could only be described as one of the Blood God's own. A mighty horned daemon, standing many times taller than an Adeptus Astartes and hate-wrought from ancient enmity, had appeared out of the night like a colossus. Where it walked, the ground shook beneath its cloven hooves. Its wings hung about its massive shoulders like the plate shielding of a battleship, and in one huge claw it clutched a flint axe, roughly hewn in its entirety from daemon world bedrock. With the razor edge of the weapon, the primordial beast swept the necroplex and battlement, ripping through scores of cultists and Charnel Guardsmen with equal indifference and creating small lakes of spilt blood. The monstrous greater daemon jangled with brass plate, mail and chain, and bawled its unquenchable fury from eyes, anger-flared nostrils and a snarl-retracted mouth, which glowed with the elemental fires burning within.

Omar watched cemetery worlders flee before the great beast, only to be cut down by another rubble-grazing sweep of its axe, while Second Whip Azareth stood his ground. The Scout's heart beat with Chapter pride as the Excoriator took the fight to the furious behemoth, dwarfed by the size of the beast and the carnage it effortlessly created. Omar looked on, sickened, as a Space Marine disappeared beneath one of the beast's brazen hooves, brought down by the monster as though he were nothing more than an irritation.

The Scout thought the gargantuan daemon might simply stride across the battlement unopposed and begin levelling the city with its primeval weapon and crushing fist. That was until the battle-scarred shape of the venerable *Gauntlet* had swooped in, drifting about the monster just out of reach of its building-cleaving axe. The gunship's heavy bolter fire danced off the greater daemon's hide, prompting the beast to cloak itself in the mighty expanse of its leathery wings, until the *Gauntlet* slammed a Hellstrike missile into the horror. The beast fell back, knocked from its hooves by the force of the explosion. Hundreds of the Blood God's slave-soldiers were crushed beneath its ancient form, and hundreds more were thrown from their feet by the quake of the monster's descent. Shaking its appalling head, a wing blast-shattered and aflame, the daemon had scrambled furiously to its feet. The pilot of the *Gauntlet* expertly gained altitude, keeping the Thunderhawk out of the flint axe's considerable reach, while at the same time drawing the enraged beast away from the city. Like some reptilian death world predator, mindlessly consumed with the pursuit of its prey, the greater daemon trailed the venerable *Gauntlet*, its battle-ire continually stoked by the annoyance of the gunship's heavy bolters, the burn of its lascannons and intermittent flooring by the Thunderhawk's Hellstrike missiles.

Kush screamed.

As Omar pulled the magnoculars from his face he saw the sniper suddenly pass before him in an ugly blur. Showering masonry told the Scout that something had struck the bell tower, taking out Brother Kush as the sniper had so many others. The Excoriator hadn't been struck by a las-bolt or marksman's bullet. A winged monstrosity had hit the belfry wall like a thunderbolt, smashing through the stone gap that had served Kush's aim so well, and cannonballing into the Scout. As both Excoriator and beast came to a savage halt against the opposite wall – Kush wrapped up in the creature's talons and bat-like wings – Omar heard the Scout scream again. The scream swiftly became a gargle and then a crunch as the monster bit out the Excoriator's throat.

The thing left Kush's corpse and, still streaming with masonry dust, crawled horribly across the belfry at Omar. The Scout managed to get off a couple of bolts from Squad Whip Keturah's pistol before the beast was upon him. Using the weapon as a knuckleduster, Omar slammed the fury's gargoylesque head to one side. Its dagger-teeth came straight back at him, and it was all the Excoriator could do to clutch his fingers around its lower jaw and keep it from his face. Omar felt himself instinctively kicking out with legs that weren't there. After the momentary strain of a struggle, with the daemon's warp-fuelled strength getting the better of the Excoriator's bulging arms, Omar clicked the bolt pistol to fully automatic with his thumb and nestled the squat muzzle of the weapon under the beast's chin. Yanking on the trigger, Omar sent a continuous stream of fire through the monster's head. Bolt-rounds tore through the fury's infernal brain and out the top of its gnarled skull. Seconds later, the thing was a deadweight of flesh on top of him – the murderous gleam gone from its eye.

Thumbing a stud, Omar ejected the spent bolt pistol clip. Heaving the beast off his torso, the Excoriator pushed himself onto his chest and, trailing lines and drips, crawled arm-over-arm across to Kush. He stopped momentarily as the fire soul-storm tore out of the fury's leathery remains and scorched its way up through the belfry. As Omar reached Kush it was obvious that the Scout was dead. His head hung limply from his torso by his spine and a ribbon of flesh.

Omar's chin dropped. Without Kush, and with his battle-brothers fighting for their lives, the Scout would not be leaving the bell tower. He prised a chunky grenade from Kush's hand. During his brief struggle with the beast, Kush had snatched it from his belt but never got as far as priming the krak grenade and blowing both himself and the daemon-monster to oblivion. Omar slipped the grenade down into his carapace. Snatching up Kush's sniper rifle, he grunted. For a neophyte, he wasn't particularly good with a rifle, close-quarters combat being his chosen specialism. Sliding the weapon along the belfry floor, he made for the hole in the wall made by the daemon's entrance. Pushing himself up against a balistraria pillar, the Excoriator primed the rifle.

As he was doing so a bright twinkle in the sky drew his attention. At first he thought it must be glimmer of lance-fire in orbit, but as it began to streak down towards Obsequa City and was joined by a busy constellation of other ominous lights, Omar recognised them for what they were. Adeptus Astartes drop-pods. A swarm of them, deployed from some Cholercaust cruiser and raining down like a storm of death.

There was little Omar could do about the audacious enemy assault. His rifle could not hit a rapidly descending insertion craft and would not penetrate its armour even if it did. All the Scout could hope for was that whatever came out of the pods would oblige his questionable marksmanship on the ground.

The Scout aimed the sniper rifle down into the tight alleyways, stepwells and cloisters. Adjusting the magnification on the powerful scope for his eye, Omar nestled the weapon against a bruised shoulder. He brought his finger off the trigger as a fleeing member of the Charnel Guard flashed before the scope, running for his life down a posternway. An armoured beast thundered past, zigzagging its way across the narrow alley, crashing its shoulders into the masonry of bordering buildings. The thing lowered its head, and with a furious charge, gored the unfortunate Guardsman before stomping on. The monster passed out of sight. Leaning into the stone of the belfry wall, Omar felt the tower shudder as the beast collided with the abbey's foundations.

With dust raining down about him, the Excoriator concentrated on his rifle's cross hairs and the heretic prey that might pass before them.

THE DREADCLAW'S ROCKET roared its kamikaze delight. The drop-pod was ancient, corrupt of spirit and falling apart. Its nameplate had once read *Darkheart*, but was now a flashburned smear – the result of an ill-advised insertion through the caustic cloud-cover of the Kassandrun hiveworld. The *Darkheart* had later been appeased by the blood of innocent hivers, battle-splashed and splattered across the Dreadclaw's malevolent plate.

As another atmospheric stabiliser was ripped from its hull by the raging descent, the craft began to pitch and wobble. The sickening motion tore at the Dreadclaw's superstructure, and the pod gave a metallic whine of internal agony. Inside the craft, amongst the swaying chains, trembling brass strutage and the stench of old gore, eight sons of Angron strained against their descent cages. Their plate was brazen horror, embellishing the blood-red sheen of gore-speckled ceramite. Spikes – both metal and warped bone – adorned their battle-blessed forms, and their helms were ghastly and extravagant. Weapons ached in their racks for the taste of first blood.

Umbragg of the Brazen Flesh stood with a brain-dashed boot on the long defunct guidance runebank that occupied the centre of the compartment. It mattered little to the Traitor Legionaries that the runebank was dead and silent. The *Darkheart* would guide them to slaughter as it always had. The World Eaters champion held on to ceiling chains with both gauntlets – his only descent precaution. As the Dreadclaw had tumbled away from the battle-barge *Rancour*, part of a low orbital swarm delivering the shock troops of the Blood God to the cemetery world, Umbragg had indulged his psychosis. The cybernetic implants buried deep in the primordial depths of his brain flushed the World Eater with a hatred unbound. His mind was an open wound, a twisted knot of psychosurgical scar tissue, only good for killing.

The World Eater loathed the long sub-light journeys between massacres. The *Rancour* was an adamantium prison, Lord Havloc their craven watchdog. Havloc was indeed blessed of Decimate Khorne – but Umbragg could not find it in himself to feel similar appreciation. Wars should not be fought from the command throne of a battleship. The weakling Imperium was an empire of dirt – dirt that it was Umbragg's murderous duty to saturate with the coward-blood of the False Emperor's subjects. To baptise with the teeth of his axe and the wrath of the Blood God's grace. But the Cholercaust followed the Pilgrim, and the Pilgrim – the Right Claw of Khorne – followed the crimson comet, the corporeal manifestation of the Blood God's will. Therefore, the sacrilegious inactivity of the armada's progress had to be endured. It had to be suffered – like the slow passing of the blade across the flesh – until finally, the comet led the chosen of Khorne back to Ancient Terra and on towards an empire's end.

On the approach to the tiny Ecclesiarchy world, Umbragg had felt the stirring. The Cholercaust's communal desire to kill. The infighting. The self-slaughter. The flaying of flesh from decapitated skulls. The disciples of the War-Given-Form, at one with their true purpose. The brute simplicity of mass invasion. The slaughterous advantage of strength and number – the Blood God's potency realising and realised in the tsunami of gore spilt before his warrior-subjects' blades.

Like magma churning inside the rock prison of a volcano, the exalted rage of the berserker built within Umbragg. He watched the unworthy slave-soldiers of the Blood Crusade fall on the planet in their thousands and thousands – all hate-twisted, battle-hungry and eager to catch the Blood God's eye. With them went Khorne's blessings – the daemonic expression of the War-Given-Form's presence on the field. Carnage-fired beasts, engines, powers and princes, killing shrines to the Skull Lord's decimate will. With unbearable restraint – his ancient bones literally shaking with the desire to war – Umbragg watched the aspirant champions of the Cholercaust take their place in mob-ranks of common killers. Warlords and butchers, their prodigious taking of life had warmed the Ruinous overlord to them.

Amongst these were bands of tainted Angels. A young and fallen brotherhood. Warriors whose shame it had been not to see the slaughter of the Heresy and the apocalypse wrought on the sacred soil of Ancient Terra: Goremongers, Skulltakers, Angels Apocrypha, the Blood Storm, Thunder Barons. It was only after the renegades – young in the ways of the blade – had thinned out the enemy, leaving only the worthiest skulls for the taking, that the Pilgrim unleashed his warbands of World Eaters.

Ancient, superhuman flesh within Traitor plate, driven by a mind without doubt or fear. The World Eaters were the very

ROB SANDERS

living expression of the Blood God's destructive power. His daemons might be a bloodthirsty essence, tapped directly from Khorne's primordial fury, but it was thousands of years of bloodshed, committed in the Blood God's name by the death-defying sons of Angron, that fuelled such ancient power. In this way, daemonkin might be part of the War-Given-Form, but the War-Given-Form was part of Umbragg and his XIIth Legion brethren's desire eternal to see the galaxy burn.

As the Dreadclaw gave another sickening wobble and the fresh screech of lower atmospheric descent assailed the drop-pod's exterior, Umbragg's berserker fury broke its banks. The enemy was close. His axes would sing through priest-flesh. The red glory of lives ended would fountain about him in glorious, hateful celebration. A roar built within his cavernous chest – a raw unburdening that was matched by the caged warriors of his warband, the *Clysm*. The *Darkheart* shook with the World Eaters' rage. Umbragg began to smash his spiked elbows into the compartment wall and his fists into the brass ceiling. The dim memory of an ancient alarm fired and the craft's interior flashed a pleasing alter-nation of red emergency lighting and darkness. The World Eaters howled their savage frustration – their cybernetically enhanced hatred for the constraints of the *Rancour*, for the rattling Dreadclaw, for the cemetery world victims-to-be and the Imperium they represented, for their fellow Blood Cru-saders, for each other, and for themselves.

Like a redirected torrent, murderous thoughts and desires flooded Umbragg, flowing through his psychosurgically sav-aged brain. The Brazen Fleshed warrior no longer wanted to kill; he needed to kill. The *Darkheart* was bleeding. The World Eaters had smashed the compartment plating and torn out cabling, hydraulics and mesh-hosing. Blood and ichor sprayed from the damaged section, bathing the Traitor Angels in a crimson shower. Forcing his pack to the wall and wrap-ping thick ceiling chains about his arms with savage circles of the wrist, Umbragg prepared for the Dreadclaw's landing.

Before the World Eater knew it, the *Darkheart* had buried its gear-talons in cemetery world earth. The shock of the

350

brutal landing was forgotten instantly, swallowed whole by the berserker instinct to break free and kill. With the bone-shattering impact of the landing still reverberating through him, Umbragg of the Brazen Flesh had unthinkingly hit the disembarkation stud and snatched his blessed chainaxes, *Pain* and *Suffering*, from their compartment mounts. Freed from their descent cages, the World Eaters berserkers of the *Clysm* dropped down through the retracting bulkhead.

As soon as their ceramite boots hit the planet surface, the Chaos Space Marines' helmet optics scanned for life signs and heat signatures. The *Darkheart* had punched its way through a cathedral roof, and the Dreadclaw's landing talons were buried in the stone floor of the nave. Their optics cut through the dust and debris to reveal warm bodies running down an ambulatory parallel to the cathedral wall. The warband broke into a run, the World Eaters pounding across the nave at the stone wall with an insatiable appetite for violence.

Umbragg reached the wall first, shouldering his power armoured way straight through the masonry to appear like a conjured daemon before the shocked and terrified stream of Charnel Guard and armed cemetery worlders flooding into the passageway. The mortals were already running for their lives from something, and Umbragg feasted on their fear. They ran straight at his axes. Gunning them to full furiosity, the World Eater cut, cleaved and butchered his way through the screaming mayhem. The *Clysm* joined him, slaking their own thirst for blood effortlessly spilt. The World Eaters descended into a brutal frenzy, chainswords hacking off limbs, axes biting through bodies and bolt pistols taking off heads. Umbragg felt the release of carnage accomplished, the god-pleasing sensation of blood pattering in sheets and sprays across his Traitor plate.

Bolts from lasfusils sizzled pointlessly off the champion as wall-to-wall Certusians were sacrificed on the twin altars of *Pain* and *Suffering*. Suddenly the source of the cemetery worlders' panic appeared, crashing into walls and pulverising the cobbled ambulatory. A brazen-plate beast with a serrated crescent horn and armoured hump charged up through the Guardsmen and fossers, eyes ablaze with animal anger, a monster out of control. It gored and trampled a path through the fleeing crowd, stamping and swinging its razor-horn to the left and right. Umbragg watched the ripple of bodies as they bounced off and over the daemon's hump. As the kill before him was stolen by the creature's stampede, the World Eater stepped to one side and buried his chainaxes, in quick succession, in the living metal flesh of the beast. The Chaos Space Marine's weapons chugged deep into the monster. The juggernaut crashed on, bouncing from one smashed wall into another until it collapsed, the beast's momentum ploughing its horned head through the dust, debris and cobbled floor. Streams of brazen flame erupted from its fallen form, funnelling through chinks and rents in its armoured hide. The dark energy spiralled upwards, carrying fragments of clinker plate and great brass rivets with it.

Umbragg turned back with a triumphant bellow of rage, his fists to the sky. About him World Eaters continued to cleave through the Charnel Guardsmen. Two cemetery worlders were suddenly before him, dappling his chestplate with rifles that were loud, annoying and pitifully ineffective. Looking down on the taller of the two fossers, the World Eater swung out the back of his gauntlet. Swatting the puny mortal aside, Umbragg took off his head with the backslash.

'Donalbain!' the second Certusian yelled, his voice shot through with the weakness of useless human emotion. Shock turned instantly to anger – a feeling Umbragg of the Brazen Flesh could appreciate – and the fosser ran at the armoured giant, smashing at his ceramite plating with the scuffed butt of his rifle. Within his helm, the World Eater licked his cracked and aged lips. Clasping the weakling mortal by both his head and shoulder, the World Eater tore in two different directions. With ease the Certusian's screaming head broke from his thrashing torso. Tossing both aside, Umbragg showed his bloody palms to the sky. With the massacre coming to an end about him, Umbragg of the Brazen Flesh snorted.

'Find me Angels!' he bawled at his dark brethren.

CHAPTER TWENTY
ENDGAME

I can feel the city slipping away from me. I am Adeptus Astartes. Sentiment is nothing to a demigod. Death is a way of life. That the citizens of the Imperium fall is of no consequence to an Angel of the Emperor. We save as many as we can – as I have here on the cemetery world. Men fall, but the Imperium endures. The city is slipping from me as a game of regicide from a master. There is a difference, however, between feeling defeat and knowing defeat. I am warrior enough to know I am beaten. My heart beats for my Emperor. I will never lay down my weapons. I will never give up. While I live, my enemies' lives will pay forfeit. My spirit is unbreakable. These things I feel. What I know is the difference between strategic success and tactical failure – and I have failed.

I see now, as I fight pauldron-to-pauldron with my Excoriator brothers, the anatomy of a world's demise. I see now how the Cholercaust Blood Crusade sundered planet after Imperial planet, and how it will go on doing so – right up to the Vanaheim Cordon and beyond. Through Segmentum Solar and the core systems; right up to an unsuspecting Ancient Terra. Unsuspecting, because none know what I know now. They will underestimate

353

the Keeler Comet and its strange ability to turn a population against itself, creating reinforcement for an army as yet unarrived. What they will see as an astral body – a returning visitor – I know as a gateway to Chaos. They will not call for reinforcement, as others have failed to do, until far too late. They will fail to appreciate the Cholercaust's number and overestimate their own. They will make a stand – as I have done – because that is what warriors do. They will stand aghast, as I do now, at the Cholercaust's speed and hunger for annihilation. They will not imagine that a force could end a world in all but a day, overrunning an entire planet with heretic, renegade and daemon. Finally, with Traitor Legionaries – the Blood God's chosen – falling from the stars and hunting them for sport, they will see how easily they have fallen and the horror that awaits others for whom the same mistakes are equally inevitable.

We are trapped.

Falling back from the perimeter it became swiftly apparent that all other sections had failed to hold as I had. The Charnel Guard are decimated and many of my brothers have fallen. Palatine Sapphira and several of her Sisters remain, along with a small collection of Chapter serfs – including my own. Beyond that, only Excoriators survive. The sons of Dorn, who fought their hardest and made the enemy pay in blood for every retreating step. The remaining Angels of the Fifth Company, holding off impossible numbers, as they pair and group up. Brothers finding each other, protecting each other's backs, knowing in their hearts that here in these tight ambulatories and posternways – in the shadow of Umberto II's great Mausoleum – they are to die together.

With a cultist army – even with an Adeptus Astartes contingent – we might have stood a chance. The Blood God sends us monsters, daemonic entities against which our weapons know limitation. And now, pushed back into the steep streets and narrow alleys, with the full force of the Cholercaust swallowing Obsequa City, we find our retreat compromised. From the sky they send us their best. Shock troops to finish off the most stalwart resistance. To end us quickly. The Eaters of Worlds. Now I know we are doomed.

'What now?' Skase calls above the din of battle. The air is thick with the chug of chain weapons, including my own, and Brother Boaz and Squad Whip Joachim are using the last of their grenades. The cloistrium is open but the cacophony bounces off the walls right back at us. We have heard nothing from the northwestern contingents. Second Whip Etham and Brothers Lemuel and Zurion sighted Sisters of Battle in the St Gorgonia district and received some surviving support from Keturah's Scouts. Nothing has been heard from any of them in over an hour, and drop-pods did seem to hit the far side of the city hardest.

'The Mausoleum!' I yell back, but my words are drowned by the whoosh of Sister Casiope's heavy flamer. The good Sister has been doing the Emperor's work with the weapon, using it to greatest effect in the cramped environs of the narrow city streets. Flame has gutted the alleys and archways of our uphill escape route, forcing back countless hordes of cultists baying for our blood or else flash-stripping them of their flesh and turning them into corpses dancing and flailing through an inferno. Sapphira and Sister Zillah finish off any warp-spawned malevolents creeping through the flames, while my absterge holds up her wounded brother, blasting the occasional cultist who makes it over a roof or through a building with her chunky laspistol.

'What?' Skase calls back, his gladius twanged back off the teeth of a World Eater's chainsword.

'Close quarters!' Brother Simeon calls, dropping his empty boltgun. One of the Blood God's armoured disciples falls before the last of the weapon's wrath, only for another berserker to come straight at Simeon with an axe. Bringing his gladius out of its sheath, my battle-brother's blade is smacked aside by the raging action of the Chaos Space Marine's chain weapon. The last few bolt-rounds from my Mark II go into buying Simeon a few moments of time, my offering glancing off the World Eater's pauldron and helm, knocking the Traitor to one side and off balance.

'The Mausoleum roof!' I yell to Skase. 'It's the safest place for a pick-up.'

Brother Eliam dies horribly before me, the thrashing axes of several World Eaters brothers hacking his armoured body apart. With his blood across my face, I send the butt of my empty pistol

across the faceplate of the nearest of his berserker killers, only to
have the hallowed weapon smashed out of my grip with the flat
of his axe. I turn. As I do, I unclip my chainsword and bring the
flared blade to gory life. Bringing the blade around and up, I
chew through the World Eater from the navel to the throat.

'Novah can't raise the Gauntlet,' Skase insists, his gladius
blade having found its way past the chainsword and into the
madman's neck. As he twists the gladius there is a crunch and
the World Eater's grip goes slack, silencing his weapon.

'Still the best holdpoint,' I bawl as my chainsword tangles
momentarily with a World Eater's axe. 'Thick walls, and Sister
Sapphira claims that the ceremonial gate is an adamantine
alloy.'

The bastard-sons of Angron are among us. World Eaters pour
into the cloistrium, wolfishly drawn down on us by the stench
of our loyalty. Bolt-rounds don't stop them. Grenades don't
stop them. They push on fearlessly through our bottlenecks and
gauntlets, stepping through the mangled corpses of their Traitor
brethren to get to us. Each maniac Angel sustains the grievous wounds of two of his loyalist kind. They hear nothing but
pain and see nothing but victims. They feel… nothing. Duty is
not enough for them. They live for battle, but even that seems
insufficient to satisfy the kill-wired berserkers. They want our
blood. They want our skulls for their Ruinous lord and nothing,
it seems, is going to stop them.

Squad Whip Joachim fights for his life – a gladius in each
gauntlet, a World Eater on each flank. One of the Traitors has
been blessed by his merciless god with a bone-spiked club on one
arm. He swings the flesh-weapon at the Excoriator but hits his
mindless compatriot by accident. The Chaos Space Marine turns
on his afflicted battle-brother with his axe, and moments later
the madmen are fighting each other. This is a small mercy since
already there is another of Angron's supersons swinging his ravenous blade at the squad whip.

I feel the moment. I feel the city slipping away on the regicide
board, and then I feel the pieces swept from the board by an
angry fist. It's the heavy flamer. I hear it chug, gasp and run dry.
I can hardly be surprised. Sister Casiope has roasted a legion

of slave-soldiers in the alleyways leading into the cloistrium. As the flamer falls silent, the Sister unhooks the support straps and shrugs off the weapon, bringing the half-clip she has left in her boltgun to bear. We all feel the heavy weapon's absence, the beginning of an end. Even though the alleyways are still flame-filled mayhem, cultists and Blood Crusaders sprint through the inferno – blades held high. Bubbling and crackling, writhed in orange tongues of hot fury, the slave-soldiers of Khorne make their doomed assault.

The palatine and her Sisters drop the killers with merciful rounds, but as the bodies begin to trip, tumble and burn, others run the gauntlet of the firestorm alley. Blood-red daemons of the Ruinous pantheon sprint horribly through the flames. They look similar to the herald-thing I faced in the Obelisk, but no two of the monstrosities look truly alike. They leap and land on the Sisters with arachnid precision, gutting and stabbing the Adepta Sororitas with supernaturally frenzied thrusts of their hellforged blades. Flashes of light and the bark of Sapphira's bolt pistols force the monsters from her prone form. As she blasts away, one of the things thrashes this way and that. Rounds tear off horn-tips, claws and a foot, but it doesn't stop the beast leaping straight back on the Sister and savaging her again.

Crackling energy suddenly leaps across the open space of the cloistrium. The searing soul lightning had passed through the bodies of several slave-soldiers crowding a side-alley. The mortals explode on contact, their torsos detonating in a fine shower of blood-spittle. The silver arc of warp-drawn power slams into the lesser daemon, as it huddles over the Sister of Battle, and throws it into the far wall. It struggles, thrashes and claws against the stream of power until it too is vaporised in an explosive gore-cloud of red mist.

Epistolary Melmoch and Chaplain Shadrath burst into the cloistrium from the alleyway. Melmoch isn't smiling. He looks tired and drawn – his eyes sunken and his talent a burden. He carries his force scythe in both hands, discharging another soul-scalding burst of energy at the daemons picking over the remains of the dead Adepta Sororitas. Second Whip Azareth is behind them, plugging the alleyway with single discharges from his boltgun. Priming his last grenade, the second whip bounces it down the alleyway at their rabid pursuers. The alleyway flashes and collapses in a rolling dustbank of masonry and pulverised rockcrete.

My heart lifts at the sight of the three Excoriators, but the reinforcement is not enough to save us. More howling World Eaters barge into the cloistrium, their pauldrons clashing in an effort to push past one another and get to us first. I choose my targets and favour manoeuvres for economy. My chainsword flicks and jabs, cleaves and slices. World Eaters get my attention for barely a moment. Just enough for the thrashing teeth of my blade to turn their own aside, take off a gauntlet at the wrist or excavate a hole in the chest. For a moment I imagine the horror before the walls of the Imperial Palace, the onslaught of the World Eaters and the lives they must have taken with their devastating combination of martial skill, fearlessness and bottomless hatred. Few of my opponents drop to the floor. I don't have the spare seconds it would take to finish them, and before I have turned to face another Traitor Space Marine, his berserker brother – who had the attention of my chainblade moments before – is back on his feet and hacking away.

The hellish melee has forced us back together. Skase and I find ourselves back to back, slapping aside angry blades coming for each other's plate while at the same time negotiating the murderous thrusts and slashes of multiple World Eaters assailants. The moment that began with Sister Casiope's flamer continues to unravel. I feel the bite of a chainaxe through my thigh plate. The teeth of some other unseen weapon glances off my shoulder plate, ripping up the ceramite but failing to reach flesh. Brother Simeon's serf Amos runs before me towards the body of his fallen master. A hulking World Eaters champion steps on Simeon's armoured form and pulls free the daemon battleaxe he buried there. I see Amos hacked cleanly in half by the soul-hungry weapon.

As Amos falls aside in two pieces, Chaplain Shadrath appears – his midnight plate glistening with the serf's blood. Holding his crozius arcanum up like a religious icon he commands the hulk and his cursed weapon back. The monstrous World Eater seems *uncertain for a moment – a trait I have yet to experience in my Traitor opponents. Suddenly furious with itself, the battleaxe comes up over its head and down on Shadrath. The Chaplain knocks it to one side with his crozius, which seems to glow with a spiritual luminescence, before smashing at the giant's ancient plate with his sacred staff of office.*

World Eaters Space Marines continue to flood the cloistrium, each more blood-hungry than the last. I can hear the gunning of chainblades echoing in the ambulatory beyond, indicating even more of the Traitors, eager to cut up what is left of us. Epistolary Melmoch's unnatural powers continue to be a boon, dwindling though they might be with the Librarian's building exhaustion. Streaks of soul lightning keep a gathering horde of lesser hellions at bay, the furious monsters seemingly drawn down on Palatine Sapphira and her affronting badges of faith. Sapphira is run through and can barely get up, but Melmoch continues to fight over her struggling form, his force scythe sweeping the space about them, the psychically-charged weapon sparking off hellblades and lopping off daemon limbs.

Brother Novah stands at the centre of the chaos. The Adeptus Astartes holds the company standard proud and high, a heart-stabbing provocation to the World Eaters degenerates roaring their way into the cloistrium. Novah clutches his boltgun in his other hand and appears to be the only Excoriator with any ammunition left for the bastard warriors of Khorne. They come at Novah – at the standard, really – screaming their obscene oaths and swinging their raging axes. Second Whip Azareth goes down under the blitz of blades, pieces of the Excoriator flying out of the frenzy. Novah puts bolt blasts into several Chaos Space Marines, but the irresistible draw of the standard drives the mindless warriors on, World Eaters running straight into the blazing path of the Excoriator's murderous gunfire.

It is a massacre. I don't know what I expected. The carnage about me is all the Cholercaust came to Certus-Minor to do. The swift and bloody annihilation of the Blood God's enemies. A world, dead in a day. The flames have died down in the alley-ways and wall-to-wall cultist warriors race for our skulls. Red, reptilian hellhounds bound over their number. The beasts spit and hiss, their brazen claws tearing up the cobbles as the daemon mongrels run at us. A pack of the monsters spreads out across the cloistrium, the black leathery sail-skin of their neck frills erect and aggressive. They sink their fang-filled jaws into our ceramite, tearing at legs and hanging off our arms. Two of the beasts snap at Brother Boaz, causing the Excoriator to swipe at them with his blade. He slashes the first beast across its horn-buds and scaly face. The second is saved by the spiked, brass collar around its neck. As the gladius sparks off the collar, the moment's distraction costs the Excoriator – a mangled World Eater getting back off the ground and to his berserker's feet. I call out, but by the time Boaz turns, the Traitor Legionary's chainsword has already taken off the Excoriator's head.

Fury builds inside me. I feel something dark and unseen wrestling for my soul. My anger and frustration feed it. A question without words chimes through my being like the clash of two blades. A proposal. A dark bargain. The unrivalled power of my enemies. The fearless, mindless instincts of a predator – with all the bloodthirsty prowess and indestructibility that comes with them – in exchange for my surrender. Not to my enemy, who deserves my enmity, my skill and my blade, but to my rage. I see the World Eaters – once the Emperor's Angels – live the benefits of such surrender. I envy their power and certitude. I see their blades butcher the supermen under my command and wonder what I might be able to do with such fury. Might I, the Scourge, be able to turn the tide of battle? My boundless wrath and the desire to avenge my brothers, forged into a weapon. My body a raw lump of brazen metal – able to withstand anything the enemy might throw at me. My mind an instrument of vengeance. My arm the executor of divine will…

A chainaxe buzzes past my head. There is blood. I think I might have just lost an ear. A World Eater, with a brass, mechanical claw for an arm, snaps out for my head. I retract, but the Traitor's brazen pincer snaps closed about my chainsword – stopping it dead. The claw cuts through the weapon, rendering it a tip-sheared, chugging mess. I abandon the weapon, slipping my Scourge's gladius from its scabbard. I spin the sword around the index digit of my left gauntlet before bringing the weapon down on the claw. The blade rings off the obscene bionic attachment. The World Eater's axe comes for me again. Claw. Axe. Claw. Axe. Each time, the gladius drives them aside. I know I can kill this monstrous combat machine. I have seen his death flash before my eyes. I know the fury I will have to unleash in order to end him. In order to end all of them. I am a moment away from damnation and I know it. A scream brings me back to my senses.

Out of the corner of my eye I see Bethesda. My lictor, Oren, is on the floor, two of the daemon hounds feasting on the serf. A third has the tips of its teeth around Bethesda's ankle, dragging the absterge away. My dark desire to kill the World Eater is greater than ever. Somehow I resist it. Instead of driving my blade through the gore-speckled degenerate, I turn in close and slam my shoulder into the Traitor's chest. He gets my elbow across his faceplate before I grab the heavy metal claw and heave the Chaos Space Marine over my pack and pauldron. He crashes into the cobbles.

I watch Bethesda screaming, her body dragged away through the gore, the whites of her eyes bright and pleading. Without ammunition and the serf too far away for my blade, there is only one thing I can do. Slapping my gauntlet down on my belt I find 'the purge' where I left it, coiled over the hilt of my other blade. Like my plate, the whip's braided length is smeared in blood-drizzle. I crack the length of the leather flail. It fails to wrap itself around her wrist as I might have hoped and instead snaps against the cobbled floor nearby. This should not surprise me. 'The purge' is not exactly the weapon of choice for an Adeptus Astartes. In her desperation and fear, the absterge strikes out with her fingers and snatches at the tip of the weapon with her pale fingers. She yelps in agony as I pull on its length, hauling her back towards me. The fiendhound bites further up the serf's leg and scrabbles against the stone floor with its brass talons.

I feel an immediate pressure on my leg. Looking down at the World Eater on the floor I see that he has his claw around my knee. The bionic shears through my plate under hydraulic insistence and I feel its crushing attentions on my flesh. Turning the gladius back around in my left hand, I stab down into the Chaos Space Marine's shoulder. Slipping the tip of the blade between the monstrous bionic attachment and the warped flesh of the Angel, I thrash back and forth with the sword hilt like a gear-stick, cutting through tendons and hydraulic piping. As the claw releases me I bring up my boot and stamp down on the World Eater's extravagant helm. The helmet twists and something snaps. I hope it is the Traitor's neck.

I heave at the whip's length, but two further daemon beasts have sunk their maws into Bethesda's flailing legs. They drag at her, and my boots skid across the cloistrium floor. She screams again. The blood-smeared 'purge' begins to slip through my power-armoured grip.

'Melmoch!' I call. I hate to. Palatine Sapphira's body has been snatched by fleet-of-claw blood-heralds. The Epistolary doesn't even know, since he is surrounded by cultists and slave-soldiers, which he cuts down like a reaper with his force scythe. The psyker spots me and my desperate tug of war with the hounds. He angles the shaft of the scythe at the beast, and with his kindly face now a hollow mask of exhaustion, desperation and fury, the Librarian sends an energy storm of arcing power at the hounds.

Impossibly the destructive stream deviates and crackles harm-lessly about the savage monsters. Furious, the Librarian sends another blast of soul lightning at the beasts, but it too sears wide. The spiked collars the creatures are wearing glow with an unnat-ural energy, seemingly protecting the hellhounds from Melmoch's psychic barrage. The whip slips from my fingers and the monsters drag the shrieking serf into a narrow alley.

The terrible cacophony of battle grows. Skase, Chaplain Shadrath and I do what we can to prevent the storm front of mulching axes and Traitor bolt-fire from turning us into Escha-ran chum. Melmoch sweeps the sizzling blade of his force scythe repeatedly through the meat-grinding crush of the cultist crowds, slicing through torsos and daemonflesh in a desperate attempt to hold the Cholercaustians back. Novah drops his empty boltgun, and his gladius joins ours, the company standard held high above our heads. Only Squad Whip Joachim fights on alone in the centre ground, beating back three rapid World Eaters with his remaining blade and a steel nerve alone.

A shockwave of revulsion and otherworldly dread passes

through me. A face has appeared at an ambulatory entrance. As the cultists thin, a colossal hand grasps the brick corner of a block-domicilia. Muscular fingers of daemonflesh terminate in metal claws, and the tough hide of the palm is etched with blasphemous runes and symbols. Heavy chain adorns the wrist, and moving up behind it, peering through the ambulatory gap and into the god-pleasing bloodshed of the cloistrium, is the face of a greater daemon, old as murder and ugly as an eternity of sin. It's all ferocity-taut flesh, flared nostrils, bared tusks and canines. I can feel its destructive power in eyes that burn with the infinitely-focused heat of hatred. Amongst the din of battle I did not even notice the distant thunder of the great being's approach.

The long reach of its palm goes out and it seizes Joachim from behind, its fingers wrapping around the struggling Excoriator, his arms and his weapon. With ease, the greater daemon squeezes. Joachim screeches. The squad whip's pack and plate crumple, and with nowhere else to go, the Angel's flesh and blood erupt from the daemon's tight-closed fist in a fountain of unspeakable horror. I die a little inside myself. It ends here, it seems. Drowned in cultist mayhem while being hacked apart by the Traitor World Eaters, with daemons picking over our bones and the fearful semblance of the Blood God himself looking on with primordial satisfaction.

This would be a distracting notion enough, amongst the bolt-rounds and roaring teeth of chainaxes – but then the sepulchre wall behind me explodes.

SHARP FRAGMENTS OF ancient brick, stone and mortar flew across the cloistrium like shrapnel. The remainder of the sepulchre wall fell away in large pieces, revealing the interior of the repository to the stars. Chewing up the rubble and masonry on the polished sepulchre floor, *Punisher* rolled out on its rugged tracks. The Thunderfire cannon's quad-barrelled muzzles smoked with the demolishing blast, and the targeting reticula mounted on its back blazed with the life of its machine-spirit through the billowing dust cloud.

During the initial assault, with *Punisher* having received

its locking and loading libations, ritual targeting protocols, prayers and appeasements from Frater Astrotechnicus Dancred, the Thunderfire cannon had dutifully held its part of the perimeter. Dancred had attached a caterpillar flatbed trailer to the itinerant cannon to aid self-loading and assigned *Punisher* its own part of the battlement to defend. Unconcerned by fleeing cemetery worlders, dying Guardsmen and the horror of otherworldly threats, the machine prioritised enemy targets according to a simple equation based upon size and closing distance. This had seen the Thunderfire cannon through the horror of the immaterial assault and helped the ordnance hold the line all but alone on its eastern section of the battlement.

Following the invasion, with no further catechisa or protocol forthcoming in the wake of Techmarine Dancred's death, the cannon had merely continued its still, silent vigil of the eastern battlement. Dancred had provided the cannon's machine-spirit with modus-contingencia, including an inner-city 'hunt and destroy' protocol, should the battlement be overrun in the initial assault. Since the perimeter had held, *Punisher* simply waited – quiet and unnoticed by forces re-fortifying the section in preparation for the incoming Cholercaust. Charnel Guardsmen, Sisters of Battle and Excoriators assumed that the cannon was dead, like the Techmarine it had taken to following like a faithful hound.

With the resurgence of hostilities on the eastern perimeter, the *Punisher* returned to automotive and explosive life. As the Cholercaust swamped battlements all over the city, including the one upon which the cannon was unsuspectingly stationed, *Punisher* fell to its 'hunt and destroy' duties in the small, sloped streets and alleyways of the cemetery world city.

As the dust cleared, fresh targets presented themselves in profusion. Heretics. Daemonic entities. Enemy Adeptus Astartes. The completion of a cold equation prompted *Punisher*'s quad-barrel to start cycling and its trailer feed system to begin loading the rotating breeches. A large etherform attempting to enter the cloistrium received *Punisher*'s initial attention. The creature received an explosive shell in the face as well as several follow-up shots that momentarily drove it back to a less threatening range. Lesser entities attempted to rush the cannon, but the *Punisher* stopped them in their tracks with a succession of volleys at the kill zone before the cannon, turning the creatures into scraps of smouldering daemonflesh. The cannon targeted the foundations of a nearby building in order to economically stall the advance of multiple heretic signatures. The old hermitage wall to which the foundation belonged collapsed, burying the heretics in an avalanche of stone as well as temporarily blocking off the entry point, which the Thunderfire cannon's machine-spirit had swiftly designated as tactically significant.

The enemy Adeptus Astartes closed with the cannon, but *Punisher* detected only small arms and close-quarter weaponry. The Thunderfire cannon sent a rhythmic barrage at the advancing contingent, blasting power-armoured bodies apart and around the confines of the cloistrium. The assault defied the machine-spirit's calculations, and *Punisher* found itself turning its barrels time and again back to the enemy Adeptus Astartes, who even with body parts blown off, continued in their attempts to reach the cannon.

As the Thunderfire cannon blasted the cloistrium to rock dust, it felt the surface contact of a gauntlet pat it on its ceramite exterior shell. Several Adeptus Astartes in Chapter colours were exiting the cloistrium up a stairwell situated in the building through which the Thunderfire cannon had just passed. Discounting the gesture as non-threatening, and confirming plate markings as those belonging to Excoriators company command, the cannon decided to hold its current station and carry out the spiritual necessities of its 'hunt and destroy' protocol.

'ANYTHING FROM PADRE Gnarls?' Commander Heiss of the *Apotheon* demanded. She sat on the edge of her throne, her slender hands forming a pyramid over her nose and mouth. Midshipman Randt had a vox-speaker to his ear.

He shook his head. The small bridge was silent. Ensigns clung grimly to pulpit rails, listening to the sound of murder and mayhem in distant parts of the ship. Even sickly servitors had stopped chattering their lingua-technis. Deck lamps flickered on and off, and pict-screens displayed ghostly static. The lancet viewport had a spidery crack running through it from the *Apotheon*'s last ramming attempt.

'Last transmission reported boarders on all decks,' Randt said. 'Nothing from the padre or the boatswain since then.'

'Gun batteries?'

'All gun crews assigned to the repelling parties.'

'Enginarium?'

'The enginseer and his menials have barricaded themselves in. They confirm critical damage to the mainstage engines due to sabotage and vandalism.'

'What do we have?'

'Life support – for now,' the midshipman informed her. 'Vox-comms, auspectia and targeting all still on line. Limited manoeuvrability through docking thrusters and, of course, the lance… But that depends upon the enginarium holding out.'

Heiss nodded slowly.

The lone defence monitor had made good on its promise to take the fight to the invading Cholercaust fleet. The *Apotheon*'s lance had visited crippling damage on a score of bloated troop transports, Adeptus Astartes frigates and daemonic vessels, as well as destroying outright an Infidel-class raider displaying traitor colours. The monitor had also managed to damage several other craft with strikes from her reinforced Voss prow. The larger vessels, including a Traitor battle-barge, paid the *Apotheon* no heed. No Cholercaustian would offend their Blood God with distant and cowardly thunder from their cannons. Nearly the entire Chaos fleet was now in equatorial low orbit around Certus-Minor, having disgorged their bays and freight compartments of all description of overladen landing craft. Several smaller ships, piratical marauders and assault boats had managed to acquire the defence monitor, deploying grapnels and hull-mounted harpoons to entangle the *Apotheon* before cutting her open and flooding the Adeptus Ministorum vessel with cannibalistic killers.

Heiss jumped as a solitary impact struck the command deck bulkhead. They had been expecting it and still it had made her heart leap in her chest. She had ordered the bulkhead sealed off and put two members of the Naval security team on the door. It seemed ridiculous now as the two flak-armoured figures backed from the thunder building on the bulkhead with their lascarbines clutched to their sides. The boarders had reached the bridge – which meant that they must have finished their slaughter spree and picking through the innards of the repelling parties. The bulkhead was designed to resist the void in the event of a hull breach and so had a fair chance of holding the fists, rifle butts and improvised rams of the cannibal marauders. Still, all eyes remained on the metal and pressure wheel of the door. All but Midshipman Randt's. He was looking at the *Apotheon*'s long range auspectral scope, and up at the cracked lancet bridge port. For a few moments he could not speak. He simply looked back and forth between scope and armaplas.

'Commander...'

Heiss looked at him, and then at what he was looking at through the viewport. She got up out of her throne.

'W-what is it?' she murmured. Others turned and saw.

The prow of the defence monitor was drifting around from the creamy curvature of the cemetery world to the darkness of the void, where the Keeler Comet was making its unnatural pass, the bloody smear of the comet's tail tracing its almost sentient change of direction and parabolic turn around the planet. This, like the colossal fleet that had been following the wandering comet like an omen, had been startling enough. Out beyond the melt-streaming surface of the bloody berg of ice, rock and metal, though, was something truly shocking. A colossal vessel. Larger than anything Heiss had witnessed over Ultrageddon, Cypra Mundi or Port Maw. Everyone on the bridge stared, and for a moment the horror that awaited them behind the bulk-head was forgotten.

'Dimensions...'

The midshipman had already checked. 'Estimated six hundred and seventy cubic kilometres.'

Heiss shook her head. It was bigger than the Keeler Comet, bigger than Certus-Minor's dwarf moons.

'What is it?' Randt marvelled. 'A hulk?'

'Magnification!' the commander snapped, and Randt had the portside lancet bring up the craft in greater detail. Beyond its sheer size, the glorious architecture of the craft was breathtaking. Colossal lancets, arches and stained-glass observation ports. The clean lines of Gothic design and detail: mullions, transoms, fan vaults, spandrels, quatrefoils and clerestory layering. Void steeples and etherspires reached up from great halls, cathedrex and monasterial superstructures all nestled between sensoria, the elongated barrels of long-range lances, nova cannon and squat plasma cannonades. The magnificent weaponry, as well as the gargantuan Scartix engine coils upon which the structures and emplacements sat, was long lost to the Imperium. Cutting the behemoth in four were solar wings of burnished adamantium, giving the vessel the bold and unusual design of two Imperial aquilas – one slotted within the other. Four armoured wings. Four engine coil talons. A monasterial body of supra-Gothic splendour. Four sculpted heads of aquiline majesty, between which the vast craft hid a far larger weapon, the yawning mouth of an enormous torpedo launch tube.

'Closer...' Heiss ordered and the screen rendered maximum magnification.

Close up the craft's Gothic magnificence assumed the macabre and chilling status of a ruin. The vessel seemed completely without power, as evidenced in the expanse of black glass, the tall dark arches and empty lancet ports. The vessel was running without lamps or nav-strobes and seemed devoid of the kind of pods, hump shuttles and barges that might be expected to swarm around a structure of its size. The cold stone and metal of its massive construction was stunning from a distance, but close up was gaunt and weathered. The stone was cracked, granular and disintegrating, the victim of an eternity of etherical erosion. The solar inlaying was shattered, and the great adamantium expanse and detail of the wings was tarnished with even greater age. In places, it seemed the only thing holding the integrity of the structure together were the growths of warpsidium and immaterial deposits spreading out from the nooks like a sterile cancer. Stranger still, the craft wouldn't have been visible at all against the backdrop of the empty space were it not for the spectral fire that burned across every surface and suffused the derelict vessel with a golden, phantasmal glow.

'Chaos reinforcements?' Randt asked finally.

Heiss snorted at the thought that the Cholercaust actually required reinforcing.

'Looks like an Adeptus Astartes vessel. A monastery or star fortress,' she replied. 'Any signature readings, identicoda, hell – a nameplate?'

The midshipman moved along the runebank and put his eye to a monocular viewer. He double checked his reading with a nearby cogitator. 'Nothing.' he said. 'She doesn't match any known records. As far as the Imperium is concerned, she doesn't exist.

The incessant hammering on the bulkhead door grew as the corridor beyond filled with Khornate raiders. A nearby servitor's jaw suddenly went to work on a stream of code-chatter that drew Randt to its runescreen.

'I have a power signature,' the midshipman called. 'It's arming torpedoes.'

The commander sat back down in her throne. 'Ready thrusters for evasive manoeuvres.'

'Aye, commander.'

'Charge the lance for return fire.'

'Aye.'

The bridge watched the ruined star fortress as the eyes of the colossal aquila heads lit up. The dark orbits of the colossal structures were vents for the great torpedo tube running between them, and they flared brightly as the spectral gleam of a warhead erupted from the star fortress's primary weapon. Heiss watched the ghostly torpedo fly straight and true towards Certus-Minor. As it streaked away from the mobile monastery, she watched the aurulent ghostfire of its appearance suddenly intensify to a halo of plasmic propulsion.

'Did you see that?' Randt said. Heiss nodded in silence, heart in her mouth, as she watched an illusion sear into reality and that reality rocket into the side of the Keeler Comet.

'God-Emperor...' she mumbled, but it had already happened.

The Keeler Comet, which had been traversing the galaxy for aeons and had last passed through the Imperium ten thousand years before, exploded. The flash of the torpedo's impact picked out the irregular shape of the Ruinous object before the destructive force of detonation ripped through the body, wracking it to its frozen core and smashing it into a billion astral splinters. Within moments the comet was no longer there, just the bloody reminder of its void-smearing tail. Instead, the comet had become a rapidly tumbling apocalyptic heaven-fall of blood-black ice shards, enormous rock fragments and rare metal nuggets, accelerating towards Certus-Minor at the speed of a bolt-round. The violently transformed Keeler had changed direction once again, this time blasted towards the cemetery world's all-embracing, gravitational pull.

Heiss and Randt stared at each other in horror. The flesh-hungry marauders at the bulkhead were forgotten. None of them would survive the coming armageddon.

'Thrusters, now!' Heiss shouted. The *Apotheon* might not have very much manoeuvrability, but what it did have the commander intended to exploit in getting the lance in position to blast incoming fragments of ice and debris on course to hit the vulnerable ship.

'Enemy vessels disengaging,' Randt reported.

Heiss took a deep breath of satisfaction. The pirate captains of the raiders and armed freighters that had grappled the *Apotheon* had no intention of weathering the coming storm with the defence monitor, and were doing their best to haul off. The Cholercaust fleet below, stationed in low orbit, would not be so fortunate. Unlike the marauders, they would not see catastrophe coming. The ravenous raiders swarming the blood-splattered decks of the *Apotheon* had been abandoned by their Chaos captains and continued in ignorance to breach the bridge bulkhead. The degenerates would not be denied their last supper and communion with the dark lord of blood and vengeance. They would get through the bulkhead eventually and when they did, it would be carnage on the command deck.

'Randt,' Heiss called.

'Commander?' the midshipman answered, a tremor in his voice.

'Get me the Adeptus Astartes.'

'The Excoriators haven't been responding to our vox-hailing,' Randt told her. Heiss could imagine why.

'Get me somebody. Anybody. The Excoriators have to know what is happening up here.'

UMBRAGG OF THE Brazen Flesh hunted like an animal through the lonely maze of ambulatories and tight alleys that was the cemetery world city. Like a predator of the deep, a clawed fiend stalking through the night or a mythic Fenrisian wolf, blood-tracking its doomed prey. He felt his ancient skin tighten over his blood-engorged, muscular frame. His brute biceps, globed shoulders and rockrete-hard chest pressed against the constraints of his World Eaters plate. He could feel the Blood God's blessing – slabs of bronze, threading through the engineered tissue of his superhuman body like streaks of fat. Part flesh, part unfeeling lump of brazen indestructibility, Umbragg had served his master well.

With his warband, the *Clysm*, the World Eaters champion

had fought on a thousand worlds, butchered human and alien alike in the name of wanton carnage, and brought glory to Khorne's name through his prosecution of crusades, the slaughter of the Dark Prince of Pleasure's perverse followers and the taking of skulls on an obscene scale. He had killed at the great Doombreed's side, slayed with Skarbrand, murdered his own with Khârn the Betrayer and fought in every Black Crusade to ever strike fear into the weak heart of the Imperium. He had served with his daemon-father, the Primarch Angron himself, during the Dominion of Fire, on war-torn Armageddon and before the walls of the Imperial Palace on doomed Terra. Now, he served the Pilgrim – daemon prince and Right Claw of Khorne – leader of the Cholercaust Blood Crusade, who would take the Blood God's disciples back to Ancient Terra and finish what they had started.

Blood-furious, Umbragg slowed to a trembling halt, his chainaxes like two silent scorpion claws held at his sides. They trembled not through fear – his scarred brain knew nothing of the emotion, bar what he saw others feel in his maniac presence – but through fury. His body quaked. His gore-rusted plate rattled. Elsewhere in the city, his brothers had found their quarry. He heard bolt-fire and the scream of axes. He felt the death of innocents only streets away and glory stripped from him by lesser World Eaters. Warband brothers of the Anointed, the Crimson Covenant and Sons of Skalathrax had killed and been killed in a battle that had stricken the killer-crowded city like a blood clot to the heart.

In common with all of the Cholercaust's victories, the cemetery world had fallen swiftly and easily. Such a god-honouring burden was the World Eaters' to shoulder. They were the victims of their own vicious success. This was why the Pilgrim had led them on the blood comet's path. Only the heavily fortified worlds of Segmentum Solar and Terra itself held the challenge Khorne's servants demanded. Somewhere on the cemetery world, however, the Emperor's Angels were surviving, and this filled Umbragg's flesh with simultaneous rage and desire. The False Emperor's pawns had to be destroyed, but they had to die at Umbragg's hand. Only He of the Brazen Flesh deserved such a sacrifice.

His murderous instincts had led him away from the havoc and carnage, out through the cobbled, labyrinthine slope-streets of a district already torched and sundered. The tall walls of chapels, hermitages and domiciles smoked and curled with flame. Blood splattered the streets in acts of violence past enjoyed. Guardsmen with antiquated weaponry, thin flak and dressed in sombre and ridiculous ceremonial robes littered the gutters. The ease of their butchery was evident. Umbragg felt the fluttering heartbeat of a dying Certusian nearby.

A mindless slave-soldier, naked and smeared from head to foot in gore, burst from an alley and raced across the cobbles with a nail-spiked club. By the time Umbragg had stalked up to the scene, the feral world cult conscript had beaten the brains from the broken body of the Guardsman. Umbragg felt the mortal's heart hammer in his chest and then stop. He savoured the moment, but it only served to stoke his fury and remind him of the emptiness inside his own chest that should have been filled with the murderous delight of gluttonous life-taking and the slaughter of heroes. Without even bringing the chainaxe to life, the World Eater bludgeoned the slave-soldier into the ground with the razored weight of the weapon.

The feral worlder died instantly. His heart stopped with sudden efficiency. Beyond, an Adeptus Astartes hung from the shattered, skeletal metalwork of a burned-out building. His helmetless face was black with blood and the severity of mob-issued beating. His plate had been rent and punctured. An arm was missing. The clean pits of bolt-rounds mottled the ivory of his armour. The emblage of his Chapter could just be made out on his axe-cleaved shoulder plate. The Excoriators. Umbragg snorted. Dorn's breed. A hateful derision started building in his twisted mind, but it died moments later. The World Eater's instincts had not brought him to the eye of the storm for nothing, to savour the abhorrent calm of aftermath. He felt the Blood God's eye on him, judging this wasted time. Here, away from the rush of daemoniacal destruction that the Cholercaust was bringing to other parts of the city.

Umbragg bridled. On the light breeze, he felt the fearful beating of other hearts. Out beyond the ancient stone of the walls, the burning buildings and the raging multitudes of tainted mortals, armoured slaughterkin and daemon madness. Amongst the overpowering stench of the tomb, the stale tang of old rot and the death-saturated scent of grave dust, Umbragg detected the sweet perfume of life and the living. There were mortals here – thousands of them – hidden from the inevitable and hoarding their skulls. Like a carnivore, enraptured at the prospect of fresh hunting grounds, Umbragg stood, his fists tight about his axe shafts; the primordial darkness of his brain struggling with what he could sense but could not see; his blood coursing with rage at the prospect of plots, scheming and trickery.

The World Eater did not see the ghost behind him. The darkness of a shadowy alcove that become a silhouette in the street smoke. The silhouette that became armoured detail. The revenant that became reality at the Traitor's back. Umbragg never saw the rachidian horror of bone-moulded plate or the auric flame that danced off the ceramite's bitter, black surface. He never saw the rent faceplate of the damned legionnaire appear over his brain-speckled shoulder, nor the burn of unnatural life glowing within the skull-socket of the being within. All the berserker heard was the nasty chatter of teeth before the cursed edge of the legionnaire's short sword slid across the World Eater's armoured neck. Passing through the plate like an apparition, the blade assumed its lethality within, its keen edge – honed to eternity – slicing through the World Eater's brazen flesh and cutting his throat to the bone.

Chainaxes clattered to the cobbles. The World Eater crashed to the floor in a heavy metal avalanche of ceramite and hatred. His killer had gone – vanished back into the smoke and ether from whence it came. Umbragg of the

Brazen Flesh – World Eater, Traitor, mass-murderer and champion of Khorne – bled his remaining life into the gutter. Alone, the infamous monster and warrior-tyrant died an unknown death, his warped hearts beating their thunderous last in a street so small and insignificant to the rest of the galaxy that it didn't even have a name.

ZACHARIAH KERSH COULD have little idea what had started in the streets below. The corpus-captain stomped along the roofside, his boots smashing through the tiles and punching into the lead and strutage beneath. The Excoriators had made good on their escape from the cloistrium, ascending through the floors of the sepulchre before smashing their way up into the roof using their fists and blades. A messy climb had taken them up through the balconies of a block-domicilia where, out of the range of pistol-fire, the Adeptus Astartes had watched the great *Punisher* silenced.

The honoured war machine had done the bloody work of ten immortals, blasting behemoths, turning cultist hordes to flesh-spatter and driving back hell-spawned daemons. It was the World Eaters that finally beat the cannon. It took a fair number of their brethren with its cold, calculating barrage of rhythmic havoc. The cloistrium became a smouldering pit of twisted ceramite and flesh that refused to die. World Eaters stormed the Thunderfire cannon's position, crawling, limbless, overcome with fury and frustration. Bastard-brothers of the Traitor Legion – attracted by the roar of battle and the copper-tinge of death on the air – threw themselves into the chaos, climbing over their wounded brethren who filled the ordnance-pounded crater the space had become. Other warbands visited their fury on adjoining walls, smashing through old brick and mortar with their hammers, axes and shoulders. It was through such an opening that heretic Angels of the Crimson Covenant gained access to the rear of the sepulchre and came up behind the itinerant cannon, hacking into its armoured shell and ammunition feed with their chainaxes.

Kersh leapt from the edge of the domicilia and across the

street to the mezzanine of an opposing tower-obsequium. The mezzanine floor cracked and shuddered as Melmoch followed – the Epistolary looking like pale hell as he demolished a stained-glass window with his force scythe and climbed through. Novah, still clutching the company standard, helped the grievously injured Chaplain on the take-off. Kersh grabbed Shadrath's armour where a World Eater's battleaxe had opened up his plate, and helped him to the window. Beyond, the Epistolary smashed and clambered his way up through the tower.

With Brother Novah and Skase across, the Scourge risked a glance down at the street below. The roaring rose up to meet him. All he saw were the maniac multitudes. Thoroughfares and posternways crowded with cultist fighters, World Eaters and their armoured renegade cousins stomping barbarously through the throng, and daemons crawling up walls and bounding fiendishly between ledges.

Obsequa City was a testament to insanity. Churches, chancelleries and frater houses were raging infernos, lighting up the necroplex beyond – still a wild ocean of charging heretics and Chaos cultists. The night sky flashed with the occasional streak of lance-fire, although to Kersh's knowledge only the Adeptus Ministorum defence monitor *Apotheon* had remained.

'Corpus-captain!' Novah called, prompting the Scourge to duck in through the smashed window and follow the trail of destruction up through the tower. Every rooftop and steeple was an opportunity to climb higher. Every box-stoop and maintenance portico took a superhuman leap of faith, across the narrow spaces of cultist-filled streets and quads. Gargoyle-encrusted walls, drain conduits and masonry scaffolding helped the Excoriators work up through the steep, climbing architecture of the city and on towards the imposing structure and distinctive dome of the Umberto II Memorial Mausoleum.

As the Adeptus Astartes edged around cupolas, ran along apexes and braved the vertiginous heights of gable walls and slender diameters of bridging supports, they could hear the Cholercaustians below, screaming up the cobbled passages and stairwells to get ahead of them. Where slave-soldiers ascended the fussy architecture of the heights in their path, Kersh and Skase had stamping boots and the finger-slicing tips of their blades waiting. Daemons were a much bigger problem, with the horned heralds of the Blood God's pantheon forced to leap further and further as Epistolary Melmoch demolished spires and walkways behind the escaping Excoriators. A huge flock of winged furies had taken to circling the towertops surrounding the Mausoleum, occasionally forcing the Space Marines to take cover in alcoves or press themselves flat to roofs in order to escape a swarm-mauling of wings and daggered claws. The monstrous myriad plunged through minarets and thrashed their thunderbolt course through belfries and cathedral lunette windows. Kersh saw blasted specimens fall from the flock as they ritually circled an abbey tower on the out-skirts of the city, las-fire cutting daemons down with each pass. With horror the Scourge realised that one of Keturah's sniper Scouts had escaped attention and had maintained his isolated defence against the countless masses.

As he hauled himself up a steeple maintenance ladder, Kersh noticed that the almost clockwork circling of the daemon flock had failed to materialise. Peering around the copper tiling, the corpus-captain saw the flock molesting the abbey tower, crawling about the exterior and clawing through a balistraria. It became obvious to the Excoria-tor that this was how the Cholercaust had dealt with the Tenth Company sniper threat. As he ascended the ladder, the remaining Excoriators behind him, Kersh saw the bell tower light up. An explosion – a grenade, the Scourge sus-pected – had taken out the belfry, the sniper and a number of the daemons, which plummeted towards the ground on what was left of their smashed, flaming wings. Pausing on the ladder, Kersh rested his forehead against the cool metal and mouthed a cult observation – a ritual thanks for a brother's sacrifice. Sickened to the bottom of his stomach, the corpus-captain realised how many observances he had missed during the Long Night of the Cholercaust invasion.

As he reached the top of the maintenance ladder, Kersh leapt for the stone guttering of an adjacent shrine and hauled himself up onto the waterlogged expanse of its flat, modest roof. There the corpus-captain waited, both for his brothers and the daemon swarm's clawing dive through the rooftops.

'Chaplain!' Squad Whip Skase roared as Shadrath's flailing form was snatched from the ladder. It was sudden and shocking – even for the Adeptus Astartes warriors. The Scourge watched the Excoriators Chaplain dragged off into the night sky, tossed between the predatory daemons in the infernal flock. Shadrath was still fighting, but his crozius arcanum fell into the street below, ringing off the wall-clutching metal stairwells.

'Keep moving!' the Scourge called at the remaining Excoriators as they watched the Chaplain disappear.

PREOCCUPIED WITH NOT falling to their deaths, and fighting off daemon aerial assaults with nothing but short swords, the Emperor's Angels had little idea what was happening in shadowy streets storeys below their boots. Amongst the hallowed halls of sepulchres and sanctuaries, and in the ambulatories snaking between them, butchers were being butchered – and not by each other.

World Eaters of the Foresworn were lured into the pillared crypts below the Vault of Divine Transcendence, where ghostly apparitions stalked the armoured brutes, taking them one by one – infuriating their dwindling number further and making them ever easier to slaughter.

Slorak the Undying failed to live up to his name after unloading his bolt pistol's entire magazine into an advancing, flame-swathed revenant and having his horned skull cleaved in two.

Berserker-brothers of the Bloodstorm issued their crude battle-cry before charging at two power armoured shadows in a corner of the Serenity Square. The World Eaters clearly thought the Angels were formerly encountered Excoriators.

Their axe-wielding frenzy only served to hew rents and bloody gashes in each other's plate, however, with the adamantium-toothed weapons passing clean through the warrior shades. Slave-soldiers, foaming at the mouth, found the Bloodstorm corpses gutted and piled at the centre of the square.

Techmarine Tezgavayn – more flesh warped over twisted machine than superman – was sent into a mechanical fury by phantom auspex returns amongst the statues of Imperial saints on the Boulevard of the Nine Sorrows. Smashing the statues to pieces, Tezgavayn was drawn to a solemn sculpture of Corvus the Sabine, where a clutch of ghostly grenades were waiting for the mechanical monstrosity. The grenades might have burned with a phantasmal glow but the armour-cracking explosions that issued from them felt very real to the Traitor Techmarine, as his body and workings were blown across the boulevard.

Skull-draped Kronosian Warlords simply disappeared whilst trailing the progress of the Slaughterfiend daemon engine *Fellclaw* as it hunted for Adeptus Astartes sighted in the Viaticus Quarter. Lord Drakkar – Blood Champion and Traitor Angel figurehead for the Hellion Dawn sadists – was torched along with a hundred of his depraved followers in a blind alley known as 'The Quietus'. Charred cultist survivors reported sightings of silent warriors in sable armour who corralled the Chaos lord and his sadists with flamers before cremating the crush.

With World Eaters stalked and slaughtered across the city by the revenant crusaders, and daemonkin instinctively giving the empyreal intruders a wide berth, Kersh and his Excoriators reached the Memorial Mausoleum ahead of the anarchy swallowing the city.

Sliding down the steep roof of a monastic cell-block, the tiles shattering before the toes of their boots, the Adeptus Astartes reached the edge of the St Aloysion Hospice. The porch balconies of individual cells looked out on the Mausoleum's impressive architecture, and a narrow strait ran between the brother and sister wings. Plunging down onto the top floor balcony, Kersh led the way, dropping back and forth across the open space, the Space Marine crashing through some porches, while bounding between others. The descent was similarly awkward amongst his brother Excoriators, but with the cultist hordes of the Cholercaust surging up the streets and closing on the Mausoleum, every moment counted.

Kersh dropped the final few floors and skidded on the cobbles as he raced for the great metal doors of the Umberto II Memorial Mausoleum. He felt Brother Novah close behind, the standard still clutched feverishly in his gauntlets; an exhausted Melmoch trailed behind the bearer, and Skase brought up the rear. The arterial boulevards and thoroughfares released a deluge of cultist madness on the open ground before the Mausoleum. The roaring had returned, as had the killer glint of a thousand eyes. Kersh felt the chill of cowardice shiver down his spine. He was not comfortable running from such a feeble foe, but numbers alone would prevent the Excoriators closing the Mausoleum's great doors if all four Space Marines did not get there first.

Kersh hurdled several bikes, the chunky, armoured cycles having been parked in an orderly row around the Mausoleum before their riders had been assigned their doomed sniping duties. Melmoch once again brought his devastating warp-drawn power to bear on the enemy. Flailing arcs of distilled death erupted from the Librarian's scythe-shaft. The energy danced across the front row of sprinting maniacs, detonating body after body and turning the riotous vanguards into a curtain of gore through which following slave-soldiers ran. The very essence of death was everywhere, like something you could touch and harness. The Excoriators Epistolary roared his denial and sent the second row the stomach-churning way of the first.

Kersh was in. Novah followed, the two Space Marines slamming their packs into the adamantium alloy of the massive door and heaving it across the tomb egress. Skase shot past Melmoch, literally skidding through the blood lapping against the exterior wall and in through the closing gap. Down on his chest, with Kersh and Novah putting their backs into the door, Skase yelled back furiously at the Librarian.

'Melmoch, get in here – now!'

An Excoriator flashed through the opening, slipping down onto his side. It wasn't Melmoch. It was Squad Whip Ishmael. 'Ishmael…' Skase began, but the greeting died in the Excoriator's throat. Propping himself up on the tip of his crackling lightning claws, Ishmael looked up. Gone was the Escharan nobility of his calling and the eyes of a battle-brother and friend. Ishmael's eyes were claret red. His head was a nest of purple veins and arteries, throbbing with blood and darkness. He was now Ishmael the animal. The animal that wanted to kill.

Both Excoriators scrambled to their feet on the cold marble floor of the Mausoleum antechamber. Ishmael came at his chief whip with savage sweeps of his power talons. Skase lightly deflected the blade tips with his gladius, not daring to risk the short sword against the full cutting capabilities of Ishmael's claws. Grabbing at the gall-fevered wrist of the squad whip, Skase turned and slammed the gladius straight through Ishmael's armoured palm. The squad whip took little heed of the bold move, chesting the Excoriator forwards and driving the claw-tips of his right gauntlet through Skase's suit pack.

Weaponless, the brute Ishmael expected his chief whip to back away and proceeded to slice off the gladius blade-length protruding from the back of his talon with his other claw. By the time he feasted his blood-swamped eyes on the Excoriator, Skase was coming straight back at him. The chief whip slammed the sole of his boot into the animal-Ishmael's chestplate, unbalancing the deviant and knocking him back towards the door.

The full weight of the advancing Cholercaust was behind the thick metal, with row upon blood-crazed row charging forwards against each other and the Mausoleum door in an effort to earn the Blood God's favour and end an Adeptus Astartes. The Scourge and Brother Novah continued in their desperate, marble-grazing efforts. Ishmael turned his unseeing eyes on his brothers. Novah was nearest, so Novah died first. Ishmael spun around and buried a crackling claw all the way up to the knuckle in the Fifth Company standard bearer. The standard itself jangled to the floor, and as Ishmael retracted his devastating talons, the butchered Excoriator followed it. Kersh immediately felt the effect on the door as hundreds of the Blood God's servants lent their weight to an irresistible entrance. A tattooed hiver managed to slip his emaciated and gore-slick form through the gap, along with a mass of clutching arms. The hiver screamed his demented triumph, but Ishmael silenced the annoyance with a savage headbutt that brained the cultist. As the hiver scum dropped like a sack of lead weights, Ishmael swung back on the Excoriators. Skase ran at the blood-mad squad whip as Kersh tried to reach for his gladius. Ishmael spat his fury at both – the Excoriator's murderous mind struggling to choose between the pair.

A stream of soul lightning struck the degenerate in the side, smashing him across the antechamber and into the thick stone wall of the Mausoleum. Ishmael clawed at the immaterial energy and snapped like a trapped beast. Melmoch was through the door. The Librarian was on his ceramite knees, still dripping with cultist blood from the carnage outside. Scrabbling beneath the warpstream, Skase joined his corpus-captain on the door. Launching their armoured frames at the adamantium alloy with renewed fervour, the Excoriators slammed it closed, shearing off the twitching limbs of slave-soldiers clawing their way through. As Skase held the great door closed, Kersh hauled at the pinion mechanism that drove a heavy adamantium bar across the portal and into the wall.

Warp lightning arced off Ishmael's plate causing the dried blood that covered it to smoulder. Ishmael screeched his hatred of the psyker and his unnatural powers, flicking his claws out and leaning into the soul-scalding stream of energy. Melmoch's face was similarly contorted, the Epistolary trying his best to angle the shaft of his force scythe and the otherworldly energies spilling from it at the squad whip. Blood bubbled behind Ishmael's eyes and his nostrils split with snorting exertion. Pure hatred alone drove the squad whip's canine teeth down out of his gums like fangs. Veins and arteries split his skin, and the Excoriator issued a horrifying scream. Ishmael exploded. Shards of ceramite shrapnel flew in all directions, *pranging* off the surface of the door and embedding themselves in the stone of the wall and floor. It rained blood inside the Mausoleum as what was left of Ishmael coated the antechamber and the Excoriators within.

As the goremist settled, Kersh could see Melmoch on his knees. The Librarian's head was lowered and he was leaning against the shaft of his devastating weapon. The corpus-captain and his chief whip slid down the wet surface of the metal door beside Brother Novah in exhaustion. Kersh checked the Excoriator for any signs of life, but there were none. Ishmael had finished him.

The hammering was awful. The Cholercaust had run its course. Only the Excoriators remained, and every slaughter-crazed servant of the Blood God was either outside the Mausoleum's mighty walls or on their way there, to claim the few remaining skulls on the cemetery world in the name of their dark overlord. Kersh could imagine the tsunami of fists, boots, weapons and foreheads slamming against the unfeeling alloy of the great door. The nightmarish vision scarred his mind, the murderous crush of slave-soldiers, cultists, renegade Angels, daemons and World Eaters, all desperate to find a way inside.

Palatine Sapphira and the pontifex had told Kersh that the great door was the only entrance to the memorial tomb, and the corpus-captain believed them. He was not concerned about the ground floor. However, dotted across the Mausoleum's exterior architecture were ornamental embrasures and aquila-shaped boltslits, apertures through which the Sisters of the August Vigil might defend Umberto II's remains and his great Mausoleum from raids and civil unrest. Neither Palatine Sapphira or the tomb's architect

ROB SANDERS

could have imagined the defensive necessities required to hold a host the size and devastating capability of the Cholercaust at bay. The walls were strong and Kersh had some limited faith in the great entrance door, but the Excoriator knew that the Blood God's disciples would find a way in – the unmanned boltslits and embrasures in the upper storeys seemed a likely weakness.

Kersh's gaze settled on the Fifth Company's battle standard, still clutched in Novah's gauntlet. Skase was staring at the blood-speckled banner also. The two Excoriators looked hard at one another. Snatching up the standard, Kersh slipped Novah's gladius from his ceramite grip and handed it to the unarmed Skase.

'Melmoch, watch the door,' the Scourge ordered amongst the thunderous din of howling and shoulders striking the metal egress. Still on his knees, his eyes on the floor, Melmoch raised a weak hand.

Kersh ran through the anteroom and across the marble expanse of the Holy Sepulchre. Skase followed with difficulty. Ishmael's lightning claw had raked through the chief whip's pack, damaging the plant and some of the motive function hardware. The plate's power supply was waning and the unsupported deadweight of the ceramite was slowing the Excoriator.

As the Space Marines crossed the open space of the Mausoleum the funereal beauty of the building was lost upon them: the intricate scrolling on the wall internments; the silver lettering adorning the floor slabs, recording the names of past pontiffs and cardinals; loggia supports and fat sculpted pillars reaching up to the exquisite detail of the Mausoleum's domed ceiling – each hand-painted illustration a depiction of Umberto II's long and spiritually-productive life. Candles and incense burned from a thousand suspended sconces, and stern statues of ecclesiarchs already elevated to sainthood adorned the sepulchre space in a ring around a simple block-crypt of obsidian brick. A silver-plated elevator was used to transport clerics and Adepta Sororitas deep below the sepulchre to a small complex of condition-controlled crypt chambers residing behind a thick vault door.

Within, laid out for private pilgrimage and display, were the surviving remains of Umberto II – Ruling Ecclesiarch of the Adeptus Ministorum and High Lord of Terra. A circular gallery spiralled about the sepulchre's exterior, made up of marble steps and landings, providing access to the wall-combs, vaultia and the upper storeys of the Mausoleum. It was the infuriating length of the gallery – winding around the sepulchre – that the Scourge and Skase negotiated. As they ran, the Excoriators could still hear the furious multitudes outside, echoing about the great dome, and could see the warp-spent Melmoch on his knees at the centre of the antechamber.

'What now?' Skase barked, as he drove his failing suit on along the gallery. Kersh didn't respond, but he did keep pausing at intervals to stare out of the embrasure boltslits and allow the chief whip to catch up. Just before the locked entrance to the Sisters of Battle's mission house, Kersh stopped and stared out through the stone aperture at the chaos beyond. The Memorial Mausoleum commanded the best view of Obsequa City that anyone could expect. The cemetery world capital wasn't much to look at now: an inferno-tormented, partially demolished ruin, tainted with innocent blood, and a rockrete menagerie for murderous deviants, traitors and filth-entities from the warp. 'Kersh!' Skase said, soaking up the hopelessness beside him. 'What are we going to do?'

The Scourge looked blankly at the Excoriator. He heard Melmoch call weakly from the sepulchre floor. Ignoring them both, Kersh took the mission house door off with a single strike of his boot. Striding across the small transeptory and past the cell-cloisters, Kersh moved swiftly through the sacristy and Lady Chapel. Near the palatine's solitoria, Kersh found what he was looking for: the mission house armoury and the vox-berth.

'Raid what's left of the armoury. Grab us some weapons and grenades – something with punch,' Kersh told Skase as he went to work on the frequency matrix of the vox-bank. Kersh heard Melmoch call again over the boom of the door assault below.

'What for?' Skase seared. 'It's over.'

Kersh dropped the vox-hailer and stormed at the chief whip. 'I'll tell you when it's over!'

Skase fixed the Scourge with a gaze that was pure reason: no fear, no despair or sorrow.

'The city's lost,' Skase shouted, 'the Fifth is gone. You hear that?' The chief whip let the rumble of mayhem intrude from outside. 'They will get in, and when they do – no matter how hard we fight, no matter what honour we bring to the primarch or our Lord Katafalque – our blood will be theirs. They will end us, and those people out there, whom you confidently placed in the bosom of the earth, will rot there...'

Kersh roared his recriminations at the Excoriator, and Skase roared back.

'Corpus-captain!' Melmoch called. The two Space Marines burned into each other with accusatory eyes. Kersh looked out at the Holy Sepulchre and then back at Skase.

'There is no dishonour in doubt,' the Scourge told him. 'You think Katafalque didn't have doubts, out on the walls of the Imperial Palace? You think Dorn was not crippled by the deep melancholies of the unknown as he stood over the Emperor's shattered form? There is no dishonour in doubt,' Kersh repeated. 'The measure of a primarch, a Chapter Master, a battle-brother, is what he does next. We are Excoriators. This is our burden. These are our trials. Trials of the mind, the spirit and the flesh. War through attrition. Victory through endurance, and we shall endure.'

Skase's gaze drifted to the floor. He nodded, slowly and to himself.

'Yes,' he said, unlocking the seals on his gauntlets and slipping them off.

The vox crackled discordance before erupting with a solitary voice.

'...please respond. This is His Beneficent Majesty's

planetary defence monitor *Apotheon* hailing Obsequa City – Fifth Company Adeptus Astartes Excoriators Chapter… Please respond.'

'*Apotheon*, this is Corpus-Captain Zachariah Kersh of the Fifth. We receive.'

'My lord,' the voice crackled, 'we've been trying to raise you. The interference…'

'Listen to me carefully, mortal. I do not have time to ask you twice,' Kersh boomed at the vox-hailer. 'I saw your vengeance in the sky. I need to know your status.'

'My lord, there is something I need–'

'Mortal, believe me when I tell you that many lives – including my own – depend on the choice of your next words. Your status – have you been boarded?'

'This is Commander Heiss,' a female voice responded after a pause. 'We have been boarded.'

'Do you have steerage way and power to your weapons systems?'

'Not for long, my lord. There has been a strange development up here,' the commander replied.

'Get ready for another one,' Kersh told her, staring at maps and schemata located about the vox-berth. He proceeded to stab digits into a glyphpad on the vox-bank with the ceramite tip of his finger. 'I'm sending you coordinates for a location on the planet's surface. After examination of them you will reach the conclusion that the coordinates reside within Obsequa City, just outside the Umberto II Memorial Mausoleum, to be exact.'

'My lord…'

'You will target these coordinates and manoeuvre your lance into position for an orbital strike in exactly fifteen minutes' time.'

'I can't–'

'You can, commander, and you will. That is a direct order. A great deal rides on whether you can find it within yourself to obey that order. Let me be clear. I am ordering you to destroy the Memorial Mausoleum.'

'And a good part of the city,' Heiss shot back.

'Don't concern yourself with that,' the Scourge told her. 'There is nobody left in the city.' Kersh looked at Skase who was standing in the berth entrance holding a multimelta beside him in one hand and a heavy bolter in the other. Without his gauntlets he could only just get his thick fingers through the carryholds of the Sisters' weaponry. The chief whip humped a pyrum-petrol fuel pack and had draped his battered shoulder plates with bandoliers of grenades and 1.00 calibre ammunition. The two Excoriators held each other's grim gaze. 'There is no dishonour in doubt, commander. The measure of us is what we do next. Fifteen minutes, commander. Good luck. Obsequa City out.'

As Heiss tried to interject, Kersh cut her off and dropped the vox-hailer.

'That's your plan?' Skase said as the pair travelled back through the mission house transeptory.

'I don't plan on any of us being here in fifteen minutes,' Kersh replied, the battle standard clutched tightly in his hand.

'It took a lot of lives to get here,' Skase said.

'And now we've got the enemy where we want them, we'll take a lot more.'

'What about the people in the vault?'

'The vault's deep and the door's thick. It will hold. If it could survive a meteorite impact, it'll weather an orbital bombardment. Just.'

'You can't stop the Cholercaust with a single lance strike.'

'No, but it will give these murderous bastards something to think about while we make good our withdrawal. I don't care what they say about the Cholercaust. We have to endure – we have to survive this. Those people out there, counting on us, in the dark beneath the earth, have to survive this.'

'Why? No planet ever has.'

'But worlds will, once they hear of survivors. We will not stop the Cholercaust, but somebody will, somebody with hope in their heart, resolution and belief – all three of which our survival will have put there.'

As Kersh and the chief whip stepped back out onto the gallery, the corpus-captain called, 'Melmoch – we're leaving.' Kersh expected some kind of protest – a question at least – but it didn't come. Looking over the balustrade, the two Excoriators saw the Librarian still on his knees on the antechamber floor. He was vomiting projectile streams of blood down onto the marble floor, a copious pool of which had built up around the psyker. 'Melmoch!' Kersh called. The roaring cacophony of the mob outside died to silence.

'The gateway called Melmoch no longer resides in this vessel,' the Excoriators heard the hordes outside drone in unison. The stone of the Mausoleum hummed with the chorus of voices. 'His witch's soul burns for eternity in the fires of my master's ire, and it drowns in the boiling depths of his bile. I am the Pilgrim, the Prince of Pain and Right Claw of Khorne. My gene-breed flesh remembers slaughtering your kind on the ramparts of the False Emperor's Palace, on distant Terra, many lives-taken ago. It wishes to remember again.'

Melmoch's body began to rise above the bloody pool. Cloven hooves on thick, red legs erupted from the Librarian's armoured knees. Great infernal claws punctured the Excoriator's plate at the elbow, unfolding into appendages of red sinew and brazen talons. Melmoch's armour disintegrated about the materialising beast, shards and fragments becoming embedded in the obscenely muscular daemon-hide. A blood-drenched pauldron remained, the Stigmartyr symbol of the Excoriators briefly bursting into flame before smouldering to the blasphemous World Eaters jaw-glyph around a paint-bubbling globe. The Epistolary's afflicted gaze and precious skull disappeared, swallowed whole by the Pilgrim's gulping, dagger-toothed maw, which emerged like a surfacing ocean behemoth from the Librarian's back and shoulders.

Shaking the freshly-morphed head from side to side, a pair of bullish horns speared their way out from the monster's temples. The thing itself did not speak, simply resorting to a foundation-shaking wrath-bellow of full realisation. With ease, the Pilgrim ripped the statue of a nearby saint out of the floor with his great claws and flung it at the Mausoleum door. The stone flew at the door, hitting the metal surface with infernal force. The door blasted open on its colossal hinges, crushing a score of slave-soldiers whose bodies were stamped into the ground by the flood of cultist pandemonium that raged into the Holy Sepulchre.

Kersh snatched a bandolier of grenades from Skase's shoulder as the Excoriator bent down to load the belt feed into the heavy bolter's breech. He snapped off several and tossed them across the breadth of the chamber, where they hit the gallery and bounced down the steps leading around and down towards the ground floor. The steps detonated, blasting the spiralling first floor gallery to dust along with the drove of blood cultists who had immediately mounted the stairwell.

Slapping shut the breech and balancing the heavy bolter on the balustrade, Skase began to hammer the endless hordes with blistering firepower. The Pilgrim tore another statue from the floor and tossed it through the air at the Excoriators. Skase leant aside and Kersh ducked as the sculpture of Saint Vatalis crashed through the embrasure behind him. Looking down on the hideous thing that had been Melmoch, Kersh came to understand the dire physical and spiritual dangers the psyker had been trying to avoid, when he put himself out during the Keeler Comet's arrival. Lifting his gaze, Kersh began to feel about his plate for the ornately decorated urn Melmoch had used. The negatively-charged dust within was used by the Sisters for consecrating Umberto II's shrine. The Epistolary had stolen the precious relic from the Mausoleum, and Kersh had intended on giving it back. Which he decided to do now.

Taking it in his hand, Kersh lobbed the urn like a grenade, over the balustrade and down onto the daemon World Eater. The pot smashed against the Pilgrim's horns, dousing the monster in the fine dust. The particles seared into the Pilgrim's daemonflesh on contact. The beast howled and screamed its torment as the psychic negativity not only broke down the horror's warp-crafted flesh but also ate away at the thing's tenuous link with reality.

'Die, you monstrous thing,' Kersh spat, as Skase continued to chew through the cultists swarming the chamber. The creature of Chaos clawed at its own dust-infected muscle and sinew, raking through its face and armoured chest. Cultists about the dissolving cage of bones screamed also and began savaging the beast with blades, nails and teeth. The surrounding slave-soldiers fell on the inner circle, tearing them apart, and before long the scene was a horrific orgy of butchery. Skase concentrated his mulching gunfire on the doorway, accompanied by throng-blasting grenades tossed by the Scourge, down through the antechamber.

A new and sickening sound rose up from the sepulchre floor. It sounded to Kersh like a thicket of trees all bending and breaking at the same time. The corpus-captain could hear snapping, fracturing and splintering. Below, at the heart of the carnage, the bodies of the dying and those who had killed them were being drawn into a bloody maelstrom. Bones were breaking and reaching out of cultist bodies, intertwining with the skeletal mesh of others in a macabre fusion, a daemon cage through which the shredded flesh and spilled gore of the cultists bubbled and swirled. Beneath the Excoriators, the Pilgrim was finding a new form. Feeding on the souls of his blood-pledged, the monster fought through the agonies Kersh had visited upon it and refused to release its terrible hold on the material universe. As more and more of the Blood God's disciples flooding the chamber were gore-assimilated by the thing, it grew. The Pilgrim's skin-rent skull emerged from the top of the carcass mountain, its devastating claws also – although being a flesh-frame of grasping, scratching, flailing limbs, it was not short of such appendages. As it rose on its murderous altar of butchered bodies, the Pilgrim's eyes blazed white with hate and it reached out for the Emperor's Angels on the gallery.

'Let's go!' Kersh bawled, tugging at Skase's shoulder, but

the chief whip shrugged him off, burying a fresh volley of bolt-rounds in the Pilgrim's grotesque embodiment.

'It's not going to happen,' Skase shouted between staccato blasts. He threw a thumb behind him. 'The pack's shot. Power failure. My plate will only slow the both of us down.'

'We can make it!' the corpus-captain returned.

'You can make it,' Skase said, blasting at the Chosen of Khorne. 'You must make it. Like you said, somebody's got to survive.'

With the Pilgrim growing horrifically before them, the Scourge stared at his chief whip. Skase nodded at the battle standard fluttering in Kersh's hand. 'Keep it flying,' he said. 'I'll keep them entertained until the lightshow begins.'

Nodding silently, Kersh knelt down and primed the multi-melta, cycling the pyrum-petrol mix and activating the sub-molecular reaction chamber. Leaving the fuel pack on the floor, Kersh placed the heavy weapon on the balustrade. Without a word or a glance, Skase silenced the heavy bolter and moved across to the melta. He punched a vaporising beam of intense fusion through the howling Pilgrim-monstrosity before recalibrating the weapon and turning another patch of its flesh-armour to molten slag. With the bandolier in one hand and the Fifth Company's battle standard in the other, Kersh left the occupied Skase and stepped through the hole the statue had made in the wall.

Sidling out along the ledge, the Scourge looked down. The darkness below swarmed with movement, killers attracted by the bloodbath within the Mausoleum and eager to be part of it. Above, the sky was stranger still. In low orbit Kersh could see the telltale signs of obliteration, vessels he could not see suddenly flaring into fireballs of destruction. With the *Apotheon*'s lance hopefully aimed down over his head and Naval assistance light years away, Kersh could only reason that the insane captains of the Chaos fleet had decided to turn their guns on each other. It was certainly not unknown amongst the savage servants of the Blood God.

A sole winged fury swooped past, snapping at the Excoriator with its jaws. As it banked and tried to savage him again, Kersh swung the bandolier of grenades like a flail and smashed it in the wing, sending the thing careening off into the side of a building. Kersh could feel the precious seconds passing. Priming one of the grenades he let the bandolier drop into the unsuspecting crowd below. Giving the belt a few seconds advantage, and with the banner in his hand, Kersh too stepped off the ledge. There was simply no swift way down off the side of the colossal tomb. Kersh's plate buckled and cracked as he struck lower ledges and the unforgiving stone of architectural flourishes. He reached out with his hand to grab rims, boltslits and the limbs and wings of gargoyles. His boots found brief and occasional footing on carved ridges and representations that could not support his weight or the gathering force of his fall. The paint on his ceramite chipped and scuffed as he grazed the building's side.

Everything suddenly became white below as the grenades detonated in a chain reaction. The moment seemed to hesitate and Kersh felt himself momentarily slow as fiery lumps of flesh and masonry were rocketed skywards by the blast. The Scourge found himself suddenly winded as he landed on a pillartop, stomach first. He felt several things break inside. The impact had at least reined in the gathering speed of his fall, and as he rolled off, the few remaining storeys down the pillarside were uneventful. Taking in a breath, Kersh realised that he'd dropped the battle standard, and that the pole and banner had gone on ahead of him. When he struck the cobbles beside it, the epicentre of the devastating fragstorm moments before, something snapped in his leg. The hot glow of agony washed up the limb. Getting up off the crumpled plating and pauldron on his arm, the Scourge looked down at the injury. The ceramite had split at the knee, as had his flesh, allowing a bone from his leg to erupt through the rent.

His face a mask of suppressed torture, Kersh scooped up the company standard and used it as a staff, taking the worst of the weight off the wounded leg. Reaching for his Scourge's blade, the corpus-captain clutched it feverishly in his other hand. The explosion had not gone unnoticed in the immediate vicinity and silhouettes were already running out of the smoke at him. Kersh had no time for strategy, skill or etiquette. Economy was imperative. As cultists rushed him they lost limbs and were barged aside as the Excoriator hobbled through the burned mist. A Gore-mongers Chaos Space Marine lost half his head, and before a World Eater had the chance to bring up the incredible length of his struggling chainsword, Kersh had turned the gladius over in his hand like a dagger and stabbed the Traitor Legionary straight through the helm with it.

Limping around the exterior of the Mausoleum as fast as his agony would allow, Kersh found what he was looking for: Keturah's Scout bikes. No longer parked in a neat line, the corpus-captain found that they had been knocked down both by the clambering hordes and the grenade detonations. Leaving the first two, which had received the worst of the grenades' attentions, Kersh hobbled around the third. Righting the vehicle and slipping his smashed leg over the saddle, he brought the bike's powerful engine to life. He hadn't ridden a bike since he was a neophyte himself, but it immediately came back to him. The solidity and weight of the vehicle. Its thick tyres and aching power, and the satisfaction derived from clinging to the handlebars as the galaxy streamed effortlessly by. It almost made him forget his leg.

Slipping the length of the company standard through the empty shotgun rack and down the side of the bike, Kersh flicked on the vehicle's powerful arc lamp. The beam cut through the acrid murk, but where Kersh had expected to find demented cult-soldiers and renegades he found only a solitary armoured figure amongst bodies. His midnight revenant, the haunter of both his daydreams and nightmares. Kersh levelled his eyes at the silent Angel. The Scourge thought he knew now what the phantasm meant. At times he'd thought that it was a further affliction of the

Darkness, at others some manifest damage to the brain inflicted by Ezrachi and his apothecarion aides. He'd questioned whether he'd gone mad; he'd heard of other forms of madness. Prophets, prognosticators and sometimes plain mortals who had glimpsed a little of a doom to come – in the same way as the soul-bound servants of the Adeptus Astra Telepathica with their tarot, or the solemn members of the Librarius. Certainly the death that Kersh had seen on Certus-Minor – the end of an Imperial world – warranted some kind of omen, and the dark revenant had been his. A chill warning of the brothers lost and the deaths to come.

Kersh drew his gladius and held the blade out across the handlebars, while providing support with his fingertips to the other grip. The revenant stood and watched him, the sinister light of its eye glimmering through the rent and across the darkness.

'Better get out of the way,' the Scourge told it, 'because I'm not stopping.'

As Khornate warrior-wretches ran at the Excoriator, Kersh let the back wheel of the bike screech and slide on the cobbles. Releasing the brake and allowing the vehicle to catapult away from the Blood God's minions, the Scourge blasted across the open space. Keeping his wheel straight and his accelerator at full wrench, the bike cannoned towards the ghostly Space Marine. The corpus-captain braced for impact. Seconds away from the phantom Kersh heard the rasping click of its teeth chattering. It was the last thing he heard before the bike passed straight through the revenant. Swinging his head back, Kersh saw that the apparition had gone. It had disappeared, leaving only smoke swirling in the bike's wake.

Gunning the engine, Kersh rode the bike off the blind apex where the Mausoleum plaza met the downhill slope of an ambulatory. He'd been fortunate. He recognised the thoroughfare as an arterial route called the 'Via Ossium', the Road of Bones. Although bordered by the high walls of buildings and alleyways on both sides, the ambulatory was straight and steep, and was a ceremonial course running from the Memorial Mausoleum down to the Saint Bartolomé-East Lych Gate and out onto the necroplex.

As the heavy bike came shearing down, it crushed several unsuspecting cultists. Several others were brained against the wheelguard, lamp and the twin-linked boltguns adorning the handlebars, before their broken bodies were tossed aside by the merciless progression of the vehicle. The cobbled ambulatory was steep, and despite being one of the wider streets, was still cramped and narrow. The Scourge kept up his speed, allowing gravity to add to the bike's murderous velocity. Kersh held the handlebars straight and true as the thick wheels ploughed through limbs, bounced the scrawny bodies of slave-soldiers like rag dolls and crushed skulls.

A sudden explosion ahead sent a cold streak across the Excoriator's hearts. He spat in anger. For a moment he thought that the *Apotheon* had struck too early. The detonation blasted the side of a hermitage across the Road of Bones, throwing the bodies of feral warriors into the air and showering the area with brick. Resisting the urge to brake, Kersh rode the debris out, the bike lifted from the ground by a ramp of rubble. With fragments of stone blasted out before the wheel, the Scourge angled the soaring vehicle through a throng of disorientated daemon worshippers, decapitating several of them. Like the Excoriator, the warrior-acolytes had been wondering where the explosion had come from. Another, several streets across from the Via Ossium, revealed the heavens as the impact origin.

Looking up into the night sky, the bloody trail of the Keeler Comet still smearing the firmament, Kersh saw a crowded constellation of fireballs. Something devastating was happening far above the city, and the Scourge could only imagine that some minor skirmish or competition for prey had prompted all-out war between vessels in the Cholercaust fleet. Meanwhile, shooting stars – which Kersh took for battle damage debris – streaked towards the planet surface like a deadly pyrotechnic display. The fiery hailstorm had already started hitting the necroplex and pieces were now striking the ruined city.

Most cultists were blinded by the bike's powerful lamp and the impossibility of an Adeptus Astartes hurtling towards them on two wheels at lethal speed. Others had the presence of mind to throw themselves and their weapons at the escaping Excoriator. Stub-rounds and scattershot rained off the Scourge's plate, while the bike shot through a forest of poorly timed blades and blunt weaponry. Hammers and spiked clubs bounced off his battered pauldrons prompting the Scourge to hold the handlebars steady with one hand, while holding out his gladius with the other. The short sword wasn't an ideal weapon to use mounted, but the partial impacts and opportunistic assaults were so close that it didn't seem to matter. Revving through mobs and maniacs, wheels slipping through blood and wreckage, Kersh hacked, slashed and lopped off body parts. As mayhem blurred past, he smashed jaws and broke faces with his fist, the blade still clutched within his fingers.

A Blood Storm Chaos Space Marine saw Kersh coming, and with a double-handed daemon blade, glowing with infernal possession, stood his ground in the middle of the ambulatory. The renegade assumed a striking stance and held the blade up behind his modest helm. The Scourge narrowed his eyes and risked the tiniest of course corrections. Sweeping left across the road, Kersh brought his body and the gladius down low to the right. The skull-hungry blade sailed straight over the Excoriator, but as the bike accelerated away, the Blood Storm heretic tumbled, his leg sheared off at the knee.

As Kersh blazed down the ambulatory, away from the Memorial Mausoleum, he saw more of the impossible. Angels haunted the shadowy streets, passages and alleyways of the cemetery world city. Not Excoriators. Not the War-Given-Form's Traitor World Eaters. Not the heretic brothers of renegade Chapters and warbands that pledged their blades and superhuman efforts to the Blood God's cause. At first, Kersh though he was seeing his phantom again, but as he shot past macabre butchery and ghostly gunfire, he realised that his revenant was not alone. His wraith-like brothers were seeping from the shadows, cutting daemons and Ruinous champions down with cold efficiency.

The damned legionnaires burned with an ethereal fire, their bone-sculpted armour a stygian nightmare of darkness and gilt flame. Every stride they took, though silent, was a step of fearless determination. Whereas World Eaters degenerates came at them with the heat of mindless fury and angry blades, the accursed crusaders were cold to the point of repose and ruin. They moved with the certainty of the grave and killed with the indomitable will of beings who already knew what it was to lose life and know the end. Their unnatural presence gave birth to a fear in their enemies that they had not known, an antiquated darkness beyond petty notions of survival or an agonising death. A nightfall of the soul. An eventuality so hopeless and final that their victims didn't dread the end of their existence – they feared not existing at all.

The daemon heralds of Khorne hunted phantoms in the labyrinthine expanse of the city, ethereal warriors who became one with darkness, only to inkblot into reality behind the spindly bloodletters and stalk towards them like otherworldly execution squads. Stampeding daemonstock, driven beyond madness, demolished an empty city as they gored and charged at evaporating shadows – their brazen clinker-hide punctured and bolt-riddled with an aurelian storm of shot that was incorporeal as it left phantom weapons, only to cross the barrier into reality as it mauled its Ruinous targets. The spectral Angels strode through ravenous mobs of traitor Guard and war-thralls, the insubstantial nexus of enraged crossfire, swinging the brute angularity of their heavy barrels and magazines about them like clubs, smashing heads and spilling brains. World Eaters warbands and their blood-blessed champions were decimated by vaporous gunfire – the plate-ripping teeth of their axes and the gaping death of their pistols nothing against a Legion of the Damned who seemed incapable of dying.

Daemons leapt at Kersh from the roofs and sides of

buildings, several gangle-limbed forms coming close to tearing the Adeptus Astartes from his saddle with their hooked claws. He fired the twin-linked bolters on the front of the bike, clearing a bloody path through the cultist-choked ambulatory. A female slave-soldier, attempting to get out of the bike's path, ended up clinging to the front of it – eye to eye with the Scourge. Pulling on the trigger, Kersh blew the soldier off with the twin-linked bolters.

Riding through the bloodhaze and aftermath, the Scourge didn't see the chainaxe coming for him. The weapon shredded up his shoulder just beneath his pauldron, and blood began to leak down the side of his plate and the bike. As he tore away from the threat, his hand momentarily uncertain on the handlebars, he heard the deep roar of boltguns, fired in spectral unison, blasting apart the axe-wielding renegade and the death cult assassins in amongst whom he was standing.

As Kersh's bike tore out of the chapels and dormitories of the city and into the smouldering devastation of Saint Bartolomé-East, the heavens truly fell. With a trail of soot streaming behind the bike from the cremated district – the result of the *Impunitas*'s earlier bombing raids – Kersh bled and watched material that was clearly not ship wreckage rocket from the sky. Unnatural blocks of blood-black ice were raining down on the district and necroplex beyond like artillery fire. Easing the speeding bike around craters created by tumbling rock and exotic metal fragments, Kersh suddenly became aware of a monstrous hound bounding up behind the bike and attempting to tear at the back wheel with its knife-point teeth. Swiping unsuccessfully with his gladius, the Scourge attempted to barge the reptilian beast into the walls of gutted derelicts.

The beast either bounded over the obstacles or crashed its bony head straight through them. When the thing almost took his arm off with a jaw-rearing snap, Kersh turned away from the daemon hound. Standing in the road were a trio of damned legionnaires, their bolters aimed straight at the advancing Kersh. As the ghastly Angels blazed coldly away,

Kersh brought up his arm instinctively. Unmolested by the immaterial rounds, the Excoriator brought down his arm, only for it to jump back up as he rode straight through the line of revenants. Holding on to the screeching bike, the Scourge cast a glance behind him to see the accursed crusaders melt into nothing, revealing the bolt-blasted carcass of the daemon dead on the cobbles.

Gunning down clots of cultists with his bolters as he rode on, Kersh was almost knocked from the bike by a meteorite strike that demolished what was left of a burning hospice. Out across the ravaged district, the corpus-captain's attention was arrested by the spectacle of a creature that had been less fortunate. Out in the wastes, the hulking greater daemon that had terrorised the Excoriator earlier stood impaled on a shard of ice which had fallen and speared the bloodthirster into the ground. Kersh sickeningly recalled the death of Squad Whip Joachim and thanked the Emperor for the daemon's spectacular misfortune.

With the bike's engine gunned excruciatingly to maximum speed, Kersh finally spotted the Lych Gate marking the limit of the city. A World Eater ran towards the road from a smashed chapel, his brass bolt pistols blazing – until a damned legionnaire stepped out from behind a blackened altar and gunned the Chaos Space Marine down from behind, ethereal bolts searing into his pack, through his warped body and out of his chestplate. The World Eater fell down by the roadside, one of his ornately crafted sidearms still aimed across the cobbles. As Kersh passed he felt a pair of bolt-rounds bore into his side. With the bike wobbling and the mauled Scourge fading fast, the sky lit up behind him.

A colossal stream of energy struck the city. For a moment, time seemed to stop. The ground seemed to shift below the wheels of Kersh's bike. As darkness returned, buildings were blasted apart by a ring of concentric destruction spreading throughout the cemetery world city. As Kersh shot through the open Lych Gate, destruction cascaded after him, an avalanche of masonry, flaming bodies, blood and dust.

With little left to destroy in the blitzed Saint Bartolomé-East district, Kersh avoided the worst of the debris-storm. A rolling dust cloud rapidly swallowed the bike and Excoriator, however, blinding the grievously wounded Scourge to the danger ahead. The bike's wheels left the ground without warning. Since Kersh hadn't hit anything, he reasoned that there simply wasn't any ground beneath him. The lychway had been pounded by a falling piece of the Keeler Comet minutes before, turning the width of the road into a crater. The bike began to fall, the front wheel not making the other side of the pit. As the front of the bike struck the crater wall, Kersh was flung like a piece of wreckage across the lychway. Bouncing and breaking along the track at all but lethal speed, the Excoriator tumbled to a plate-crushing stop by an ornate gravestone.

The half-dead Scourge blinked gore from his remaining eye. A gash across his face kept flooding the socket with blood. He might have lost consciousness, but if he had, he didn't remember. As he moved his neck, pain streaked through the back of his head. Something was cracked or broken there. It was a living torment to move, but Kersh felt he had little choice. He was out on the necroplex. He sensed danger all about him.

Obsequa City lay behind him, a devastated mess of flaming wreckage and settling dust. The magnificent dome of the Umberto II Memorial Mausoleum was now a mountain of masonry. Many of the city centre cathedrals and temples had been wiped from the face of the cemetery world, but a good part of the city remained, albeit as a firestorm wracked ruin. Torched and shattered disciples of the Blood God who refused to give up the fight wandered the night with their murderous instincts still intact, even if their bodies were roasted and smashed. Damned legionnaires, incorporeal and impassive, hunted down such degenerate specimens without mercy, finishing what the lance strike had begun. The revenants had been unaffected by the city-levelling, star-hot beam of energy, with even those Angels directly below the orbital strike going about their vengeance oblivious to the destruction wrought around them.

Kersh limped agonisingly along the darkness of the lych-way, daemon-haunted burial grounds on either side. He no longer had the company standard and had lost his Scourge's blade in the crash. Drawing his remaining gladius – his back-up blade – the Excoriator hobbled on. With blood leaking from both sides of his mangled plate and the gleaming sword held limply in a shattered hand, the Scourge didn't think to last long.

Destruction rained from the sky. Shattered pieces of ice had tumbled and rolled a path of annihilation through the Cholercaust fleet, cleaving vessels in half, destroying others outright and scattering smaller wolfpacks of raiders and pirates. Rock and immense warp-frozen shards of blood pounded the burial grounds – devastating the rabid hordes, blasting daemon entities back to the depths of the warp and laying waste to Khorne's most frenzied warriors, decimate champions and able butchers. World Eaters raged at the heavens with their axes roaring and swords held high, shot through with white-hot metal nuggets that thunderbolted from the sky.

Kersh stomped on, blood-shod. A daemon herald leapt out over a crypt at the Scourge. He remembered raising his gladius but little else. Fading in and out of consciousness, the Excoriator found the daemon dead at his feet. Traitor Angels charged at him with oversized weapons and war cries, only to end up dead and bolt-punctured before him. An infernal predator swooped overhead, dive-bombing the corpus-captain, but that too found its way to a swift death on the ground. Kersh's failing sight revealed only movements in the murk. He heard deviant hordes fighting with each other. Warbands at war. Infernal rivalries settled in blood. All he recognised were the flame-swathed Angels of his salvation. A Legion of the Damned, moving about the graves like an army of ghosts, taking the fight to the Ruinous, executing the tainted and delivering doom to the Emperor's enemies.

The Scourge had fallen several times and stubbornly regained his feet, but as he collapsed once more, he found that he couldn't get up. With the cold creeping through his shattered plate and into his wounded body, Kersh found himself lying across a grave, his head propped against its stone marker. There, he hugged the polished, unbloodied gladius to his chest and waited for death in the battle-torn darkness.

Above, the blackness of the star-speckled firmament was still dotted with glowing embers, Cholercaust vessels that had lost their fight with colossal chunks of rock and ice and fallen into an explosion-wracked, decaying orbit around Certus-Minor. Such fragments still tumbled from the sky and obliterated the servants of Chaos still wandering the night. Squinting, Kersh thought he saw a vessel pass overhead. At first he thought it was falling to the cemetery world surface, growing larger as it descended. But from its movements and the twinkle of cannon fire he realised that it was in high orbit, mopping up fleeing members of the Chaos armada. The Scourge watched it for a few moments, entranced – the vessel appeared to him like an Imperial aquila, passing across the heavens. He blinked, reasoning that he must have imagined the spectacle in his concussed and skull-fractured state. The vessel would have had to have been colossal in size to appear to him as it did, at such a distance.

Kersh closed his blood-crusted eye for a moment of peace, but when he opened it again his armoured revenant was standing above him. The damned legionnaire blazed an ethereal radiance over its rachidian plate. It was staring down at the Scourge through the crack in its helm, the warp-lustre of a sentience glowing from its skeletal eye socket. It said nothing. It did nothing for a while, not even chatter its teeth. In its midnight gauntlet it held the Excoriators Chapter's Fifth Company battle standard. Stabbing it into the earth beside the grave, the revenant let the blood-spattered banner flap in the breeze. In its other hand, between two exposed, skeletal digits, it held something else. The damned legionnaire dropped it on the Scourge's chest and walked away into nothingness, leaving Kersh on the field of battle. Alone.

MYSTERIUM FIDEI

EPILOGUE
GOD-EMPEROR

Approbator Vaskellen Quast dropped the distance between the Valkyrie's ramp and the carpet of burial ground carnage. With his meme-vox in his hand he bounded between bolt-mangled bodies and ran through the spoiling gore. Inquisitorial storm troopers from the 52nd Ranger Pelluciad were not far behind him, attending on the Ordo Obsoletus acolyte from a respectable distance.

Excoriators Thunderhawks had little trouble beating the Ordo Valkyrie across the festering necroplex to the reported location of the sole survivor, and by the time Quast trudged up behind them, Santiarch Balshazar and an honour guard of Excoriators Angels had surrounded the warrior – scattering the frater burn team who had almost incinerated him and the Sister Hospitallers who had barely begun attending to his grievous wounds. With Adeptus Astartes gunships circling overhead, the approbator slipped between the forest of hulking giants. Rounding their ancient, scar-annotated plate, Quast found the only living witness to the mysterious destruction of the Cholercaust Blood Crusade. The approbator was bursting with questions, but like the

Excoriators Space Marines stood solemnly about him, he remained silent.

Propped up against a tombstone, his armoured limbs laid out across grave dirt, was a mauled Angel. An Excoriators captain of the Fifth Company. His plate – formerly an ivory edifice like that worn by his brothers – was stained the red of death. Its inscriptions and preserved battle-scarring had been obliterated by the mutilation of recent carnage. The Angel's power armour was a rent, bolt-blasted shell of buckled ceramite, and the earth about him glistened with the moisture of his life quietly leaking away. His face was similarly plastered with blood – his enemies' and his own – and dusted with the soot of raging fires. His tonsure-shaven hair was matted and singed, his ear was missing and the dull glint of a ball-bearing shone out from one eye as evidence of former atrocities suffered. Breaking the crust of blood that had dried across the other eye, the Excoriator stared at them. His gaze was weak and uncomprehending, sensitive to the burgeoning Certusian sunrise.

The breeze ruffled the captain's battle standard, leaning slightly out of the ground as it was above him, playing with the brown-speckled material. At the sight of hulking silhouettes, cut out of the morning sky, the survivor clutched his gleaming short sword to his ruined chest. Unlike the wrecked Excoriator, and everything else on the cemetery world, the gladius was unblemished and unblooded. Quast was not a warrior, like the surrounding Space Marines, but the resplendent weapon held even his attention. The spartan honesty of its unadorned and heavy blade. The crafted angularity of its pommel. The three simple numerals stamped into the breadth of its cross guard: VII.

The approbator looked about him, his instincts taking his gaze to the Santiarch's own. The Excoriators Angels were looking at the sword rather than their wounded brother.

'Captain, I...'

'Approbator!' Balshazar boomed, the warning in the Chapter Chaplain's words irresistible. The Santiarch stepped forwards, drawing a gladius of his own. Kneeling before the survivor he offered the captain the blade. 'I believe this belongs to you, Corpus-Captain Kersh.'

Kersh took the blade from the Chaplain and clutched it to him with the other. The second was equally bare, but while similarly functional and austere, lacked the clear craftsmanship of the first. The Santiarch went to reach for the other gladius, but the unspeaking warrior tightened his grip, holding the weapon to him. Quast looked from Balshazar to the one they called Kersh and back again.

'You came for the sword?' the approbator marvelled.

The Santiarch ignored him and addressed one of his gathered brethren. 'Brother Japhet, signal the *Cerberus*. Inform Chapter Master Ichabod that we have discovered the Dornsblade. Tell him that it remains in Corpus-Captain Kersh's care and will be transported to the battle-barge with the Chapter Scourge directly.'

'No astrotelepathic appeal. No request for assistance. You were already on your way to Certus-Minor,' Quast said. 'To reclaim a sword?'

Santiarch stood to his full, imposing stature.

'This is not any blade, approbator. This is the Sword of Sebastus. The Dornsblade. A sacred relic to the genetic progeny of Rogal Dorn. It was carried by the primarch himself during his trials in the Eternal Fortress and used to spill Traitor blood in the Battle of the Iron Cage. It is a symbol of our unbreakable unity and the sacrifice shared by the sons of Dorn despite the Legion-splintering accords of the Codex Astartes. It is a piece of Imperial history, sculpted, beaten and honed to a razor edge.'

'And the captain stole the relic blade?'

'Corpus-Captain Kersh earned the Dornsblade,' Balshazar corrected the approbator, his gaze meeting the Scourge's. 'He won the honour of a year's custodianship at the centennial Feast of Blades. It is the corpus-captain's by right.'

'Then why reclaim it?'

'Kersh should have sent the Dornsblade back to the safety of our home world, Eschara, on the frigate *Scarifica*. Instead, he kept the blade and sent that one in its stead, an inception sword, given to neophytes in recognition of their ascension to true brotherhood.'

'Why would he do that?' Quast asked before kneeling down in the blood-soaked earth beside the silent Scourge. 'Captain, why would you do that?'

Kersh said nothing. He just stared up at the Santiarch.

'To force an audience with the Chapter Master, possibly,' Balshazar said, his deep voice finding its way to an accusatory edge. 'He'd been formerly denied one. His act could be one of Chapter politics. The corpus-captain's reasons are best known to himself. I know only this – if our passage had been easier and swifter here, then we might have faced the terrible odds evidenced about us as brothers, the Sword of Sebastus, thousands of years on, still bringing the sons of Rogal Dorn together.'

Quast leant in. The stink of gore rising from the Scourge's plate made the approbator recoil slightly.

'Corpus-captain, I am here representing the interests of the Holy Ordos. I must know what happened here. These are strange happenings indeed and explanations must be sought.'

Kersh moved suddenly, causing the approbator to retract further. In an agonising movement, and with fresh blood gushing from his ripped plate, Kersh dropped his neophyte's inception blade and reached for the gravestone behind him. It was torment to watch. Both Balshazar and the approbator wanted to assist the wounded Space Marine, but had little idea what he was doing. Slowly, the Scourge's ceramite fingertips reached for the sculpted stone of the grave marker. The stone was inscribed with a name: *Erzsebet Dorota Catallus*. At its heart, like the thousands of gravestones surrounding them across the necroplex, was a small bell. Quast frowned, assuming the instrument to be part of some Ecclesiarchy ritual or cemetery world custom. With an effort-trembling fingertip, Kersh prodded the bell, sending out a tinny chime across the steaming burial grounds. He did this a second and a third time until suddenly, and surprisingly, the bell began to ring of its own accord.

Quast and the Santiarch looked at one another. About

them, bells started ringing everywhere, each of the gravestones peeling with chimes of urgency and insistence. The approbator moved in closer to examine the grave marker. He saw the openings for air supply and the wire running from the bell and down into the earth. He turned back to Balshazar.

'The dead are rising, Santiarch. Miracles indeed.'

'Approbator!' the Ranger Pelluciad sergeant called, standing next to a vox-pack-carrying storm trooper. 'Dig teams report knocking from beneath the ruins of the Memorial Mausoleum. The new pontifex has begged assistance from the ordo and the Adeptus Astartes in excavating the survivors and the relic-remains of Umberto II.'

'Inform the pontifex that we are going to need shovels,' Quast called back. 'Lots of shovels.'

As the chorus of bells rang across the killing fields, the approbator's eyes settled on an object, half buried in the bloody earth. Picking it up and wiping it off, Quast discovered a crystalline wafer bearing a name and illustration. He had seen astropaths use such cards to divine possible futures – a tarot card. On the bottom of the wafer it stated *Deus Imperator* and pictured their corpse-lord, sat on his Golden Throne, amongst ancient apparatus of gold, steel and brass.

'God-Emperor...' Quast mouthed.

Looking down, the approbator saw another tarot wafer, and another – both amongst the carnage, sitting on the earth of newly dug graves. Burial plots all about were marked with the cards and each bore the holy image of the God-Emperor. Quast shook his head. He had seen Guardsmen drop playing cards on enemy dead as a signature of their success – a practice of certain regiments – but never wafers deposited on the living; on battle survivors. Returning to the wounded Excoriator, the approbator showed him the cards.

'What happened here?' Quast asked the Scourge. He held up the crystalline wafers. 'I must know. Tell me everything.'

'...or the teachings of our lord-founder, Demetrius Katafalque. I know not what I saw on Certus-Minor. I'm not sure that I'm the best instrument of elucidation. I have lived a warrior's life. A simple but essential existence of death and darkness, so that the light of the Imperium might shine brightly. What I experienced, others have known. Brothers who bear witness to a Legion of the Damned. An intervention from beyond. Aid unexplained, yet offered in silence and with the fury of ethereal vengeance – vanishing as swiftly as it appeared. I shall let Imperial scholars and the sophists of the Holy Ordos assign an explanation to this strange but welcome phenomenon, whether that be brothers lost on the Sea of Souls, a corruption beyond our understanding or the manifestation of a divine Will. I think that another Chapter – I forget which one – said it best. Their motto was In dedicato deus imperatum ultra articulo mortis: For the God-Emperor beyond the point of death. Perhaps these damned legionnaires had pledged themselves as such. Perhaps one day I shall know. There are worse fates in the galaxy for a battle-brother, intent on serving one's God-Emperor into eternity.'*

From *Damnation's Calling*
By Chapter Master Zachariah Kersh, of the
Excoriators Space Marine Chapter

413

ABOUT THE AUTHOR

Rob Sanders is a freelance writer, who spends his nights creating dark visions for regular visitors to the 41st millennium to relive in the privacy of their own nightmares.

By contrast, as Head of English at a local secondary school, he spends his days beating (not literally) the same creativity out of the next generation in order to cripple any chance of future competition. He lives off the beaten track in the small city of Lincoln, UK. His first fiction was published in *Inferno!* magazine.

More legendary tales from the Space Marine Battles series

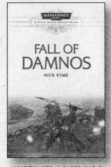

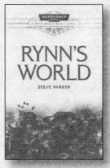